"I'm not interested in becoming one of your conquests..."

"I'm not sure what you're used to, but I promise you, I'm not it. I have no need for what you offer."

Patrick quirked one side of his mouth up into a roguish grin and looked down into Charlie's dark eyes. "Are ye certain of that, lass?"

"Aye, I'm certain. In fact, I'd rather be drawn and quartered than find myself bound in an unwanted relationship."

He was taken a bit back. He'd just never been rejected so wholeheartedly. And what was it exactly about him that she found so unappealing?

"Goodnight, Mr. Campbell." She walked away from him. Just like that.

He liked her. He liked the sound of her voice, even when she was reviling him. He liked the way she moved, as if her feet weren't touching the ground but gliding over it. He liked that she didn't need a man to make her happy, and that she was willful and braw.

What he didn't like was that she found him undesirable... and that he gave a damn.

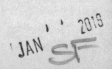

The Scandalous Secret of Abigail MacGregor

"4½ stars! A page-turner. Quinn twists and turns the tale, drawing readers in and holding them with her unforgettable characters' love story."

—*RT Book Reviews*

"A wonderful book...Paula Quinn has raised the bar even higher with this newest novel in the MacGregor saga."

—*NightOwlReviews.com*

The Wicked Ways of Alexander Kidd

"Paula Quinn has done it again!...If there ever was a book that deserved more than five stars then this one is it. I was absolutely captivated from start to finish."

—*NightOwlReviews.com*

"The Scottish highlands and a pirate ship provide the colorful setting for this well-written, exciting, and action-packed romance."

—*RT Book Reviews*

"Vivid...Quinn's steamy and well-constructed romance will appeal to fans and newcomers alike."

—*Publishers Weekly*

The Seduction of Miss Amelia Bell

"Plenty of passion, romance, and adventure...one of the best books I've read in a long time...a captivating story from beginning to end."

—*NightOwlReviews.com*

"Delicious…highly entertaining…a witty, sensual historical tale that will keep you glued to the pages…This beautifully written, fast-paced tale is a true delight."

—RomanceJunkiesReviews.com

Conquered by a Highlander

"Rich, evocative historical detail and enthralling characters fill the pages of this fast-paced tale."

—*Publishers Weekly* (starred review)

"What a conclusion to this fast-paced, adventure-filled story with characters that jump off the page and will capture your heart." —MyBookAddictionReviews.com

Tamed by a Highlander

"Top Pick! Quinn's talents for weaving history with a sexy and seductive romance are showcased in her latest Highlander series book. This fast-paced tale of political intrigue populated by sensual characters with deeply rooted senses of honor and loyalty is spellbinding…Top-notch Highland romance!" —*RT Book Reviews*

"A winning mix of fascinating history and lush romance… Readers will be captivated by the meticulously accurate historical detail." —*Publishers Weekly* (starred review)

Seduced by a Highlander

"*Seduced by a Highlander* is sparkling, sexy, and seductive! I couldn't put it down!"

—Karen Hawkins, *New York Times* bestselling author

The Scot's Bride

Also by Paula Quinn

The Scot's Bride

PAULA QUINN

FOREVER
New York Boston

Copyright © 2017 by Paula Quinn
Preview from *Laird of the Black Isle* copyright © 2017 by Paula Quinn
Cover design by Claire Brown
Cover illustration by Alan Ayers
Cover copyright © 2017 by Hachette Book Group, Inc.

Forever
Hachette Book Group
1290 Avenue of the Americas, New York, NY 10104
forever-romance.com
twitter.com/foreverromance

First Edition: October 2017

Forever is an imprint of Grand Central Publishing. The Forever name and logo are trademarks of Hachette Book Group, Inc.

The publisher is not responsible for websites (or their content) that are not owned by the publisher.

The Hachette Speakers Bureau provides a wide range of authors for speaking events. To find out more, go to www.hachettespeakersbureau.com or call (866) 376-6591.

ISBN: 978-1-4555-3533-0 (mass market), 978-1-4555-3531-6 (ebook)

Printed in the United States of America

OPM

10 9 8 7 6 5 4 3 2 1

MacGregor/Grant
Family Tree

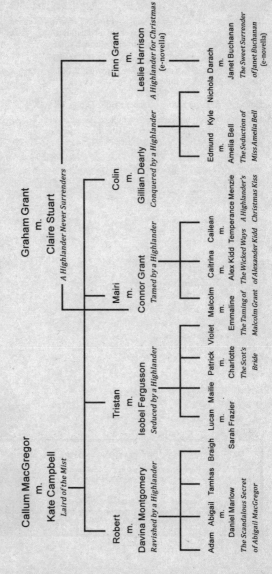

Graham Grant
m.
Claire Stuart
A Highlander Never Surrenders

Callum MacGregor
m.
Kate Campbell
Laird of the Mist

Finn Grant
m.
Leslie Harrison
A Highlander for Christmas
(e-novella)

Robert
m.
Davina Montgomery
Ravished by a Highlander

Tristan
m.
Isobel Fergusson
Seduced by a Highlander

Mairi
m.
Connor Grant
Tamed by a Highlander

Colin
m.
Gillian Dearly
Conquered by a Highlander

Adam Abigail Tamhas Braigh Lucan Mailie Patrick Violet Malcolm Emmaline
m.   m.   m.
Daniel Marlow   Sarah Frazier   Charlotte
The Scandalous Secret   *The Scot's*
of Abigail MacGregor   *Bride*

The Taming of
Malcolm Grant

Caitrina Cailean
m.   m.
Alex Kidd Temperance Menzie
The Wicked Ways *A Highlander's*
of Alexander Kidd *Christmas Kiss*

Edmund Kyle Nichola Darach
m.   m.
Amelia Bell   Janet Buchanan
The Seduction of *The Sweet Surrender*
Miss Amelia Bell *of Janet Buchanan*
(e-novella)

Chapter One

*Y*e're undressing me with yer eyes, rogue."

Patrick MacGregor, the *new* Devil of the Highlands, slanted his mouth into an unrepentant, dimpled grin that made the serving wench's hands tremble and the jug of ale she carried slosh and spill onto the floor. He reached out to capture her wrist in his fingers. She'd been teasing him all night with her swaying hips and veiled, come-hither glances. He'd rather get himself a room and sleep for the next two days, but he wasn't one to turn down a willing maiden.

Up for the game, he pulled her into his lap and plucked the jug from her hand without spilling a drop.

"'Tis well beyond that, lass," he told her dipping his mouth to the jug and then her neck. "Ye're already bare in m' arms and I'm aboot to fill m'self with the sweet taste of ye."

She giggled and groaned and nestled her rump deeper into the nook of his thighs. "I should slap ye fer yer boldness, stranger."

"If that is how ye like to play the game," he replied burying his face in the folds of her russet hair at her nape.

Another woman in the pub caught his gaze for an instant, mayhap longer while she moved through the light and shadows of the tavern. A stray lock of hair, black as onyx, fell over a high, pale cheek. Her dark, beautiful eyes captivated him, commanded his attention while they passed over him, moved through him, and then came away, unimpressed. He thought about getting rid of the lass in his lap for the one in the shadows. But she was gone, taking the only spark left in the room with her.

The lass in his lap tugged on his sleeve urging his attention back to her. He obliged, liking the full dip of the wench's lower lip and the promise of pleasure in her hooded eyes.

But pleasure was fleeting when the chase ended before it began; surrender, rather dull.

"What are we doing still sitting here then?" she asked.

Aye, what were they still doing here? He swigged his ale, wiped his mouth, and called to the tavern owner for a room.

"This isn't a brothel," the taverner blustered beneath his bushy brown moustache. "I run a respectable establishment."

"Good thing." Patrick rose from his chair with the lass in his arm and gave the taverner a pat on the shoulder with his free hand. "I'm certain this lovely lass would cost more coin than I carry."

She lifted herself on the tips of her toes and whispered to Patrick that he didn't have to pay her and to follow her to her room abovestairs.

He did, tossing the taverner a wink as he went.

On the way up the stairs, Patrick set his gaze on the wench's well-rounded rump and thought of all the things he'd like to do with it. It didn't startle him when he could think of only two. He'd fought twelve fights today. His muscles still ached with tension. He smiled at her when she turned, catching the direction of his gaze. Mayhap she'd understand if he changed his mind.

When they reached the second landing, she stopped, looped her arm through his, and leaned in close. "I've been thinking about how ye taste as well."

He felt his blood heating his veins. He'd been a fool to reconsider. "Lead the way."

Inside her room he watched her run to her moldy-feathered bed and slip off her shoes. Hell, he wanted to sleep on something soft. Sleeping on his plaid in the grass stopped being pleasant after three hours with pebbles in his back. He undraped his plaid and pulled his léine over his head, groaning at his sore muscles as he stretched and then tossed the shirt to the floor.

He heard a little sound escape her lips. He looked at her from beneath the inky sweep of his lashes and found her gaze fastened to the thick muscles in his arms, his taut, rippling abdomen. He wondered if he could convince her to rub him down with some oil. He'd been hit a few times in the ribs and the belly, but mostly his arms were tired from his expert defense.

"Don't ye want to know my name?" she asked, tugging at the laces of her stay.

"Nae," he said, giving her a slow half smile while he moved toward her, unbuckling his belt. "'Tis less to ferget."

She pulled the laces loose and her breasts spilled forth like ripe apples from a basket.

Well, that helped fire up his blood a bit. They were free apples and he was hungry. But that was all this was and in truth, he was beginning to lose his appetite. There was no chase, no seduction, and no challenge. There hadn't been for a long time.

Until tonight when he'd been struck by the disdainful gaze of a lass trying to remain unseen in the nooks and crannies of the tavern. He'd wanted to chase *her*.

She smiled and it struck him, as it always had, how most lasses didn't mind his detachment—until after, which was why he tried not to remain in one place too long.

He pulled one leg out of his leather breeches and then stopped to think about what he was doing here.

He wanted sleep. He'd left Camlochlin with enough coin to last long until he'd arrived at his uncle Cameron Fergusson's Tarrick Hall. But women and whisky didn't come cheap and he'd stopped in almost every town for all three while he traveled to Colmonell, using up his supply.

To earn coin to eat, drink, and be merry, he'd fought for the past sennight in competitions using his fists, and in tournaments with swords. He fought better than most, with or without a weapon, well enough to avoid being struck too often in the face or head, and to earn enough tender to eat and sleep in the best inns. Usually he liked to enjoy the delicacy of a lass's sheath tight around his shaft, her arms and legs coiled around him as if his body possessed the solution to all her cares. But it didn't. It sure as hell didn't help him with his. Lately he'd been less inclined to prove it to any of them.

He didn't really want to be here. All his bravado belowstairs had just been his usual play of getting the gel. He was tired of always being victorious. Hell, even fighting would soon grow dull if he won every match.

"Lass, I—"

She looked him over like a hungry cat and leaped at him. He laughed, catching her in his arms, and bent his head to brush his mouth over hers. If she wanted him this badly...

The tight little groan he pulled from her made his blood rush to his loins like liquid fire. He hauled her into his embrace, parting his lips and molding his hungry mouth to hers to devour her with leisurely demand.

She pushed him down on the bed and he smiled on the way, liking her boldness and her eagerness for him.

But hell, the bed felt good under him.

A knock came at the door. Patrick ignored it and continued kissing her. As he'd suspected, her lips were soft, yielding to his masterful tongue. Aye, he knew how to kiss a lass. He'd been doing it since he was a lad of thirteen summers, practicing the art almost as often as he practiced fighting.

The knock came again, harder than before. Patrick leaped from the bed and yanked his bare leg back into his breeches.

A kick followed, tearing the meager bolt away. The lass screamed at the giant figure of a man blocking the doorway.

"Unhand her before I rip the head from your shoulders."

Patrick cast the wench a sour glance. The intruder was either her husband or her brother or some other damned guardian she'd failed to mention. He held up his palms to ward the brute off. He didn't want to fight. He wasn't sure if his strength would hold up.

"I'm certain we can—"

The brute didn't care about talking and came at him swinging, giving Patrick no choice but to fight back.

Patrick ducked with ease and struck the first blow, and then the second. He quirked his mouth in a feral smile when he felt the ogre's nose crack against his knuckles. All right, so he fought even better than he kissed.

Shaking off the pain of his broken nose, the man threw another punch, bringing a slight breeze close to Patrick's face as he warded off the blow.

Legs planted, Patrick bent to the left and then backward, avoiding two more punches to his jaw.

Coming back at him, Patrick delivered a left to the beast's guts and a right hooking strike to the jaw, then ended the combination with another fist to the belly.

Pain seemed only to enrage the brute further.

Surprised that his blows had done so little damage, Patrick blinked and took a fist to the jaw that snapped his head back and loosened a tooth.

As he rolled the tip of his tongue over his teeth, his eyes widened and turned a darker shade of green. This wouldn't do. A broken, slightly crooked nose was one thing. A missing tooth and no profit for it was foolish.

"Let's talk aboot this." He held his hands up again, but his opponent showed no mercy and rammed his fist into Patrick's side.

Hell, he thought as he hunched over trying to catch his breath, the blow might have been a little low.

"Hamish, enough!" the lass cried out.

Paying her no heed, Hamish yanked him up by the collarbone, hauled him out of the room, and then over the balcony. Patrick's back shattered the table below. He almost blacked out, but tempting as it was, he fought to hold on.

Amidst the startled screams from some of the women present, he groaned and then tested the movement of his arms. The pain was bearable, and good thing because Hamish was barreling down the stairs and coming at him again.

Pushing the splintered wood aside, Patrick rose and faced the resilient bastard once more. He had a dagger in his boot, but why kill a man when it was unnecessary? His father's voice echoed within him. Hamish was big and dangerous, but Patrick wouldn't give him the chance to cause him harm. He wouldn't kill Hamish, but he was going to have to put him out quickly.

The instant the giant reached him, Patrick landed his left fist into his face, followed by his right. He swung his fist upward, lifting Hamish's feet a little off the ground with a tooth-crunching uppercut. Another man would have succumbed to Patrick's onslaught, but not this one.

He answered Patrick with a punch to the jaw that made Patrick shake his head to stay upright. Hell, he was tired from fighting all day. He just wanted a damned bed!

From the corner of his eye he saw his bedroom wench hurrying toward them with a wooden jug clutched against her haphazardly laced stays. Patrick sighed with relief. It was just what he needed. He swiped it from her hands as she reached him and, ignoring her cry of surprise, swung the jug across Hamish's temple.

The ungainly oaf hit the floor with a crash that shook the walls. The lass hurried to him while Patrick watched. He knew the jug had been meant for *his* head. Thankfully, his reflexes were quick. He didn't ask her who the man was or why he'd kicked the door in to get to her. Patrick didn't care. But why had she taken him to her bed when she knew there was a giant brute prowling about, waiting to protect her from rogues like him? He'd almost had a tooth knocked out. And for what? A bit of pleasure and a warm bed? He had neither. Women were trouble.

He stepped around the wench and her fallen hero and looked around at the faces in the tavern. Each wore the same expression of stunned disbelief. He parted the silent crowd with a step toward the taverner, tossed him a few coins to pay for the table, and then left, cursing his sore muscles. There would be no bed for him here tonight.

* * *

Charlotte Cunningham, along with the other patrons at Blind Jack's, had heard Beth's door ripping from its hinges when Hamish had reached it. Everyone knew Hamish loved Bethany. Well, she allowed, the stranger hadn't known. No one had moved while listening to the two men fighting abovestairs. She, along with poor Ennis the taverner, watched the stranger sail out of Bethany's room and destroy the table beneath him.

Charlotte thought he was dead, and was surprised when he wasn't. What stunned her more though was when he stood up and readied himself for another onslaught from his larger opponent. His plaid and the léine he'd worn under it had been discarded, likely to the floor inside Bethany's room. His long, bare torso rippled with coiled muscle. His broad chest was well-defined by a dusting of hair a few shades darker than his auburn crown. She liked his courage and marveled at his skill when he landed a series of brutal blows to Hamish's face. She wondered who he was. Word usually spread quickly when a stranger arrived in any of the neighboring villages.

She wasn't able to wait around to find out. She'd been there too long already. If one of her brothers or her father woke and found her gone, they'd make her life hell for the next month.

She left the pub before the victor was crowned. It wouldn't take long to reach home if she pushed her horse.

As she raced toward Pinwherry she cursed herself for lingering about earlier, watching the rogue at work. She'd noticed him when she'd first arrived at Blind Jack's. It was difficult not to notice a fallen star illuminating the dark tavern. Utterly at ease with his surroundings, he'd laughed with some of the other customers and flashed a roguish dimple

at the serving girls. His hands were quick when he caught
Bethany in one and her jug in the other.

Charlie would admit, she thought as she thundered toward home, that the stranger was without doubt the most
wickedly alluring man to ever cross her path. He'd drawn
her from her table where she'd sat with a patron who'd just
given her a well-received bit of information.

She'd followed the sound of the stranger's laughter. She
watched him from the shadows while he pulled Bethany
into his lap. She suspected he was the worst kind of rogue,
the kind she'd been warned about, but she'd moved closer
while he bent his mouth to Bethany's throat. She hadn't expected him to look up and find her in the shadows. His eyes
smoldered, a fire contained with measured control. His full,
intoxicating lips slanted with arrogance and victory when
she pretended disinterest.

He was a knave and a very dangerous one. She couldn't
help but wonder how he had managed to beat a furious man
who was twice his size.

She didn't care. Thankfully, she'd never see him again
after tonight. She'd stop thinking of him now.

The next day Patrick traveled south toward the village of
Pinwherry on his way to Colmonell. The journey alone gave
him time to consider the things that had recently begun to
prick at him. For instance, when had wenches begun to lose
their luster and his interest? Why, despite the hard earth beneath him, had he been relieved to sleep alone last night?
Was he ill? What had changed? Normally he wouldn't have
given it a second thought. Change was good. It helped one
grow. But not this time.

His lack of interest in marriage was something he'd often
had to explain to his kin. Patrick knew what was expected of

him. But he liked his life the way it was, with no one to answer to, no one to be responsible for but himself. He didn't want it to change.

At night, alone in the beds he'd paid for, he'd been examining his life more thoroughly. Being an outlawed MacGregor, he didn't fear much. But love? Now there was a power he would confess scared the hell out of him. Love had the power to change a man, to change the course of his life. He'd seen it happen so often at home. Mighty warriors were reduced to heather-wielding, wife-pleasing pansies. Even Malcolm and Darach had traded in chasing skirts for chasing their bairns. It was pitiful really. He didn't want to live a life dictated by commitments and duty to anyone. He didn't want to fall in love. He'd grown up hearing extraordinary tales of it, of seeing the effects of it in his kin's lives. It wasn't because he didn't believe in its power. It was because he did.

If he were to fall in love, he'd have to be prepared to give up not only his heart, but his soul as well. He had no interest in that kind of life. He was young and virile and he was enjoying it.

He reached the river Stinchar when the afternoon sun formed golden flashes of light on the rippling surface—and on a goddess wetting her toes in the water, her skirts hiked up to her thighs.

Patrick wasn't sure she was a mere lass. Playing in the glistening rivulets, she looked more like a self-indulgent forest fairy lit up by the sun. She didn't wear layers of heavy wool, or even a jacket or arisaid, but a gown of billowing blue linen with threads of gold sewn in around the neck and sleeves. Matching laces kept her corset tight around her slim waist and full breasts. He watched behind a stand of trees while she spun in a circle with joy in the day, her skirts flaring slightly at her hips, the fabric thin enough to expose the silhouette of her long, shapely legs beneath. He forgot to breathe when her raven locks fanned out around her, a crown of daisies upon her brow.

He couldn't move. He could think of nothing but mayhap joining her, but his legs felt heavy, his thoughts muddled by the vision of her skipping over the water as if she were a veil in the summer breeze. His heart leaped at the sight of her lost in her own reverie, freedom personified. Had he happened upon something otherworldly, sent to seduce men to sin with her large, dark, feline eyes and dainty ankles?

He wondered what being seduced by her would entail. What might she want from him in exchange for time in her bed? What would he be willing to give such a delicate beauty?

His sister would have scolded him for spying on the nymph unseen. He almost laughed, giving away his position. She was made of mystery and whimsy, of daisies and darkness. How could he *not* stare at her? A tiny, nagging voice—likely from one of Kate MacGregor's books on knightly behavior—compelled him to make his presence known, but Patrick decided against it. He'd left Camlochlin and the notions his kin lived by so steadfastly. Honor would deny his desire, rebuke it.

So he watched her, unashamed and curious as to how to win the favor of a forest nymph.

Chapter Two

*C*harlotte kicked up her feet splashing water upward. She laughed when droplets fell over her face.

Oh, what a glorious day!

She adjusted the daisy circlet around her brow and tilted her face toward the sun. The water from the river was especially warm today, soothing away her anxious thoughts. She basked in the sounds of nature around her and nothing else. The chatter of birds filled the trees, bees buzzed while they hovered over daisies, water rushed over rocks. She drenched herself in the time she had alone, away from her father's strict, or so he thought, confines.

Her only regret today was that she hadn't insisted on taking Elsie along. She would make it up to her sister later.

She heard a sound to her left and hiked up her skirts to turn. She searched the branches of an old birch for the lark that had landed in it. When she found it, she whistled, smiled, and then headed back to the bank with a song on her lips.

She looked around for her brothers Duff and Hendry.

Not that she wanted them to hurry with their hunting. She loved being out of their company, free to do as she pleased, which was to make a crown of daisies and go into the water. But their father would be angry if he knew how long they'd left her alone. She was a troublesome daughter, far more defiant than Elsie, but she hated her father's fears, and endless rules and ambitions. He'd tried to marry her off several times for some profit or another. But she'd managed to convince every prospect so far that she wasn't fit to be a wife. She had faults, and plenty of them. One being that she liked to make her own decisions—a heinous offense to most men. Her last suitor, Geoffrey, Baron of Ardrossan, had needed a bit more convincing.

She leaned against a tree and stared out at the river glimmering against her eyes, the mountains far beyond. One day, she would travel across them with Elsie, both of them liberated from tyranny and the empty promises of men who couldn't measure up to a boy.

She heard another sound and reached under her skirts for her sling. She could take care of herself. A lass didn't frequent pubs and the seedy allies behind them without learning to protect herself.

Why was her heart suddenly pounding? No one in a hundred-league range was foolish enough to trespass on Allan Cunningham's land. Her father, like both his sons, didn't care who he killed, especially if the trespasser was a Fergusson.

But no sooner did she convince herself of her safety than she heard rustling in the foliage. It could be a deer. Oh, she hoped it was. She looked around for a stone.

Her heart near stopped when she looked up to find a man rising from his crouching position in the thick bushes. And not just any man, but the apparent victor of last night's brawl! In the full light of day, donned in nothing but a pair of snug-fitting woolen breeches, hide boots, and a purple jaw, he appeared as big as Hamish and fit enough to out-run her. The hands he held up were large enough to confine her with little effort. She knew how powerful he was, how fast. The slight tilt of his mouth almost convinced her that it would take even less effort to arrive at her throat to devour her as he had devoured Bethany.

She looked around. Where were her brothers? What was this stranger doing here? Had he followed her? She should be afraid of him, but she had her sling. She was more afraid of him telling her brothers that he'd seen her in the tavern. "Stay back!" she shouted and lifted her weapon. The man went still, eyeing the leather sling in her hand.

Something in his gaze sparked with recognition. Damn!

"Lass, where did ye—?"

She didn't wait for him to finish, but whirled her weapon over her head. She knew nothing about him, save that he was strong, he'd been hiding in the bushes, and he was a rogue. She wouldn't take any chances.

"Wait!" he called out, lifting his hands higher in surren-der. Sunlight dripped over his carved arms. His shoulders flexed, a ripple of movement and a promise of pure, solid power. "Allow me another moment to take ye in to convince m'self that ye're real."

She didn't breathe in the waiting stillness. She'd grown up among men, learning from her beloved Kendrick not to trust them, from her father to fear them, and from her brothers to keep her tongue leashed. She knew from her visits to different pubs what men were like when they wanted something. But none of them had ever spoken to her this way and with boldness and audacity to spread his appreciative gaze over her from her crown of daisies to her bare, tanned feet.

Even with the small meadow between then, Charlotte felt as if he touched her with his piercing jewel-like eyes.

She lifted the sling again. He was nothing more than a silver-tongued scoundrel who was likely here to force himself on her.

"I beg yer mercy, Angel," he called out then lowered his chin to his chest like a repentant servant. "But if ye must shoot, aim fer m' head and then pray over me that if I awaken, I have no memory of ye."

She smiled at the fool when he looked up. "You're a clever scoundrel."

She wished she were closer just to see if his lashes were as long and lush around his green eyes as they appeared from a distance.

But a face, no matter how ruggedly appealing it was, didn't mean anything to her. Flowery words meant even less. Duff and Hendry were handsome devils and they used their good looks to get what they wanted from women.

She wasn't so foolish.

"What do you want?" she demanded. "My brothers are just over that ridge." She motioned toward the small hill to their right.

"Just a moment more to gaze at yer beauty." His smile darkened with humor and something else that deepened his lilting voice to a smoky timbre. It worked its way down her spine and made her blood boil.

Knave. She'd seen him at work. He was a slayer of hearts, but he wouldn't have hers. No one would ever again. She had more important things to do than fawning like a twit over a man. Besides if she hit him now, he'd fall into the bushes and remain unseen by her brothers when they returned for her. No reason to get the rogue killed for admiring her. "I'd rather knock you out." She swung her sling over her shoulder and let her stone fly.

"Charlie!" her brother Hendry, having finally arrived a moment too soon, shouted from his saddle. They both heard the rock meet its target and the subsequent thump of a body hitting the ground.

Charlotte chewed her lip watching her brothers lift the man and haul him over his saddle.

"Who is he?" Hendry demanded as they headed home. "And why does he wear no shirt or coat?"

"How would I know?" She did her best keep the bite out of her question. "He appeared while I was waiting for you and Duff to come fetch me."

That rattled him, as she'd hoped it would. Her brothers were afraid of their father.

"Why didn't you call for us?" Duff asked her while a breeze lifted his dark hair and dragged it across pewter eyes. He wasn't as vile as Hendry or their father. The eldest of her siblings at a score and six, he had the most patience—mainly with her and Elsie. Sometimes his eyes warmed on Charlie and she remembered how he'd adored her as a child—despite their father's teachings to never grow weak over another person, even kin.

Though she would never return it again, she used his affection for her to her advantage. "I did," she lied then sniffed. "Father will be angry with me for having been alone, when it was you and Hendry who left me." She didn't give a damn that her brothers had left her, but her father would. "I thought you'd forgotten me."

"We wouldn't forget you, Charlie," Duff reassured her, softening his tone just a wee bit and moving his horse a little closer to hers.

Hendry's golden hair blew across his dubious smirk. "Is that why you felled him to the ground with that sling of yours?"

The slash of Duff's brow cast shadows over his eyes. "You used your sling?"

"Aye," she confessed, "and if you and Hendry will agree to keep my sling secret, I will also agree not to tell Father that you left me long enough for this to happen."

She prayed he would agree. Her father had forbidden her to use her sling. He had no problem expecting her to know how to protect herself against strangers, but not with her sling. It had belonged to a boy she'd once loved more than life itself. A boy she thought of often and would never forget. She'd been ten when he finally agreed to teach her how to use it. She'd practiced every day since his death five years ago until her skill was unmatched.

She'd crafted many duplicates of her sling over the years, mostly because her father always demanded she relinquish it whenever he found out that she had used it. She always gave him a replica. She'd never give up the original. It was all she had to remember Kendrick Fergusson.

"What choice did I have? Let him rape me?"

Duff set his black glare on the stranger tossed over his gray stallion. "He sought to rape you?"

She looked at the Highlander, still unconscious, and recalled how his gaze had fallen on her today and last night, when he'd looked up from devouring Bethany's neck with those simmering green eyes, like she was a slab of roasted venison and he hadn't eaten in a fortnight.

"Nay. I meant..." Damn it! Hendry hadn't killed the stranger and she wanted to keep it that way. "I don't know what he was after. I wasn't going to stand around and wait to find out."

"Mayhap, if you didn't dress like a trollop—"

"Hendry," Duff warned in a low growl.

"Come now, Duff," Hendry argued like the fool he was. "She's odd and you know it. She's always seeking to come hunting with us, but she doesn't hunt. Instead she slinks off by herself and splashes around in the river like some—"

"That's enough," her older brother warned, this time with more meaning. "You'll leave her alone or I'll break your nose again."

Charlie grinded her jaw to keep from telling Hendry what she thought of him. It wasn't her fault that laboring all day in the oat and wheat barns, cleaning the stables, planting, harvesting, and feeding the chickens was enough to exhaust her. She was ten and nine and she liked basking in the sun and laughing with old men.

"Do you think he's a Fergusson, Duff?" Hendry asked, changing the topic.

She groaned inwardly, hoping he wasn't. She may have just instigated another Fergusson attack.

Her gaze fell to the bold rogue again and the warm autumn colors in his hair. Burnt orange and bronze set ablaze by the sun, nestled within more earthy chestnut hues.

Kendrick's hair had been the same color. Perhaps just a bit redder. She smiled remembering the boy who still held her heart, making it impossible for any other to take his place. Once he was out of her life, her father had made certain she'd never lose her heart to a Fergusson again. He hated them over some ridiculous feud whose beginning neither clan could recall. And after the terrible thing had been done, and almost his entire family had escaped unscathed, her father didn't trust any stranger who happened on his land not to be a Fergusson assassin sent to finish what they'd started. And if the Fergussons returned, who would stop them this time?

"Let's hope he isn't a Fergusson," Duff said in a flat tone. He kicked his mount and muttered as he passed his sister. "Imbecile."

Charlie didn't respond, since he was speaking to himself and not her. But she agreed with him. They should all hope he wasn't a Fergusson since she'd injured him and would likely start another war. And Hendry was an imbecile.

As they rode onward toward Cunningham House the landscape spread out before her into rolling hills and shallow vales dotted with grazing sheep and thatch-roofed cottages beyond.

Crossing the old drawbridge, they approached the two-story house, in need of a new whitewash and a few stones to replace the crumbling ones. The stable and henhouse were also in need of repair, duties usually carried out by her father's serfs from the village, but Allan Cunningham preferred his tenants to pay for what little protection or aid he provided, with coin rather than labor. Most of the villagers in Pinwherry were poor or ill, or both.

Charlie looked up at Bhaltair and Kevin, the two guardsmen keeping watch from a high tower to the west of the house. Another two patrolled the perimeter—surely not enough men to counter an attack should the Fergussons ever return. They'd come only once, but no one had forgotten the dead they had left behind. Especially Charlie. The men in the surrounding countryside had been warned not to guard the Cunninghams. And when Cameron, John, and Tamas Fergusson warned a man of something, the man listened. Cunningham House had no bailiff, no reeve, and the only priest in attendance lived in the village.

As they neared the small outer gate, the intruder began to move. Hendry noticed and rode his horse to him.

Charlie's blood went cold when her brother kicked the man in the head, knocking him out again.

She recoiled and glared at him. "Your needless violence makes me ill, Hendry." She ignored his murderous gaze. He wouldn't try to strike her with Duff here. "One day, someone is going to give you the beating you deserve."

"Not likely," he drawled and continued on.

Forgetting her brother for now, Charlie waved to Alice, the Cunninghams' cook, when she stepped out of the small servant's house built inside the inner gate, this "gate" fashioned with short sticks and shrub.

Charlie headed her horse toward the stable, but Duff called her back.

"Hendry will take care of your mount, Charlie."

"Why do I have to tend to her horse?"

She tossed Hendry another glare that heated her large coal eyes and dismounted.

She didn't argue though. Why provoke him to getting even with her later? She bit her tongue until it almost bled, but she'd learned that sometimes it was better to tame the tongue than wield it.

"Charlie," Duff called out again. "Your sling."

She spun on her heel and stared at him, her eyes wide. "You will tell Father and have me disarmed then?"

He shook his head. "I'll get you a pistol in the morning."

"I don't want a pistol."

He held out his hand for the sling. She gave him one last glare then hiked up her skirts over her left leg and yanked the counterfeit free from where it was secured. After handing it over she turned, smiled, and left him with Kendrick's sling still secured to her right leg.

When she entered the house, she spotted her sister bobbing down the stairs, her heavy petticoats lifted in both hands.

"Thank God, you're back! You were gone all morning!" Elsie exclaimed with her flare for the dramatic. Her golden waves bounced over her diminutive shoulders, her blue eyes wide with apprehension. "I was beginning to fear something terrible might have happened."

"I told you, darling," Charlie cooed and took her sister's hand. "Nothing will take me from you."

And nothing would. Their mother had died five years ago. Elsie was the babe by a year and was often ill and needed mothering. Charlie had happily taken up the duty. The village physician had treated her with various concoctions but none of them helped Elsie's condition. Most of the time the poor darling lost her breath, sometimes she struggled through each one. It was difficult to witness, especially when her attacks made her weak and pale for days. There had to be a way to help her. According to the physician, keeping her indoors and safe from the elements was all they could do. Charlie refused to believe it. There were other healers out there. She'd found some. She would find them all, and not stop looking until she found the one with the cure. Until then, she did her best each day to teach Elsie how to be a strong, confident woman.

"Charlotte!" Their father bellowed from the parlor. "Get your arse in here, gel!"

Charlie closed her eyes. Damn her brothers for telling him anything. He always overreacted and she was weary of it.

"I'll come with you," Elsie offered, biting her lip.

"Nay, dear," Charlie smiled tenderly at her. "Wait here for me and we shall do something exciting when I'm done with him."

"You mean after he's done with you."

Charlie shook her head. Five years of his bellowing had

taught her that agreeing with her father was the best way to mollify him. She would handle him, but for now she preferred to waste no more time on him.

"I made this for you." She removed her daisy circlet and placed it over her sister's brow then stepped back to admire it. "You look like a fairy queen."

"Charlotte! Damn it!" their father shouted.

Elsie stopped her when Charlie turned to answer his booming expletive. She stepped closer and kissed Charlie's cheek. "I made something for you as well." She took Charlie's hand and placed a small leather hilt inside it.

Charlie looked down at the short, curved blade, black as a moonless sky. "What is it?" she asked running her finger along the edge. She pulled back as the blade cut her skin and drew blood.

"'Tis very hard glass," Elsie told her in her soft breathless voice. "'Tis called obsidian. Like your eyes."

They smiled at each other, kissed again, and then Charlie hid her dagger beneath her skirts and ran off.

"He did not tell me who he was, Father."

"Well, what did he tell you, Charlotte?"

Allan Cunningham sat across from her and to the left of her brothers in the private parlor. The "parlor" was nothing more than a stone and timber chamber with a small hearth and several cushioned chairs. But according to Lachlan Wallace, the village tanner, Cameron Fergusson's Tarrick Hall had a parlor, so her father had to have one as well.

"He didn't have time to say much," Charlie told her father, trying to remain patient. She hated having to stand before him in his stuffy parlor and give account for everything she did. She'd much rather be outdoors soaking up the sun. "He begged me not to strike him.

"Duff has my sling, as you already know, and I request it back."

"I didn't know," he informed her, sparing his son a surprised glance.

Charlie turned to him as well. She wouldn't smile or thank him for not telling their father, but she was glad he hadn't. He was still loyal to her. It broke her heart a little to remember how much she'd loved him. That she'd not only lost Kendrick but him too. He'd always been a better brother to her than Hendry, who was jealous of any attention their father gave anyone but him. Duff had been a better person, or so she'd believed. His part in Kendrick's death hurt more than the rest. She couldn't forgive him.

"I shall consider it." Her father's dark eyes narrowed on her before he spoke again. "You struck him down after he pled your mercy?"

She nodded, keeping what she truly thought of her father hidden behind a well-learned impassive expression.

"You've learned well, daughter," he smiled. She didn't smile back. "People are merciless. You must be merciless, as well. Did he say anything else?"

She'd asked the stranger what he wanted. The conquering slant of his grin had been riddled with a natural magnetism that had rattled her a bit.

Just a moment more to gaze at yer beauty.

"His name perhaps?" her father pressed.

What would he do to the stranger if he was a Fergusson? Would her father be such a fool to harm the man and bring Cameron Fergusson and his brothers back to Cunningham House? They had four guards. Four. What would four guards do when the Fergussons could take down fifty? "I didn't wait for him to say anything else."

Her father laughed then offered her a nod of approval. "Duff, give her back her sling."

She still didn't smile. They could keep it for all she cared. She had the original.

"Thank you, Father." She dipped her head and turned to her brother. He gave her the sling, and the slightest of smiles.

"You may go, Charlotte," her father called out, "and take that kohl off from around your eyes. You look like a woman from a brothel."

She remained unfazed by his insult as she turned to face him again. "Warriors used to paint their faces, Father." And she was a warrior, wasn't she? Perhaps not the kind he would prefer, but that hardly mattered. She did all she could to help her sister and the others. Defying her father and her brothers with her nightly visits outdoors. She'd fight to the death for the freedom she lost five years ago to her father's fear of the Fergussons. Sometimes she painted her eyes to remind herself of who she was.

He raised a brow. "They did, didn't they?" He looked her over from her mantle of raven hair to her long, flowing skirts she sewn herself, to her bare feet, and scowled at the last.

"You certainly don't look like one," he finally concluded. "I would prefer it if you wore acceptable layers and your earasaid. You look fragile in those sheer skirts."

He didn't know her. He used to, but not anymore. Not since her mother was killed. "Looks can be deceiving."

"So it seems." He dismissed her with a wave.

She turned to leave, refusing to remember the happier, kinder father who'd raised her until she was ten and four, the year, unbeknownst to her at the time, he ordered her brothers to murder Kendrick.

She had suffered a life with him for five long years and was determined to get Elsie away from his poisoned ways of thinking and cold, callous tongue.

But for today...She stopped at the door. There was something she wished to do and she needed her father's permission else she'd find herself locked away in her room for the next sennight. "May I take Elsie to the village? I believe the sun does her good."

He raised a gray brow. "You think to know more than Ennis Kennedy, the physician?"

She folded her hands in front of her, her sling dangling from one, and stood her ground. "I know Elsie more than he does. As for knowing what's best for her, Mother always said that laughter was good medicine."

She held fast to her stoic expression, keeping a victorious smirk hidden. If there was ever anyone Allan Cunningham loved, it had been his wife. He wouldn't disagree with anything his dearest Margaret had believed.

Charlie didn't even have to continue. He would grant what she asked. She felt mildly guilty for using her beloved mother to get her way, but she would always do what needed to be done. "Elsie doesn't laugh when she's locked within these walls."

He looked up toward heaven and pounded his palm on his thigh. "Margaret," he lamented dramatically, "why did you leave me with such a sickly creature?"

Charlie turned away from him, hating how he felt about Elsie's illness. To him, she was weak and a burden.

"Go," he breathed out as if she exhausted him. "Don't be out for too long."

Charlie shut the door behind her, glad to be away from him and her brothers. Someday, when the villagers were safe from her father and Hendry, she would take Elsie away from this house. They would live alone in a small cottage somewhere near the water. But until then, there were things to be done. One of them being finding a cure for her sister's breathing ailment. The other was even more impossible. Thinking of it, she prayed that the pouch of coins she'd hidden upstairs in one of her winter boots remained unfound until she could get out of the house tonight.

But presently there was another matter that needed her attention.

She hadn't asked her father about his prisoner. The stranger hadn't been brought into the house so he must have been taken to the stable—which was where she'd planned on going.

She wasn't afraid to be near the Highlander. Her brothers would never have left him unbound. Not if he was possibly a Fergusson. Was he? If he was, she didn't think he'd be candid about it since the only reason he would have come here was for trouble. She'd find out the truth if she could, and possibly save all their lives.

She wasn't going to help him because she liked him. She didn't know him. She sure as hell didn't like rakes. They were the worst kind of men; versed in flowery words, they seduced, took what they wanted, and then left. She'd seen the effects of it firsthand. She didn't want that kind of possible trouble to complicate her life.

If he was a Fergusson she should hate him the way her father and brothers did. But she didn't hate the clan. She wanted to forget them. She did all she could to forget them. All but one.

She'd help because if this stranger was kin to Cameron Fergusson and her father and brothers killed him, she had no doubt that this time, retaliation would include the death of everyone in Cunningham House, not just her mother. If he was a Fergusson then anything that came next was her fault. Any act of aggression would lead to bloodshed for all, and now they were holding him prisoner! If he was not kin to her father's enemy, then he had likely just wandered onto Cunningham land and was guilty of nothing more than having a fickle, foolish heart.

She'd help because it's what she did, what Kendrick had always told her to do, follow her heart. Her heart told her to right her father and brother's wrongs. To give back what they took and help whom they harmed. She wasn't completely merciless, and she wasn't fragile. Mostly, she wasn't about to change now, no matter who the man in the stable was.

She found her sister sitting on the steps and finally smiled. "Told you I'd be done with him quickly," she said with victory lacing her voice. "Do you want to ride with me to the muirs?"

"The heather muirs?" Her sister sucked in a slight breath while a faint smile hovered over her lips. "'Tis too far. Father wouldn't approve."

"I know," Charlie said, her eyes sparkling in the candlelight. "But he won't find out. I told him I was taking you to the village. He won't look for us. Will you come?"

Elsie's smile grew wide and she nodded.

Without waiting to ponder what she was about to do and perhaps talk herself out of it, she took Elsie's hand and led her to the front door. "Come. I must see to one thing before we go."

Elsie made no protest when Charlie led her out but paused on their way toward the stable.

"Are we taking horses, Charlie? Will Father notice if we—"

"I'm going to help a man who is inside. Stay close to me," Charlie warned as they neared the old structure.

She felt her sister's thumping heart against her back as they entered. Or was it hers? It didn't matter. She'd promised Elsie something exciting. What was more exciting than danger that wasn't truly dangerous?

Then again, if the stranger was a relative of Cameron Fergusson, he was dangerous indeed.

Chapter Three

*P*atrick opened his eyes and lifted his forehead away from something cool. A wooden post. Where was he? He groaned and muttered a curse at the ache in his head. The smell of hay and manure overwhelmed him for a moment while he tried to clear his thoughts. The neigh of a nearby horse confirmed that he was in a stable. What had happened? The lass at the river, he recalled. She'd brought him down with a sling and a stone! He didn't know anyone who used a sling anymore, save his uncle Tamas. He tried to ask her where she got it but she'd struck him in the head with a stone. Did she know the Fergussons?

He thought of her eyes, ringed in shadow. He'd seen them before, felt the power in them. Last night at the pub. The lass in the shadows. It was she. Hell, she was even more compelling in the light of day. He should have recognized her at the river when she not only sparked his desire, but piqued his curiosity. But what the hell was she doing in Pinmore if she lived here in Pinwherry?

He tried to pull himself up but found his movements

restricted. He glared at the rope securing his wrists to the post. Had she done this? Where the hell was he?

He looked around in the shifting light. There was hay under his arse and his head was pounding. Why was he tethered to a damn post?

He yanked on his ties to no avail. The more he yanked, the angrier he became. Whoever did this was going to regret it.

He was still pulling on his knots when he heard the stable doors opening.

"Is he dangerous?" a female voice asked.

"Nay, and I'm certain he is bound," another voice answered.

It was her. Patrick would remember the silken edge of her voice for the remainder of his days. He didn't blame her for slinging her stone and knocking him out. She did him a favor by stopping him from proclaiming her beauty one more time. Hell, it had been as if he'd fallen under a spell and every time he should have been fighting for his life, he was praising her. What the hell had come over him? Perhaps it was the smirk that curled her lips, mocking his prettiest words. There was fire in her.

He wasn't sure if he'd ever forget the sight of her, her willowy locks dancing across her face, her rosy cheeks, her arm lifted over her shoulder as she swung her sling. Her aim was precise. Who had taught her?

She was glorious, vital, and dangerous.

What was she up to? She couldn't have dragged him here alone. Damn, he recalled her mentioning something about her brothers being close by. He deduced the rest.

He heard her footsteps coming closer and he sat up straighter—as straight as he could with his bound wrists. He refused to appear weak and vulnerable to her. This was her stable. Her brothers had captured him, for what purpose, he didn't know. It had to be nefarious or he would have been left where'd he'd fallen. He'd come upon the lass, and for doing so she had almost killed him. Why bring him home?

He didn't care why. He was getting out alive and he'd use her to do it. He knew how to get what he wanted out of women.

She moved forward into the shaft of light from the small window behind him. She gasped upon seeing him there—as if she didn't know.

"Have ye come to save me?" he asked, surprising her with a wry grin.

He noticed another lass breathing hard behind the first and heaving in her friend's ear. Her golden hair flashed in the light for a moment, illuminating her pale, angelic face and the familiar crown of daisies now placed on her brow. The dark-haired one pushed her farther back.

Patrick slipped his gaze to the first once again. Her eyes were already on him, wide, curious, guarded eyes, made even darker by the thin line of black kohl encircling them.

"So what's goin' to happen now?" he asked her. He knew what he wished would happen. She'd untie him and send her friend away. Whatever concerns he'd had about growing tired of women and trouble faded when he looked at her.

He could see her shapely curves through the gauzy folds of her skirts. She was delicately formed with long, elegant arms and full breasts beneath the delicate fabric of her gown.

"That depends on who you are," she told him.

He smiled gazing at her full lower lip. She didn't smile back.

He had no intentions of telling her who he was. The MacGregor name was proscribed. Being one could get him thrown into prison with a paid reward to anyone turning him in. Her brothers couldn't know he was a MacGregor, so why was he being held captive?

"Why was I brought here?" he asked.

She shook her head and looked down at him. "That's enough questions from you, but I have one to ask. What were you doing at the river?"

His dimple flashed when his smile deepened along with his tone. "Ye know what I was doin' there, lass. But if I'm to die fer admirin' ye, then stay where ye are and let me take m' fill this time."

Hell, he couldn't seem to stop. Sure, he knew what words to use to win a lady's favor. But he'd never used so many on one lass. He was tempted to ask her to knock him out again.

She smiled, but not the way other lasses smiled when he was trying to seduce them. Hers was a pitying quirk of her mouth, like he was the biggest fool she'd ever come across if he thought she believed a word he said.

"Charlie, are we going to untie him and set him free?"

"Nay, Elsie."

Charlie? Why would any parent give this beauty a man's name?

"Untie me and ye'll never see me again," Patrick promised. Why would he come back to see her when she was clearly uninterested in him? He found it a wee bit insulting.

"I cannot," Charlie told him. She moved closer, out of the light, and knelt in the obscurity with him. She smelled of lavender and the wind and made him want to lean in and take a deeper breath.

"But I will tell you this," she whispered, sending her breath along his nape and making him taut as an over-wound harpstring. "If you are a Fergusson, don't tell them. If you do, they'll kill you."

"Why?" he asked, "And who?" But she was already gone and reaching into the shadows for her friend. Grasping her by the wrist, she pulled Elsie out of the stable and closed the doors.

Whoever this family was, they obviously hated his uncles. But why?

He didn't have much more time to ponder it when the doors opened again. This time men's voices filled the stable.

"She molds you and Father like warm clay in her hands."

"See if he's awake, Hendry."

Ah, the brothers had arrived.

Hendry appeared around the stall and stood where Charlie had been moments before. He was tall and thin, easy for Patrick to take down if his hands were free.

"He is," he called out, and then kicked some moldy hay in Patrick's direction.

Patrick coughed and Hendry laughed.

"Let me speculate." Patrick interrupted the merriment with a dark smile of his own. "Ye used to pull the wings off bugs, and now ye slap lasses around." He flashed his teeth. "Am I correct?"

Hendry answered with a fist to Patrick's mouth.

"Aye," Patrick said quietly and moved forward to wipe the blood from his lip on the ties that bound him. "I thought so."

"Hendry!" the man who had entered with him shouted, appearing in the light. "There will be time for that later. Can you not control that wretch within you for a full hour?"

Aye, Patrick wanted to agree out loud, at least with the part about Hendry being a wretch.

The other man moved forward, towering over Patrick, who couldn't stand. Unlike his brother, this one's wide shoulders blocked out the light behind him.

"I'm Duff Cunningham."

Patrick tossed him a brief smile. "A pleasure. Now can ye do somethin' aboot the rope? 'Tis beginnin' to wear on m' good nature."

"Who are you?" Duff Cunningham said as woodenly as the post Patrick was tied to.

"Patrick Campbell of Breadalbane, and ye better have a good reason fer takin' me from the road. M' uncle is the Duke of Argyll." A very distant uncle, but it wasn't a complete untruth. His great uncle Robert Campbell had once been the earl.

"You weren't on the road," the dark giant countered. "You fell at my sister's feet."

"Not that close, I'd argue. More like a target at fifty feet."

He thought he saw a hint of a smile on Duff's face. If there was one it was gone when he spoke again. "What were you doing at the riverbank?"

That seemed to be the important question of the day. Were these people feuding with his uncles?

"I was lost and thought to refresh m' horse, which ye have m' gratitude fer bringin' back here with me."

"We didn't bring it back," Hendry said. "We left it—"

"Mine is in the third stall on the left."

Duff stepped out of the stall and looked to the third stall on the left. When he saw that Patrick was correct, he hurried back to the post and bent to check the tight knots around his prisoner's wrists. When he was satisfied that Patrick couldn't have left the post to find out where his horse was, he bent to his knees and set his level gaze on him.

"How did you know?"

"He's m' horse."

Duff waited for more but when none came, he straightened again to his full height. "You're in trouble often and need to know where your horse is in case a quick exit is needed."

Patrick looked up and offered him a benign smile. "Ye make it sound so unsavory."

"Verra well then," Duff said, ignoring Patrick's light humor and producing a dagger. "If you're telling the truth you will get your horse back and leave here." He cut the rope loose from the post but left Patrick's hands tied.

"Who decides whether or no' I'm tellin' the truth?" Patrick asked while he rose.

"My father," Duff said then led him out of the stable.

Sunlight stung Patrick's eyes so he held up his bound fists to shield them. He spotted Charlie watching them from behind a short wall and a field beyond. Her dark locks snapped against her face and she cleared them. Her gaze remained on him.

He smiled at her and then fell to his knees when Duff sent his fist into Patrick's guts.

Chapter Four

Charlie's muscles twitched when Duff hit him. Fergusson or not, the auburn-haired rogue was trouble to be certain, but he'd done nothing to deserve a beating.

Unless a mere glance from him was considered so dangerous.

Judging by Charlie's weak knees, it was. The confidence he possessed emanated from his eyes and went straight to her head. They pierced her defenses and sparked her embers to life. The carefree quirk of his mouth tempted her to defy him. She had no idea how such a challenge would play out, but he tempted her to engage. Trouble; like she said.

With the sunlight behind him, she hadn't been able to get a clearer look at him in the stable than she had at the river—or the pub. Just as well, his husky voice in the shadows had been enough to stir her blood and make her feel overly warm.

Now, she watched from a short wall separating the yard from the field, as he doubled over at the force of Duff's blow.

"He's like snake rising from the pit," Elsie said of him rising from his knees, one hand on his sore belly.

A snake? Charlie thought as he stood and faced Duff head-on, his bare muscles tight and ready to respond. More like a wild stallion at its peak.

"Why," Elsie inhaled, sounding affected by the handsome Highlander in a way that had little to do with her condition, "he's as big as Duff."

Aye, Charlie had already noticed. And he was strong. He'd walked away from a brawl with Hamish.

"Do you think Father will kill him?" Elsie asked from where she sat on the wall with her legs dangling over the other side, the muirs forgotten in favor of a handsome stranger.

"I don't know," Charlie told her as the prisoner spoke words she couldn't hear and her brother laughed in his face. "It depends on him and who he is."

"I know Father is afraid that we will be abducted by Fergussons," Elsie sighed. "Do you think the stranger meant to abduct you at the riverbank?"

Charlie had told her about the encounter while Duff and Hendry were inside the barn. She'd also told her sister of seeing him at the pub the night before.

"I don't think so." Was she wrong? Possibly. She looked away when the trio reached the house. Everything she knew about men she'd learned from those who lived with her and from the kind who frequented pubs. If the stranger had meant to abduct her he would have used stealth or strength, not charm.

"I'm glad you helped him, Charlie," her sister told her when Charlie joined her on the wall.

"If we can help, we should."

Elsie pulled in a shallow breath and nodded in agreement.

"Come," Charlie tugged her sister's skirt, "let us go for a walk in the sun. 'Twill help your breathing."

"If he is a Fergusson," Elsie ignored her request, "can we still help him? I know what the Fergussons did, but mayhap they all are not bad—"

"They came here because our brothers killed Kendrick, lest you forget, Elsie."

"I haven't forgotten, but if we can help, we should, aye, Fergusson or not?"

It would be risking much. Charlie set her eyes on her sister. "Now, dearest, I would not have you do anything that might get you into trouble with Father."

"But you get into trouble with Father all the time," her sister argued.

"That's different."

"Why?" Elsie's blue eyes widened.

Charlie shook her head. She didn't want to have this conversation yet again. It was different because Charlie could take care of herself. Duff had taught her how. She'd watched him practice every day. Hidden behind the hen-house, she imitated his movements and practiced them as often as she did with her sling.

"If the stranger is a Fergusson and he tells Father, then he is a fool and helping him further will only jeopardize us."

"Of course, you're correct," Elsie sighed, sounding somewhat deflated. "But can we at least go—"

The remainder of her request was cut off by Hugh, one of their father's guards, racing his horse toward the wall. Almost a dozen more mounted men raced up behind him.

"Riders approaching!" he shouted at the girls.

What? Charlie's heart hammered in her throat as she leaped from the wall. Who were the riders? Were they

Fergussons? She turned to look back at the house. Had they come for him? Oh, what had she done?

Hugh looked pale when he reached them an instant later. His eyelids drooped. "Get…inside," he said weakly, and then fell out of his saddle, the hilt of a dagger protruding from his back and blood staining his tunic.

Kevin fell from the watchtower, an arrow jutting from his chest. Bhaltair shouted but his words were cut off when he fell next.

Elsie screamed as the riders thundered closer.

Charlie seized her sister's hand and raced with her toward the house. She felt for her sling but the men who killed Hugh were too close. She lifted her skirts and grabbed her obsidian dagger. "Duff!" she shouted as loud as she could.

Somewhere behind her she heard the riders getting closer. She'd almost reached the house when a man whose voice she didn't know shouted behind her.

"Stop, lass! Or you will share the fate of your father's guards."

Charlie stopped and pushed Elsie behind her when she turned to face him. They were close to the door. "Get inside," Charlie warned her sister.

"I won't leave you!" Elsie insisted.

Charlie grinded her jaw and made a quick note to throttle her foolishly devoted sister later. Elsie couldn't lend a hand. She didn't know how to use a sling. She'd never practiced archery or any kind of fighting. But she knew what was needed to remain safe. Charlie fingered the small hilt in her hand.

Charlie faced the eight riders dismounting from their horses, looking her and Elsie over with blatant male intent. If they touched Elsie, she'd kill them or die trying. She was sure she could get at least three of them down before she died. Were they Fergussons? Unlike the soul most likely still bound while he faced her father in the parlor, the men in front of her clearly had more treacherous intentions.

"What do you want here?" she called out, doing her best to keep her breath even. She'd never faced down so many men bent on trouble. Where in blazes was Duff? She was afraid but she'd learned well how to mask it. "I warn you though, if 'tis not forgiveness for killing my father's guards, this day will likely be your last."

For a moment the men looked surprised by her boldness and then they laughed.

"Do you intend to slay me with your beauty then?" drawled the one who'd ordered her to stop.

Charlie rubbed her fingers over the obsidian. His flattery meant nothing. She didn't want to kill. She never had before, but she would if she had to. If he touched her sister, she'd cut his throat. "If you come closer you will find out."

One corner of his bearded mouth hooked into a smirk as he held up his dagger. "Seems like I'm the one with the weapon."

"Seems like it," she allowed, standing her ground.

"I will strike a bargain with you," he called out, amused. "I will not come any closer. You will come to me." He beckoned with his blade. "Come here or I'll have my men kill her." He lifted the dagger over his shoulder and was about to motion the men behind him to move forward.

Charlie broke away from her sister and took a step forward, her heart pounding madly in her chest. If they hurt Elsie—

She almost reached him when the front door swung open and Duff appeared like an angry dragon from its cave.

The rider snatched her wrist and pulled her in the rest of the way. He spun her around to face her family and hauled her spine against him. He brought his cold blade to her throat and set his balmy breath upon her cheek.

"Take another step and she dies. 'Twould be a pity, nay? I know my brother would be disappointed."

Duff went still. His steely eyes burned with the promise of retribution. In the next instant though, he was shoved out of the way as her father stepped outside. Allan Cunningham growled a warning to Elsie, who stepped back into Hendry's chest as he, too, exited the house.

"Who are you and what are you doing on my land?" her father demanded.

Charlie hoped they weren't Fergussons because they were surely going to die for coming here and threatening her life. Duff was going to kill them. She could see it in his eyes. Damn it, but when would this feud end?

"I'm Archie Dunbar," her captor called out, "and I've come here to fetch a wife for my brother Alistair. Your daughter's beauty is spoken of throughout Galloway. We didn't know about the golden haired one though. Mayhap we'll take her too."

Not if Charlie could help it. She'd rather die than marry this brutish pig's brother, and she'd rather gut him down the center than let him anywhere near her sister.

"You'll never leave here alive," her father promised, ignoring his prisoner, the man from the riverbank, still bound at the wrists, still shirtless as he too, appeared at the doors.

"And who will stop us?" Charlie's captor asked, his lips close to her ear. "Your guardsmen are dead. If you have any sense, you'll go back inside and leave her to us."

"If he had any sense," her father's prisoner stepped forward and held up his bound wrists, "he wouldna have taken a Campbell prisoner."

A Campbell. The charming rake was a Campbell? Damn it, if her kin killed *him* they'd have the whole bloody kingdom at their front door. Charlie watched him spread his devilishly disarming smile on the beast at her back.

"I'm Patrick Campbell. Cut me loose and I'll fight at yer side."

Charlie caught the subtle shift of his gaze toward her when she glared at him, doing her best to keep her eyes above his chin and ignoring his long, sculpted physique and broad shoulders. Was he speaking to her or her captor?

Dunbar laughed at his offer. "You don't even carry a sword." He looked him over. "Or even a place to hide one."

It was true. Charlie hadn't noticed it before. Patrick Campbell spoke like a Highlander and had dressed like one when she'd first seen him at Blind Jack's, yet he carried no obvious weapons.

"I dinna need one," he claimed, his amiable smile changing slightly into something more ominous.

Charlie knew it was true. He had fought Hamish with no weapons other than his fists. What kind of Highlander didn't carry a sword? The kind who doesn't need one.

Campbell moved closer to her and the eight men behind her. His gait was wrought with ease and confidence while her brothers and her father remained still.

"I'll kill you for this, Campbell," Duff swore.

"That's doubtful," Campbell tossed back without turning around. Instead, he looked at Charlie, now only a few inches away, standing between him and her captor.

If there wasn't a blade to her throat, she would have taken a moment to admire him and all his hard angles.

"Untie me," he said to Dunbar, "and I'll fight them all with no help or risk of injury to ye or yer men." He lifted his bound wrists up, close to Charlie's face and the dagger at her throat. "The Duke of Argyll will hear of how ye aided his nephew."

Dunbar seemed to think it over for a moment and then moved the dagger away from her neck to possibly cut Campbell loose. But instead of waiting to be free, the Highlander moved in a blur of speed snatching the dagger from Dunbar's hand. In one fluid movement that Charlie almost missed by blinking, Campbell, still bound and clutching the hilt in his fingers, lifted his arms and then brought them back down to capture Dunbar's head between his forearms, and Charlie's head between his thick upperarms.

An instant turned into an eternity while he pulled Dunbar closer, wedging Charlie up against his chest. Time slowed as she looked up and he tilted his head to meet her gaze. She stared into his summer-glade eyes—ringed by lashes that *were* that long—and the evidence of Hamish's wrath on his lip. His current wounds and an older one which had broken his nose saved him from being pretty. His mouth crooked ever so slightly—just enough to flash his dimple and completely befuddle her. A rascal. That's what he was. He was helping her. But why? Before she had to ponder it further, the instant was over.

He hauled Archie Dunbar an inch closer and knocked him out with a clean blow, forehead to forehead. He moved quickly and lifted his arms to release Dunbar from his hold then gave him a powerful kick in the guts to topple him over.

"Run!" He pushed Charlie behind him and faced the rest of the Dunbars alone.

Duff reached them at the same time and an instant before the stunned expressions on the faces of Dunbar's men wore off and they rushed forward.

"Give me your hands!" Charlie commanded, tugging on Campbell's sleeve. When he obeyed, she cut him loose using her black blade.

The fool took a moment to smile at her before she tucked the dagger back under her skirts.

Hendry finally joined the fight but Charlie couldn't take her eyes off Mr. Campbell in the melee. He took down three men on his own with nothing but his fists.

Charlie was certain she saw teeth flying.

Duff sliced his sword across the chest of another man and stepped over his dead body to move on to the next opponent.

"Charlotte."

She tore her gaze from Campbell fighting together with her brothers. Pushing back the Dunbars, and saving her and Elsie. She didn't know why he did, but she was grateful.

"Aye, Father?"

His eyes on her were hard, as if this were her fault. "Bring Elsie to her room."

"Aye, Father." She began to leave but he called her back. "Meet us in the parlor when this is over. I'm curious to know how your *beauty* is spoken of throughout Galloway when you haven't left Pinwherry."

Chapter Five

*P*atrick sat in the parlor, unbound, donning a borrowed shirt, and sipping wine.

He hated wine.

Thanks to the Dunbars, who had taken their dead and left, he was no longer a prisoner of Cunningham House but a welcomed guest. Things had worked out well; then again, they usually did where Patrick was concerned. He was a lucky scoundrel else he would have been killed half a dozen times already by angry brothers and fathers. Still, he didn't like that three Dunbars had died today. Aye, the men were bastards coming here to kidnap a wife, but Patrick had always preferred not killing if he didn't have to. The Cunninghams didn't share his sentiments.

How had that boded for his Fergusson uncles, living close by? Patrick knew the two clans were longtime enemies, but the hatred with which Allan Cunningham spoke seemed fresh enough. His host wouldn't say what had kept the feud going when Patrick had asked him and Patrick hadn't pushed the issue. He'd leave and ask his uncles any questions he had.

"We could use a man like you here," Cunningham told him now. "None of my guardsmen ever fought the way you did today. That scoundrel bastard might have killed Charlotte, or made off with her, if not for you."

Patrick flicked his gaze to Cunningham's daughter seated next to Duff. He kept his expression neutral, preferring not to get into another brawl with one of her brothers, although when faced with eight armed riders who meant to kidnap her, they stood motionless. Duff, at least, hadn't moved because there was a knife to his sister's throat that could cut quickly enough had he attacked. Patrick understood and didn't fault him for it.

"I'm glad I was here to lend my aid," he answered. Was it fate that brought him here to save her? Nae, he thought slipping his gaze to her again, if no one had helped her, she would have saved herself. He remembered the wee black dagger she kept hidden under her skirts. He wondered what other weapons she possessed.

It was difficult not to aim his most charming smile on her though, for she was exquisite in every damn way. Apparently, he wasn't the only one who thought so. When her father had questioned her about how the Dunbars knew of her, she'd insisted she didn't know and then said as little as possible. Patrick guessed her father didn't know about her late night visits to Blind Jack's.

What other secrets did she keep? Patrick wanted to discover them all.

He thought about her being crushed up against him for a moment while he had taken down her attacker, the fear and anger that made her large dark eyes shine like moonlit seas. The same eyes that had cut through a crowded pub to slay him. The same nimbus mantle falling down her back. She'd looked right at him but if she recognized him, she'd made no show of it, nor had she mentioned it.

"Why were you so quick to aid her?"

Patrick blinked, severing his gaze from hers and returning it to his host. Cunningham certainly was a suspicious bastard. "Because there was a man holding a blade to her throat and no one else was moving their arse fast enough."

Patrick didn't give a damn who he insulted. He hadn't forgotten the blows inflicted upon him by Cunningham's sons.

"We had no choice," argued Hendry, a most unlikeable fellow with pinched lips and a belligerent, though striking gaze. "One wrong move and he would have sliced her."

"And yet," Patrick answered in a voice rich with sarcasm, "he did nothing when I approached him."

"In fairness to my sons," Cunningham said, dragging Patrick's attention back to him. "Dunbar thought you would stand with him."

His good mood restored, Patrick flashed him a grin. "I *was* verra believable."

Cunningham returned his smile but there was no sign of humor in his eyes. "You find ease in deceit, Campbell?"

Patrick shrugged one shoulder and relaxed his mouth as he boldly turned to look at Charlie. "Depending on the purpose, aye."

He didn't miss the slight curl of her tantalizing mouth before she looked down, shielding her midnight gaze beneath a spray of sooty lashes. Could he seduce her? Perhaps take up a true chase for the first time in years? He didn't believe she'd be an easy victory and it tempted him beyond control. He'd have to begin in the next few hours, before he set out on his way again. He'd like to reach Tarrick Hall by tonight. He'd return to finish another time.

Hendry sneered and rose to fetch himself another drink. "And you would have us believe you're a man of honor?"

"I'd have ye believe no such thing," Patrick protested watching him. "No' that ye'd know what honor was if it smashed ye in the face and broke yer nose."

Hendry opened his tight lips to say something but Duff stopped him. "Be silent, fool," he warned and then addressed Patrick. "Campbell, you have our gratitude for saving our sister."

Duff Cunningham was a few years younger than Patrick, with dark, almost black hair, which he wore loose to his shoulders, and eyes of tempered steel. He was tall and built for tossing folks around. Patrick's borrowed shirt, given to him by Charlie's bonnie sister, had no doubt come from Duff's own cabinet since he was the closest in size. Something about the cut of his jaw and the silvery tint of his eyes reminded Patrick of someone else. Presently, he couldn't place who it was.

"Of course!" Allan Cunningham agreed. "And that's why you'll stay for a few days and enjoy my food and drink."

"Ye have m' gratitude fer that," Patrick said, accepting the offer. "I could use a rest from m' travels. A soft bed mayhap." What harm was there in staying another day? He hadn't seen his uncles in a decade. Another day or two wouldn't hurt. There were things he wanted to find out, like what made Miss Charlotte Cunningham smile? He didn't want to rush.

He brought his cup of warm wine to his lips and swept his gaze back to her. Her hair fell down her shoulders and over her cleavage like an inky cloud. He wanted to touch it, scoop the weight of it off her neck and kiss . . .

"Are you looking for a wife?" her father asked, hauling him from his thoughts once again.

Patrick nearly choked on his wine and sat up in his chair. "Nae."

"Because I must tell you," Cunningham went on. "I wouldn't be against a Campbell union. I could use the influence and strength of your clan to aid us against our enemies."

"Father!" Charlie bound from her chair looking mortified and furious.

"Sit down, Charlotte. You'll do as I say. You could use a firm hand and I could use—"

"I dinna want a wife," Patrick interjected.

"Someone needs to keep you in your place, gel," her father told her, ignoring her dark, blazing eyes and Patrick's vehement refusal. "You have chased away every prospect other than Alistair Dunbar." He pointed to her brother, "And Duff here refuses to let you go to a man who sends his brother to kidnap you. A Campbell union would serve us and *you* well."

"'Twill have to be someone other than me," Patrick said, rising from his chair, demanding to be heard.

Hell, he should have said he was a MacGregor.

"Why?" Her father set his wide, insulted gaze on him. "What's wrong with her?"

That seemed to be the last straw for her. Without another word, she hiked up her flimsy skirts and stormed out of the parlor.

Patrick waited a moment when no one moved to go after her. He did.

No one stopped Patrick from following her out the door. Hell, her father was likely drawing up her dowry. They were mad. The whole lot of them, he thought, slowing his pace. This morning he was tied up and left in horse shyt by the

Cunninghams and now they wanted him to be part of the family. Mad.

What did he want with a lass who painted her eyes black like some Pictish queen and dressed herself in fabric crafted for fairies? Who cared if she was so beautiful that men risked their lives to try to capture her? He wouldn't. A wife. He laughed between his steps. He'd rather shove a dagger into his temple than be saddled down with one lass for the remainder of his days. He would win her favor and bed her thoroughly, proving to himself once and for all that he wasn't turning into some soft, needy fool.

He watched her stomp toward the vale in her bare feet, her black hair snapping behind her.

What kind of arse was her father to mortify her the way he had? She had looked angry enough to shout, but she hadn't spoken a word in her defense. Patrick doubted her father would have cared if she had. It was clear the Cunninghams were a patriarchal family. Where was Charlie's mother?

He hadn't been the one asking questions when brutes one and two had brought him to meet their father before the Dunbars showed up. Allan Cunningham had wanted to know one thing and one thing only. Was his prisoner a Fergusson?

Charlie had warned him in the stable to say no—and judging by her overly suspicious and insensitive father, she'd risked much.

Why?

He picked up his pace again, cursing under his breath. He wanted to tell her not to fret. He was leaving. He didn't want a wife, though if he did, he might admit that he wouldn't consider it terrible if it were her.

Where the hell was she going? She hadn't slowed her

pace and as he closed the distance between them, he thought he heard her voice.

"I don't want prospects, you lout!"

Aye, it was her voice. Patrick listened as he came up behind her quietly.

"And no man will ever put me in my place! I'll tell you that!"

Patrick knew they were alone but he looked around anyway.

"There is nothing wrong with me that a future without you in it wouldn't cure. How dare you offer me up to—" Her words stopped and she spun around to see him behind her. The storms in her eyes scattered as they widened with surprise. Her long dark hair brushed across her face in the cool, summer breeze as she looked beyond his shoulder to see if he'd been followed. He knew he hadn't been. When her sunlit gaze darkened on the empty field, he also knew it was somehow more insulting to her that they'd been left alone.

He held up his palms as an offering of peace before she turned that tongue on him. "I stand with ye, lass."

She let out a perfectly feminine little sigh that fired up something completely male in him. "I meant no insult inside the parlor, Mr. Campbell—"

"Patrick." He smiled at her. And it was one of his best. He liked this lass. He let his gaze rove over the rest of her, taking in the delicate rise of her breasts as he came closer. He'd like her in his bed.

He offered her an unrepentant grin when he lifted his eyes to hers again. She was even more beautiful up close, her black waves cascading down her cheeks and shoulders, unrestrained by the absence of her circlet.

He remembered her wielding her sling at the riverbank,

unfazed by his most flowery words. How difficult would she be to seduce?

"I meant none, as well," he told her, tilting his head to meet her gaze.

Her expression softened and he had the feeling that he was among the very few to see the vulnerable tilt of her mouth. "My father can be difficult at times."

If that's what she considered the bastard, he wouldn't argue. "Dinna fret. Ye willna be forced to marry me."

She lowered her eyes to her bare feet peeking out of the grass. "'Tisn't you," she said quietly then turned and continued on her way.

What was it then? He found himself wondering while she left him. He should return to the stable, get his horse, and leave. Caring wasn't in his best interest. He should leave because he wanted to touch her, kiss her, from the moment he first laid eyes on her. When he did—and he would if he stayed—he wouldn't be wed at the end of a pistol whether for her "honor" or not.

Still, she was more than beautiful. She possessed an air of mystery, a spirit of boldness even at the edge of a blade, and docility when standing before her father. She stirred up a desire in Patrick to know more about her.

He caught up and walked beside her despite all the warnings going off in his head. "What is it then?" he asked her, waiting for her to look up again. Hell, he was counting each moment. When she finally did, his eyes took in the splendor of her face, the slight dimple in her chin.

"A marriage would get ye oot of here. Would it no'?"

"And put me under the hand of a man like Alistair Dunbar," she pointed out.

Aye, men like the Dunbars didn't care about bare toes and grass, or daisy circlets and perfect aim with a sling.

Or what any of it meant about her. He shouldn't care either.

"My father might be a devil," she continued, turning to look up at him beneath the shadow of her lashes, "but I know him. I know how to appease him."

Ah, so her meekness toward the patriarch was given with guile. Clever. But why the need? He could have asked her, but instead he found himself saying, "But what aboot marryin' a different kind of man?"

"There are no different kinds of men, Mr. Campbell."

Was that laughter he heard coming from her? He'd spoken the truth. He knew the men personally.

"Oh, you disagree?" she asked letting her mirth soften into a challenging smile at his sudden brooding. "Do you think you're any different with your twinkling green eyes and devilish dimple, that you know how to use to your greatest advantage? I saw how you graced Alice our cook when she brought your cup. You even flashed your reckless grin at my sister. If that advantage is to get a woman into your bed, do you think your treatment of her is any less demeaning? You are a rake are you not?"

"Of the worst sort," he admitted, looking into her midnight eyes. He should look away, for it felt as if she were looking inside him, fussing about in places that swept old ideals to the surface. Ideals he didn't want disturbed. "But I can assure ye," he added truthfully. He wouldn't deny he was a rogue, but he was not a mindless pig. "I was no' tryin' to get yer cook or yer sister to m' bed. I was simply smilin' in greetin' at meetin' them."

"Well then," she muttered, "You're even more dangerous than I thought."

Hell, but her tongue was viperous indeed. He smiled now, though he tried not to. She was correct about him. "I wasna speakin' of m'self when I spoke of different men. There are plenty of men where I live who would never mistreat a lass."

She cut him a wry side-glance. "How did you stray from that dignified path?"

"Och, lass," he laughed, his good mood returned, and lifted his face to heaven looking for some help. None came. He guessed he didn't deserve any. "Ye're withoot mercy."

"Not if you're deserving of it." Her gaze caught his and held it. "Are you?"

His unrepentant grin intact, he shook his head. "'Tis doubtful."

Was that a smile he saw hovering over her delectable mouth? "You're truthful," she allowed, "that's something."

He didn't know whether to keep smiling or cringe when he asked, "Are we looking for m' virtues then?"

"I doubt there's time," she tossed at him and turned away, her saucy hips swaying beneath her thin skirts.

"All right then," he continued not knowing why. It could have been because it was a nice day and walking with her in it put him in good spirits. Or that her stark rejection sparked a challenge he rarely faced and sorely missed. "I didna stray," he admitted when she stopped and returned her attention to him. "I chose a different path."

"You do realize that telling me that doesn't help."

He smiled again in defense of her relaxed mouth tilted up at him. "Doesna help what?" He let his gaze linger on her mouth, not to seduce her, but because he had the urge to kiss her senseless.

Instead of looking away in modesty, false or otherwise, she set her luminous eyes on his mouth, matching his boldness. She looked away though after only an instant or two.

"Your schemes to win my favor and whatever foolish

notions you have about what will happen after you do," she answered.

He shook his head and clamped his hands behind his back. "I have no intention of touchin' ye." He wanted to do so much more than that.

"That's good to know. I wouldn't want to cause you harm after you helped me today."

He wanted to laugh again but not because she thought she could harm him. She'd already proven that she could. He enjoyed her saucy mouth and despite her rejection of him—or because of it—he found his interest in her piqued. Of course, not every woman found him irresistible, but none had ever been so vocal about it.

"Speakin' of harmin' me, yer skill with a sling is impressive. Where did ye learn to use such a weapon?"

She cut him a glance as suspicious as her father's. "I learned many years ago." The thin lines of kohl around her eyes made them appear larger and more fathomless than a hundred seas. "My father does not approve."

Aye, because she'd learned from a Fergusson, Patrick had no doubt. It had to have been a Fergusson. His uncle Tamas was the only man he knew who could wield one with perfect accuracy. Tamas, along with Patrick's other uncle, John, lived with their families at Cameron's holding not too far from here. Had Tamas taught her? One of his cousins, mayhap? Did she *know* his cousins? She likely knew them better than he did. What the hell was all the hate toward his kin about anyway? There were so many things he wanted to know, but he'd have to use caution to find any answers. He didn't want to give his identity away. Not even to her. Not yet.

"Why did ye tell me no' to admit to bein' a Fergusson if I was one?"

"The Cunninghams hate the Fergussons." She stopped and turned to him again. "Did you deceive my kin, then?"

He could tell her the truth, that his mother was a Fergusson, but strangely, the thought of Charlotte Cunningham hating him didn't appeal to him.

"Nae, I didna deceive them," he told her. "M' brother Luke is Lord of Campbell Keep in Glen Orchy."

The curl of her mouth and the playful tilt of her chin rattled his senses and tempted him to unclamp his hands behind his back and go back on his word.

"You have a brother?" she asked. "Is he very much like you?"

"No' verra much like me," he laughed thinking how different he was from Luke. "He lives by dusty, old ideals."

"Oh?" She arched her brow. "Which ideals are those?"

"Just certain...values that are more..." He paused and looked at her. What did he care what she thought of him? Why the hell was he explaining himself—and worse stumbling around it? "...knightly to m' ways of thinkin'."

"I see." She smiled but turned her attention back to the foothills.

What did she see? Did she think he lacked any ideals at all? Hadn't he saved her life? He could be chivalrous if he needed to be.

"Mayhap," he said, doing his best not to move closer to her. "I should stay fer a few days after all. The Dunbars will likely return and yer guardsmen are dead. Ye'll need protectin'."

He didn't expect her to laugh. It was a wee bit insulting. But the dulcet sound of it compelled him to remain by her side.

"You were brave and clever with the Dunbars, Mr. Campbell, but don't assume I need a protector." Her eyes gleamed with humor as she set them over his discolored jaw. "And if you stay to fight," she continued letting her gaze dip to his shoulders and beefy arms, "you are not doing it for me." She swept her waves off her shoulder and moved to leave him.

Patrick's smile faded, but only for a moment before he threw back his head and laughed and then for the second time that day, took off after her.

Chapter Six

Charlie stood before the wardrobe on her side of the room she shared with Elsie and held a gown up to her body. She looked down at the coral-colored folds falling softly to her toes, concealing them from judgmental eyes. Oh, but she loved this gown. It reminded her of the early morning dew, delicate and cool to touch. She'd sewn it herself, using several whisper-thin skirts from her mother's nightdresses to create voluminous layers that captured the sunlight, and then she dyed them to match. Of course, like most of her dresses, the bodice fit a bit snuggly. It helped keep things in their place when she ran.

But it wasn't the right dress for this evening.

She chose petticoats of heavier linen, dark blue in color, a matching stay, and a jacket that belted at her slim waist. She went to sit at the edge of her bed and pulled hose over her feet before reaching for her boots.

"You're like two different beings."

Beings. Charlie smiled hearing her sister's voice at the door. Elsie often accused her of being otherworldly.

"I'm just me," Charlie assured her, looking up from tying her laces. "Sometimes I like to feel more delicate and sometimes I don't."

Elsie gave her a bright smile and moved toward her bed. "Are you wearing your ugly boots to ward off any of Mr. Campbell's advances?"

Mr. Campbell. Charlie had tried not to think of him while she dressed. She'd tried to keep the memory of his size and all that warmth so close while he walked beside her, his easy laughter and full, sensual mouth, from making her insides go warm.

A rascal in its truest form. She knew what he was after and he wasn't going to get it. Why would she want a miserable life with a man who had a heart for nothing? But hell, he was all male and quite tempting in his arrogance—and he *had* rushed to her rescue from the Dunbars.

"What advances do you mean?" She finished and looked up at her sister when Elsie threw herself on her bed. "And my boots are not ugly."

Elsie gave the mud-baked hide-skins one last glance before forgetting them. "Only a fool wouldn't have noticed"—she paused to take a breath and then continued—"the way his gaze barely ever leaves you when you're in his presence."

Charlie laughed. Elsie was only a year younger than her, but she was so much more innocent. "And only someone wiser would see the vanity in his gaze and know what it means. He's too enamored by himself to truly notice anyone else."

"Do you blame him?"

No, Charlie had to admit, but not out loud. She also didn't tell her sister how appealing she'd found him shirtless and bound and pushed up against her with Dunbar on the other side. "What I think has nothing to do with it. We know plenty of women who think the same about our brothers. And we both know that there is no one more important to Hendry than himself."

Elsie took her eyes off the ceiling and glanced at her. "You certainly cannot compare the two."

"Why not?" Charlotte asked while she began plaiting her long locks over her shoulder. "Mr. Campbell uses his good looks and magnetic charm to win favor with women. He admitted it to me himself. He would have been gone already if…" Her voice trailed off realizing what she was about to say. He'd claimed to want to stay to protect her from the Dunbars, but she suspected he fought often and had become quite good at it, enjoyed it even.

Elsie would think it was chivalrous when it was anything but.

"If you do marry him, can I live with you?"

Charlie sighed and shook her head. "I'm not going to marry him."

"Is it Kendrick?" her sister prodded on. "Truly, Charlie, you must let him go. I know you loved him, and I understand why. His heart was stout and loyal and his face was the finest of them all. No one will ever be as good as he, but—"

Charlie held up her hand to stop her. "I have let him go, El," she promised. "But I cannot help but look for what Kendrick had in others, and they always fall short. He knew they would. He knew what lay hidden in the hearts of men.

"But that's cnough talk of Kendrick and Mr. Campbell." She smiled and reached for her sister's hand, dragging her from the bed. "If we're late for supper, Father will go on for an hour."

"Are you going out again tonight?" Elsie pulled her back

before they reached the door, her corn-silk eyes wide with her plea.

Elsie knew she sometimes left the house alone at night, but she only knew half of the story.

"Can't I please come with you?"

"No," Charlie told her sternly. "Never follow me, El. You must never leave this house alone and at night."

"But you do?"

"I can fight. You cannot."

"You cannot either," her sister argued as Charlie left the room. "Not against a man."

"Aye, my darling," Charlie stopped and turned to look at her straight on. "I can."

Charlie stepped into the great hall and found their guest seated at the long dining table with her father and brothers.

She paused when he lifted his cup to his lips and his eyes to her. Was Elsie correct? Did his gaze linger on her? And so what if it did? It meant nothing. She didn't want any more men in her life. She was tired of her father promising her to barons and other nobles, tired of having to plan ways of making them refuse her as a suitable wife. Kendrick had little to do with it. Love and marriage were two separate things sometimes. A husband would surely think to stop her from her dangerous tasks. And damn it, she wouldn't be stopped.

She wouldn't be forced into marriage either. Her father's suggestion this afternoon still mortified her. She was chattel, offered away for protection of the Cunningham holding. He needn't have admitted it in front of the man he was offering her up to, but Allan Cunningham lacked sympathy.

She spread her gaze over her brothers, who hadn't looked up, before it settled on the Highlander, his long, broad fingers cradling the bowl of his goblet. Hell, but he was nice to look at with the glow of flames in his hair and the warmth of summer sunshine in his eyes. Her gaze dipped to his lips, full and fashioned for most decadent endeavors. She found herself thinking of some of them when his eyes slid to her. One corner of his mouth quirked upward as he caught her admiring him. Her face burned and she looked away and took her place at the table beside Elsie.

"You're late," her father said looking up from his plate.

"'Tis my fault, Father," Elsie was quick to admit. "I—"

"I couldn't find my boot," Charlie spoke over her. "And I know how you frown on my bare feet. I shall consider your rules before your sentiments next time. Forgive me."

She saw the shadow of Duff's smile from the corner of her eye. If there was one thing her oldest brother had taught her well, it was how to feign submission to get out of trouble. He'd begun teaching her soon after their mother died. Dragging her to her room and locking her inside any time she lost her temper with him. After a month or two, Hendry had begun to do the same. She'd hated their treatment of her, but she'd learned to control herself, and she learned patience.

"Charlotte." Duff set down his cup and looked at her from behind a tumble of black curls. "We were just discussing you."

No! Not again! "Oh? What were you discussing?" If they were discussing her marriage she wouldn't be silent about it this time.

"Mr. Campbell was asking about our mother."

Their mother? Charlie flicked her gaze to their guest. Why would he ask about her mother, and what did it have to do with her? Why did he look so relaxed in his chair? Like he had nothing to fear from her family? She remembered how well he'd fought the Dunbars and Hamish, and decided he likely didn't have all that much to be afraid of. "What about her?"

Now that he had a reason to regard her without incurring Duff's ire, he set his warm gaze on her fully and smiled.

He made her want to smile back. She didn't.

"I inquired which of her daughters most resembled her. But when yer father informed me of her great beauty, I knew both her daughters had much to thank her fer."

Beside her, Elsie drew in a tight breath, coughed, and then thanked him.

He was indeed clever, she thought watching him. If he sought to win any kind of favor with her, Elsie was the path to take. Charlie offered him her slightest smile.

"My Margaret was a *dark* beauty," her father corrected. His insinuation didn't go unnoticed by Elsie, who shifted in her seat, though she said nothing.

"With beautiful blue eyes just like Elsie's," Charlie added then grinded her jaw when she turned her smile to her father.

"Aye," her father conceded, "Hendry and Elsie have her eyes, but of my three offspring, only you share her dark mystique."

"Three?" Patrick Campbell asked, thankfully, and mayhap purposefully veering the topic off the sisters and who was more beautiful. "Is Duff not yer bairn?"

"Nay, he is not," her father answered frankly, surprising their guest enough to make him set down his drink and move forward in his chair, his interest piqued.

"My mother died when I was six," Duff told him, "leaving me an orphan."

"Yer faither?" the Highlander inquired.

Charlie's oldest brother shrugged his brawny shoulders.

"I never knew him. Margaret Cunningham found me peddling coin on the road and took me in."

"My wife had a terribly bleeding heart," her father said, reminiscing. "If left on her own, she would have taken in every waif she came across. But in the case of Duff, she made the correct choice in bringing him home. He is like my own."

Save that he didn't include him when he spoke of his bairns, Charlie thought and looked across the table at her brother. Her heart stirred, remembering him as a boy, grimy and skinny and orphaned at the tender age of six. He was well-behaved and thoughtful and fun to play with. Her father was unkind to him when his wife was out of their presence, as was Hendry, who was a year younger than his new "brother." Duff had never cried though and he'd quickly grown to love Charlie, three summers old at the time. He spent time with her every morning before his chores began and kissed her goodnight before she closed her eyes to dream. He loved her. He loved her still. Even when he'd locked her in her room, it was to help her curb her temper with her father, or Hendry, who had taken a hand to her on a few occasions because of her sharp tongue. Duff possessed a kinder heart beneath his cold, rough exterior. What kind of man would he have become if her mother had left him on the road?

It didn't matter. He'd grown into a monster.

"Yer wife sounds like an extraordinary woman, Cunningham," Patrick complimented. Charlie fought the urge to turn and smile at him again. "Did a fever take her from ye?"

Charlie's gaze darted to her father. Would he tell the Duke of Argyll's nephew the truth? That under his order, his sons had killed a Fergusson child and the boy's father had retaliated by taking his wife? What would the Earl of Argyll's nephew do if he found out? Such a crime wouldn't go unpunished. Would she and Elsie be punished for what her father and brothers had done?

"Aye, a fever," her father said. "A terrible one. Took her within a sennight five years ago."

"M' condolences," Patrick said softly, setting his gaze on her first, and then on Elsie.

Just when the mood went sour and Charlie prepared herself for another quick, quiet supper, the Highlander turned in his chair and grinned at Duff.

"Ye fought well today. D'ye practice with the sword often?"

Duff nodded. "Every day."

"I'd like to join ye tomorrow, if ye dinna mind."

So then, Charlie thought, he *was* staying. For how long? How would it affect her and her duties? Did she want him around to continue to beguile her? He was distracting and arrogant—and he made her smile when she was blistering mad. His ruthlessly charming grin flashed through her thoughts. She wondered what it would be like to kiss him. She lifted her cup and downed what was left inside. If he stayed, he'd surely try to spend more time with her. How would she refuse his company without insult?

Really, it was no concern of hers. She had other matters to see to. As soon as everyone was asleep in their beds she could be about her task.

She listened while her father told the Highlander about the Fergussons keeping able-bodied men from working for him. Of course, he failed to mention that there were very few able-bodied men in Pinwherry thanks to his greed and punishments for their not having enough coin or crops to pay him.

When their guest took up the conversation and told them tales about folks he'd met on his journey to Pinmore for a tournament, she found herself stealing glimpses of him.

"Are you a knight then?" Elsie asked in breathless anticipation of his reply.

Charlie glanced at her and decided she'd have to protect Elsie from the captivating scoundrel.

He tossed back his head and laughed at Elsie's query. "Och, nae, lass. I just know how to fight and win."

Watching him, Charlie didn't doubt his declaration. Every movement, even lifting his goblet, was interspersed with fluid power, a current of pure energy impossible to ignore.

"We'll see about that," Duff said, bringing his cup to his lips. "I won't go easy on you."

"Good." The Highlander's eyes danced across the table and paused on Charlie. "Victory is empty withoot a challenge."

Charlie caught his eye, and though his declaration made her belly flip, she held his gaze a moment longer. The poor devil had no idea what a real challenge was like. If he thought to make her his next conquest, he would find out soon enough.

"Come, Elsie, let us retire." Without waiting for her sister's agreement, she pulled her to her feet. "Father, may we go?"

He shooed her and Elsie away with a wave of his hand and then returned his attention to Patrick Campbell. Charlie knew she shouldn't, but her eyes moved of their own volition and found the Highlander watching her.

He offered her a polite smile and a nod. When Elsie bid him good eve, he flashed his dimple at her and offered her the same.

Elsie liked him. It seemed Duff and their father liked him as well. Hendry didn't have use for anyone other than himself so it was no surprise to find him scowling.

Ah, now there was another challenge the Highlander wouldn't likely win.

Hell, she thought as she left the hall, she hated having anything in common with her brother.

Chapter Seven

*P*atrick stopped at the door and watched Charlie enter the moonlit field with fistfuls of her skirts hiked up over her weathered boots.

He wondered where she was heading tonight and set off to follow her. It was the second time in one day that he found himself chasing her. But this time it was for her safety—and he would admit, curiosity. What was she up to? Was there danger ahead? She must be mad to venture out alone at night. Again. Was she on her way to another pub? What the hell had she been doing in Pinmore? Any number of catastrophes could have befallen her. Where were her brothers? How was she able to sneak out for the second night in a row without their knowledge? She'd seemed submissive to the Cunningham men at the supper table. Was it all a ruse to appear subservient? He was certain her kin wouldn't approve of her traipsing across the land in the moonlight, else her father would have guessed how her beauty had been spoken of in Galloway.

Was it a man this time, someone in the small village she was heading toward? What other reason could there be for her to defy her family and her safety yet again?

Her loyalty to a clandestine lover pricked him in the guts for some reason. He wasn't jealous. He didn't have a jealous bone in his body. At least, he never had one before. Hell, he thought, raking his hand through his hair, he couldn't be jealous. How could he be envious of a man who could hold the heart of a woman so completely that she would risk all just to be with him, when that wasn't what *he* wanted? Was it?

He chuckled quietly to himself. Nae, he didn't need or want such devotion. Did he? Then again, he knew men from Camlochlin who hadn't thought they needed it either, until love struck them like a fevered plague and rendered them helpless.

Nae. Not him. Helplessness scared the hell out of him. Admitting it didn't help. He paused to turn back. He'd already spent too much of his day thinking about her. She was a curious wisp of veils across the cheek, darkly sensuous and elusive—with a razor-sharp tongue. She possessed a rare streak of confidence when facing down enemies, whether it was him, her father, or the Dunbars, that he found absolutely irresistible. Best if he left and never looked back. But he wanted to get to know her, discover her secrets—and she seemed to have many.

He continued, following her onward. What would he do when she reached her lover? He was a cad, he freely admitted it, but he wouldn't try to deliberately steal another man's woman. If she found herself in any trouble, he'd protect her if she wanted him to or not.

She stopped suddenly, and so did he. He looked around for a place to hide. There was none. What the hell would she think of him following her? She turned as if sensing him behind her.

Hell.

She moved toward him, stepping into view, illuminated by moonlight. She looked so damned appealing bathed in pearly light with one hand lifting the hem of her skirt and disappearing beneath it, that for a moment he forgot what she kept hidden under her hem.

"'Tis only me, lass," he said before she struck him with another stone.

"Mr. Campbell?" She released her skirts and placed her hands on her hips, her mouth pursed with indignation.

"Patrick," he corrected, taking a step closer to her.

She backed up. "What are you doing here?"

He sure as hell couldn't tell her that he'd hoped to steal a kiss from her, or that the mere sight of her tempted him to follow her to England.

"I was goin' to ask ye the same thing," he said. "Ye were attacked today, lass. D'ye no' see the danger in comin' oot here alone?" Or traveling to Pinmore alone. He wanted to ask her what she'd been doing in the pub last night, but he doubted she'd tell him the truth.

"What I do is no concern of yours. Go back to the house, or wherever it is you came from." She offered him a curt smile then turned and walked away, continuing on her path.

Patrick watched her go. She was correct. She was no concern of his but that didn't mean he was going to stand by while she stormed off in the night.

"Where are ye off to?" he asked, catching up, determined to find out her secrets. She remained tight-lipped—the way she'd gone mute when her father questioned her.

He tried another route. "On yer way to a lover then?"

"I should slap your face for suggesting that I'm that big of a fool," she answered crisply without turning to look at him.

"A fool fer leavin' the safety of yer home to meet with him, or fer havin' a lover at all?"

"Both."

He wished it were morning so he could see her more clearly; the pert tilt of her nose, the alluring cut of her high cheekbones, the beguiling shape of her mouth. He inhaled a deep breath and let the fragrance of the heather-lined foothills, and something more soothing—lavender mayhap—clear his thoughts.

"I'm surprised yer brothers are unaware of yer disappearance. They strike me as overprotective."

"They are asleep and shall remain that way until morning."

How did she know they'd sleep through the night? Unless she saw to their guaranteed slumber with an aid in their wine. It made sense since she'd had to slip back inside the house last night. He would have to watch her more closely to ensure he didn't succumb to the same tomorrow night. If he remained that long.

"Duff shouldn't have struck you today," she said quietly, giving in a bit to his company but still keeping her gaze on her path.

"I understand why he did. I have sisters," he told her quietly, thinking of Mailie and Violet at home. He missed them. "I know the desire to keep them safe from the wrong kind of men—"

"Then why are ye here with me instead of them?"

He smiled despite the thread of guilt she provoked. "They have m' faither and every other man in Camlochlin to watch over them. They dinna need me there too." But he was their brother. Shouldn't he be taking on the responsibility of protecting them too? "Besides," he shrugged it off, "m' sister Mailie would sooner fall on a sword than fall for anything less than the perfect knight."

"Poor thing shall be alone until she's old and dies."

Patrick smiled with her, but he couldn't help but wonder if any man could ever change Charlie's mind.

"I thought ye believed in those ideals," he said, remembering their last walk together and the conversation they'd shared.

She shook her head. "I was simply curious why you don't, since you're the one who claims to know men who live by them. Men are seldom gallant unless they want something in return."

Patrick didn't live by his kin's creed but he knew she was incorrect. Still, he wasn't here to prove it to her. "Ye have a difficult life with yer kin," he surmised instead.

"No more difficult than any other lass my age. My father can be unkind but I have found ways to avoid him and make myself happy."

"Like this?" Patrick asked softly. "By sneakin' off alone?"

"Perhaps."

"So will ye tell me where ye're off to?"

"If you're as stubborn as I think you are," she said, "you'll find out soon enough."

He *was* that stubborn and stayed close by her side.

"My sister tells me that your eyes linger on me."

Patrick blinked, unprepared for her confession. But he wasn't one to remain unwary by the small surprises that life threw at him. Hell, he enjoyed any challenge that veered onto his path. Most of the time.

"Yer sister's astute."

She paused and turned to him. Her thick black braid

caught light from the waxing moon, illuminating rich blues and fathomless onyx.

"Let's get this straight, Mr. Campbell—"

"Patrick," he corrected again with a smile.

"I'm not interested in becoming one of your conquests. I don't want a man whose only ambition is to make certain *he's* happy. You're only interested in your own needs and wants, and I have much bigger things to contend with."

His smiled faded. "Ye really dinna like me, d'ye?"

She looked up at him and shrugged he shoulder. "What's to like? You're pleasing to the eye."

Patrick was sometimes a heartless bastard. He knew that. He didn't usually let things affect him. But he felt as if she'd just clubbed the side of his head with a tree, knocking him on his arse.

He was a pretty face and nothing more. She couldn't think of one other thing. He was truthful. He'd saved her. Had she forgotten that? Why did it hit him so hard? Why did he care?

She clearly did not, but went on mercilessly. "I'm not sure what you're used to, but I promise you, I'm not it. I have no need for what you offer."

"I haven't offered anything," he pointed out, wounded but undefeated.

She appeared flustered for a moment. She knew he was correct and had no immediate reply. He took it as a small victory. It didn't last long. "Well, in case you change your mind then, my answer will be the same until you leave."

He quirked one side of his mouth up into a confident grin and looked down into her dark eyes. "Are ye certain of that, lass?"

"Aye, I'm certain. In fact, I'd rather be drawn and quartered than find myself bound in an unwanted relationship."

Hell, but she had a cutting tongue. It wasn't that he'd never been rejected before. He'd just never been rejected so wholeheartedly. Drawn and quartered? Well, damnation. This certainly put a damper on things. He still wanted to kiss her, but now, he felt foolish because of it. And what was it exactly about him that she found so unappealing?

He looked back toward the house, thinking he should return. But he didn't want to. He didn't want to leave her. He almost laughed out loud. What kind of fool was he becoming? What had come over him? He hardly knew her. He recognized almost instantly that that was the problem. He wanted to know her, damn it. He wanted to know where she was going that was so important she'd risk so much.

"Goodnight, Mr. Campbell." She walked away from him. Just like that.

He let her go, afraid of what he was feeling. He liked her. He liked the sound of her voice, even when she was reviling him. He liked the way she moved, as if her feet weren't touching the ground but gliding over it. He liked that she didn't need a man to make her happy, and that she was willful and braw. What he didn't like was that she found him undesirable, and that he gave a damn.

Patrick watched her veer off to the left of the village and continue toward a cluster of thatch-roof cottages.

She stopped when she came to a small run-down cottage and turned to find him behind her again. "Do you insist on coming inside?"

"Is that where ye're goin'?"

"Aye."

Who was inside? At this point, he had to know. "Then, aye. I insist."

"You will not tell my father or brothers, will you?"

He shook his head. He wouldn't do anything to cause her

trouble. "Ye have m' word to tell them nothin' of yer adventures, lass."

She responded to the quirk of his mouth with a foul glance and knocked on the door.

They waited in silence until the door opened. A woman a few years older than Charlie stood on the other side. She was short in stature, with large pale green bloodshot eyes and blond hair tucked neatly into a net caul. When she saw Patrick, she appeared frightened and withdrew into the shadows beneath the doorway.

"'Tis all right, Mary," Charlie said in a comforting voice while she reached for her and gathered her in a quick embrace. "This is Patrick Campbell. He means you no harm."

Patrick offered Mary a smile he hoped would reassure her of Charlie's promise.

Still looking a bit unsure, Mary stepped aside and allowed them entry.

"How is Robbie tonight?" Charlie asked, following her inside.

"He's feeling better. His leg is healing nicely."

"And the children?"

Patrick looked around, quiet while Mary replied. The interior of the cottage was small and dimly lit with candles placed throughout. The floors were strewn with fresh rushes and herbs, the walls absent of tapestry to keep out the cold.

"They sleep," Mary told her in a hushed voice as they approached a room housing a bed presently occupied by four small children. The quartet ranged in size with the two oldest at the edges of the straw mattress and the youngest in the middle. Golden hair splashed across their cherubic faces and rosy cheeks.

"Nonie is still having troubles with her dreams since the

incident," Mary told them. "She finally managed to settle down. Wee Jamie spent the day playing with a wooden stick, pretending it was a sword. He received a nasty splinter in his hand that took me half the evening to remove."

Patrick's gaze settled on the smallest of the four. His heart lurched at the sight of the child's bandaged hand, a pudgy little thumb resting between his relaxed lips.

"He didn't shed a tear but promised to see to his father's attacker."

"You must keep him away from Hendry, Mary," Charlie warned her gently, her gaze also fixed on the boy. "Remember what I told you."

So, Patrick surmised, Hendry, whom he'd been correct about in the stable, had attacked Mary's husband—and in front of these little ones. Why? And what was Charlie doing here with her brother's enemy?

"Come," their hostess beckoned, mostly to Charlie, but Patrick went along. "Robbie is having his midnight cup in the kitchen. He'll want to see you."

They tread along a short dark corridor until they came to the kitchen, where Mary's husband sat alone at a long wooden table. Light from the central hearth revealed a man born long before his wife. A beard covered most of his gaunt face. His left leg stretched outward from his chair, bandaged from the knee down. His dark, surprised gaze shone in the firelight when he saw his guests.

"Who are you?" he asked Patrick while he downed his cup and struggled to stand. "You haven't come to finish what Cunningham began, are you? As you can see, I'm not fit to fight you but if you mean to murder me—"

"Robbie, dear," Mary hurried to his side and settled him back down. "Charlie brought him. I'm certain he can be trusted."

Patrick stepped forward and introduced himself, determined to ease the man's apprehension. "I'm here as yer guest and mean ye no harm."

All those above and below the Grampians knew the Highland law of *Murder Under Trust*. It was the most grievous crime to kill or hurt anyone offering hospitality.

It seemed Robbie Wallace knew it as well because after picking up his cup, he offered Patrick his name and a chair.

"Mary, fetch our guest some wine."

Patrick held up his palm. "Another time, mayhap, lady."

"You will not drink with me?" Robbie squinted his eye on him like he was reconsidering his first assumption.

"Anything but wine." Patrick shrugged, meaning no offense.

"Whisky then?"

Patrick returned his host's smile and leaned back in his chair, relaxing his back against it. "That, I will accept."

"We cannot stay overly long," Charlie looked down at him and pinched his arm.

"A drink," Patrick ignored the pinch and continued to make himself comfortable. "Ye didna come all this way just to bid these good people goodnight, aye, Angel?"

"Oh, she is that," Mary hurried back to the table with a jug and a platter of honey cakes, set both down on the table, and clasped Charlie's hand. "An angel."

"Oh?" Patrick asked curiously, enjoying the blush that such a title spread across the bridge of Charlie's nose. Who was she? Why did her brothers' enemies adore her? "Long enough fer two stories then?"

Chapter Eight

I owed dues to my lord Cunningham," Robbie Wallace told Patrick over a cup of warm whisky and sweet honey cakes. Charlie had pulled up a stool, likely one of the children's, and sat beside him. If Robbie's rendition of the events that led Hendry Cunningham to beat him across the leg weren't drawing all Patrick's attention, her nearness and that damned hint of lavender would have distracted him.

"How late were ye?" Patrick asked. He wanted as clear a picture of the Cunninghams as he could get. The tenants of Camlochlin sometimes paid his uncle Rob, the chief, but they often fell behind. They were never troubled for it.

"A sennight."

Patrick passed a side-glance to Charlie but her gaze was fixed on her hands in her lap and she didn't see him. He didn't blame her for her kin's actions. She clearly had nothing to do with it.

"He is returning tomorrow to collect it," Mary told him.

"D'ye have it?"

Robbie lowered his gaze to his cup. His wife looked at Charlie.

"Aye, you have it," Charlie told her father's tenant and dipped her hand into her cleavage. Patrick's gaze followed it until she produced a small pouch. She stood up and placed the pouch on the table before Robbie. "This time, you'll use it and save your wife and children the sorrow of your pride."

Patrick watched her as full comprehension struck him and he understood what she was doing here—why it was so important for her to come.

Mary sniffed and brought Charlie's hand to her lips for a series of kisses.

"You'll send word to me if you're in need again," she told the weeping woman. "You won't wait until 'tis too late, aye?"

"But 'tis too much to ask of you," Robbie said, fingering the pouch. "You help all the folks of Pinwherry. There will come a time when you must cease. Besides, I am the provider of this family—"

"As a father," Charlie said cutting him off gently. "There are many things you provide. Guidance, for one. You need to be here to teach your sons to be the kind of men they ought to be. Not men like Hendry or your liege. Safety, for another. You keep them safe by paying my brother."

Patrick was still, barely breathing. Had he heard Robbie right? Doing this once for a family in need was one thing, helping everyone in Pinwherry was another. It was too much. Sooner or later she would get caught…or killed. He smiled at her when she turned to him. He could do nothing else. Mary Wallace was correct about her. She was an angel. Who was he to tell an angel to stop what she was doing?

"We should go."

Patrick nodded. They'd been gone too long. He wasn't the kind of man who took killing lightly, but if her father or one of her brothers laid a finger on her, he'd kill them.

After bidding Robbie farewell, they followed Mary back out.

"Ye help all the villagers?" Patrick asked Charlie as they passed the doorway to the children's room.

"When I can," she whispered back.

"Mama!" One of the children cried out.

It was the girl. Nonie her mother had called her earlier. She sat up and cried out again, disturbing her slumbering siblings. Mary hurried to her side with Patrick following close behind. He didn't think about why he went, he only knew that the child's terror gripped him by the heart. He knew what night terrors were like. He'd suffered them as a young lad after he nearly drowned in *Camas Fhionnairigh*. Many of his kin had been playing in the waves that morning, but none of them knew he'd gone under. At least, it had felt to him like no one had, for he'd swallowed two gulps of water before his mother pulled him up. He suffered with the memory of it for a year.

"Mama, they were here! They came back!" she cried, waking her brothers. "They came back!"

"Who's that?" the youngest asked, popping his thumb from between his teeth. He sat up and spilled golden curls around his little round face.

Hearing him, the girl looked over her mother's shoulder and whimpered when she saw Patrick.

He knelt at her bedside and plucked the candle from her night table and held it between him and the children. "Nonie, yer mother was findin' me."

"Who...who are you?" the girl asked, wedged deeply in her mother's arms.

Hell, but she was so damned small and her eyes were so big. How could such a wee face, a quartet of them as a matter of fact, have such a thunderous effect on his heart? He smiled at them. They smiled back. They appeared to range in age from mayhap three to six with Nonie being somewhere in the middle. Her brothers didn't concern him. Nonie did. She was terrified and he would give anything to ease her fear.

"I'm Patrick, Protector of Dreams."

Her eyes opened wide. "You are?"

He nodded and whispered. "If yer dreams frighten ye, tell them to me and I shall help ye vanquish them."

Her eyes opened even wider. She moved a little closer and he inclined his ear to her. But she reached out her small hand and brushed her fingers over his wounded jaw. "Did an ogre do this to you?"

"Aye," he told her softly.

"And then what happened?" asked one of her brothers.

"And then I vanquished him," Patrick told them all then returned his attention to Nonie. "Tell me yer dream."

"I was playing with Otis—"

"Who is this Otis?"

"He's our cat," the oldest boy told him, sitting up.

"It got dark," Nonie whispered, "the way it gets when a storm is coming."

Patrick nodded, listening.

"I heard them behind me and I looked...I looked and..."

Patrick waited patiently while she buried her face in her mother's bosom and fought back her tears. Hendry Cunningham had done much to this family. Patrick would see him punished.

"They were big and ugly and they tried to catch Otis,"

Nonie ran her tiny fist across her nose to wipe it. "They wanted to eat him. And then one of them caught him and..." She could go no further and began to cry.

Patrick deduced the rest. It would indeed be horrifying to watch a monster consume a beloved pet.

"Lass?" he whispered and tugged softly on her hand to make her look at him. When she did, her eyes gleamed with tears. "Where is Otis now?"

She pointed to a fat gray cat curled up on a nearby stool.

"Are ye certain Otis didna eat one of them? He looks as if he feasted well."

The boys laughed. Nonie smiled behind her mother's skirt. Then, "You speak oddly."

"Nonie!" her mother scolded quietly.

"But he does, Mama!" the second youngest agreed vehemently.

"All the warriors in m' land speak this way," Patrick told them. "Monsters hate it. They say the lilt of m' voice makes them cry fer their mothers."

The boys' laughter brought another smile to Patrick, but he was most grateful to see Nonie smile.

"I like it," she said.

"Good," Patrick said. "Then ye're are no' one of them in disguise." He gave her a closer look. "Are ye?" He turned to her brothers. "Are any of ye lads monsters?"

They all giggled, shaking their heads.

"So," Patrick turned back to the cat. "They didna truly eat Otis." He returned his attention to Nonie. "D'ye know why?"

"Nay."

"Because they are no' truly big at all. In fact, they're rather small, small enough to live only here." He pointed to her head. "They couldna fit a cat in their mouths, especially Otis."

"How do you know this?" she asked softly.

"I know many things. Would ye like to know some of them?"

She nodded with enthusiasm that made his heart lurch. "Ye're bigger and stronger than they are. Why, ye dinna even need me to fight them."

"I don't?"

He shook his head. "But I'll still help ye. I'm goin' to tell ye their secrets. Ye are aware that monsters and all types of ogres can be defeated if ye know their secrets, are ye no'?" She nodded though he'd just made the entire thing up.

"D'ye want to know them, then?"

"Aye, aye, I do!"

He held up three fingers. "First, they can never ever tell the truth. If ye know this secret they'll never be able to lie to ye. They lose all their power. The second way to defeat them"—he curled one of his fingers back into his fist—"is to know that the reason they are so foul is because they have never had a friend. They are monsters, after all. Who would want to be friends with a monster?" He paused for a moment to let her think about it. "This secret is good to know," he continued, "because making a monster yer friend means he can never frighten ye again."

He moved the candle back to the nightstand. Nonie's eyes, wide and curious followed the light—followed him as he went. "D'ye want to know the last way to defeat them?"

"Aye," she uttered breathlessly eager for his instruction.

Both their gazes watched his last finger curl with the rest.

"They are verra small. As I've already told ye. 'Tis why they will never come to the place where we truly reside. We would see how small they are and we would laugh." He smiled and moved a bit closer to her face. "And laughter is what they are most afraid of."

She was silent for a moment. No one stirred in the room while she counted down on three of her fingers. She closed her eyes and then opened them again on Patrick. "I think I can do it."

He smiled as his pitiful heart melted all over his ribs. "I know ye can. And until they're gone fer good, I'll be close by to help ye if ye need me."

He wasn't prepared for her small arms as they reached around his neck or her delicate sigh across his cheek. He looked up at her mother and smiled, undone by her child.

Bidding Nonie farewell, he left the cottage with a satisfied grin on his face and Charlie at his side.

"You surprised me, Mr. Campbell," she offered lightly and walked with him toward Cunningham House. "The sinner has a bit of saint in him."

Patrick quirked his mouth in the milky light of the moon. "I'm no' a saint. I'm no' a host of things, lass. Take yer pick. That's what I've been tryin' to tell ye." His grin deepened on her and he stepped closer to bump her shoulder.

He noted with a palpitation in his heart that she sprang right back to him, even closer this time.

"I'll be the judge of what you are not," she said, giving him a little bump back that didn't move him an inch.

"And what have judged so far?" Why did he care? He never had before.

"You're not altogether barbaric like the rest. You have a naturally easy way with people, beguiling at will."

"Ye flatter me, lass."

"And judging by what you think of yourself, you want me to proceed."

He threw back his head and laughed. He liked how she aimed her insults as skillfully as she hurled her stones. She thought she knew him. He was quite transparent, after all.

But being not altogether barbaric wasn't so terrible. And he did have any easy way with people. He'd much rather make friends than kill enemies. He could kill if he had to. If Hendry Cunningham ever harmed Nonie Wallace or her cat, he would. Thinking of killing her brother sobered his thoughts and he remained quiet while he walked.

"I will proceed then," she said, breaking the silence. "What you did for Nonie was kind and verra clever. My brother has caused the Wallaces much affliction and I'm sure Hendry is one of Nonie's monsters. When you first told her you'd help her vanquish them, I asked myself how you could do it. There is no way you can step into her dreams and save her. But you did something better. You taught her how to fight them herself. You"—her dulcet voice grew lighter—"made a little girl her own hero. And mayhap that makes you a hero too."

He eyed her in the soft moonlight. It pleased him that she thought highly of him, enough to consider him a hero. She was wrong, of course, but he saw no reason to tell her that. "I must start somewhere."

He was glad to hear her soft chuckle. This night had to have been taxing for her. She could likely use some laughter.

"Mayhap," she whispered in the darkness. Her sweet breath fell across his chin. He clenched his jaw with the effort it took not to bend to kiss her. "There is more to you than I first thought."

There was. But revealing it made him vulnerable, needful. Like...drowning in the water, needing to be rescued.

"Where did ye get the coin?" he asked, moving away a little. He wouldn't expose any more of himself to her.

"I stole it from Hendry, of course. He keeps his purses in a trunk in his room. He's paid for much of his wrongdoings and thankfully he's too dimwitted to realize it."

"If he brings harm to—"

She placed her hand on his arm. He looked down, wishing he could see her slender fingers.

"He would be dead before you reach him," she vowed.

"Ye share no affection fer him then?"

"I'd like him better if he were a viperous asp."

Damn it, he couldn't help but smile at her. She possessed fire beneath her subservient gaze. Fire to defy, outwit, and save a village or two while she was at it. He'd never met anyone like her. She was trouble. The worst kind.

"And Duff?"

"He's different," she told him after a moment to consider her words before she spoke them. "He had no part in this. But he wouldn't approve of what I'm doing, especially since I've taken from his purse as well."

This time they laughed together. When was the last time he'd strolled with a lass under the moon and simply spoke and laughed together? It was rather nice. Different. Better.

"Once I robbed Hendry's favorite whore to pay for a goat so that Maeve Kennedy's new babe could have fresh milk," she continued, the amusement in her voice sounding like music in his ears. "The whore refused to ever sleep with Hendry again, calling him a thief. He brooded for a month."

"Och, lass," he told her. "I'd want ye on m' side in a battle. Ye're devious."

They continued to laugh all the way back to the perimeter of the house.

She made no apologies for finding amusement in her brother's misfortune. Hendry was a hateful bastard who deserved what he got. And thanks to his sister, he was getting it good.

"Your company wasn't so terrible after all."

"Truly, ye must cease with all yer kind words."

She laughed one last time then leaned up on the tips of her toes and before he knew what she was about to do, she placed a kiss on his cheek. "Goodnight, Mr. Campbell."

She turned to proceed toward the house alone but he grasped her wrist and pulled her back into his waiting arms. She bent backward, casting her long plait of raven glory over the crook of his elbow. He followed, leaning over her, enveloping her like smoke. When she ceased protesting, he leaned over her, one hand cupping her chin to tilt back her head while he drew her closer. Her lips were soft but unyielding, wanting his kiss but set in denial. He flicked his tongue across her lips coaxing her to open for him. When she did, he felt his strength leave his body in a maelstrom that left him weak on his feet. For an instant, fear overwhelmed him. Her effect on him was most unwanted but she tasted of defiance and honey and as he spread his tongue across the hot cavern of her mouth, he knew he had to have her.

It was going to be a difficult task he was reminded when, after a tight little moan he pulled from her throat, she shook her head as if her senses were returning. She pushed out of his embrace and managed, in the dark, to slap him hard across his cheek.

"Never do that again!"

Hell, he thought while she stormed back to the house. He wanted to do far more than that.

Chapter Nine

Charlie sat on her windowsill and looked out at Duff and Patrick Campbell sparring in the front yard.

She was surprised that Duff had risen from his bed so early. She had put enough Valerian in his nightly cup of wine to keep three men of smaller size out cold for at least twelve hours. Duff was a big brute and she preferred being safe than sorry. She never wanted to take the chance of him following her out at night.

But there he was, engaged with Mr. Campbell for at least a quarter of an hour now, both men throwing jabs and different combinations of punches, as well blocking and avoiding many blows. They caused no real harm to each other, avoiding most of the blows. They used no weapon in their practice, other than fists, skill, and wit.

They appeared equally matched, but Charlie noted that her brother was slower and less fluid in his movements.

She also couldn't help but notice how the sun shone off their guest's crown of auburn hair and off the fiery hair dusting his arms. He moved like a flame, penetrating all

Duff's best defenses. The size of his arms drew her careful attention from time to time. They were well muscled and thick, built for brawling. If he ever fought with Hendry, her brother wouldn't last ten breaths.

They stopped for a break and came together to discuss the match. Patrick Campbell smiled at something Duff said. He always smiled, Charlie thought. He always appeared calm and unruffled. Even when he'd stepped out of her home, bound at the wrists, and came face-to-face with the Dunbars, his supreme confidence hadn't faltered. He had yet to offer her a scowl for knocking him out with her sling and setting him here.

"Are you going to stare at him all morn?" Elsie asked while she slipped into her petticoats and woolen stays, dyed the perfect shade of blue to match Elsie's eyes.

"I'm not staring at him," Charlie defended herself and left the sill. "I was watching them fight."

She ignored her sister's doubtful smirk and went directly to her wardrobe. But instead of choosing what to wear, her thoughts drifted back to him.

What was she to do about him? Last night he had the audacity to put his mouth on her without leave. Not that she would have given it. Although, dear saints in heaven, she nearly lost consciousness—or something just as vital—tossed into his arms like some carefree wench. If not for the strength in his arm she would have wilted right there at his feet. He kissed with exquisite care, molding her mouth and her body to his. Kendrick had kissed her, but they were young and his mouth had been awkward on hers, not hungry and not nearly as passionate.

The Highlander had also made her laugh, really laugh, and it had felt delightful. She didn't do the like often.

There weren't many reasons to. After her brothers had

killed Kendrick, after the Fergussons had killed her mother, her life changed drastically. She saw the truth in men, what they were truly made of. Kendrick's warnings were true. The first time her father tried to marry her off she was ten and five. Hendry began pushing her around more openly. Duff had retreated into a cave and tore at the throats of anyone who tried to go near—including her. She found ways to protect herself, and her sanity. Thankfully no one wanted Elsie with her breathing condition.

The only good thing left in her life after Kendrick and her mother left was their memory. She wouldn't let them go. She couldn't.

But Patrick Campbell was filling much of her thoughts. As much as his kiss and his laughter haunted her, so did the memory of him with the Wallace children, Robert, Nonie, Andrew, and Jamie. It made her think about him with his own bairns...and hers. She remembered him with Nonie, their faces aglow in the candlelight, eyes locked on each other. He'd calmed Nonie's fears with cleverness, compassion, and authority.

Nonie had ruffled the Highlander's feathers. She'd made him admit to things Charlie was certain he hated confessing. How much more was there to Patrick Campbell? She wanted to find a way around his well-aimed smiles and inviting green eyes, around his charming words and relaxed confidence.

No. She had absolutely no desire to lose the only freedom she had left to a man. Especially a self-proclaimed rake whose heart was loyal to no one. What about Bethany from the pub? Surely, he'd had no time to bed her before Hamish had shown up. But he would have. She'd seen the passion in his eyes. Was he going to return to the tavern wench? Or was she forgotten, just as Charlie would soon be? No,

Charlie wouldn't surrender all her hopes and dreams for her and Elsie to a man she hardly knew. A man who would likely be gone in another day. A man who was nothing like the man Kendrick would have been.

She'd wasted enough time thinking about him. She had sheep to tend and chickens to feed.

Thinking of her day, Charlie smiled and pulled a dress from its peg. It was one of her favorites. She'd made it herself from strips of billowing gauze, dyed piece by piece in an array of pale blue, lavender, and peach. The corset was made of soft, thin wool, also dyed in the palest purple, laced up the front, as were all the dresses she made. She didn't like having to depend on anyone to tie her up the back. Long sleeves opened at her elbows and hung in fluid splendor to her fingers. She heard Elsie sigh behind her. Her sister didn't understand why Charlie always insisted on wearing such scarce garments instead of the tight boned stays and thick stiff skirts that the other lasses wore. "What good was comfort," Elsie had often asked, "when you are freezing?"

Elsie was always cold. Poor dear.

"What about your earasaid?"

"Oh, Elsie," Charlie sang, spinning on her heel to face her, and enjoying the easy sway of her dress, "'Tis a beautiful day! What need is there of a heavy cloak?"

Her sister gave her a frustrated sigh. "You're always taking care of me, Charlie. Why don't you ever let me take care of you?"

She loved that Elsie wanted to help her, but she didn't need Elsie to do things for her.

"I'll wear a snood in my hair." Charlie smiled reaching for a thin woolen ribbon of ordinary white. "Will that please you?"

Elsie threw up her hands, conceding. "All that hair of

yours will only come loose and hang down over your forehead like that of a wild mare. Why bother?"

Charlie laughed and tied the snood around her head. She pulled her thick locks out of the bottom, and left the room without her slippers.

She was thankful when she didn't see Hendry or her father breaking fast in the hall. They were likely still asleep, thanks to the Valerian.

With Elsie at her side, she grabbed a pair of apples and handed one off to her sister on the way out of the house.

"You go tend the sheep in the meadow, El. You always have more trouble breathing around all the feathers. Stay where Duff can see you."

"But what about you?" Elsie protested, not wanting to leave her. "You'll be alone in the henhouse should the Dunbars return."

"The Dunbars will not return," Charlie reassured gently. "They cannot be that foolish. Why, I'd wager that Duff and Mr. Campbell could fight a dozen Dunbars and win. Do not worry. Duff is just around the bend."

With Patrick. She'd thought about going to watch them spar. She'd decided against it. She certainly didn't want the rascal Highlander to think she liked looking at him, being around him. She wasn't like his past admirers. His carnal appearance meant little to her. She knew what men were like on the inside. She'd grown up fatefully wounded by their pride and hatred. They were savage in their thinking. None of them were any different, not the Cunninghams, the Fergussons, or the Dunbars. They were foolishly stubborn like Robbie Wallace, arrogant and cruel like her father and brothers, lustful leeches that were often too drunk to fight her back. Was Patrick Campbell any different?

He had been different last night.

"'Twould only take Duff a moment to reach us."

"And half that time," Elsie said, her voice sounding lighter as she turned toward the pasture, "for Mr. Campbell to save you again."

Aye, Charlie thought watching her go. The Highlander had saved her once. She would make certain not to let it happen again. The only reason she'd found herself needing rescuing when Archie Dunbar thought to take her was because Elsie had been there. Otherwise, she wouldn't have hesitated to fight back. Usually, a hard blow somewhere in the groin was enough to bring a man to his knees.

She bit into her apple and coaxed by the sun, set her path for the wheat house where she would gather the chicken feed. A warm breeze wafted over her, lifting the delicate layers of her gown and spreading through her hair.

Setting her hand over her eyes for shade, she turned one last time to watch her sister reach the sun-drenched meadow. No one else was about. Her eyes turned toward the village beyond the low hills.

How are Mary and Robbie this morn? Had Patrick vanquished wee Nonie's frightening dreams?

Charlie smiled remembering his soft, compassionate voice. She would never have believed him so considerate of a child's fears, but he'd gone to Nonie's bedside as if her peace of mind were his responsibility. She hummed as she walked, swinging her arms wide and squinting at the sun. It seemed he was more than a pretty face.

Her thoughts returned, as they had numerous times since last night, to his deep, sensual kiss, the feel of his hard angles pressed against her soft ones. She cursed herself for thinking it, but she wished for another opportunity for him to do it again. No man had ever taken such liberties with her before. She likely would have killed one if he had, but instead of taking her dagger to Mr. Campbell, she'd merely slapped him. And she was fortunate to have been able to do that! What she had truly wanted to do was pull him in for more.

If she was truthful, and Charlie considered herself to be so, she must admit that the very thought of him warmed the blood in her veins.

She reached the wheat house and wiped her brow from the effects that the Highlander and the sun had on her. She fanned her face as a gentle breeze lifted a few curls off her neck.

Honestly, how did Elsie wear so many layers?

She pulled open the wide door and stepped inside. Light splashed from behind her across sacks overflowing with wheat and other grains. She plucked two buckets off hooks that were secured into the split pine wall to her right and headed for the sacks.

Tonight she would return to Blind Jack's Tavern in Pinmore. According to Mr. Will Stewart—a patron she'd met there during her last visit—a physician by the name of Malcolm Lindsay would be traveling through the town tonight. She'd learned the best way to gain information was from loose, drunken lips. Indeed, many of the same tongues that had, last winter, helped her discover the truth about Kendrick's disappearance five years ago.

It was risky to spike her family's drinks three nights in a row, but she would be there to meet Dr. Lindsay and speak to him about helping Elsie.

Set to her cause, she shoved her first bucket into the grain and listened to the spray of seed overflowing to the floor. She set the full container down then filled the next.

Unbidden thoughts returned to her of the Highlander's sure, strong voice while comforting a little girl. And then to his embrace and passionate kiss beneath the moon. Slapping him had been difficult because the last thing she'd wanted him to do was stop, and satisfying because she wasn't a wench to be manhandled and because he made a living from fighting. His cheek could take it. She imagined many women had slapped it.

But there was no place in her future for a charming rogue. Too many people needed her. And how could she betray Kendrick's memory by letting herself be seduced by a man like Patrick? It was best if she forgot him now.

Bending to the first bucket handle, she hauled up both and turned to leave. As she went, she thought she might have to spike Mr. Campbell's drink tonight to keep him from following her.

She stepped outside and set down the buckets so she could shut the door. When she saw the Highlander leaning his back against the outer wall, hands crossed over his chest, his face tilted toward the sun, she drew in a tight gasp.

The sound drew his attention and he turned his head to set his eyes on her. "I can think of nothin' but our kiss last eve. How aboot ye?"

Her knees went a bit weak—before she pulled herself together again. He was a bold rascal who was well practiced in the art of seduction. The slant of his scandalous lips proved it. He expected her to swoon. Instead, she straightened her shoulders.

"You call that a kiss?" She tried to maintain a serious composure while he laughed. "What is it truly that possesses you to follow me around the vale, uninvited?"

He unclasped his arms and stretched them outward. "I've been askin' m'self that verra question."

"And?" She turned away and pulled on the door.

"And," he replied, pushing off the wall and bending to her buckets, "the answer still eludes me."

What was he trying to say? What was so difficult about deciding why he followed her? She glowered at him and snatched one of the handles. He let her take it.

"I thought at first," he continued, picking up his pace to walk beside her along the path back to the henhouse, "'twas the way the sun spills over ye like ye were created to dance in the light."

Oh, but he had a masterful tongue. It worked like soothing ointment to a wound that had been opened too long. Her lips ached to form a smile. Her heart raced, wanting to let go and fly. She loved to fly.

"I considered if 'twas the challenge of winnin' a mare as wild as the wind in winter, or a naggin' affliction to want to know who ye are, that possesses me to follow ye."

Affliction?

"But I'm still undecided."

So, getting to know her was an affliction. She flicked her eyes to him. As for his confession of being undecided, could he possibly be as guileless as his current smile implied? Oh, but he had other smiles, ones that were tainted with trouble.

It frightened her. Allowing him, or any man for that matter, to distract her from saving Elsie. She couldn't lose sight of her task. Not even for a man whose kiss curled her toes and scorched her blood.

She had to keep her head clear and her heart well guarded. This Highlander, with his dancing eyes and full, decadent mouth was temptation incarnate. But she didn't want to be tempted. She didn't want to note the height or breadth of him so close, or how his easy smiles put her at ease. Or how he'd snatched the power from Nonie's monsters and given it back to her. But he didn't want a wife.

Hadn't he told her? He was a rake of the worst sort. She'd seen him with Bethany. He considered integrity and honor dusty ideals.

"Did you ever consider," she put to him, "that the reason you want to win my favor has nothing to do with me, but with you?"

He quirked his brow at her, his dimple flashing.

"Your victory," she explained, "would be another notch for your belt."

He paused and looked down at his belt. She kept walking until she reached the henhouse and entered it. When he caught up, she should have insisted he leave, for the small shack was dimly lit and being alone in it with Patrick Campbell wasn't wise. But when she heard him enter a moment later, she inhaled a satisfied breath.

"Ye think ye know me."

His voice was like feathers falling over her skin when he spoke behind her. The hairs rose off her nape while the feathers continued down to her belly. She took a step away and turned to face him.

"I do know you, Mr. Campbell, and many men like you. I know your ultimate goal is to have your way. You think to flatter me into submission, but you will not succeed."

He grinned, addling her senses. What in blazes was wrong with her? He was a man, just like any other man—only he wasn't.

"I disagree."

Perhaps she was wrong. She wanted to slap him again. "You think me weak?"

"No' at all," he said lifting his fingers to her face. "In fact, I think ye're quite extraordinary."

He mesmerized her. That was the only logical explanation she could come up with to explain why she remained in her spot, why she closed her eyes at the touch of his large callused palm against her face. He must have spoken these words to a dozen other women. He'd probably spoken them to Bethany. She wanted to laugh at him and his well-practiced words and tell him she wasn't fool enough to believe them but the thought of him and Bethany made her grind her teeth. What did she care? He was a rogue and this is what rogues did. In her rational mind, Charlie knew what she should do. Stay clear of him until he left.

But there was nothing rational about the heart, and she feared she could lose hers to him. To a careless knave.

"You flatter me, Mr. Campbell," she said, gathering her strength around her and returning her attentions to the hens. "You don't have to. I will not be won."

"By anyone?" he asked, sounding amused beside her.

She slanted her gaze to him. He didn't bother concealing his dark, dubious smirk.

"No' ever?" he asked.

She didn't know. She hadn't thought about *ever* before. "Perhaps in time, after I've lived life with Elsie the way I've dreamed of for many years. Why?" she asked with the arch of an eyebrow and a smirk of her own. "Would you wait?"

"Would ye consider me if I did?" he countered with a grin.

"If you waited for me that long," she told him letting out a soft laugh, "I'd consider you a fool."

Chapter Ten

He was a fool.

A fool to linger in Pinwherry, to linger here...with her. Why didn't he leave, even now, after she professed her deep desire to be left alone? Out of all the women in Scotland, he wanted a lass who didn't want to be won.

He wanted her. Not just in his bed. He ached for the sight of her, the interaction with her. He enjoyed her company and he didn't want to leave it just yet.

How much longer would he stay?

Her fingertips settled on his ear and tightened the muscles in his abdomen.

"You're bleeding."

"Duff is a brute."

She smiled with him and he fell captivated, as if he were under some sort of spell. As if he couldn't control his own thoughts, only his actions. And why was he keeping himself from sweeping her into his arms and seducing her senseless? Because he didn't want to jeopardize the life she'd dreamed of.

Hell, was he ill? Had he caught a fever? Was he delirious? Was he truly not going to kiss her?

Damn honor and integrity!

He decided to stick with the topic he was more comfortable with. Her brother, for instance. It was safer and there was something about Duff that bothered him, like a nettle in one's boot, pricking at his thoughts. Sparring with him this morn proved that Duff knew how to fight. Not only that, but he enjoyed it, smiling when his fist collided with Patrick's body while they had sparred. It was that smile... that smile Patrick had seen somewhere before. But where?

"I'm surprised Duff didn't break your jaw," she said, dropping her fingers to her side and returning to the hens. "He likes to break jaws."

"Whose?" Patrick asked, tossing seed from his bucket to the hens.

"Men who deserve it," she granted. "Men whose names I will not speak, who'd harmed some of the children in the village and the next. Duff broke their jaws before he killed them. He shows no mercy."

So then, he thinks like a Highlander.

"D'ye know who his faither is?" Patrick asked her, wondering if he knew the man.

"If Duff wanted you to know his father's name, he would have told you."

His gaze took in the splendor of her alluring profile while she denied him in the splintered light. "Ye're loyal to him."

She shook her head but then her dissent faltered. "Duff had no part in the circumstances of his childhood, no say in who fathered him."

There was mercy in her. It pleased Patrick. She shared no fondness for her brothers. She'd made it perfectly clear. Her disdain for Hendry was understandable, but Duff had not laid a finger on any of the villagers, at least, according to Duff when Patrick had asked him earlier.

He admired her loyalty for compassion's sake, but he wanted to know more. "Was his father so terrible that Duff would find shame in acknowledgin' him?"

She shrugged her dainty shoulder and turned back to the chickens. "Terrible enough to ride through Pinwherry and stay long enough to father a child and then leave, a child who grew up defenseless in this merciless world with only a mother to protect him. I saw what having a rogue for a father did to Duff. He fights well because he was forced to learn at a young age."

So, Patrick thought, this was where her disdain for rogues was born. It was understandable.

She'd drawn her walls back around her when she thought he didn't comprehend what Duff's father had done wrong. He could. He hadn't wanted to think on such things before. Was he ready now?

"Aye, ye have it right," he admitted. "'Twas terrible to leave a lass alone with his bairn."

She slipped her dark gaze to him once again while she bent to the hens. A thin beam of light fell upon her, illuminating the skeptical quirk of her lips.

"Something you've been careful to avoid?" she asked.

He began to answer with a resounding aye, but he found himself unable to follow through.

Hell. He didn't want to think about any babes he may have left behind, who would live out their lives fatherless. He had never witnessed the aftermath of his carefree, selfish way of life. According to Charlie, she had with Duff.

"In truth," he confessed quietly, dipping his gaze to the fowl, "I dinna know fer certain what I've left behind."

Silence passed between them for a moment that lasted

an eternity for Patrick and left him feeling heavy with remorse.

"I see." Her voice played like a sultry breeze over his skin. "You think little of me to believe I'd toss myself over *that* precipice."

He knew he should feel defeated, but damn it, she was quick and genuine and she didn't give a damn if she injured his feelings. She forced him by deed and by word to face the man beyond the reckless smiles. The man he had allowed himself to become. And while self-examination brought him to a darker place he preferred to avoid, she pierced the gloom and made him smile.

"I dinna think little of ye, Charlotte," he told her, unable to stop himself, not wanting to. "In fact, I think more of ye than anyone I've ever known. Ye're braw, no one's fool. Yer compassion and wise counsel with yer neighbors last eve convinced me that ye are a far better person than I."

Had her smirk softened into a smile? Was that the sound of her shallow breath that tempted him beyond reason? He reached out and swept a wavy lock of her hair away from the apple of her cheek. He let his fingers trace the soft contour of her face and felt his chest expand beneath his tunic when he thought her gaze went warm on him, her breath faint. He wanted to hold her, kiss her. He'd never wanted anything as badly. He stared into her eyes, fearing he was close to losing all. She was everything...

But he thought too much of her to take her to his bed and then leave. He thought of her more than he should.

"I...I should be goin'." Did he just deny himself his desire? Did he stammer doing it? Hell. What was she doing to him? He didn't want his heart to stir because of her. He didn't know what to expect and if his current condition were any indication, he was in deep trouble. He wasn't ready for this. He feared giving up his veneer and succumbing to the duties of devotion.

"I told Hendry I would ride with him to the village to collect Robbie's rent. I want to make certain he terrorizes them no further."

Her tight little gasp tempted him to toss his fear to the wind, lift her in his arms and kiss her breathless.

"How did you get Hendry to agree to let you accompany him?"

He grinned and stepped away, setting down his empty bucket. "I didna ask."

Following him out, she stopped him with a hand on his arm. He looked down at her slender fingers, able to hurl a sling or offer comfort. He knew he shouldn't, but he raised his gaze to her sunlit face and then over the rest of her gloriously garbed in a dress that looked like it had been fashioned by a host of sprites.

Hell, she was bonnie.

"What will you do if Nonie or the boys see you?"

The children. He hadn't thought of that. They'd likely mention seeing him last night and mayhap Charlie, as well. Hendry would discover that she'd sneaked out. "Mayhap, I shouldna' go then. I dinna want to put ye in jeopardy if—" His eyes narrowed on her. "Would he put his hands to ye? Would Duff, or yer faither?"

"You should go," she told him, ignoring his question. "We need to make certain he doesn't bring any more harm to them. Let me come with you. I will gather Mary and the children and keep them inside."

His smiled widened and before he spoke, her smile matched his. "'Tis a good plan."

Damn it, but she was radiant in the full light of day, dazzling him senseless with her excitement.

"But ye dinna need to ask m' permission, lass. Do what ye wish."

"Hendry will—"

"—no' be given a choice."

"You would cause him harm?"

"No' if I dinna have to."

Her smile remained while her fingers stroked his arm. "Thank you, Mr. Campbell."

Aye, she made him smile. "Patrick," he corrected.

Charlie had thought he would try to kiss her again, but he hadn't. She should be thankful, instead she felt disappointed. It was only because he'd told her it was all he'd thought about. There was no other explanation, and no other reason to dwell on it further.

She'd admit that watching him take control over Hendry, having to insist only once that she be allowed to accompany them to the village, made her want to smile. Hendry had never allowed her to ride with him when he collected rent. She wondered if her brother's acquiescence had anything to do with Patrick's bloody knuckles from his sparring with Duff earlier.

She didn't care why. She was going. Her heart beat hard and fast over the excursion. She loved unexpected adventures—even if she was going only to help keep the wee ones silent and away from the men. Though she would love to allow Nonie a glimpse of her fearless defender, ready and able to defeat the gel's monster, Charlie couldn't chance the child calling out to him and rousing Hendry's suspicions. She doubted there would be any trouble with Hendry this time, thanks to Patrick's presence, so it really wasn't too dangerous.

She realized that the last thing she should be doing was spending more time with Patrick Campbell. He was finding a way around her defenses. She didn't want to end up like Duff's mother, but her heart still thumped because she was going with him.

She cast him an appreciative smile when he turned to her and flicked his reins to go. His wink thrilled the breath right out of her.

For the first time since she met Patrick Campbell, she didn't want him to leave.

She trotted her horse a bit closer to Patrick's as they rode at a leisurely pace. He turned to her, blocking Hendry's view of his face on the other side, and smiled.

Could he see her thoughts in her eyes? In the involuntary curl of her lips? She suspected he was a better man than he led her to believe. She wanted to believe it.

But her mind fought to deny it lest she become the kind of fool she detested. There were no better men. Mr. Campbell likely had something to gain by coming. She thought about the first night she saw him—dragging a serving wench into his lap and dipping his mouth to her neck. How many women had he seduced with the facets of his emerald eyes, the devilish slant of his smile? Or was it his polished prose that beguiled them?

She despised the thought that she could be so easily misled, and worse, distracted. When his gaze fell to her soft skirts blowing over her thighs, she suspected she'd been correct all along.

"Have ye given any more thought to m' inquiry?" he asked her in a hushed voice.

Pity he didn't know that Hendry had perfected the art of eavesdropping during his many hours hiding behind curtains.

"What inquiry is that?" her brother asked, a snide lilt tainting his tone.

"I asked her fer the name of Duff's faither."

He surprised her again by answering honestly.

"'Twas Will MacGregor who sired him," Hendry supplied without so much as a shred of loyalty to their brother.

"Hendry!" Charlie kept her voice down though the struggle to do so clenched her teeth. "He never told you. How do you know that?"

"Duff's voice resonates through the halls, dear sister. He's easy to hear if you aim your ear in the right direction."

Eavesdropping, irritating little weasel, Charlie thought, while Patrick drew her attention.

She couldn't be certain, but he fidgeted around in his saddle as it were on fire. It was no mystery that Campbells and MacGregors were enemies. Every Campbell knew about the proscription against the Highland clan. What would he do with this knowledge? Would he turn Duff in as an outlaw to collect a reward?

"Why are you curious about Duff's father?" Hendry put to him, dragging the Highlander's gaze to him.

"I have met many men in m' travels. He bears a strong resemblance to a man I met in Argyll last month. But my acquaintance went by the name of Alex MacLachlan."

Charlie peeked around Patrick's shoulder to see Hendry. He looked to be mulling over the explanation, then shrugged and set his blue eyes on the road. "Whether you know him or not, Duff still remains a bastard."

Charlie wanted to sling a stone at his chest, but best not put him in a foul mood before he reached Robbie Wallace's house.

Patrick must not have given a damn about her brother's mood. Why should he? He'd already compelled Hendry to give up authority over her, not to mention the family secrets. He wasn't afraid of what Hendry might do. Patrick would simply stop him.

"Better to be a bastard than the tyrant son of a liege lord."

Hendry smirked. "If you think to come at me with your self-righteous indignation, don't bother. I would rather be the tyrant."

"I surmised that much the moment I met ye."

"And," Hendry braved another sneer turning to Mr. Campbell, "you remember my fist in your mouth during that same meeting."

"Aye," Patrick laughed. "And m' hands were bound. I'm no' bound now. Want to give it another go? I warn ye," he said, his smiling fading, "fer the next few months, mayhap a year dependin' on how hard I hit ye, ye willna be able speak or eat withoot aid."

Behind Patrick Campbell's broad shoulder, Charlie smiled. No one had ever dared speak so to Hendry. She'd wished so many times that someone would. People feared her brother almost as much as they feared her father.

When it became apparent that Hendry had nothing to further to say, Mr. Campbell turned his attention back to her, his easy smile returning.

She was careful to conceal what she thought of him at this moment. God help her, he was so handsome just looking at him made her doubt all her convictions. Did she truly want to spend her life trusting no man? Could Patrick ever be loyal only to her the way Kendrick was? Would living alone with Elsie be enough?

She looked away and spread her gaze over the cottages coming up over the hill.

He said nothing. Good, she didn't want him to speak to her. What would he think of her gushing all over him the way Bethany had after one smile tossed her way? She had higher goals to aim for than being in this man's bed.

They rode the rest of the way in silence.

But she liked what he did to Hendry. She wouldn't lie.

Chapter Eleven

S he was pleased.

Patrick hoped she wouldn't be angry with him for threatening to beat her brother senseless. He wished he didn't care. But he did. It hadn't stopped him from threatening to do it though. He didn't like Hendry Cunningham for more reasons than he could list.

He would ponder Charlotte Cunningham's effect on him later—and how bonnie she looked with her raven tresses bouncing around her shoulders—shoulders she squared now as if bracing herself before she turned her fading smile away.

Will was Duff's father! Will MacGregor! Truly, Patrick wasn't surprised. Now that he knew it was Will, their resemblance was so much stronger, the similarities more apparent, and the differences, as well. Will was often found filling Camlochlin's hall with laughter. Duff barely smiled. Hell, Duff was his cousin. How would Patrick tell him? The lad had a right to know his father. Patrick could even take him back to Camlochlin.

They reached Robbie Wallace's cottage, giving Patrick no more time to think on what to do. He was here to protect Robbie and his family from any more tyranny... or nightmares.

He hadn't considered what the children's reaction to seeing him would implicate. Charlie was wise in joining them.

He watched her spring off her horse and hurry to the door as it opened.

Patrick inhaled a steadying breath. He noted the quickening of his heart, the rush of blood through his veins, the world moving slower. What the hell was happening to him? He'd faced three MacPhersons coming at him with their muscles bulging and he hadn't felt this kind of apprehension.

But this wasn't a fight between willing opponents.

Robbie Wallace limped forward, his affliction brought on by the man saddled beside Patrick.

"Do you have your lord's rent?" Hendry called out over his lifted nose.

"I do," Robbie called back, his eyes slipping briefly to Patrick. He reached for the pouch at his belt.

Hendry looked surprised and a bit defeated, causing Patrick's heart to warm on the lass who'd just entered the house for what she'd done.

Eyes squinted and lips pinched, Hendry asked, "How did you come by it?"

"What does it matter to ye?" Patrick turned to him on his horse. "'Tis paid. Let's be on our way."

"He likely robbed it," Hendry argued.

Well, he had it half right. The coin had been stolen...

"And my father wouldn't take kindly to thieves on his land."

"Nor would I take kindly," Patrick told him, keeping his

voice evenly toned, despite his desire to knock Hendry's teeth out, "to any harm coming to this man."

"What concern is this of yours?" Hendry snarled at him. "When you asked to accompany me, you claimed you were interested in holding competitions here so you could rob the village men blindfolded."

"I never said blindfolded," Patrick corrected lightly. "With an arm secured behind m' back 'twas what I said."

"Then go about your task, Campbell."

"Come with me," Patrick said in a low voice, bringing his mount closer to Hendry's, "or I shall drag ye away, tied to m' horse." He blinked, turned to Robbie, and gleamed a smile at him. "Just a moment and we'll be off."

Robbie nodded and looked back. His family was not there.

Patrick returned his gaze to Hendry. He didn't care how many times he had to threaten this grunting boar, sooner or later Hendry would no longer be warned.

"Another moment and I might insist that ye thank him fer payin' ye fer the verra little ye provide him and his family."

Hendry wanted to challenge him. Patrick could see the signs of it in his shadowy eyes, his still smirk. But he didn't have the heart.

"Next month don't be late," he warned Robbie instead then tugged on his reins and moved off.

Patrick would make certain Hendry was paid next month.

"Good day to ye." Patrick tossed Robbie one last smile before following his host. When they passed the front of the house, Patrick shouted, "Miss Cunningham!"

They lingered a moment longer waiting for Charlie to return to them. Patrick wasn't sure who hid their smile best when he and the lass set their gazes on each other. He suspected he'd failed, since he'd never had a reason to conceal his pleasure before.

"I'm going back to the house. I have things to discuss with my father," Hendry declared with an eye on Patrick while Charlie gained her saddle. "Come, Charlotte."

She shot a glance at Patrick. "Are you not returning?"

He shook his head. "I've something to see to first."

"Oh?" she asked, slinging the full potency of her gaze on him.

He hesitated giving her a more thorough explanation only because the sight of her was so distracting. Hendry seized the opportunity to answer for him.

"He wants to pick fights with the villagers."

Patrick cast him a frown but then returned his smile to her. "Inaccurate. Why dinna ye accompany me and see fer yerself?"

A moment of indecision passed over her elegantly spun features and then disappeared. "I think I shall."

"I think not!" her brother demanded, breaking the spell she weaved over her admirer.

Patrick turned his horse around to face Hendry head-on. Hell, but he'd had enough of this little worm. Normally, Cunningham's nose, at least, would have been broken by now, but he didn't want to worsen the feud any further. And if he did what he wanted, the feud would get worse. The trick was in concealing his true hesitation and making Hendry believe his threats.

Luckily for Patrick, he was as good with his words as he was with his fists.

"She'll be safe with me. If not, and she accuses me of layin' a hand on her, I'll take her as m' wife, giving yer faither what he wants, a Campbell alliance. Is that an opportunity in which ye truly want to get in the way? What will yer faither think when I tell him yer distrust has sent me on m' way?"

He didn't think it would be over so quickly but Hendry left without another word. Pleased with his work, Patrick turned back to Charlie—and her hand flying toward his face.

He could have ducked and avoided it. He was fast enough, but he stood his ground. Her palm cracked across his cheek, stinging like the edge of a blade.

"A chance to molest me is an *opportunity*?"

"Is it no'?" he asked her, rubbing the side of his face with his palm. "Yer faither wants a union between us. What harm is there in danglin' that possibility before his face?"

"To get what you want," she accused.

"And to get what ye want, as well," he countered. "Did ye want to return home with Hendry or come with me?"

She dipped her head and veiled her eyes behind her long lashes, but he could hear in her voice the smile she tried to deny him. "I chose what I wanted, did I not?"

"Aye, lass, ye did." He ached to kiss her. His muscles twitched with longing to seize her in his arms and tell her how braw and beautiful she was to him.

"Now will you tell me where we're going?"

He wanted to ask her where she wanted to go. He would have taken her anywhere. He recognized that he was in danger. He felt his resolve falter every time he looked at her, spoke to her. He felt himself molding to become more...worthy of her. It was a condition he should worry over. But he hated worrying.

"I want to earn some coin," he said, flicking his reins and trotting his horse away.

"Why?" she called out, bringing him back. "Are you leaving?"

Was that disappointment he heard in her voice? So what if it was? He couldn't stay indefinitely, just long enough to earn enough coin to keep the Wallaces safe for a time. With enough fights, he could make the required coin in two or three nights. "Soon, most likely."

"You're verra clever."

He quirked his brow at her. "How so?"

"You know I don't want a husband. You believe if you manhandle me, I won't tell my father."

His gaze on her softened. "I willna manhandle ye, lass."

"Good, because I would tell him without fear of a marriage," she said, tilting up her chin and looking away. "He would not force me to marry a corpse."

He thought nothing was more splendid than her face but when she turned her profile to him, he grew entranced. How could she be so delicate, yet so strong? Like the winter heather that lined the braes around Camlochlin.

"Why did ye no' stab me last night then?" Last night when he'd tasted the sweet desire in her kiss.

Her knuckles tightened around her reins. Was her memory of it as pleasurable? To hell with the future. He wanted to taste more of her, kiss her until her defenses fell around his arms.

"You caught me off guard," she said, turning to stare right back at him.

He saw the flash of warning in her eyes. If he tried kissing her again there would be consequences. They would be worth it. Hell, she was a delight to his senses, his soul.

"And now ye'd fight me?" he asked with a fierce smile. "And win?"

"Aye," she told him confidently. "I'd win."

Something in her declaration made his blood sizzle in his veins, made him want to leap from his horse and drag her from hers. The thought of taking her down and straddling her between his thighs excited him. "I'd like a demonstration of yer skill later."

"You shall have it."

"Good, now tell me, where is the nearest pub?"

She turned to him. Her face was pale.

"The pub?" Charlie asked him, trying to swallow. Why did he want to go there? People knew her there.

"Where else am I to find men willing to fight me?"

"Is that how you intend to earn coin? By fighting?"

"Dinna worry," he assured her. "I willna fight anyone a few years older than me."

No! They couldn't go to the pub. If he discovered that she'd been there often and alone, he might remember seeing her in Pinmore. He might tell her father. He certainly won't let her out of his sight again.

"There's a pub in the village, aye, Charlie?"

She nodded and wiped her brow. He'd want to know how she knew all the patrons. He'd want to know everything. What she was doing was extremely dangerous. He would try to stop her.

What did he need to fight for anyway? If he wanted to leave so badly, why couldn't he earn his coin building or repairing, by doing something useful? She looked him over, set upon his horse, drenched in the spring afternoon sun. The man was powerfully built for certain. His strength and stamina could see to more than just fighting.

"You will find no worthy opponent in the pub, or in this village," she told him. "More are sickly than strong. You would be better off visiting farms. In fact, why not begin with the Wallaces?"

"I wouldna fight Robbie," he insisted with the sting of insult in his voice. Did she truly think so little of him?

"I know that." Her lips curled like a silky veil in a breeze. "His hay hasn't been baled in a fortnight. He could use your brawn."

"Balin' hay?" He looked utterly disappointed.

"Aye." Her smile deepened as she dismounted and tied her horse to the post in front of the Wallaces' small cottage. "Shall I knock, or will you?"

"How can I gain a purse by balin' hay?" he said, dismounting and tying his horse as well. "I dinna want payment from men who have nothin'."

She paused to consider how she should take what he just said. She was glad he wouldn't take from the poor, but was gaining a purse so he could leave all he thought about? If so, what would it make her to fawn over him? And, if that wasn't bad enough, he hadn't even considered what she was asking him to do. She turned away and started toward the front door. "You'll be helping," she called to him over her shoulder.

He joined her quickly. "That's what I'm tryin' to do."

She knocked, ignoring his defense. "I'm sure these good folks can use your aid."

"'Twill take all day. I could be—"

She blew out a gusty breath. "You can hone your skills on weaker men later, Mr. Campbell—" She paused to watch him glance up at the heavens. "Patrick," she amended.

His smile returned almost immediately. "And just so ye know, the men who choose to fight me are strong."

"According to you, you win often," she told him as Mary Wallace opened the door. "So they are still weaker than you."

His dimpled grin made her senses reel, and her nerve endings raw. She tossed him her darkest scowl an instant before turning to Mary and smiling. "Mr. Campbell has come to offer his help."

"What?" Patrick asked following her inside the house. "Why are ye angry? Is it wrong of me to be pleased that ye think me stronger than any other man?"

She kept walking, her arms stiff at her sides, and her chin tilted slightly upward. "That is not what I said. My *presumption* was formed by *your* claim as champion." She turned so he could see the truth in her eyes. But he wasn't there.

He'd remained by the door, now on one knee and holding little Nonie Wallace's hand in his.

Chapter Twelve

hat brings you back, Mr. Campbell?" Robbie Wallace held himself steady by clutching the back of his chair. "Has Cunningham—"

"Nae," Patrick assured him, holding up his hands while he entered the kitchen. "'Tis nothin' to do with him. Miss Cunningham has asked me to offer ye m' services."

Robbie shifted his gaze to Charlie at Patrick's right. Patrick wanted to look at her too. Was she still angry with him? Why did he concern himself with it? What did she have against fighting when she boasted of her own skill? Fighting—and winning—filled his purse, and presently, that's what he desired.

But instead he was getting ready to work for nothing, doing what she had asked simply because she'd asked it. He hadn't wanted to deny her request. The desire to please her should have left him feeling stripped and afraid of losing control of his good senses, but oddly enough, he felt rather pleased with himself. Helping Robbie for the simple sake of helping him felt right.

Mayhap, he wasn't such a selfish bastard after all.

Miss Nonie Wallace didn't think so. Convincing Charlotte Cunningham was going to be a bit more difficult. And he wanted to convince her. Damn it. He wanted to protect her—though he wasn't fool enough to ever tell her. He wanted to stay and get to know her better. She was all finely spun threads of strength and softness. Those threads were winding around him the way ivy clings to stone. He wondered how long he would allow it to grow before no more stone could be seen.

"Your services?" Robbie asked, surprised and grinning now at Charlie. "You mean like baling the hay?"

Patrick almost sighed out loud. "Aye, like balin' the hay."

"That's verra kind of you, Mr. Campbell." Robbie's fingers uncurled from around the back of his chair. "I'll see that you're fed well for your help."

"Please, call me Patrick."

"I'll make fresh rabbit stew!" Mary exclaimed with excitement. "And Charlotte, you'll stay for supper, as well."

It seemed this wasn't such a poor idea, Patrick thought, accepting the invitation. A good meal and a day with Charlie—

"I'm afraid I must return home." Charlie spoiled his reverie. "My father—"

He turned to her. "—Knows ye're with me, a Campbell."

He knew his words cut by the way she veiled her gaze. Her worth to her father was based on what she could give him. An alliance with a powerful clan. Patrick was sorry, but she already knew the truth of it. She was not a fool.

"Use it to *yer* advantage," he whispered, reminding her of her power to make her own choice. "Stay here with me."

He looked down at her slender shoulders relaxing around her neck. "Verra well." She lifted her eyes to him, her gaze softening and robbing him of rational thought. "I shall stay then."

He had only a brief moment to offer her a purely heart-felt smile before Mary pulled her attention away with offers of allegiance and refreshment.

His gaze lingered on Charlie until Robbie cleared his throat. "Aye," Patrick agreed and clapped his hands together turning back to the farmer. "Where d'ye want me to begin?"

Charlie looked out Mary's kitchen window and watched Patrick enter the barn. Robbie limped behind him while Nonie skipped along the rear.

What was she to think of Mr. Patrick Campbell? He didn't want to spend his day in and out of a barn. He could have easily refused her. He would have refused her if he were nothing but the dispassionate scoundrel she first thought him to be.

She thought back to him—as she was sure she would do for the next half a century—on bended knee before Nonie like some kind of fabled champion before his queen. And though he didn't want to bale hay, he was willing to do it for Charlie. What kind of man was he under all that charm?

There had to be more to him.

If he ever wanted to win her heart.

What would he do with it if he did? Did she want him to keep trying? She liked being with him, slicing away at his rakish defenses, and watching him take the blows with a sturdy chin. He kissed her like she was the only lass in the country and he, the one who possessed her. She wanted more of his mouth—but the danger was in wanting more of *him*.

Could she toss aside every conversation she'd had with Kendrick about Duff's father and trust this self-proclaimed rogue wouldn't do the same to her? What if she was wrong and he was like all the rest? What if she was correct and he tempted her to give up her plans with her sister?

"Charlie, you're spilling the water!"

Charlie's attention snapped back to what she was doing. Pouring refreshment for those outside. She corrected the tilt of her pitcher and managed to get some water into the cup. "Oh, forgive me, Mary!"

"What is it that steals your attention and unsettles your heart?"

Charlie wanted to stop her when Mary leaned up and looked out the window.

It was already too late. Mary saw him and smiled.

"I see," she said, barely concealing her smile and then reached for her tray. "He's quite pleasing to the eye."

Aye, he was. "Is that all?" Charlie didn't realize she'd spoken out loud until Mary answered her.

"Nay, not all, else I think you would not have stayed."

Charlie smiled. Had they spoken about it so many times that Mary knew her this well? They had become quick friends long before Robbie's injury. She guessed she knew Mary just as well. At least enough to know that beneath Mary's prim exterior dwelled a strong, bold spirit.

"I see a man with a good heart. A man who taught my Nonie to slay her monsters and then showed up here to keep them from returning. That's all I know of him, but 'tis a good start."

A good start to what? Charlie snatched up her tray, spilling even more water, and followed Mary out.

"I would have you know I have no feelings for Mr. Campbell."

Mary turned on her heel to face her. "Och, forgive me for assuming. If you've no interest in him, I think he would be a good match for Eleanor Kennedy. Poor gel has no help since her husband died last spring."

Charlie stared at her then blinked. What was she supposed to say? Eleanor Kennedy? Patrick would like the young widow. She had long red hair and a saucy mouth.

"He isn't staying. In fact, he's trying to earn coin for his journey."

"Well, Eleanor doesn't have much coin but I'm certain she will come up with a way to pay him if he ploughs her soil before he leaves."

Ploughs her soil?

Charlie looked over Mary's shoulder at Patrick beginning his work. He bent to a large mound of hay and stuck his fork in it.

She swallowed and raised her hand to her throat. She didn't want him to plough Eleanor's soil. What if word spread that he would work for coin and old Ramsey hired him? What would he think of Bonnie and Brenda, Ramsey's twin daughters? They were of marriageable age and were looking for husbands. Caitriona Cunningham, Charlie's cousin, was also without a husband. Caitriona was beautiful, with wheat-colored hair and striking blue eyes. Before Kendrick died, Cait barely left their side. She'd even learned to wield a sling. After the Fergussons had attacked, and Charlie had become a prisoner on her own land, she barely met with Cait anymore for leisure.

Patrick would find her pleasing.

She didn't care. Why should she? He wasn't staying.

She didn't care whose fields Patrick Campbell ploughed.

"Verra well then, on to Eleanor Kennedy's farm tomorrow!" She stepped around Mary and proceeded toward him, her tray shaking in her hands.

She didn't make it to him with a full cup. Nonie and her

brothers, who appeared from inside the barn, snatched up the three cups she carried.

"Robert," her father called to his eldest son. "Fetch Miss Cunningham a chair."

"Aye, Papa!"

"There's no need," Charlie protested as the lad ran off to his chore. "I won't sit while you stand, Robbie. Take the seat or give it to your wife, I will stand here for a little while."

"As you wish," Robbie replied and accepted a cup from his wife.

"Here, bring this to Mr. Campbell, will you?" Mary handed Charlie a full cup and smiled.

Charlie looked her petite friend over. She wondered if Robbie knew the spitfire who dwelled within his wife. Judging by his growing family, she suspected he did. She would ask Mary next time they talked. Now, she would demonstrate that *her* fire would not be so easily doused.

"That's kind of you, Mary." She graced her hosts with a smile, accepted the cup, and turned her back on them.

Her composure though, could not withstand the sight of the Highlander pulling off his shirt and tossing it aside. Drenched in sunlight with sweat glistening over his flexing muscles, he looked like some mythical warrior crafted in bronze. Her eyes basked in the sight of him and the strength of his hands and bruised knuckles, the shadow his shoulders cast as he bent to another mound and jabbed his fork in deep. She took a step toward him, trying to deny his mesmerizing effect while she watched him lift the pitched hay in the air, turn, and smile at her. He took the heavy fork in one hand and reached for the cup with the other.

She tried looking around at the land, but her gaze returned to him tipping the cup to his lips. She watched the tilt of his jaw as he drank. His throat was thick and corded and made her think about what it would be like to bite it. She'd heard some of her brothers' whores talk about things they enjoyed doing to men. She bit her bottom lip instead.

He finished quickly, taking only a sip and then handing her back the cup. "'Tis goin' to be a long afternoon. I heard ye tell Robbie ye were goin' to stand fer a wee bit? Aye?"

She nodded, wondering what color exactly were his eyes? Green, like life unleashed? Or burnished gold, forged from liquid fire? They changed often. Humor skipped across the surface of his gaze but something more primal lurked beyond the shadows cast by his dark lashes.

He quirked one corner of his mouth, along with the brow above it. "Charlie?"

She blinked, and realizing that she'd been staring into his eyes like some stricken fool, she felt her blood rush to her face, and then to her head. But she couldn't pry her eyes away from his.

"If ye dinna mind bringin' me another cup later," he said with his gaze going warm over her.

The urge to smile at him proved that his guile could charm even her. It frightened her. She'd never had a problem harnessing her emotions before. In fact, she was a master at it. It's what kept peace at Cunningham House. Worse though was that she hadn't been tempted to abandon herself to anyone since Kendrick. She was afraid to abandon herself to Patrick. She'd seen the result of a rogue's seduction.

But Patrick made her breathless and hot.

Too hot. She tried to swallow but her throat felt like dry tinder. She couldn't surrender her heart. She wouldn't.

"Will ye stay and bring me m' water?"

What? What did he ask? She'd been in the sun too long, fighting too many frightening emotions. She was having trouble thinking clearly. She wanted to nod, but her head was spinning and she felt...No! She didn't want to collapse at his feet like some weak-willed nymph. But her knees buckled and she felt her head knock against his chest and his arms close around her.

Did many lasses fall into his arms just as easily? For an instant Charlie understood why any woman would, for he loomed above her, gleaming with the sun behind him like some deity come to life, his strong hands steadying her.

She shouldn't let him touch her. He was too dangerous. "I'm fine. You can let go of—"

Darkness prevailed and ended, at last, her humiliation.

She awoke sometime later in Robbie Wallace's favored kitchen chair, which was more like a cushioned throne, wide enough to seat two of her. She and the chair had been set before the back door, which was open and allowing a soft cool breeze to waft through her hair.

She heard voices around her and sat up. It was bad enough that she'd fainted, she wouldn't remain slumped over like a wilted herb. Oh, she'd fainted, fallen at Patrick Campbell's boots. How would she face him?

Mary was coming toward her with a wet rag in her hands. Her husband limped in behind her.

Charlie glanced around for Patrick and found him leaning against the wall, watching her.

Her face burned. Mortified, she turned away, but not before she saw concern in his gaze.

"You had us worried," Mary said softly as she bent over the chair and dabbed at Charlie's face with the cool rag.

"I'm fine," Charlie reassured her gently. "'Twas just the sun."

Mary leaned down to her ear. "'Twas more than that."

Before Charlie could scowl at her, Mary was gone and Patrick appeared in her place—almost as close.

"'Tis good to have ye back."

"The sun...I was..."

When his dimple deepened, she offered him the scowl she'd missed giving Mary. "You had nothing to do with it!"

His damned grin curled even wider. Hell, but he was arrogant. Her fainting dead away in front of him only convinced him that what he thought of himself was correct.

"I'll never speak of it again," he whispered on a silken pledge. He shared a brief, furtive smile with Mary before she walked her husband out of the kitchen then returned it to Charlie when they were alone. "If ye promise no' to ask me to plough Eleanor Kennedy's farm."

Chapter Thirteen

Satisfied that he pulled a smile from her, Patrick reluctantly moved away. Not too far. Not yet. Hell, he was glad she returned to him. To all of them. Her father's tenants needed her.

It had taken every ounce of control he possessed not to lean in and kiss her plump, parted lips. But stepping back gave him a fuller view of her, slumped in an oversized-overstuffed chair, a few strands of her black hair lifting softly off her shoulders in the slight breeze. He would be happy to stand here and gaze upon her for the next sennight.

"Who am I," she asked with a spark of playfulness flickering in her dark eyes, "to keep you from ploughing any farm you desire?"

Aye, this lass possessed fire. It attracted him, captivated him, and made him want to play along. "Why would I want to go anywhere else, when I'm needed where I am?"

She tossed him a dry smirk. "What makes you think you're needed?"

He laughed softly. "Balin' hay? Have ye fergotten why we're here?" His mirth turned into a smile of uncertainty. "Ye are speakin' of the Wallaces' farm, are ye no'?"

The flash of his dimple proved he knew exactly what she was referring to.

She kicked him in the knee. "You're a fool if you think I need you."

He caught her foot and held it. Boldly, he swept his fingers over her bare ankle and contradicted her with a lazy grin.

Her face flushed and he laughed and let her go before she fainted again.

"Who d'ye want to be, Charlie?" he asked growing serious again.

"No one special," she answered softly.

He raised a skeptical brow upon studying her. Did she mean no one special to him, or to the world around her? "That will be a difficult endeavor, lass. Ye'll always be noticed."

"Such a silver tongue you possess, Patrick Campbell," she said while he reached for a stool and set it before her. "Tell me, where did you learn to wield it so flawlessly?"

"Everywhere," he told her as he sat, facing her. "The words are imbued in the wind at Camlochlin—"

"Camlochlin?"

He realized his error too late. If she already knew the name of the MacGregors of Skye's homestead, then he'd just about admitted he was one of them. He waited an instant to see her reaction. When no fear came to her features, he decided to continue. "M' home in the Highlands."

Her eyes danced on him as she settled deeper into Robbie's chair. "Tell me of it."

He'd never spoken of Camlochlin with anyone who

didn't live there. Asking for a description made him ponder its grandeur and glorious history.

"'Twas built in the mists by a true chief, determined to keep his clan safe and hidden from the world."

Mayhap, he could convince her in the telling that this clan wasn't made up of savage killers bent on trouble. If she did find out who he was, mayhap she wouldn't see him as a danger.

"He built a fortress of stone and resilience and brought the daughter of his enemy there to be his wife."

Her eyes widened and shone with interest. "Did he take her against her will?"

"Nae," Patrick assured her. "I'm told she almost reached the castle before he did, so eager was she to arrive there. She became a mother to many and a tutor to all. She taught a beast to be gallant and turned Highlanders into knights."

"With dusty old ideals," she teased gently.

He smiled. How could he not? She'd dragged him into the light again, made him look the careless, reckless rogue straight in the face.

He didn't dislike who he saw. It was him—the man he was, the person he knew. He just didn't know if he wanted to continue being that man. The idea of such change though, well, damn it, it scared the hell out of him.

"Everyone in Camlochlin was taught them. The ideals of honor were as deeply planted as love fer country or swordplay. Whether or no' all her children practice them, they are impressed upon us all."

At the sight of her curling her lips, he grinded his jaw to keep from cursing himself. She had the most damned delectable mouth. What the hell was wrong with him? Why wasn't he there? Kissing her?

"You will have to prove that to me, Mr. Campbell."

His smile warmed on her for a moment before he laughed and shook his head. "I know. I know I do."

He didn't shrink away from her challenge. She wasn't going to be easy to win, and that made trying more exciting. That is, if he decided to try.

"You still have hay to bale."

Nodding, he stood up. "I'll get to it then." He didn't want to leave. The fever was obviously getting worse.

"Mr. Campbell?" she said, stopping him as he stepped around her chair. "Before you go, tell me a bit more of Camlochlin, where the wind is infused with virtuous poetry. Is it pleasing to the eye?"

He almost wished one of Camlochlin's bards were present so that he could sing of its beauty. He could never do it, but his words would have to do. "It looks like God's fury and splendor collided on earth. 'Tis like the crowning glory upon the world. 'Tis unforgettable once 'tis seen. That's why so few have ever seen it."

She stared up at him with a fanciful tilt to her smile and he never wanted to look away again. "Where is this soul-wrenching place?"

"Far into the clouds."

"It doesn't sound real."

He felt the words bubbling to the surface. Before he thought about why he would utter them, they poured forth from his mouth. "'Tis. I can prove that to ye too, lass."

Patrick left the cottage spilling quiet oaths before him. Did he just offer to bring her home? How could he have spoken such a thing when he had no intention of ever doing it? Bringing her home meant he was promising something to her—his devotion and his love.

What was wrong with that? a part of him asked. Charlie

was different. Hell, she was so unlike any lass he'd ever known. She wound herself around him in strips of colored veils, some painted with compassion and wisdom, others in courage and confidence. She was delicacy draped in regal robes. Watching her with Robbie Wallace the night she supplied his rent was like being caught up in the radiance of a star—and in the light, he was revealed.

He felt neither pleased nor displeased with himself. He knew he could be a different kind of man if he was willing to work at it. He didn't know if he was willing. And Charlie would make him work.

He was a selfish knave who thought only of his own happiness. Even now.

Damn it, that was hard to admit. He would have never done the like a few months ago, too caught up in the fulfillment of his desires to consider himself further. He'd known there was something different about him. He'd felt the change. The emptiness. But he hadn't truly stopped to examine who he was until he met Charlie. And now that he had, he knew he wasn't good enough for her. But could he be?

Why did she make him want to be? Another part of him argued as he reached the haystacks. Did he want to give up so much so soon? He'd just met the girl. What did he know of her, save that she had good aim and a kind heart? He'd help her mission as much as he could and then he'd be away from here with or without Duff, free of cares and duties, with no desire to change for anyone.

"Are you going to live here, Patrick?"

Torn from his thoughts, he looked down to find Nonie following him and smiled. Should he tell her what she wanted to hear, or the truth?

"I'll stay until the bad dreams and the monsters in them go away."

"You won't leave?" she asked. Her large blue eyes stared up at him.

"No' until ye let me."

"You promise?"

"Aye, I promise." He bent to her as if she held reign over him.

"Nonie," her mother called, coming toward them. "Leave him to his work. What has your father told you about loitering around the pitchfork when work is being done?"

"To be away," Nonie repeated somberly. She looked at Patrick one last time, returned his smile, and wandered off.

"She's fond of you," Mary told him, reaching him.

"As I am of her."

"'Twill be difficult for her when you leave."

Patrick dipped his gaze to his boots. He didn't want to think about leaving Nonie, at least until her and her family were safe from Hendry Cunningham.

It didn't bode well for him. He didn't want to lose his heart to anyone, especially a lass. He didn't want to live a predictable life or have a syrupy heart. If he didn't leave soon, he might not ever want to. He should leave tonight. He lifted his gaze and looked over her shoulder at the cottage. The sooner he left, the easier it would be to forget Charlie.

"I canna stay—"

"She will likely be wed this time next year."

"Who?" he asked, turning back to her.

"Charlie."

Charlie would likely be wed this time next year? Aye, he realized, Mary was correct. Patrick knew firsthand how eager Allan Cunningham was to hand his daughter over in exchange for safety.

The thought of her with another man churned his guts.

And she wouldn't be happy about it either. Another man would try to tame her spirit. What a pity that would be.

"Last month," Mary continued mercilessly, "her father offered her the Baron of Ardrossan when he passed through. I thank the Good Lord the baron didn't find her to his liking. Of course, what man would when she drops a bowl of hot soup in his lap and then blames her poor strength on her illness?" Mary paused to giggle. "She confided in me that 'twas no accident and that she was in perfect health."

Patrick found himself smiling. Clever lass, he thought, looking over Mary's shoulder again. "Is she so determined to remain unwed then?" he asked before he could stop.

"For now," Mary told him, bringing his gaze back to her. "But I suspect if the right man came along, her mind could be changed."

"The right man," he laughed without any trace of humor. Who was worthy of such a radiant prize? He shook his head and jabbed his fork into the hay. "A woman like Charlotte Cunningham deserves m' grandmother's Sir Lancelot. No' me."

Mary shrugged her slender shoulders and turned to leave him to his work. "I don't know who Sir Lancelot is," she called out, "but if he's anything like Patrick, Protector of Dreams, then I think Nonie would disagree with you."

Patrick carried his hay into the barn. He *had* protected Robbie today. He *was* helping Robbie with their work. He'd already decided to fight to earn some coin for the Wallaces' rent next month. Mayhap, he wasn't *that* terrible.

The rest of the day, baling hay and all, was quite pleasant.

Chapter Fourteen

After a mortifying afternoon, the day had been quite pleasant for Charlie as well. Once she'd assured her gracious hostess that she was completely recovered, Mary had agreed to let her help prepare supper. They'd shared wine and laughter while they worked. Charlie had even blushed a time or two when Mary teased her about the way Patrick's eyes followed her. Elsie had told her almost the same thing.

She decided to find out for herself and chose a stool opposite his when he sat down to eat.

He looked at her and smiled, then just as quickly turned his smile on the deep bowl of hot rabbit stew Mary set before him.

She realized quickly that if she meant to catch him, it would mean she had to watch him. She didn't think she'd be able to stop herself if she wanted to. Cloaked in firelight and shadows, his green eyes danced with a passion for life. His irresistible grin hinted of decadent pleasures and effortless confidence. Like a flame he drew her into the temptation of wanting to share her life with him.

Robbie said a prayer over the table and then reached for the loaf of baked black bread his wife delivered next. He tore off the first piece and then handed the loaf to Patrick, who did the same.

"Taste the stew, Mr. Campbell," Mary offered, finally taking her seat and swiping Jamie's thumb from his mouth. "Charlie helped me prepare it."

"I must warn ye," he said, his dimple flickering between shadows and light as he lifted his spoon to his lips. "M' mother is known as the best cook from Dumfries to the farthest reaches of the north."

"Oh?" Charlie raised an eyebrow. "Your mother is from Dumfries?" Was his mother a Kennedy, Gordon, Dunbar? Why hadn't he told her his mother had lived in this region?

"Glasgow," he answered, lowering his gaze to his stew.

Was he keeping something from her? She decided to ask more questions. He was practically still a stranger—except that he'd kissed her. "How did you come to live in the Highlands?"

He set down his spoon and picked up his cup. After a drink, he returned his eyes to her. "M' grandmother, a Campbell, married the man who built Camlochlin within the mountains. M' kin have lived there fer many years."

"Well, we are glad you're here now," Mary said then turned to her. "Aren't we, Charlie?"

Charlie blushed to her roots, not because of Mary's obvious matchmaking, but because she *was* glad. So glad. He'd brought a gust of fresh air into her life.

"So far," Charlie admitted and caught his soft smile and lingering gaze.

Conversation and bread were shared amidst rounds of laughter and two pitchers of ale.

"Nonie tells me that you are here to help her in her dreams," Robbie said, turning to his guest.

Charlie looked at Nonie sitting between her brothers and couldn't help but smile. The child was quite beautiful with sunlit locks tumbling around her pink, dimpled cheeks. She quibbled with her siblings and laughed easily, as a little girl ought to do.

Last night Patrick had promised Nonie that he'd remain close by. How long would he stay?

"Even though m' true identity as a dream protector is to remain secret," Patrick replied, putting a finger to his lips and winking at Nonie. Her eyes opened wider and she nodded, silently promising to keep his secret. "I will tell ye this, Robbie," he said, turning to Nonie's father. "I dinna think she'll be needin' too much help from me. Yer daughter is courageous."

"Aye, I am, Papa!" Nonie called out, scratched behind her ear, and then returned to her bowl.

Patrick's smile widened and he cut his gaze back to Charlie. She blinked away guiltily from her appraisal, but not before feeling a tingle in her kneecaps.

The others were correct, his gaze fell back to her often during supper. She caught him looking over and over again from beneath the veil of her lashes, the slant of her glance. She didn't need to see though. She could feel his attention on her, merry, mischievous eyes, and something more, something deeper and more primal aimed only at her.

What they may or may not have noticed was that Charlie looked back at him often. She couldn't help it. His good humor was infectious, his rich, robust laughter inviting. Even his hearty appetite and the way his mouth moved when he chewed drove her to distraction. Soft light from the hearth spilled over the cut of his auburn-bristled jaw. A jaw strong enough to withstand Duff's mighty fists—and Hamish's. The curled dip of his plump lower lip taunted her with memories of how it felt against her mouth, her teeth. She wanted more. Her desire made her feel flush—or was it the ale?

She had to take hold of herself. She refused to faint again. She had to stay focused, see to her plans. She didn't want—

"Is there a woman waiting for you to return home?" Mary asked. Charlie listened.

He soaked up the last bit of stew on a piece of black bread and put it in his mouth. "I'd like to believe m' mother and sisters, well." He paused his words and his chewing for a moment as if a thought had just popped into his head. "Violet at least," he continued, swallowing, "would be *pleased* by m' return. M' aunts and cousins, as well, but there is no lass who *awaits* m' return."

"You have two sisters, then?" Charlie asked, feeling overwhelmingly relieved and trying to conceal it from him by asking about his kin. Why did sitting with him around the Wallace supper table, sharing food and drink and laughter, feel like everything had finally come into place? Like she fit. Did she want this? What about her plans with Elsie?

"Why won't Mailie be pleased by your return?" she asked, her pulse racing at her thoughts.

He laughed, and she watched the muscles in his throat flex. "I was hopin' ye wouldna remember m' mention of her and ask me that."

"Now you must answer," Mary told him, getting up to pour her husband more ale.

Patrick conceded, sitting back to think more about his answer. "Mailie," he began, "grew up with her head hidden in books, where men behave in a certain manner and honor rules the day. I dinna behave like those men and it vexes her greatly. I confess I've gone oot of m' way to frustrate her. She hasna lost hope though. She is sure she can change me."

"Can she?" Charlie asked him with a smile teasing her lips.

He looked at her with a spark in his eyes that proved what he said next was true, "I'm no' the romantic type."

Charlie already knew it. She didn't need him to make any confessions. He oozed sex and sensuality in everything he did, whether he was winning hearts, or trying to win hers. Was he succeeding? He dazzled her eyes with his laughter, the arch of his playful brow, the quirk of his sinister mouth—sometimes at the same time—all seemingly unimportant, but meant solely to entrance, just as his pretty words did. He was rough and unrepentant, captivating in his charms.

And he refused to be tamed. Just as she did.

When supper was over and the table cleared, Patrick thanked Mary for a meal his mother would have enjoyed and promised Robbie to return tomorrow.

"Will you carry me to bed, Patrick?" Nonie asked, rubbing her eyes with her knuckles.

He couldn't refuse her, even though he couldn't wait to be alone with Charlie. A moment or two would make no difference. The wee lass was too tired to walk herself to bed. What choice did he have? Bending, he scooped her up into his arms.

"Me too!" Jamie insisted and lifted his short arms to him.

While he bent to take up the boy, his brother Andrew climbed atop Patrick's back and wrapped his arms around his host's neck. Patrick made a show of his struggle to regain his stature and laughter rang out all around his ears. He smiled.

"And tell us a story!" Robert insisted, tugging on the rim of Patrick's sleeve when he straightened.

A story? he thought while he carried Robbie Wallace's bairns to bed, with Charlie and Mary trailing close behind.

What stories did he know, save for the ones involving antics not fit for children's ears? He glanced over his shoulder at Charlie. He certainly didn't want her to hear any of those stories.

"Don't you know any stories?" Robert asked as they reached the room and their bed.

"Of course I know stories," Patrick replied and dumped the children, laughing into bed. "I'm simply thinkin' of the right one. Let's see now—" He tapped his finger to his chin while he backed into the seat nearest them. He held up his finger, remembering one his father used to tell him.

"All right then. This story involves an old crone and a legendary knight called Sir Gawain. He was nephew to a verra great king. He was well-known throughout the land as a formidable defender of the poor and of maidens, and the most trustworthy friend."

"I like Sir Gawain," Nonie said looking up at him.

"Then ye'll like this story." Patrick grinned, looking up at Charlie in the doorway, watching, listening.

"The tale goes that one Christmas the great king was accosted by a verra dangerous warrior. To avoid a fight, he agreed to a challenge. He was to return to the warrior in a year with the answer to this question: What thing is it that lasses most desire? If the king didna return, or if he couldna answer the question, he would lose his land and liberty."

"What's liberty?" Robert asked, finally lying back in the bed.

"Liberty is freedom," Patrick told him, then continued.

"The year passed and the king still had no answer. But he kept his vow and rode off to find the warrior. On his way, he met an old crone. Och, but she was ugly. Hunched over, her long nose near hit the ground!"

The children laughed and Patrick took his time elaborating on the witch's unfortunate features.

"The king, bein' great as he was, suspected the witch knew the answer to the question, so he offered her his knight and nephew Sir Gawain as a husband in return fer the answer. She agreed and a bargain was struck."

"Sir Gawain had to marry the ugly crone?" Robert asked, looking horrified. Jamie and Andrew responded with loud squeals of disgust.

Patrick's smile deepened. He usually didn't have much use for children, but he liked the ones he was with now. The sight of them and the sound of them worked their way around him like one of Charlie's veils.

"Did I mention," Patrick answered, "she had a wart or two, dark ones with hairs shootin' oot every which way."

More laughter. He felt another pair of eyes on him and tilted his head to catch Charlie looking serenely enchanting in the soft candlelight.

"What did he do then?" Andrew asked.

"Well," Patrick tore his gaze from hers and returned his attention to the children. "With his land and liberty secured, the king found the warrior and gave his answer. The warrior was verra angry because the witch was his sister and she'd helped the king."

Patrick was surprised by how much of his father's tale he remembered. He was pleased to see the lads rubbing their sleepy eyes.

He smiled at Nonie when she yawned and then softly asked. "So, did Sir Gawain marry the crone?"

"I will finish the story another night, lass. Tonight, ye will dream of knights."

He waited another moment until she fell asleep and then followed Mary and Charlie out, where they bid their hostess goodnight.

The sun had set, casting a light indigo hue on the fields and muirs in the distance. The horses were where they'd left them and he headed toward them with Charlie at his side. He wanted to kiss her. He could think of nothing else all night. Every time she moved her lips, whether she ate, or sipped from her cup, or laughed, or spoke, he thought about kissing them.

Denying the temptation was becoming extraordinarily difficult.

"Did Sir Gawain honor his king and marry the crone?" she asked, tilting her face to him.

"He did," he told her as they reached their horses. He stopped and gazed down into her eyes, lit in a glint of the fading light. "And on the night of their wedding she transformed into a beautiful woman."

She quirked her lips and her dark brow at him. "So he was blessed for having honored his king?"

"Nay, lass. Fer she wouldna remain beautiful in the morn. She'd been cursed to spend half her life as a crone. And only the man who knew the answer to the great question could break it. The king didna tell the knight the answer."

Her brow dipped with disappointment.

"But there was another way," he continued, pleased at her interest in the tale, and even more at how he enjoyed remembering it. "His wife loved him fer marryin' her despite her ugliness. She thought him a good man and hoped he would answer the riddle on his own. So she asked him if he would rather she remain in that likeness by day or at night. He replied that he would rather she be beautiful at night. But his wife would prefer her beauty by day. Sir Gawain then allowed her to choose. In doin' so, he broke the curse cast on her by another witch. He had answered the warrior's question. The thing lasses most desire is the freedom to make their own choices. From that day... and night on, Sir Gawain's wife was beautiful."

Neither one spoke for a moment while he basked in her soft sigh. "I think," she said, stepping closer to him and rising up on the tips of her bare toes to kiss him, "tonight I shall dream of knights, as well."

Chapter Fifteen

Charlie didn't let herself think about all the reasons it was wrong to do what she was doing. The noble knight had given his wife the freedom to choose. Just as Patrick had done for her. That reason alone was enough to make it right.

She would give him a chaste kiss on the mouth and then gain her horse. Just a peck. She closed her eyes when her lips touched his. A...peck...

He brought his palms to her face and cupped her tenderly.

She went soft, falling closer, pressing deeper against his full lips.

Pulling her closer still, he caressed her face then broke their kiss to stare deep in her eyes. "What is this power ye have over me, lass?" He didn't wait for an answer but dipped his mouth to hers again.

He tasted like sweet ale, his tongue sweeping into her like a hot brand. His arms came around the small of her back and drew her in tight against his hard curves and planes.

She felt lost in his embrace, abandoned to his power. She'd wanted this, had waited all day for it since the henhouse. His lips wreaked havoc on her, molding her to him in an intimate dance that played across her tongue. His hands stretched over her back, learning and relishing the shape of her until she felt consumed in flames.

But she wasn't ready to relinquish all control.

With a slow smile that made her own insides burn with the pleasure of teasing him, she took his full lower lip between her teeth.

His muscles grew more taught against her. She gasped at the movement of his stirring desire between them. His kiss deepened pulling from her unbidden thoughts of tearing at his clothes, of…

"Charlie?"

At the sound of Duff's rigid voice, Charlie leaped away from Patrick and took a moment to plant her feet firmly in the grass before she faced her brother.

"What the hell is going on?" Duff asked, setting his cool silver gaze on Patrick and dragging his sword from its scabbard. "Campbell, you had better start talking."

"Duff!" Charlie leaped between the two men. "Put away your sword! He hasn't done anything wrong!"

Her brother's eyes widened with disbelief. "If our father had seen this instead of me, Campbell would be your husband by morning."

"But Father didn't see. *You* did." She wasn't sure what he would do. She knew Hendry would tell had it been him who caught them. She knew Elsie would not. She suspected, in times like now, when she challenged her brother without losing her temper, that he liked who she'd become. "I don't wish to be forced to marry so I ask you not to speak of this. It will not happen again."

Duff offered her a doubtful look but then nodded, giving in to her. His eyes settled on Patrick next. "Nay, it will not. Campbell, I'll give my father your apologies for not thanking him for his hospitality and leaving in the night."

"I wouldna hear of it, Duff." Patrick's practiced smile shone forth, charming at least Charlie's hose off—if she'd been wearing them. "I may look like a man who can fight off a bear, but I'm a Campbell, and Campbells are well mannered. I'll ride back and see yer father m'self."

"Verra well," her brother allowed, "but you would do well to remember that I am not that bear."

Patrick's smile remained. "Thank ye fer the warnin'."

All right, Charlie had had enough of this foolishness. She'd put an end to it now. "Duff, why are you out here looking for me? Didn't Hendry tell you and Father our arrangement?"

"He did," Duff told her as they began walking their horses back. "Which is why 'tis a good thing I found you before anyone else did."

"Aye," Charlie agreed, her eyes finding Patrick's as he led his horse behind Duff. "A good thing."

A good thing that Duff's presence had interrupted their kiss else God only knew what she might have done next. Patrick tempted her to abandon her virtue, her fate, and her future, to him. He was dangerous to Elsie's well-being because Charlie's thoughts were too filled with him.

She tugged her horse forward.

As much as she enjoyed her day with Patrick, save for fainting at his feet, she should have returned to Cunningham House with Hendry.

Perhaps, giving her the freedom to make her own choices was not the best decision. She'd still be in full control of her emotions if she'd gone home.

No. She didn't care what consequences came from her decisions. She was happy she'd made them. She loved being in control of her own life. Safety was precarious since Cameron Fergusson had accused her father of killing Kendrick when she was a young gel. She'd lost her mother at the hands of a madman who had lost his youngest son. After that day, she understood what fear and hatred could make a man capable of doing.

She didn't need another man in her life. They didn't understand her. They smiled at her with desire shining their eyes, but none of them could ever tame her. Not anymore. And they wanted to.

But…She glanced at Patrick again, walking beside her now. He didn't seem interested in taming her. He laughed at her opinions of him. He didn't appear to find fault in her manner of dress, and he not only offered her choices that defied her brothers and her father, but he encouraged her to make them.

When he turned to have a look at her, perhaps sensing her gaze, she smiled at him and then, just as quickly, scowled at her brother when he spoke her name with a sharp snap.

"Gain your horse and return home," he commanded, turning fully to face her. "I know the short journey alone doesn't frighten you, so be on your way. I wish to have words with Mr. Campbell."

"Duff, I—"

"I will not argue with you on this, Charlotte," he said, his gray eyes hard as twin swords on her. "Go home."

"Lass, if ye're worried aboot me…"

She turned to set the frosty gaze she'd offered her brother on Patrick. Did the man truly think everything had to do with him?

Ignoring her incredulous stare, his mouth curled in the subtlest of smiles. "...dinna be."

Should she be? She looked at Duff again and bit her lip. What would he do to Patrick when she left? Would he turn up gone in the morning like Kendrick had? Had she been so infuriated over being dismissed that she didn't recall what a threat her brothers were to someone she loved?

Did she love Patrick Campbell? She lifted her hand to her pounding heart and tried to swallow. It was difficult.

She felt ill. Over all of it.

"You don't know what he's capable of," she told Patrick though her eyes remained on her brother.

"Charlie," Duff said, all traces of anger gone from his voice, "it would seem that you also don't know."

She shook her head, barely hearing him. Nay, Duff wouldn't kill him. Patrick wasn't a Fergusson. He belonged to a powerful clan that extended over half of Scotland and England alike. Her father wanted a union with the Campbells. Was Duff going to demand Patrick marry her because they'd shared a kiss and a smile?

"If you want to prove I'm wrong, don't demand a marriage of me, and let me stay."

"I will do one and not the other," her brother allowed. "Goodnight, Charlie."

Och, but she wanted to kick him. Still, she wouldn't be forced to wed. Although...She bit her tongue and nodded.

"Goodnight." She leaped into her saddle and rode off before she said anything that would change Duff's mind.

Besides, she had dozens of other things to think about, like being in Pinmore before midnight.

And the way Patrick's hard body felt against hers.

* * *

"You told Hendry that you were considering Charlie as a wife," Duff said eyeing him with a glint of menace in his dubious gaze when they were alone.

Patrick sighed. Was Duff going to try to force him to marry Charlie? He hoped not. He didn't want to beat the senses back into his cousin.

"Yer sister didna want to return home with Hendry, so I told him what he wanted to hear."

Duff chuckled moving into the moonlight. "An art you have no doubt perfected."

His cousin was perceptive, Patrick noted—with a bit of a sting. Was that who he truly was? A man with no values or ideals? A man who used a deceptive tongue to gain him favor among the people? It was nothing to boast about, so he didn't.

"The only art I've perfected is with m' fists." He punched the air ahead of him and then turned to smile at his cousin.

"Then you don't want her as a wife?"

Patrick knew that if he wanted to stay at Cunningham House, at least for a little while longer, he shouldn't make Duff his enemy. Nor did he want to fight with his cousin. He wanted to get to know Will MacGregor's son. Was Duff anything like his father?

"I dinna know what I want," Patrick answered. It wasn't untrue.

"You kissed her. Do you mean to tell me that you won't do so again?"

"That's what I mean, aye," he agreed. "But tell me, if yer faither wants her married, how could any interested man discover if she would be a suitable wife if he canna spend time with her?"

Duff's gaze was all the more menacing by the glint of

moonlight shooting across his eyes. "Are you telling me you're interested?"

It wasn't the path Patrick had wanted the conversation to take, but then, he had to remember this wasn't Hendry. Charlie's eldest brother wasn't a fool so easily swayed. He also wasn't as concerned with what his father wanted.

"I'm curious," Patrick admitted. "Aye, m' interest in her is piqued." It wasn't an untruth either, but Patrick would go no further than that. There wasn't any further to go, was there? He wasn't ready to give up his rakish way of life for her. He should leave. Hell, he should have left the instant his wrists were unbound.

But then he wouldn't have known the taste of her lips. He missed it already and longed to kiss her again. Only one thing stood in his way. Duff.

Good thing Patrick had a knack for winning favor even with his enemies. Good thing also that Duff was Patrick's cousin or what he was about to say would have tasted bitter.

"I'd like to remain here fer a few more days and get to know her a bit more, if ye'll allow it."

Duff looked at him. "Shouldn't you be asking this to my father and not me?"

"But we know what yer faither's answer would be," Patrick told him, glancing back when he began walking toward the house. If they weren't going to fight, there was no reason to stand here. "I'm a Campbell," he told him, not ready yet to tell him his true name and have Charlie denied him for it by her father. "He'd toss Charlie into m' arms while he hurried to fetch the priest. But ye care more aboot her than that. So 'tis yer approval I seek."

Silence again while Duff considered him. Patrick had to grin turning away from him. He loved confounding others' opinions about him, winning them over to his side. If that was a flaw, he didn't give a damn.

"I do care for her," Duff confessed and began walking the trek home. "She doesn't want a husband."

"Aye, she and I spoke of that."

Duff glanced at him. "What else did you speak with her about?"

"Mostly Hendry. She had harsh words fer him."

"And me?"

What did Duff care what his sister had to say about him? Few sisters had anything favorable to say. Why did Duff watch over her so carefully? Was he a protective brother or was there something more?

"Do ye love her?" He didn't know why he asked. His mouth had a way of getting the best of him.

"Of course I love her, you fool. She's my sister!"

"No' by blood."

Patrick barely saw him coming and when he did, it was too late to do anything but stay on his feet.

"She is my *sister*." Duff shook his hand that had just punched Patrick in the jaw. "If you ever suggest anything other than that again, I'll remove your head. Understand?"

Patrick felt his jaw to make sure it wasn't broken, and then nodded. He let the blow go unanswered. He deserved it, after all, asking such an insulting question. But he didn't get hit in the face often and he intended on keeping it that way. If Duff ever tried it again, Patrick would lay him to the ground. Kin or not.

"M' apologies," he offered.

Duff nodded, then looked away. They walked their horses back in silence for a little while before Duff spoke, his voice lower, softer. "Our lives grew more difficult after the death of our mother. The duty of protecting my sisters fell to me, and I have never failed in it. I won't begin now. I don't care who you are." He stopped and looked toward Cunningham House in the distance. "I have some questions to put to you, but presently I have business in a tavern not too far from here. Join me and we can discuss things over a tankard of whisky."

Chapter Sixteen

What the hell were they doing in Blind Jack's Tavern? Patrick wondered, following Duff's hastened footsteps inside.

Duff's choice to sit at a table in the corner far from the hearth light drew no dispute from Patrick. If the shadows would conceal him from Hamish and his serving wench, Patrick would prefer it. It wasn't a good idea to fight the same man twice. Hamish would know what to expect this time around and would likely use harsher tactics to ensure that he didn't wake up again on the floor with a broken jug around his head. The brute's wench was likely just as dangerous with any stoneware around.

But why were they here? Why was Duff hiding?

"Are we meetin' someone?" Patrick asked, curious at the way Duff's gaze spread over the inhabitants, as if he was searching out someone in particular.

"Nay." Duff severed his gaze from the tables, and turned it to him. "We're waiting."

Patrick was relieved when Duff called over a serving

wench who wasn't the one he'd almost lost a tooth over. He'd told Duff that his interest in Charlie was piqued, that he wanted to remain here to possibly win her favor. Duff's discovering that he'd been here a few nights ago, ready to bed a wench, wouldn't be in his best interest.

"Two whiskies," Duff told her then sent her on her way before she had time to fall into either of their laps.

"Now, tell me," he said, returning his gaze to Patrick, "Where were you with my sister all day?"

The truth was the only answer to give him. If not to visit a tenant, where would he have taken her until the evening?

"We spent the day with the Wallaces."

"The Wallaces?" Charlie's brother asked skeptically. "What business do you have with Robbie Wallace that you spent the day with him and my sister?"

Patrick couldn't tell him that they had visited the Wallace holding the night before to help this family survive his brother. Duff didn't know his sister stole away from the house at night to help the villagers. If Charlie wanted her brother to know about her selfless adventures, she'd tell him. But Patrick had to tell him something.

"His hay needin' balin'," he said with a casual shrug.

Duff's smile was as sharp as his gaze. "Why did you insist on Charlie accompanying you when she should have gone home with Hendry?"

Damn it. How many questions was Duff going to ask? He'd learned interrogation well from Allan Cunningham. Patrick didn't blame Duff for his concerns, but he was growing weary of having to pull up the right answers. He let it be known in his deep exhalation of breath before he answered. "She wasna particularly pleased aboot goin' with him. His presence was intolerable in the short time we traveled so I know why."

"Hendry is unpleasant," Duff agreed and barely looked up at the serving wench when she returned with their drinks. "I sometimes wonder if I have other brothers somewhere who aren't..."

He stopped and drank from his cup. Patrick wanted to say something. Duff did have other brothers. Four of them.

"Did Charlie put you up to baling his hay?" Duff asked, setting his cup down. "She doesn't think so, but I know her well."

How well? Did he know that she'd robbed him to feed others?

"She has her mother's kind heart," Duff told him in a mild tone, his love for her softening his smile.

He did know her then. He'd know Patrick was lying if he denied her involvement. "She asked," he admitted.

"And for her, you agreed."

"I did."

Duff nodded, looking pleased but doing his best to conceal it.

Patrick looked into his cup and smiled. "Whisky is a verra strong trait among Highlanders."

Duff knew he had Highland blood. He knew he was a MacGregor. Patrick would have him be proud to bear the name, but it was outlawed. And though the laws against his clan weren't as strictly adhered to as they had once been, MacGregor was still a dangerous name with unsavory implications. Duff wasn't going to confess to being one, not to a man he'd only met a few days ago.

"Highlanders are stubborn," Patrick continued, "and extremely possessive and protective of their kin, as ye are."

Duff looked away. "Men don't frequently travel through Pinwherry. What I know of Highlanders are things I've been told. They have not always been favorable."

Hell, the poor lad was starving for some knowledge of his heritage.

"What have ye heard?"

"That they are troublesome," Duff said. "They enjoy the sport of fighting. That's why so many of them have given their allegiance to the Jacobite cause. I know also that one of them visited Pinwherry, fathered me, and then left."

Aye, that. Patrick looked into his cup. He could not argue that truth.

He thought about how he would tell Duff while he lifted his cup. He took a swig and cringed. "Hell! This must be what unholy tastes like."

Duff spared him a slight smile. "I fear 'tis of poor quality compared to what you're used to."

Patrick nodded, setting the cup down. "I'll make certain ye taste Angus's brew if I have to deliver it to ye m'self."

"Angus?" Duff asked, one raven brow arched over his silver eye.

"Aye," Patrick told him. He wanted Duff to know about his kin. Every man deserved that much. He wanted Duff to know that they were kin. Did Duff know the MacGregors were tied to the Fergussons? If Patrick told him that he was, in fact, also a MacGregor, it wouldn't take Duff long to deduce that Patrick was a Fergusson as well and that he had likely been heading to Colmonell to visit Tarrick Hall at the time Charlie had struck him with her stone.

The time for *that* confession didn't feel right just yet. First, Patrick needed to learn more about the feud between his kin and the Cunninghams—and what Duff might do to him for being the enemy and being interested in courting his sister.

That didn't mean he couldn't tell Duff about his father.

He deserved to know. "Aye, Angus," he told him while Duff lifted his cup to drink. "Angus MacGregor."

The cup paused at Duff's lips, though he quickly righted himself, careful not to reveal too much. "You know MacGregors?"

"I do," Patrick replied, smiling, and then shattered Duff's resolve like a canonball through mortar. "But more importantly, I know yer faither, Will MacGregor."

As he expected, Duff looked as if he was about to leap to his feet, or purge the contents of his belly. He did neither but sat and stared at Patrick with eyes like hammered steel.

"Charlotte told you."

"Nae, 'twas Hendry," Patrick supplied then called for more whisky. Duff was going to need it.

"I should break Hendry's jaw," Duff growled, ignoring the serving wench and the plunging cleavage she dangled before him while she refilled his cup.

"I admit," Patrick told him when the wench turned to him next. "I often find m'self longin' to do the same thing."

"Can I get you something else?" The gel leaned her face in closer to Patrick's.

She was bonnie, with intensely blue eyes and pale yellow hair. Just days ago Patrick would have taken notice of the rest of her, and frankly, he wasn't pleased that he found no interest in her whatsoever.

A very telling sign, that. Exactly how much trouble was he in?

"How do you know him? My father?" Duff asked after Patrick dismissed the wench.

To keep Duff...and ultimately, Charlie from discovering that he was a Fergusson, he made up a tale. "I was travelin' home from Dunvegan last winter when a fierce blizzard hit.

I was snowed in fer a month with the MacGregors of Skye. 'Twas there that I met him."

"Skye?" Now Duff reacted. His color faded in the dim light until he resembled an apparition. "Are you telling me that my father is of the clan MacGregor of *Skye*?" When Patrick nodded, Duff wiped his hand down his face and swore a quiet oath. "The MacGregors of Skye are kin to the Fergussons of Ayrshire."

So, he did know. "Are they?" Patrick asked, feigning surprise. "The Fergussons ye're feudin' with?"

Duff nodded. He seemed to be turning something over in his mind, something that urged him along. "How do you know he is my father, and not a man with the same name? I'm certain there are many Will MacGregors in Scotland."

But few with the same sharp cut to his jaw and cool, merciless eyes.

"Ye share his face and his expressions," Patrick told him. "Hell, I suspected ye were his the moment I knew Cunningham wasna yer faither. I tell ye the truth, ye wear his face."

It didn't look to be as satisfying for Duff as Patrick had hoped. His color hadn't returned. In fact, he looked mildly ill. "Speak of this no more," he said turning his face toward the shadows.

Patrick wished he hadn't mentioned it in the first place. But hell, if he never knew his father and someone showed up in his life who did, he'd want to know. He could appreciate the emotions that must be surging through his cousin at this moment.

"D'ye want to know anything aboot him?"

Duff remained still. He wasn't ready to learn such things. Mayhap Patrick didn't blame him. If his father had abandoned his mother he might not be interested after all.

"What is he like?" Duff asked, giving in to every human need.

Patrick might be a careless, reckless rake who just happened to enjoy life too damn much, but he understood the magnitude of his answer. He had the task of shaping Duff's first impression of his father. This had been his idea, hadn't it? He'd wanted Duff to know. Why shouldn't the duty of telling fall on him? But how does one tell a man about his father? Should he tell Duff everything; that there were a few men in Camlochlin who didn't particularly adhere to its unspoken call for chivalry and Duff's father was one of them. At least, he had been before he too fell ill to love when he met his wife, Aileas MacLeod, and became father to four of his own defiant hellions. Sons he'd chosen to raise. Would Duff hate his father for abandoning him and not the others?

"He's a master archer…and he's…" Patrick grinned and rolled his eyes at his inability to speak. He held up his cup, as if the watered-down whisky was the reason. Should he tell Duff that Will enjoyed agitating his cousins with his sharp tongue and playful smirk? "He's the MacGregor clan chief's cousin and closest friend." Aye, that was the truth, and it sounded better. "In his younger days, he was known to be reckless with lasses and dangerous to have as an enemy. Despite the pepperin' of gray hair, he is still dangerous but less reckless since he took a wife. He laughs often—and often at the expense of others. He fears nothin' save his wife's ire, and is the only man at whom Brodie MacGregor, yer grandsire, smiles."

Duff's expression lightened. He may have even smiled in the dim light. "You sound like you know him well."

"One doesna spend time with the MacGregors of Skye without gettin' to know Will. He's friends with all."

Duff swigged the remainder of his whisky. He wiped

his mouth with the back of his hand and called for more. Finally, he turned back to Patrick. "Does he have other bairns?"

Hell, Patrick needed a stronger drink than what they were serving here. "He has...four sons."

Duff's eyes went heartbreakingly soft. "I see."

Again, Patrick regretted telling him anything. Was not knowing you could have had a different, better life more merciful? Hell.

"An hour ago, I had no brothers. Now, I have four. What are their names?"

Patrick closed his eyes and breathed a sigh before opening them again, "Brodie, Beathan, Ailpein, and Niall. They are all younger than ye and will likely be the death of him."

Duff stared into his cup and shook his head. "I would be the death of him."

Patrick leaned in closer. "What was that? Ye would be? Why ye?"

Duff's forced smile in the fluttering candlelight offered anything but assurance of his sincerity when he spoke. "I'm certain that discovering he fathered a fifth son, one of whom there is a lifetime he knows nothing about, would at least make him *wish* he were dead."

He had a point. Patrick laughed and raised his cup with him.

They talked over two more drinks before Patrick found himself offering to bring Duff to meet them if he ever wished to. Patrick wasn't sure what the hell had come over him, but he missed his home. It was because of Charlie. Because she reminded him of Camlochlin, untamable and as steady and sheltering as a fortress. His kin would...

Was that...Charlie he saw just walk through the door?

Forgetting his thoughts, he blinked at Duff to find him rigid and alert in his chair, his eyes fastened to his sister.

So, Duff knew about her nightly ventures. What the hell would she think of that? What was she doing back here? What had she been doing here the first time he saw her, dressed in shadows and candlelight? Why hadn't he asked her? Why hadn't he told her he had seen her that night? He didn't want to care and especially not to the point of wanting to start tearing heads off any man who'd touched her.

"What is she doin' here?" he asked, keeping his voice low, steady, and remaining in the shadows with her brother.

"She's keeping her promise."

"A promise to whom?"

"To our mother," Duff told him while Charlie smiled and waved to the serving wenches and even the taverner. She'd changed her gown into heavier wool and an earasaid draping her delicate shoulders.

Patrick didn't care about breathing. She was so very bonnie to him with her long glossy tresses a bit haphazardly plaited and drawing his eye to her breast where it fell.

"Does she know that ye follow her?" Patrick asked him.

"Nay, and I want to keep it that way. It wouldn't make a difference though, she'd still come but I'd prefer not to fight with her about this." Duff sipped from his cup without flinching. "She's been visiting pubs for the last sixteen months, at least."

A year and a half? Why? Was she here trying to find a way to earn coin to pay her a tenant's rent? What the hell was he going to do about it?

"What is the promise she made to yer mother?"

"To care for Elsie. The others, she has taken on of her own accord."

"Then ye know aboot the Wallaces."

Duff nodded. "I know she's friends with Mary Wallace." Duff looked at him from his drink. "What else is there to know?"

That she sneaks out and to visit them and pay their rent? Patrick didn't speak his thought out loud. Duff didn't know. He couldn't know how often he'd been drugged or he would not have put up with it.

"There's nothin' else to know," Patrick assured him. "I assumed from yer earlier question to me aboot the Wallaces that ye didna know Charlie and Mary were friends."

"Hmm," Duff murmured and gave his attention back to his sister. "While you decide about her, you should know that she will always do what she wants. She will use whatever means necessary to see her desires fulfilled. She will defy you as she defies my father, silently and methodically. As much as I would like to see her find her own happiness, I don't think she is a good candidate for—"

"She is perfect," Patrick finished. Aye, damn it, it was his voice that just spoke—and worse, sounded like a lovestruck fool.

"I don't think she will be as easily won as you hope." Duff watched her bend her ear to two patrons, smile, and then pat their backs as she moved on to someone else.

"I dinna want an easy victory."

"Is that what she is?" Duff asked, turning to look at him. "A victory?"

"Aye," Patrick said candidly, "a victory fer me to have won the heart of such a lass. A victory fer m' kin to welcome her as their own. A victory fer yer faither because his daughter belongs to the most powerful clan in Scotland."

"And for Charlie?" her brother asked, convincing Patrick, by his dedication to her well-being, that Highland blood did indeed run through this lad.

But this conversation was going too far. Patrick had wanted to stay for a few more days, and with freedom to be with Charlie. All this talk of marriage was making him feel antsy.

"I dinna know what she would think of it...if I decided to marry her."

"Well, you heard her," Duff told him, setting down his cup. "She doesn't want to marry. She has refused all and chased them away. I don't think she will ever be happy with anyone again."

Patrick smiled remembering the tale Mary had told him about Charlie's last suitor.

Then his smile faded.

"Again?"

Charlie had been in love before? He didn't know why it fired a streak of jealously through his insides.

"Aye," her brother told him. "She hasn't loved anyone since him—and it has been a long time." His eyes settled on his sister again and his gaze took on a faraway look. When he spoke, his voice was low and riddled with something like regret. "I haven't spoken of him for many years. Too long."

"Who is he?" Patrick wanted to know who had held her heart for years and stopped her from loving anyone else.

Duff wrenched his gaze back to him and shook his head. "No one. He's gone, and 'twould be best if you don't bring him up to Charlotte."

Bring who up? How the hell was Patrick not going to talk about him if he didn't know who he was talking about?

"But how do you know she still loves him?" Patrick asked, undeterred.

"Because she still carries his sling around as if it were a part of him."

Patrick stared at him while his belly sank to his boots. Her sling, given to her and taught how to use by a Fergusson. She'd loved a Fergusson. According to her brother, she still did.

She'd spoken of him the first time they walked through the field. She'd mentioned learning how to use the sling and her father disapproving. Had Allan Cunningham forbidden the two from being together? Did her heart belong to one of his cousins? Was it one of Cameron's sons? Shaw, or Tam, or mayhap Kendrick? Surely Tamas's youngest son, Aidan, was too young. John had all daughters.

"It seems she's found whom she came to see."

Patrick followed Duff's gaze to find Charlie sitting at the table of a well-dressed older man. They were engaged in what appeared to be a serious conversation.

What was she up to this time? Patrick wondered, watching her, unaware that his gaze had gone soft.

"You still consider her after finding her here in a pub in the dead of night?"

Patrick understood that most men wouldn't want such a troublesome, defiant wife. But he had to admit, the idea of it was pleasing. She was a rose made of many petals and he enjoyed watching each unfurl.

"Is it no' apparent enough to yer eyes," Patrick asked, glancing at him, "that m' interest in her is sparked?"

But which one of his cousins had claimed her heart?

"You don't strike me as the kind of man who stays in one place too long," Duff countered. "What becomes of her when the spark fades?"

Patrick wanted to tell him that it wouldn't fade. But how did he know? What if it did? What the hell was he doing? Her heart was lost to one of his cousins. He couldn't tell Duff who he was now.

His gaze shifted back to her and her companion still speaking. He'd stared at Charlie's face and studied it enough in the past two days to know that she wasn't pleased by the man's words.

"Who is he?" Patrick asked and shifted in his chair. What bargain was being struck between them? What did she want? What did she have to offer? He wanted to leave his table and go find out.

"A physician, I imagine," Duff replied. "Most of them are. None of them help though."

What the hell was Duff saying? Patrick turned to him. "Why does she need a physician?"

"She doesn't. Elsie does."

Chapter Seventeen

$\mathcal{I}$t sounds to me as if your sister suffers from asthma, a humor of phlegm that attacks the respiratory organs."

Charlie withheld a sigh of frustration while she glanced up at the ceiling. He wasn't telling her anything she didn't already know. Elsie had been seen by several physicians from an early age.

"I know what ails her, Doctor. I need to know what can be done to help her."

Dr. Lindsay beckoned for another cup of wine. His heavy mustache dipped around his chin when she once again refused his offer to join him.

She'd come for a cure, not a lover—or a fight. She needed to get it and go home. Sneaking out without disturbing not two men, but three, was difficult.

She hadn't seen Patrick or Duff before she pretended to ready for bed. She hoped neither of them was lying hurt in the fields. Or worse, awake and aware off her absence.

But she'd had to get to the pub. For this moment. The small hamlets just off South Ayrshire's coastline didn't see many visitors and especially not many true physicians. It had taken dedication and perfect timing to ensure that she had this opportunity to meet Dr. Lindsay. If there were any new medicines available to treat her sister's condition, Charlie would get them. "I've tried many things, but nothing has helped. I am desperate."

He eyed her with dark, piercing eyes beneath his gray brow.

Charlie beseeched the heavens again, praying that she wouldn't have to prove her words by killing him.

"I have something that will help."

"Oh?" she lifted a skeptical brow. "What is it?"

"An elixir made from certain herbs that will induce vomiting."

Charlie's heart sank. Vomiting? Over the past two years she'd heard of and had tried every treatment from honey to tobacco, the latter taking her half a year to obtain. She'd tried different types of oils soaked in tree bark and rubbed on Elsie's chest, along with various meats and herbs. She'd passed her sister under the belly of a horse, and smeared deer grease on the soles of Elsie's feet. How was vomiting going to help her breathe? Had this all been for nothing?

Still, he hadn't suggested that Elsie was possessed by demons, as the previous charlatan had diagnosed.

For that, she would listen to his explanation.

"How would vomiting help her?"

His reply sounded convincing and intelligent. Something was indeed blocking her sister's "airways." What did she have to lose?

"I will take it."

"It is in my bag. Abovestairs in my room."

Judging from the hungry glint in his gaze, this exchange wasn't going to go smoothly.

"Go get it," she warned impatiently. She couldn't linger here tonight.

His mouth cocked into the smirk of a man who'd never been told what to do before this moment. He crossed one leg, encased in fine wool trousers, over the other and let his gaze rove over her with unabashed desire. "What of payment?"

She lifted her arms over her head and reached to the back of her neck. She unclasped the stone necklace her mother had given her and held it up to him. She didn't want to part with the gift, but her mother would have understood and been happy with her decision.

"Is that all your sister's good health is worth to you, my dear?"

Damn it all. She reached for her skirts under the table and found the opening and the small dagger she had secured to her thigh. "What else did you have in mind, Doctor?"

His smile deepened along with his voice. "A kiss. Perhaps a little more?"

She gave him an icy smile. "I'm afraid not. This will have to suffice."

"It doesn't."

She'd waited to meet him for days, hoping he would be the one who could help Elsie. She'd risked much coming here. Should she leave before she was forced to hurt him? But what if he did have something in his bag that would help her sister? When would another physician come along? It could be months, a year. Charlie didn't want to wait that long.

Before she paused to consider what she was doing, she drew her dagger and reached across the table to hold the tip to his throat.

"I'll pay you by letting you leave here alive. Do we have a bargain?"

He whimpered when she poked him a little, pricking his

skin. The world was a hard, merciless place. She could be hard and merciless too. "I want that elixir. Do you under—"

She was interrupted by a man—or two men—exiting the shadows and then a powerfully built body whisking Dr. Lindsay out of his chair.

She leaped to her feet and watched Patrick fling the doctor into the wall.

What was he doing here? Her first thought was that he'd come to visit Bethany again, but the fire in her veins cooled when she saw Duff.

"What the hell are you both doing here?" She turned her glare on Patrick. "And why did you knock out Dr. Lindsay?"

He shrugged his wide shoulders and stepped away from the physician's limp body and came closer to her. "It appeared ye were finished with him."

Why did the low pitch of his voice send fissures down her spine? Or was it his close proximity that caused her to temporarily lose her mind? Patrick was the one she should be stabbing, not the doctor. Patrick was the one who tempted her to give up everything.

"I wasn't finished with him," she told him. She didn't want a protector in her life. She wanted her sister to be well and free of the confines of her breaths—or lack of them. "He has something I need."

"Does he carry whatever it is on his person?" Duff asked. Duff! She turned her glare on him next.

"Most physicians who travel bring medicine with them. Now tell me what you are doing here." She pointed at Patrick. "Did he bring you?" Oh, if he had, she would shoot him with an arrow first chance she got. Why here, on this night of all nights?

"I brought him," Duff admitted. "I knew you were coming and I didn't feel like sitting here alone again."

What did he mean, *again*? "Do you mean you followed me here on purpose and this isn't the first time?"

This time, she didn't think she'd be able to control her temper. What would he do if she picked up Dr. Lindsay's cup and flung it at his head? If, once started, she couldn't finish until she cursed him for his part in Kendrick's death?

"Charlie," her brother began and sat in the previous occupant's chair. "Do you truly think I'd forget my promise to our mother to watch over you—the same promise you made her for Elsie?"

He held out his arm, offering her back her seat. She accepted it, glancing at Patrick while she sat. Naturally, he smiled.

Had Duff been following her all this time? Waiting alone, unseen by her at least, and then making certain she arrived safely home? She'd been frequenting pubs for more than a year trying to find cures. How long had he known? How long had he let her believe he knew nothing? Did he also know about her visits to their father's tenants? Or that she'd robbed him? What did she think of all of it? It didn't change anything.

Aye, promises had been made, but didn't Duff understand that he'd already broken his promise when he followed their father's orders and killed Kendrick?

"What are you trying to gain from this man?" her brother asked her, his eyes gleaming like polished steel beneath the slash of his black brows.

When she didn't answer him, he answered for her.

"Medicine for Elsie."

Astoundingly, he didn't sound angry. There wasn't going to be a fight. Her temper would remain leashed another day. She was relieved, but still angry with him for not telling her.

"If you already know, why are you asking me?"

"I was curious about your answer," he replied mildly.

She sat back and folded her arms across her chest. She could feel Patrick's eyes on her. Amused, glittering green eyes that found humor in everything she said and did—even when she woke from fainting at the Wallaces'. She was tempted to look his way, but her conversation with Duff took precedence. "What do you think you're going to do about it?"

He stretched out his arms on either side of him. "Same as I've been doing. What?" he asked when her expression darkened. "Is following you to make certain you're safe so terrible?"

"Where else have you followed me?"

He sat up straight in his chair and eyed her. "Where else have you gone?"

She almost sighed with relief. "To The Red Rooster tavern in Pinwherry." It wasn't an untruth.

He smiled and nodded. She knew he cared about her. That had never changed, though he'd grown harder, along with their lives. But the Duff she'd once loved had died with Kendrick. After Kendrick had gone missing and before the Fergussons killed her mother, Duff had become quiet and more detached. He'd grown worse over the years, snapping at her often and breaking Hendry's nose twice. Morose even after years had passed, Duff rarely smiled.

Last winter, in a busy pub in Colmonell called Hecker's Muse, Charlie had finally found out why.

The folks of that town knew chieftain Cameron Fergusson well. They had known his son, and according to many, they had seen Kendrick riding off with her brothers—never to be seen again.

Up until then, she'd always wondered why the Fergussons had accused her family of the vile deed. Finding out the truth had turned her heart cold toward the men in her family. The men who were truly responsible for her mother's death.

"How long have you known what I've been doing?" she asked, refusing to be moved by his concern. "And why did you keep your knowledge from me?"

"For about a year and a half and there was no reason to tell you. Once I discovered what you were after I knew you wouldn't stop until you found it. It was simply more peaceful this way."

He had that right. Trying to stop her would have been useless and taxing for them both.

"How did you find out?" It didn't matter, but she was curious just the same. Had she been careless and let him see her leave the house? She'd have to be more careful.

"Elsie told me. She said you go out every sixth night. She was concerned because she loves you."

Damn it! Elsie! She should have known her sister would worry over her. But at least Elsie hadn't told him that she goes out far more often than every sixth night.

She was still deciding how angry she should be with her brother when Patrick touched her shoulder.

She hadn't forgotten he was there. His presence demanded attention though he hadn't spoken a word. It had been difficult trying to give Duff her full attention with Patrick standing over the table the entire time.

"What ails Elsie?" he asked gazing down at her.

His eyes, changing from green to deep amber in the firelight, captivated her. Or perhaps it was the curiosity and concern making his eyes gleam behind his spray of long lashes that made her stare at him like a fool, unable to form a logical thought.

"Does it have to do with the way she breathes?"

Charlie blinked out of her brief reverie. Was he simply

observant or had Elsie's sickness become so obvious to an untrained eye? Had it worsened without Charlie's notice because she saw her sister all the time and missed any small changes?

"What way does she breathe?" Charlie asked him so she could know if what he saw was the same as what she saw. Or worse.

"She lifts her shoulders to pull in shallow breaths."

She nodded. "You're observant."

He shook his head. "No' observant enough or I would have known the seriousness of her condition and could have helped sooner."

Helped? Did she hear him right? He could help? Was this another ruse to win her? It seemed too providential that Patrick Campbell would be the man to save Elsie... to save them both.

"How do you know about this illness enough to help Elsie?" she asked doubtfully. He was no physician, after all.

"Its symptoms appear similar to an ailment from which m' mother suffers. Thankfully, she is all but cured, but winters in the mountains can be hard."

Charlie could no longer remain in her seat. She sprang up and searched his gaze for the truth. "Did you say, she is cured? From asthma? You said the winters were hard. Does your mother's condition worsen in colder months causing her to wheeze?"

"Aye."

Could he truly help or was she dreaming? Was it the same condition? Perhaps his mother's condition wasn't as serious as Elsie's. "Has your mother ever labored until you feared she was going to turn to ash before your eyes?"

His gaze on her went warm and soft, like a gentle caress. "I heard tales of m' faither almost losing her, but 'twas many years ago. Now, she breathes with no trouble fer three full seasons of the year. The last time she was set abed from it I was ten and two."

Charlie wanted to fling her arms around his neck. She wanted to laugh and weep at the same time. There was hope! Real hope for Elsie's good health! She'd vowed to find a cure, but it had become difficult to believe there was one with all the failed remedies they'd tried. But if Patrick's mother suffered the same illness...and was well now...

"What is the cure?"

Her heart thumped so wildly she felt a bit light-headed. She'd searched for so long. Was she truly about to get the right answer?

"There are several ways to ease her breathin'," he told her, lifting his fingers to her face as a tear fell. "But the main source of relief is her tea."

"Tea?" Her heart sank a little. What kind of tea could cure asthma?

"Aye, butterbur tea," he replied as simply as if he were telling her the weather and not answering her prayers. "'Tis a plant that grows in certain regions between Ayrshire and Dumfries. One such region is no' far from here."

That was it? Tea from a single plant? Not a concoction of powders and elixirs with a high price attached? Was it truly that simple? Had Patrick Campbell just given her what she'd been praying to find her whole life? She smiled, and then she did what she wanted to do and threw herself into his arms.

Chapter Eighteen

$\mathcal{H}$ is arms closed around her and she nearly sighed out loud with the pleasure of it. There was no seduction in his embrace, only comfort, making it all the more sensual, captivating and capturing her in a whirl of emotions she'd never felt for anyone else, not even Kendrick.

But now wasn't the time to be afraid, not with him.

"What region close by carries this butterbur?" Duff, whom she'd completely forgotten, interrupted.

Patrick's arms fell away as she opened her eyes to her brother. She stabbed him with a sharp look before returning her gaze to Patrick. It was because she was studying every nuance of his roguish beauty that she noted hesitancy shadowing his eyes. What did he resist telling them?

"Where does it grow?" she asked, needing him to tell her, holding nothing back for payment.

"The closest is in Colmonell." He stopped again and looked away for the briefest of moments before settling his apprehensive gaze back on her. "'Twould be best if I travel alone to gather the plant. 'Twill be too dangerous fer either of ye to go."

"Not for me," Duff assured him immediately with a subtle flick of his shoulders squaring.

Charlie wanted to declare the same, but best if her brother didn't know *all* her secrets.

"Nae," Patrick insisted. "I'll go alone."

"Why?" Duff pressed, rising to stand. "Where is it that 'tis so dangerous?"

Patrick met his gaze straight on, looking determined to defy that edge of trepidation still darkening his features. "Just west of Tarrick Hall."

"The Fergussons' land?" Duff asked, sounding as stunned as he appeared.

"Aye."

"How do you know of it?" Duff asked, sounding much like her father when he questioned her. "What else do you know about the Fergussons?"

"No' much besides that ye're warrin' with them. Would ye care to tell me why?"

"No," Duff grumbled and began to turn away. "But you're correct. 'Twould be dangerous to go. I would likely kill them all."

Charlie stared at her brother. She knew Duff hated the Fergussons as much as her father did. But to kill them all? And what if their kin, the MacGregors, rode down from the hills to exact vengeance?

Wasn't that what her family had always tried to avoid, ever since the first MacGregor, Tristan, as named in the tales she'd heard as a child, had threatened her father's brothers with retaliation after her uncles had raided a Fergusson holding?

Was Duff truly so foolish?

All traces of his usual easy nature faded from Patrick's expression at Duff's declaration. He did nothing to conceal it this time as he laid his hand to Duff's shoulder, stopping her brother from rising from his chair.

"And be hanged fer murder?" he asked. "How would ye protect yer sister from the dangers outside Cunningham House and in it after that? Ye didna strike me as the kind of man who rushes headlong into a battle he canna win."

Charlie breathed a sigh of relief that finally Duff had a man of some sense to speak with.

Her brother laughed but looked as miserable as ever. Did he regret what he'd done to Kendrick? Was his regret and shame the punishment he'd been living with for five years? Did it make any difference? What kind of man, young or old, could take the life of a boy barely into his sixteenth year?

"Ah, but I do think first, Campbell," Duff said. "That is why the Fergussons still breathe." He called out for another tankard of whisky before settling back into his chair.

"Tell me," Patrick said, pulling up a chair and sitting between herself and Duff. "What have they done to—"

"You have bollocks to return here, Highlander!"

Damnation, it was Hamish, escorted by two of his friends.

Charlie shook her head at him. Bringing friends to a fight proved that he wasn't confident in a victory without aid. "You're without courage, Hamish," she charged while Patrick rose from his chair. She could feel his eyes on her like hot brands, but her gaze remained fixed on Hamish and his friends.

"Stay out of it, Charlie," Hamish growled at her. "Unless you're here with him in the hopes of being his next conquest. Mayhap," he said, his gaze moving to Duff, "you're hoping for both of them."

Patrick moved in a blur of speed. One moment he was standing near her and the next, he was snapping a leg off the nearest chair with his boot heel, and then moving toward Hamish with it.

He didn't hesitate or pause to say a word. He walked with a purpose, and when he reached the giant, he swung the wooden leg with such power, Charlie wasn't sure if it was the wood or Hamish's ribs that cracked. She realized it was the latter when the giant grasped his side and fell forward to his knees.

Patrick wasn't done with him, but Charlie had no more time to watch when one of Hamish's friends came at her.

Patrick tossed the wood aside, rooted his feet to the ground, and smashed his fist into Hamish's jaw. He watched the brute go down and shook the pain from his hand. It had to be quick else Hamish could have knocked out a tooth this time. Besides, the brawny villager was fortunate to be still breathing after the insult he caused Charlie. Patrick may not live by Camlochlin's ideals but they were inside him, engrained in him, and they were correct ideals. Aye. What kind of man stands idly by while a lass, and one he was thinking of courting, was so slighted? Not he.

Where were the other two bastards? He turned to find them and saw Duff's fist fly into flesh and bone again, and then again until his opponent crumpled at his feet.

Patrick smiled and then looked around for the third man.

To his horror, Patrick found him fighting Charlie! In truth, it wasn't much of a fight. The scoundrel swung at her. She ducked and rammed her knee into his groin. He collapsed instantly and while he was going down, she clasped both hands together and swung—much like the way he had swung the leg of the chair at Hamish. The man's head snapped back and he sank the rest of the way to the floor.

She looked up from her work to find Patrick watching her. He wanted to smile, to hurry to her and take her in his arms. Women who knew how to fight were nothing new to Patrick. His female cousins had always been welcomed to practice with the lads. His cousin Caitrina was a pirate for hell's sake! He didn't look down his nose at women warriors. No man in Camlochlin did.

"I don't think we should linger here," she said, dragging him back to the present.

"Aye," he agreed. She was correct. "Come, let's be off."

They left Blind Jack's in a hurry and made their way to their horses.

"What was that about?" Duff asked him. "Who was that man?"

Reaching for her reins, Charlie shook her head and said acidly. "Honestly, Duff, do you mean to tell me that you don't get to know anyone in the times you're spying on me?"

"I'm not here to make acquaintances."

His sister tossed him a disapproving glance and gained her saddle. "His name is Hamish. He's a villager from Pinmore who loves a lass called Bethany. A lass Patrick took to a room."

"Where nothin' took place," Patrick defended.

"How do you know about him taking anyone to their room?" Duff asked her, horror dawning on him. "You were here recently. Without me. You put something in my drink."

"I had no choice," she confessed.

So, Patrick thought, giving their conversation half his attention and coming to his own conclusion, she'd recognized him all this time and said nothing.

"I didna want Bethany," he said, feeling the need to ex-

plain to them both. "I didna even know her name until...
now."

Hell, he pondered the truth of it. He was as bad as Will,
mayhap worse. Mayhap he too had bairns scattered all
through Scotland. The thought of it made him feel ill. Children going through life without him. Just like Duff.

"Well, you will need to put an end to such behavior if
you want to court my sister, Campbell."

Charlie looked down at them from her saddle. "Court
me?" She spread her dark gaze over Patrick. "You want to
court me?"

Patrick glared at Duff. Now what was he supposed to
say? He'd never courted a lass before. Hell, he didn't know
how to go about it. He didn't know if he wanted to now. "I,
well, I—"

"You've piqued his interest, Charlotte," Duff supplied.

"Oh, have I?" She cocked her brow at Patrick as he
mounted.

It was either go along with it or punch Duff in the face.
Patrick had had enough fighting for one night. He stared at
Charlie instead, taking in the sight of her. Remembering the
way she'd brought down her attacker, the reason she was
here, the reason she'd been here before, and likely to other
pubs besides this one, putting herself in danger. For her sister. Always for others. What did she do for herself? What
made *her* happy?

"Tell me, lass," he said, sounding to his own ears lost and
sickly, "are ye truly surprised that ye would pique m' interest? Any man's interest fer that matter?"

She smiled and his muscles went hard. "You wield your
tongue as well as your fists."

He shook his head. "Nae, I find m' tongue has a mind all
its own when it comes to ye."

Duff cleared his throat. "Mine doesn't." He swung his steely gaze to his sister. "We'll speak about your fighting skills and where you learned them when I've had a chance to consider what it means."

"It means I can take care of myself, Duff," she said woodenly, her smiling fading.

Silence spread over them as they raced toward home. Patrick listened to the booming sound of it, louder than any disagreement. Duff seemed to truly try to gain his sister's favor, short of falling to his knees and begging her forgiveness for whatever it was he'd done. Charlie's anger toward him was evident in her eyes, her tone with him. But she didn't hate him. She remained loyal to his secret and had never equated him with Hendry.

But the rift between them was wide. What had Duff done to cause it?

"When will you get the butterbur?" she asked, turning to him and making Patrick thankful that she liked him. He never wanted to see disdain in her eyes when she looked at him. Hell, he felt feverish when he looked into her eyes.

What had she done to him? What was he going to do about it?

"Tomorrow," he told her.

She smiled and he feared there wasn't much he *could* do.

He was glad he could help Elsie and if the truth be known, he liked that he could give Charlie something so important. He hoped that once she had what her sister needed, she would stop visiting taverns in the dead of night, but he didn't suspect she would. If another need arose, she'd do what she could to see to it. He looked at her riding slightly ahead. How did she carry so much weight on her delicate shoulders? He'd have her be free from all of it. He'd begin with her brother. Whatever Duff had done couldn't have been so terrible as to carry the burden of so much anger. They returned to Cunningham House and walked to the stable.

"Might I have a word alone with yer sister, Duff?" Duff looked about to refuse but his eyes settled on her. It had to be clear to Duff that his sister liked Patrick. He'd told her about butterbur, though he'd had no idea she'd been searching for it. She'd offered him her smiles, more than poor Duff could pull from her. He hoped his cousin would remember his words and grant him time with Charlie alone.

"Verra well," Duff grumbled. "I'll brush the horses down. You have until I finish and I bring her inside."

Patrick smiled at him. They would get along well in Camlochlin.

"Go," Duff ordered. "Before I change my mind."

Patrick took Charlie's hand and led her out of the stable.

"How did you do that?" Charlie asked when they were alone.

"What?" He liked holding her hand. He'd never done it before with any lass. He'd never wanted to walk and talk and be content to simply stare at any other lass before.

"How did you get him to agree to this?" she asked, moving her finger between them.

How should he answer? With the truth, as wretched as it sounded? "I asked him fer time alone with ye to decide if I want a wife."

He thought she'd be angry but she threw back her head and laughed. "And he believed you?"

Patrick wanted to laugh with her but he suddenly felt feverish again. What did she find so amusing about him wanting to mayhap...possibly wed her? Did she see nothing but a rogue when she looked at him? Why did her reaction hook him in the guts? He didn't let women affect him this way. He was becoming someone else because of her—a little lass's defender, a champion for the ill and the poor. He liked who he saw now, not any more or any less than who he'd seen before. This man worried him though. For he no longer found Camlochlin's ideals dusty, but shining in the heart of a lass. In her, those ideals came to full radiant life, drawing him, beckoning him to walk with her along her path.

To what lengths would he go to win her? What would he do once he did? He would surly ponder these matters, but not now.

"Dinna fear," he reassured her, his playful smile returning. "I'm no' here fer a wife."

"Pity," she sighed and moved closer to him while they walked, rattling his good senses when her arm brushed his. "I think you and Eleanor Kennedy would make a handsome pair."

His lips widened into a toothy, dimpled grin as he bent his head to hers. "Ye think me handsome then?"

She shrugged and broke away from him, leaping back like a playful mare. "I've seen worse."

He didn't give chase but continued on toward the house, confident that she liked what she saw. "But am I handsome enough fer Eleanor? Mary said she's quite beautiful. Mayhap I should call on her."

Charlie's smile grew stiff and she pinned him with a glare, all traces of lightheartedness gone. "You're free to do as you wish."

She was jealous. It delighted him.

Reaching out, he snatched her hand and pulled her with him around the side of the kitchen entry. Hidden from the stable—and anyone possibly watching from it, Patrick dragged her in close against him. He coiled an arm around her slender waist and traced the outline of her elegant neck with the other hand.

"Then I think," he whispered, dipping his head to her throat, "I'll stay right here with ye."

His mouth hovered over the rapid pulse-beat in her neck. He kissed it and she trembled in his arms. Or mayhap it was his body that was trembling with desire for her. He found her lips, eager for his, and cupping his hand around her nape, he tilted her head so he could take her mouth more fully. He swallowed up her gasp and swept away her fears and misgivings with a stroke of his tongue.

She looped her arms around his neck and ran her fingers through his hair, answering pleasure's demand with a tight groan and a shift in her body that made him go hard.

A sound to his left caught his ear and he withdrew, expecting to see Duff.

A flash of golden hair proved it wasn't Charlie's brother who saw them, but her sister.

Elsie?

"Elsie!" Charlie cried out, breaking free of Patrick's embrace. "What in the world are you doing out here at night! You'll catch—"

"Nice to see you, Mr. Campbell." Elsie looked around her shoulder and offered Patrick a pleasant smile.

"Elsie," he replied with a friendly smile of his own.

"Charlie," her sister blinked back to her, "I will not tell Father if you don't."

Charlie's mouth fell open. "What should I not tell him?" She looked around, noticing for the first time the direction from which her sister was coming. "Were you in the village?" she asked, stunned. "Were you with someone?"

"Charlie," her sister replied, stepping around her, "do I ask you whom you meet when you disappear at night?"

"You know perfectly well where I was. You told Duff!" Charlie defended. "Who, by the way, is just inside the stable and will be here any moment."

"That didn't stop you both from sharing a moment of passion," Elsie pointed out with a soft smile. "Are you going to marry Mr. Campbell, Charlie?"

"What? Nay, I . . . We . . ."

"Were locked in a most passionate embrace," Elsie finished for her. "Kissing."

"It meant nothing!"

"Mr. Campbell," Elsie lifted her sparkling blue eyes to him. "Did it mean nothing to you, as well?"

She was clever veering the topic away from herself. If it were daylight, he would have smiled and played along. What was wrong with a lass running off to meet her beau for a kiss? But it was night and both of them should be home. "I enjoyed it," he admitted, "but yer sister's correct to be concerned. Ye should have an escort."

"Perhaps," Elsie allowed with a shrewd curl of her lips. "And perhaps Charlie should have an escort as well."

Aye, mayhap she should, Patrick agreed silently. He sure as hell couldn't be trusted to keep his mouth or hands off her. Even now, all he could think about was her sweetly salacious kiss, the taste of her breath, her bold, curious tongue. She drove him mad with desire and he wasn't sure how much longer he could control it.

"Elsie," Charlie said now, tempering her reaction with a steady tone. "You know who I was kissing, now you will tell me who you were with."

When Elsie coughed into her fist, Charlie went pale in the dim light. "Are you unwell?"

"I am fine, sister," Elsie assured her gently.

There was nothing gentle in Charlie's voice when she demanded, "Who were you meeting? What if you had fallen ill in his care?"

"Truly, I'm fine, and you don't know him," Elsie said, dipping her gaze to her boots. Patrick recognized the deception she tried to conceal. He looked at Charlie, curious if she saw it too. "Can we return to the house so Duff doesn't see me? If he knew I've been slipping out when he follows you, he would—"

Charlie looked horrified. "This isn't the first time? Is that why you told Duff about me seeking your cure? So that he wouldn't be here to see you sneaking out?"

"Don't be angry, Charlie," Elsie said breathlessly. A noise sounded from the stable. She looked nervously toward it, then turned to head back to the house. "Don't tell Duff, I beg you."

With her hands fisted on her hips, Charlie watched her sister go, and then turned to Patrick with stunned disbelief. "I don't believe it. She's been sneaking out!"

Patrick smiled at her. Damn it, he couldn't help himself, despite her fury. She was utterly, ravishingly beautiful to his eyes, his poor soul. If he never kissed another lass, he'd be satisfied to remember this one for the remainder of his days. But he wanted to do more than remember her. He wanted to kiss her again.

He nodded, doing his best not to smile at her overprotective nature over her sister. For an instant he felt as if they were the parents of a disobedient child. He liked how it felt.

"She's no' a child, lass," he said softly, wanting to ease her apprehension.

"But I'm to take care of her," she told him.

Patrick was quiet while she walked away. She took on every responsibility herself, so unlike him, who ran from it. He wanted to run now at the thought of it all, but he wanted to comfort her more.

He caught up in two long strides and took her hand in his. "She'll be all right, lass. I'll see to it in the morn."

Chapter Nineteen

Patrick reached Colmonell early the next day.

He rode toward the line of trees that separated the sparse woods from the western edge of the Fergussons' large farmstead.

What if they no longer grew butterbur? His mother hadn't needed it in years. No, it had to be here. Was his memory correct and this was the area where the plant had previously grown? He knew what butterbur looked like. Large white leaves, sometimes three feet in diameter, heart-shaped with scalloped edges topping tall fleshy stalks. They shouldn't be too difficult to find.

His thoughts brought him back, as they had all morning, to last night and Charlie's kiss. Patrick hadn't wanted to let her go. Her lips, so soft and sweetly yielding drove him daft. He wanted her. He wanted to bring her home or stay here with her—he didn't care which.

But the cold dawn brought with it misgivings. Did he want to promise her things he wasn't sure he could give her? Did he want to change his life so drastically? Did he want a wife? Being a husband was the highest of duties, and, as he'd learned throughout his life from his kin, the hardest.

But hell, he was ready for a hard fight. He hadn't had one in so damn long.

But did she want something else? Someone else?

Did she still love whichever of his cousins had given her her sling? Who had it been? And what kind of fool was he to have let her go? Patrick could ride to Tarrick Hall and find out. But he'd promised Charlie he'd make haste after Elsie awoke this morn with labored breathing. He also didn't know how he'd tell his uncles, whom he hadn't seen in a decade—that he was falling for the daughter of their enemy. The same lass one of their sons had fallen for. Hell, he could barely admit it to himself. And what if his cousin who had taught her how to use a sling still loved Charlie and was staying away to quell the feud?

Was it heroic or cowardly? Would Patrick have to fight him?

"Why would I?" he asked himself, moving over a worn path toward clusters of tall stemmed plants where he believed the butterbur to be.

What else would Patrick do about permanently losing her? Had he truly ever pondered a life of needing her— and not being able to have her because she belonged to his cousin? He pondered it now. It wouldn't be pleasant, that was for damn sure. How could he put a halt to the effects her smile, her spirit had over him?

Patrick spotted the leaves and breathed a sigh of relief. He wasted no time gathering what he needed and packing it up. He was surprised none of his uncles were out patrolling the farmland—and even more surprised that he hadn't been struck in the head with a stone from someone's sling.

How were his uncles? What had happened between them

and the Cunninghams that caused Duff to hate them? He'd make it a point to discover why when he returned to Pinwherry. And then he'd come back and visit his kin.

Gaining his mount, he looked toward Tarrick Hall. It hadn't been finished when last he'd visited and MacGregors and Grants had been everywhere. Now, the Hall, complete with lattice windows of lead and animal horn, stood like a strong fortress nestled within the flower-carpeted hills.

It was quiet.

Too quiet.

The hair on the back of Patrick's nape stood erect. He wasn't alone. He looked around and held his hands up in surrender.

"Who are ye, and what are ye doin' on my land?" a man called out, appearing from a tight stand of trees a stone's throw away.

It was his uncle Tamas—and a stone's throw was all he would need to fell Patrick to his arse. His face and red hair hadn't changed. Nor had the sling in his hand. Said to be one of the most fearless, defiant, hellion sons ever to be fathered, Tamas had been fostered in Camlochlin in an attempt by Patrick's mother to instill some manners into him.

Patrick had gone on his first cattle raid in Sleat when he was a lad of seven, thanks to Tamas taking him along. His uncle had fought his way out of many confrontations. Patrick had been there to witness many of them.

"'Tis I, Uncle, Patrick MacGregor, son of yer sister, Isobel, and her husband, Tristan. Put away yer sling, I beg ye."

"Patrick? Wee Patrick?" His uncle hurried toward him and stopped when he reached him to give him a good looking over with eyes as blue as the heavens. "Hell, 'tis ye, lad. Ye're no' so wee anymore."

"It has been long, Uncle," Patrick said as he dismounted.

"Too long," Tamas agreed and leaned in to offer his nephew a quick embrace and a pound on the shoulder. "What brings ye here now? Is that butterbur ye're takin'? Is it fer Isobel? Is m' sister ill?"

"Nae, nae," Patrick was quick to assure him with a hand to his uncle's shoulder. "M' mother is in good health. This is fer...a friend."

"Nothin' serious I hope."

"Nae, I—"

"Good, then come greet yer uncles." Tamas flung his arm around him. "Cam just returned from visitin' yer uncle Alex in Ballantrae. Neither him nor John would fergive me if I let ye get away withoot greetin' them. Ye're Isobel's son. They will want to see ye, lad."

He wanted to see them too, but he wouldn't stay long. He wasn't one to make promises, but he'd made them to Charlie.

Was that a good enough reason though to refuse time to his kin and bring shame to his father?

Faced with the cumbersome task of doing the right thing, he fully appreciated the strength it took his father to live according to his ideals. He also recognized that no man alive meant more to him than Tristan MacGregor. He'd brought up his children well. Luke and Mailie were proof of it. Violet, the youngest, had a cheek toward rebellion, like him. Patrick would talk to her when he returned home. Resistance was pointless. The teachings, led by example by their father, their kin, were planted deep in their hearts and sooner or later the heart takes over.

It wasn't that he'd never wanted to emulate his father. He did, but he was afraid he'd fail.

"Of course, Uncle. I wish to meet yer bairns as well."

Tamas gave him a hefty chop to the shoulder to show his

satisfaction then shouted across the fields. "Aidan! Go fetch yer uncles!"

Aidan was too young to be the one who'd given Charlie the sling. At ten and three, he was a scrawny-boned, pumpkin-haired lad without a hair on his face longer than fuzz.

Patrick watched the lad run off to do his father's bidding and followed Tamas to the house. He wanted to get to know this part of his family and realized, after having met the Cunninghams, that there was much he didn't know.

The next two lads to leave the large Hall were older than Patrick by a few years. He smiled and greeted his uncle Cameron's sons Tam and Shaw. He remembered playing with them as children but nothing after that.

Shaw, the younger of the two, looked him over, his eyes lingering on Patrick's hair, the same copper color as his. "Have we met?" he finally asked.

How the hell was Patrick to know that? He'd met more people than he could ever count. Before he could venture an answer, a man exiting the house next called out.

"Is it true?"

Patrick turned to smile at him. He was taller than Tamas and a few years older. His hair had darkened over the years to a dark golden brown but his eyes, as they took in the color of Patrick's hair, were as wide and perceptive as Patrick had remembered.

"'Tis good to see ye again, Uncle John."

"Aye," his uncle drew him in for a hefty embrace, "ye're Bel's son. How is my sister?" he said, stepping apart but keeping his hands on Patrick's shoulders. "Has she given yer faither any more bairns?"

"Violet remains the last," Patrick told him. "I understand from yer letters to m' mother that ye have five daughters."

They spoke of their families while they entered the house. Patrick met three more of his cousins, Donella, Eithne, and Izzy, two of John's daughters and one of Cameron's.

They sat him at the head table and served him food and good whisky. Soon, his aunts, Annie and Eleanor, joined them, the latter receiving a kiss from her husband, John, before she sat.

"Cameron should be along any moment now," Annie informed them. "He's not returned yet from seeing to Roddy Fergusson's new roof. You know how he likes to keep himself occupied."

Patrick looked around the table at his uncles, who for a moment let silence reign. These were men his mother had raised and taken care of after the MacGregors had killed their father and made them orphans. She adored them and spoke of them often.

"What is Uncle Patrick doin' these days?" Patrick asked of his namesake. He'd like to bring home news to his mother. He missed her. He missed them all. Thanks to Charlie. "And how are Lachlan and Alex?"

"Patrick still lives at our family homestead," John told him, perking to attention again. "He is a husband and a father to eight bairns."

"Eight!" Patrick laughed and raised his cup. "To makin' bairns then."

He didn't know why Charlie popped into his mind at that moment, or why the idea of having eight bairns with her wasn't an altogether unpleasant one.

"Lachlan lives in Girvan," Tamas said. "We see him from time to time. In fact, he's due to arrive here in a sennight or so."

Patrick made a mental note to return to see him.

"Alex still resides in Bran—"

They all heard the entrance door open and the footsteps that followed. A man entered the hall, but Patrick didn't recognize him right away. He was tall and able-bodied dressed in breeches and a coat. His auburn hair was streaked with gray, his green eyes dull and shadowed by the weight of his life.

"Cam." John stood to his feet and urged Patrick up next to him. "'Tis Patrick MacGregor, Bel's son."

It was his uncle Cameron. Patrick could scarcely believe how much he had aged. Did he carry the burdens of all the villagers on his shoulders? Patrick had seen what the same weight had cost Rob, the MacGregor clan chief. He didn't want to see Charlie bear the same burden.

"Patrick," Cameron greeted with a warm smile, joining them. "What brings you here. How is your mother?"

"She's well," he assured him, then explained that he'd come to gather butterbur for a friend and met up with Tamas.

They drank together and shared stories about Patrick's mother. His uncles loved their only sister dearly and they enjoyed hearing about her life with Tristan. An hour passed quickly and Patrick thought about leaving.

But there was a cousin he remembered whom he hadn't yet met, a lad a year or two younger than him.

He turned to Cameron sitting beside him. "Will yer son Kendrick be joinin' us?"

The hall grew quiet. His uncles' daughters excused themselves from the table and left. Their wives followed shortly thereafter, dragging Aidan with them.

What the hell had he said? Had some tragedy befallen Cameron's youngest son? Patrick closed his eyes and prayed that he hadn't just brought up a man's dead son.

"We lost Kendrick five years ago." Cameron's raspy voice chilled the air.

Nae.

"Fergive me," Patrick said quietly. "I didna know. Ye never wrote to m' mother aboot it."

"There was no reason to bring her such terrible news," Cameron explained, his tone shallow and empty. This was what haunted his gaze. "Let her go on thinking her nephew lives."

"I will say nothin' if that's—"

Five years ago? Did Charlie's mother die five years ago? Allan Cunningham said his wife died of a fever. Did the two have anything to do with each other?

"If ye can speak of it," Patrick said with dreaded hesitation, "what happened to him?"

"The Cunninghams," Tamas answered, setting Patrick's heart to ruin. "They killed him."

Patrick wanted to leap from his seat. He wanted to know the full tale, and at the same time, he wanted to flee the house and never hear the rest. The Cunninghams? Which Cunninghams? Why? Why would they kill Kendrick? He was naught but a boy five years ago! Was it Duff? Did Charlie know?

"Why?" he blurted. "Who took him from ye?"

"Allan Cunningham's sons," Cameron told him, downing the remainder of his whisky and looking into his empty cup with misty eyes. "By order of their father. They took him away and disposed of his body. We know not where."

Nae. Patrick shook his head. He couldn't be hearing this right. Duff? Duff was his cousin! Kendrick's cousin! They had to be mistaken. But…he thought raking his fingers through his hair…Charlie knew. She knew what her brothers had done to the lad who'd taught her to use the sling. The cousin she loved. Kendrick was the reason for Charlie's scorn toward her brothers.

Hell. He felt ill. This was too big. Too unforgivable for the feud to ever end.

"There were witnesses who saw Kendrick being led away by Cunningham's sons," John revealed as if he could read Patrick's hidden thoughts.

Witnesses. There was no doubt then. Duff had done the unthinkable and killed a man's bairn. He should never have told him that he knew his father. He would never tell Will that they'd met.

"Why did ye no' kill Allan Cunningham? His sons? Whoever was responsible?" he asked them while his blood boiled in his veins.

"I wanted to," Tamas answered, his knuckles white as he gripped his cup. "The man who ordered Kendrick's death still lives."

"They should die as Kendrick died," Tam, Cameron's eldest son bit out. "Alone, in an unmarked grave."

Patrick closed his eyes and prayed it didn't get any worse than it already was.

"There are lasses involved," Shaw reminded them. "Even if there is no intention, they could be hurt or killed. None of it will return our brother to us."

"Nay, it won't," Shaw's brother agreed. "But 'twill bring some—"

Cameron held up his palm and set his angry gaze on his son. "I'll have no more talk of this. It's been settled for years now. We've done enough. I've made orphans of children once. I will not do it again."

Patrick knew what his uncle was speaking about. Traces of guilt that had consumed Cameron as a lad still laced his voice. He'd been but a child when he shot his arrow into the night and killed the then Duke of Argyll, Robert Campbell, the Devil MacGregor's beloved brother-in-law, and brought the wrath of the Highland Chief down on his entire clan. Archie Fergusson had taken the blame for killing Lord Campbell and had suffered the consequence for it.

Cameron's father was killed before his eyes because of what he had done.

It would be a difficult thing for any lad to live with and the somber glaze in his uncle's eyes had always been deep.

Lifting his cup to his mouth, something occurred to Patrick and he paused before the rim touched his lips. Did his uncle say they'd done enough?

What had they done? Why did Duff hate them and want them all dead?

"What did ye do?" he asked in so quiet a voice, he was asked to repeat it. "What did ye do to the Cunninghams?"

Cameron's eyes were wide pools of deep regret. He lowered them to his cup and expelled a heavy sigh. "I killed Margaret Cunningham."

Chapter Twenty

It was nightfall when Patrick left Tarrick Hall. He'd promised his kin he'd return soon but told them nothing about where he was going. He didn't know why he kept quiet. He should have told them everything, including who Duff's father was. He should have burned the butterbur and stayed where he was.

Why was he going back to Cunningham House? His uncle Cameron wanted no more fighting. It wouldn't take much fighting to kill Cunningham and both his sons. He'd have his uncle Tamas's blessing if he did. He could do it without harm to Charlie and Elsie. But how would they live without any men to protect them? He didn't care if Charlie knew how to fend for herself against one man. What if the Dunbars or men like them ever returned? He couldn't avenge Kendrick and leave Charlie and her sister at the mercy of savages. Another reason he couldn't plan on killing them was because his uncle already lived with so many burdens. Patrick didn't want to be the cause for another.

He wasn't going back to kill them, though he couldn't promise he wouldn't beat them to within an inch of their lives. He was going back for answers. He would continue to be Patrick Campbell until he learned where Kendrick's body was. Then he would go gather him and bring him home to his father for a proper burial.

He was going back because Elsie needed butterbur, and for the Wallaces and their wee bairns...and for Charlie.

He knew there could be nothing between them. His kin here and on Skye would never accept her. He knew the MacGregors were no strangers to marrying their enemies, but none had ever been sister to a man who killed one of their children. He also knew that Charlie would never forgive him for deceiving her. Still, he wanted her to know the truth about how her mother died and how the man who'd killed her had pled her forgiveness before he left her. It might not make losing her any easier, but his uncle was no monster. Patrick would tell her before he left, before he told her who he was and who his uncles were.

She would hate him, and he suspected he'd miss her, but there was nothing to be done about it. He'd find Kendrick and do what he could for Elsie and the Wallaces, and then he'd leave and never think of Charlie or any of them again. He realized it wouldn't be easy and he blamed himself for giving in and giving a damn. Now he remembered why he'd steered clear of the burdens of responsibility.

By the time he reached Cunningham House, he was feeling quite miserable. He didn't want to go inside. He didn't want to see Duff. He was afraid of what he might do. He remained in his saddle for a long time, torn between staying and leaving. He didn't know how long he sat there trying to decide when Charlie pulled open the front door and hurried out to him.

"Where have you been, Patrick?" she asked, wringing her skirts in her hands. She looked almost bloodless in the pale moonlight, her eyes were wide and filled with worry. "You've been gone overlong."

"What is it?" He leaped from his mount. He forgot everything else when he looked toward the house.

"'Tis Elsie," she answered in a hollow voice. "Her breathing has grown worse since this morning. She still will not tell me who she was meeting last night, but I just know she is sick today because of it. Did you get the butterbur?"

Elsie was worse. If it was too late to help her, it would be his fault. He knew without a doubt that the butterbur would have worked if he'd delivered it sooner.

Nae. He wouldn't let it be too late.

"Aye, 'tis here." He hurried to show her. "Return to yer sister. I'll take care of the plants."

"Duff is with her. I want to help."

He reached for the sack. He wouldn't let the thought of Duff and what he'd done distract him now.

Charlie stopped him with her hand on his arm. "Will it help her?" Her voice was laden with distress and weariness.

He didn't want to look at her and see it in her eyes. Why had he lingered at Tarrick Hall when he knew Elsie needed the plant? He could have been reunited with his uncles any time after he saw to Elsie. But he'd let loyalty dictate to him, and for the sake of Camlochlin he'd remained and found out things he didn't want to be true.

"Aye, 'twill," he said, pulling the sack free and tossing it over his shoulder. "Dinna fear."

"Do you know how to prepare it?" she asked following him into the house.

He prayed he remembered. "We must clean the roots in

cold water. Once they are completely dry we must soak them fer a few hours."

"How many hours?" She tugged on his sleeve as they entered the kitchen.

"Six will be enough." He dumped the sack on the chopping table and opened it.

"Six more hours until she can be helped?" She stared at him with wide, terrified eyes. "My remedies offer her no comfort."

Hell, there must be something. He thought of his mother's jars lining the kitchen wall. "Is there any chickweed in the kitchen?"

"Nay." She worried her lip.

He thought about it a bit longer. "Daisies!" he blurted.

"What about them?"

"They are no' as strong as butterbur, but they will help until the butterbur tea was ready."

"Daisies?" Her beautiful eyes grew wider along with her smile. "Elsie has the daisy circlet I gave her in our room!"

She turned to run off but then whirled on her heels and flung her arms around him. "Thank you, Patrick."

Her long loose tresses brushed over his fingers when he stretched his arm around her waist.

God help him, he didn't want to let her go. Couldn't they just run away somewhere, away from their names, from duty, and responsibilities? He was good at running away but what of Elsie and Nonie? What of Kendrick's empty grave? He couldn't run this time, but he would have to let her go.

She tilted her head so he could feel her breath on his chin, fragranced in spice when she spoke again. "I feared you weren't coming back."

What was he to say? That he'd considered it? His heart ached because she didn't trust him. Why would she? She was raised with murderers and she associated with drunkards and men who put pride before their family. She didn't believe there were any "different" men because she didn't know any.

"Fergive me," he whispered, looking into her eyes, longing to kiss her. *Fergive me fer everything.* "I couldna find the butterbur."

"Of course," she allowed and with a smile, broke free from his embrace and ran off to get the daisies.

Patrick watched her go. He thought he might be a different man, but he'd chosen to remain at Tarrick Hall, despite Elsie. If Charlie ever discovered all the things he kept from her she would consider him no different...nae, worse because he'd broken through her armor. He'd felt it in her sweet surrender when he kissed her. He'd penetrated her defenses and she let him kiss her. She would never forgive him for that.

But how could he keep the truth from her, from Duff? If he told one, the other would find out. He should go now before everything was out in the open—with her father probably dead.

His gaze dropped to the butterbur needing to be cut and cleaned.

He reached for a knife and slammed a root on the table. Why was Elsie his responsibility anyway? Or Nonie Wallace? Hadn't he kept himself from this kind of burden? The guilt? Hell, he never wanted this. He had to get Elsie well, find Kendrick's remains and exact a little Highland vengeance on the guilty, and then he had to get the hell out of Pinwherry.

Stay with the plan. He heard his cousin Cailean's voice in his head warning him while he chopped and carried the pieces of root to a pot. As lads, they had fallen into as much mischief, if not more than the rest of their cousins, but only the two of them had escaped with the least punishment... because they always planned out their actions carefully.

He would not veer off. He would not...

She returned to the kitchen and stood at the entrance with the daisy circlet in her hand and a hopeful smile on her lips. "She's feeling a bit better."

For a moment, Patrick forgot their names, the innocent, and the guilty. He could only stand captured and captivated by the sight of her in her flowing skirts and obsidian waves falling around her shoulders. He never wanted to stop looking at her, at her face, her slender shoulders that bore the weight of her world. He could make her happy.

His sorry condition only lasted for a moment before his attention was pulled to Duff appearing at his sister's side at the entrance.

"She's asleep," he told Charlie, then turned to Patrick. "What can I do to help?"

Ye can get oot of the kitchen before I rid ye of all yer teeth. "We need water."

Duff hurried to fetch two buckets and set out to the well. Watching him, Patrick wondered if he could take a blade to him if he had to.

"What troubles you?" Her silken voice brushed across his ear as she came near.

He looked away from the path Duff had taken and ran his palm over his chin. "Ye thought I wouldna return."

She moved around him like a breeze and lifted a piece of the root to her nose. "What kept you?"

"There was no butterbur in Colmonell," he told her, widening the divide between them with more deceit, but not seeing any other choice. It was either this or the truth—and that would only make her hate him sooner. "I had to travel to Craigneil."

She accepted his word without further question. "Forgive me then for doubting you. You've shown me with Nonie—"

"Nae." He looked at her. He couldn't have her thinking he was some kind of hero. He wasn't. It was odd, really. He had found a certain ease with her that he'd never felt with any other lass, as if he could tell her anything. And yet, everything she knew about him was false. "Dinna think I'm someone I'm no'. 'Twill be easier fer ye when I leave."

She went still and dropped her gaze to the circlet. "'Twill not be difficult either way."

He smiled at her bent head. He would miss her sharp tongue. But it was better this way. Seeing Duff proved to him that he wanted revenge on her family. There was no hope for anything between them. The sooner he left, the better.

Still, when she turned her back on him, he reached out to stop her. His fingers brushed down the length of her hair.

Duff returned with the water and then thankfully left again to see to Elsie. He was being generous about leaving his sister alone with Patrick, but Patrick was glad just to have him out of his sight.

He remained with Charlie and helped her separate the water into smaller pots and then add the daisies to one and butterbur root to the other.

"'Tisna that I want to go," he began while he lit a small fire beneath the pot with the dried daisies. He didn't like this silence between them, as if they were strangers.

"Does your mother know many remedies?" she asked him, veering off the topic he'd brought up.

He was happy to comply. "M' mother knows everything

there is to know aboot foliage of any kind. No' only does she have a remedy fer every ailment, but her expertise in the kitchen is withoot rival."

"Did you learn much from her?"

"I learned everything she taught me aboot her healin' plants. While m' brother practiced the art of courtly behavior, and m' cousin learned how to wield a spoon, I spent m' nights up late with m' mother, learnin' her remedies."

He missed her. Isobel Fergusson was a good woman, and she taught her daughters to be the same. Saucy mouthed Mailie was the only one to tell him what she thought of his disreputable ways. He missed her too. He wanted to tell Charlie about the women in Camlochlin—and about his father.

But to what purpose? He should be relieved really. He had no reason to stay after he got what he came back for. The decision was already made for him.

But he felt like hell.

"I havena seen m' kin in a long while. I want to—"

"You have no obligation to explain anything to me," she cut him off, holding up her palm. "You're free to leave without quarrel from me." She folded her arms across her chest and turned to stare into the pot of daisies, her defenses returning like a tower around her.

Patrick stared at her profile illuminated by the flames and cursed the temptation to veer from his plan.

"Ye expect me to believe ye wouldna miss me?"

She blinked at the steam rising before her face, and then slanted him an incredulous look. "Is that so difficult to imagine?"

"Aye," he said, "'Tis. Ye've shown no displeasure in m' company."

"Ha!" She tossed her head back and laughed. "You wouldn't have believed anything I told you."

He tilted his mouth into a smile. Damn it, he couldn't help it. She delighted him. He liked this side of her better than her angry silence.

"Ye told me I was no' altogether barbaric like the rest," he reminded her while the daisy tea began to boil. "That I had a naturally easy way with people, 'beguilin' at will' were yer exact words. Ye told me I was kind and verra clever, mayhap, even a hero, and I believed ye."

"Of course you did!" she said, all traces of amusement gone. "Those are all good qualities!"

His dimple deepened. "Were none of them true then?"

"None of them," she said icily, rejecting his truce. "I was tired and not in my right frame of mind when I said those things."

"*Now* I dinna believe ye."

She looked like she wanted to hit him. He grinned at her. It was all he could do to stop himself from tossing his plan to the wind and kissing her senseless. "Tea's ready."

Chapter Twenty-One

The daisy tea helped Elsie's labored breath—that and Duff's quiet voice at her bedside while they waited for the butterbur to soak.

"I cannot believe we've had"—Elsie stopped to cough then sipped more of her tea—"daisies right here all along. Thank God for you Mr. Campbell."

Aye, Charlie had thanked God often when Elsie's color returned. She also asked why He'd bring a man like Patrick Campbell into her life, only to watch him leave?

But wasn't that what she had wanted? He wasn't included in her life with Elsie. Besides, she'd known from the beginning that his heart was true to no one. Why had his words created such turmoil inside her? So, he was planning on leaving. It came as no surprise. So he'd kissed her last eve and set her heart to ruin. It was her own fault to allow it.

Instead of being angry with him, she should be thanking him for riding all the way to Craigneil for Elsie.

She turned to look at him now standing at the doorway.

Sensing her, he turned his hard gaze from Duff and let it soften on her and then on her sister.

"Ye'll be well soon, lass."

Had he truly done it? Had he brought her sister a cure? Answered her prayers?

She hadn't meant what she said earlier. Everything she thought of him was true. He *was* beguiling. He *was* a hero—to Nonie, to Elsie…to her.

"You brought back a good amount of roots," Duff said, standing up to stretch. "How long until we need more?"

What was that flash across Patrick's eyes when he looked at Duff? Now that Charlie thought about it, Patrick appeared angry at Duff since his return tonight. She wondered why.

"Ye'll have enough," Patrick bit out and then excused himself and left the room.

Something wasn't right. Charlie wanted to go after him and find out what it was, but Duff went to the door and followed Patrick out first.

"Charlie?" Elsie asked, pulling Charlie's attention back to her. "I'm glad Patrick came here, aren't you?"

Elsie's clear blue eyes were wide with anticipation. Her cheeks and lips had returned to their natural pink hue. She was going to be well.

Because of him. Whether he left or not, Charlie knew one thing. Soon, perhaps within the year, Elsie would be well enough to leave Cunningham House. Thanks to Patrick Campbell, a scoundrel with a knight's heart she would soon be free to live her life alone with Elsie.

Thanks to him, she wanted more.

Aye, she trembled where she sat, she was glad Patrick had come here.

* * *

Patrick headed toward the front door. He needed to get air and clear his thoughts before he took action against the Cunningham men without finding Kendrick's remains first. The sight of Duff, the sound of his voice enraged Patrick. Why had he done it? Why had he killed a young lad? He wanted answers. He was thankful Allan and Hendry Cunningham had gone to bed before he'd returned from Tarrick Hall. Apparently, Elsie's condition hadn't concerned them. Tonight, if he saw them, he might kill them.

Were these the men by whose standards Charlie judged them all?

"Patrick."

He stopped at Duff's call and blew out a long breath before he began to turn to him. He'd learned over the years that the best way to keep from killing a man was to smile at him.

"I was goin' to check on the butterbur," Patrick told him and turned toward the kitchen.

"May I join you?"

Patrick grumbled his consent and kept walking. Duff sure as hell didn't get his manners from his father.

"I wanted to thank you for caring about Elsie and bringing back the butterbur," he said, hurrying to catch up. "This attack was worse than the others. When I heard Charlie weeping in the hall…"

Charlie had wept in the hall? He didn't want to give a damn.

"…I did what I could to help."

Patrick cut him a quick side-glance. So, he wasn't the most heartless of the three. "What did ye do?"

"I just spoke to her. I kept my tone gentle as it seemed to calm her, despite the topic of my words."

Patrick nodded. A soothing voice was a remedy for many things. "What did ye speak aboot?"

They entered the kitchen and Duff reached for a jug of wine and two cups. "I told her I wasn't a monster." He looked down to pour the drinks, casting his solemn gaze into the shadows of his lashes. "Though I don't know if she believed me." He looked up and handed Patrick his drink. "She's heard things to the contrary."

Hell. Was Duff going to confess? It was too soon! Patrick wasn't sure he could endure hearing the details without losing control of his temper. He could take Duff down right here and then go take care of the other two.

"Who has she heard them from?"

"Charlie, I'm afraid. She believes I killed someone she loves."

Patrick set his cup down on the chopping table. Whether he was ready or not, he was about to get the information he wanted. He'd had a plan. What was it? Make friends and find his cousin's remains. One thing he could do well was make friends. "Is she wrong to believe it?" he asked calmly.

"Nay," Duff told him, looking down again and into his cup. "Though I'd laid not a finger on him. I did nothing to stop it."

Patrick's heart thundered in his chest. Why the Cunninghams? Why was it Margaret Cunningham who'd taken him in and not another family?

"What prompts ye to tell me this?"

Duff closed his eyes, seeming to gather himself from someplace deep within before he spoke. "Perhaps, because you know who I am and that my father is kin to the Fergussons, you will understand the weight which I carry." He stopped and shook his head. Patrick thought he wouldn't continue. "Not only because he was my kin—though that knowledge makes my shame even more unbearable."

"Do the Fergussons know that ye're a MacGregor?" Patrick asked him.

Duff shook his head. "Charlie told Kendrick but he never told his family. He was verra loyal to her. He was a thoughtful lad," Duff told him, looking like he might begin weeping. Patrick felt no pity for him. "He had a particular disdain toward my father for abandoning me. Charlie discovered for certain last winter that I was involved with his death. I've tried to tell her that 'twas not by my hand, but she will not listen. Perhaps you might consider telling her what I am telling you."

Patrick almost refused to believe what he was hearing, it was so outlandish. Duff wanted *him* to convince Charlie that what he'd done wasn't so wretched?

Patrick wanted to break something, preferably a jaw, or a nose. But he wanted directions. "Who was he?" He wanted to hear Duff speak the lad's full name.

Duff guzzled the contents of his cup and then reached for more. "Vile stuff," he said, concerning the wine.

Patrick agreed.

"He was called Kendrick...Kendrick Fergusson. He'd visited often with his father and uncles. Our mothers were friends. My father was always cordial for my mother's sake, but he didn't like them and he didn't trust them. The boy..." He paused and Patrick looked away. "Kendrick and my sister had grown very close during these visits and their love was obvious to all. My father was against a union."

So Kendrick had been killed to keep him away from Charlie.

"He was yer kin."

Duff lowered his head. "I didn't know, though it changes nothing. He had done nothing wrong. He was a lad."

"What was done to him?" Patrick didn't want to know. He didn't want to hear what Will's son had done—or not done—to Cameron's son.

"Hendry and I were to take him away and...dispose of him." His voice had become almost dreamlike and distant, as if his memories were lost in a fog.

Patrick felt as if he was in the same fog. It was one thing to think about his young cousin's murder, but to hear Duff describing how they were to "dispose" of him shook him to his core. He fought every urge to spring forward and close his hands around Duff's throat. "Where did ye take him?"

"Dumfries."

Dumfries. Patrick's heart sank. It would take at least two days to ride there and more time to find Kendrick's body.

"When we arrived, I couldn't do it and left the task to Hendry. I should have stopped it."

"Aye," Patrick agreed, heartbroken for the lad and his parents—and for Charlie, as well, "ye should have." If only he had. Things would be so different. Patrick could have taken Duff home to Skye and Charlie...she would likely be wed to Kendrick.

He tried not to think of what would have been, and how he felt about it.

"So Hendry killed him and left his body in Dumfries?"

"Aye."

"Was he given a grave?"

Duff lifted his gaze, glimmering with tears. "I don't know."

Disgusted, Patrick turned away. He was glad Duff was contrite.

"I am haunted by his face."

Patrick hoped Kendrick haunted him forever. "And yet ye hate his faither."

"Cameron Fergusson murdered my mother with a sword to her back. She was innocent."

"As Kendrick had been." Patrick wanted to tell Duff who he was, that Cameron Fergusson was his uncle and that the Cunninghams had destroyed his uncle's life. He wanted to tell him that he'd spent the day with the Fergussons and that Margaret's death was a terrible accident.

But Duff's feelings could wait. He would speak to Hendry first and try to discover what had been done to Kendrick's body.

"I don't blame Charlie for hating me." Duff's soft, ragged voice raked across Patrick's heart. "Kendrick was the love of her life."

Och, hell, was Patrick a monster also? Why did hearing how much Charlie loved his cousin make his stomach hurt?

"D'ye think she will feel any differently aboot ye if she believes ye stood by and did nothin' while Hendry killed him?"

Duff shook his head and set down his cup. "Nay. You're right. Nothing will change."

Patrick watched him move toward the doorway. He didn't care if Duff lived with the weight of his actions. Most men did. His only concern was his uncle Cameron. "There might be something that will help," Patrick said, stopping Duff from leaving.

"You will tell her my part in Kendrick's death then?"

"You're a fool!" Charlie accused, appearing at the door. Her eyes were wide, dark pools of anger Patrick had never seen in her before. He believed in that moment that Charlie truly did hate her brother. Madly enough, it made him feel sorry for Duff a little.

"You were never to speak of it to anyone," she said to him. "Do you want to bring the Fergussons here again?"

Without waiting for an answer, she turned and ran from the house.

Chapter Twenty-Two

$\mathcal{P}$atrick went after her immediately. He didn't wait for Duff's approval. He didn't need it anymore. He didn't wait to see if her brother would go after her first. Which he didn't.

"Charlie," he called out, following her outside and into the breaking dawn.

She stopped and turned to him as bursts of gold and orange light rose behind her. She wore her thick black tresses tied into a heavy knot on the top of her head. Golden rays spilled across her bare neck tempting Patrick to distraction with the thought of kissing her there.

"Duff told you of *him*." Her shattered voice stole across his ears. "He shouldn't have. My family's gruesome history does not concern you. You should leave and continue on your journey, forgetting this part of it."

But it did concern him. He couldn't tell her why it did. Not yet at least. Surely she would think his uncle had sent him here to win her favor and then take revenge on her family. Even more though, *she* concerned him. He wasn't sure he could forget her and it rattled all his defenses. Having his heart control his logic was unfamiliar territory to him. She muddled his thoughts. He didn't know what the right thing to do was anymore—or why he even wanted to do it.

But how could he leave her here with men who'd done such a heinous thing? She would never be safe.

"I know what I should do," he told her in a quiet voice as he moved toward her. "But I keep findin' reasons to stay."

"Aye, reasons such as my brother being a MacGregor, enemies of the Campbells for what, two hundred years now? And that he killed a boy? He will bring you quite a bounty."

"I have no intentions of deliverin' him over to anyone. And besides, Duff claims he didna kill the lad." The words spilled forth before he could stop them—and now, when he tried, his tongue continued to defy him. Why in blazes was he defending Duff to Charlie? He closed his eyes and clenched his jaw. He didn't know how he would feel if Mailie or Violet hated him and never forgave him something for which he was sorry. He opened his eyes again to mutter an oath. "Though he admits to doin' nothin' to stop it, I believe he is—"

"I don't care what he admits to. It won't bring back Kendrick."

Nae, it wouldn't. She wished it would. She carried his sling. Was he truly jealous of his dead cousin? Damnation, he was pitiful indeed.

"Duff said ye love him still." Clearly, he still had no control over his tongue. But he wanted to know.

"I will always love him. He was the one I intended to marry. I miss him tremendously every day and I will never forgive those who took him from this world, either with their sword or their silence."

She turned away from him and lifted the hem of her skirt

as she padded toward the wheat house. "If you will excuse me, the chickens need to be fed."

Patrick watched her leave, his heart stuck somewhere between his chest and his mouth. Was there no room in her heart for anyone else then? And why did he feel so defeated when he wasn't staying?

"'Twas five years ago," he said, picking up his steps to walk beside her. "Why d'ye remain loyal to— He's the one who gave ye that sling though, aye?"

Her glare as they neared the wheat house stopped him from finishing.

He knew he should give her some sort of repentant look, but he hoped she'd answer. "'Tis his sling, aye?"

"Aye," she gave in with an exasperated sigh. "'Tis his sling."

He pulled open the thick wooden door and offered her entry into the wheat house first.

"I have others that I've fashioned to look like Kendrick's sling. I give them when I'm caught using it. I'd never let them take his."

Patrick tried to swallow. It felt as if something deep inside of him wanted out. Was it possible that of all the lasses he could have fallen for, he'd chosen the one who was still in love with his deceased cousin? She'd gone to the trouble of crafting decoys just so she wouldn't lose Kendrick's gift.

What kind of fool was he?

What kind of fool was *she*? Who loved a memory? That's what Kendrick was. Would she be satisfied to go through her life with no man at her side because she was still in love with a memory? It was preposterous. Even more absurd was how it clawed at his insides.

"Yer faither didna want a union with the Fergussons," he

said, stepping inside and taking the bucket she handed him. "Would ye have defied him had Kendrick lived?"

"Aye," she told him, looking him in the eyes. "I would have. I defy him every chance I get."

Patrick smiled, despite the thought of her being wed to Kendrick. He enjoyed her spirited nature. It tempted him almost beyond his endurance to take a leap into the fray and claim her as his own.

"And now, ye would live oot yer life alone?"

She paused and looked up at him as if a brighter alternative had drifted across her thoughts. "Nay." She blinked the thought away. "I would have Elsie."

Aye, the dreams of a life with Elsie she'd mentioned. How could he tell her he didn't think Elsie was enough to make her happy?

"Ye have a plan then?" he asked while they filled their buckets.

"Aye, get my sister well enough to leave, and then go."

Hell, what fool wouldn't fall for her? She had a plan!

"What aboot the villagers ye've been helpin?" he asked her, following her to the door.

"I'll do what I can to help them, but Elsie and I have to leave before he marries us off. A husband would take me away from Pinwherry and if I must go, I would prefer to leave with her."

"Where would ye go?"

"Someplace far away, where we could disappear."

He knew of such a place. Damn him to Hades. In fact, he did feel a bit warmer. Stepping outside into the cool morning breeze didn't help. "Elsie might no' want to go now that she's in love."

Charlie scowled obviously disapproving. "I will speak with her."

He nodded. "'Twill be dangerous fer two lasses travelin' alone to someplace far away."

She set down her bucket and looked at him while she bolted the door. "Are you offering escort?"

"I might be." He might be mad. He was definitely mad.

"I thought you were in a hurry to leave."

His dimple flashed. "I never said I was in a hurry."

When she smiled back at him, he lost his breath, as if someone punched him in the guts. He tried to fight it. He couldn't stay and she wouldn't want him to once he told her the truth.

He had to fight it. Even if she could forgive him for his secrets, his kin would never accept a Cunningham. The MacGregors had received many into the fold, Campbells and Menzies alike, a pirate and even a queen! But sharing blood with those who killed children was unforgivable.

And as if all that weren't enough to keep them apart, her heart was lost to Kendrick.

He could fight it. Fighting was what he did best. He turned away and began the short trek to the henhouse. He'd drop off the bucket then do his best to keep his distance from her until he left.

"Patrick?" she called out.

"Aye?"

He didn't stop and he didn't turn to look at her. He was afraid that if he did, he'd smile like some captivated fool.

"When the time comes, would you return here and take us to your Camlochlin?"

The ground was falling away beneath his feet. Aye, Camlochlin. She would be happy living there, hidden from the world. His mother would help her take care of Elsie until she was completely well...

He stopped and turned to her, bracing his feet firmly

on the ground, the way he did before any good match. "I thought ye wanted me to ferget ye."

The tips of her lips curled upward in a mischievous smile. "I never said *me* in particular."

Where was the harm in smiling at her? Damn it all. How easily did she make his resilience falter? Camlochlin was impossible. *Tell her!* "D'ye think ye could stand seein' me there every day?"

"Likely no." Her dark eyes twinkled in the sunlight as she walked past him. "But luckily for me, you don't stay home for long, do you?"

Forgetting his plan and his resistance, and his cousin, his grin widened. His gaze took in the sight of her hips swaying beneath the gauzy folds of her skirts, her bare feet peeking out from beneath the hem while they carried her farther away.

"When ye're ready to come," he called out, his good humor fully restored. "I could already have taken a wife and settled down."

She laughed at him over her shoulder. "That's even less likely."

He was happy to hear her laughter. Happy that he was the one who brought it to her. He didn't deny her assumption but followed her into the hen house.

"Ye dinna believe m' heart can be won then?"

She looked at the chickens and tossed them a handful of feed. "I think you would fight it until your dying day."

He chuckled and shook his head at himself. "I canna seem to hide m'self from ye. Ye step boldly into m' thoughts and see me plainly."

She turned to look at him where he stood behind her and offered him a knowing, solemn smile. She didn't want to be right about him. She didn't want him to fight. He wished he didn't have to. He could love this lass madly. Did he already? Was he willing to forget that her heart belonged to someone else? That her clan was the archrival of his?

He moved closer to her and she turned to face him fully. He wanted to kiss her, steal her from Kendrick's ghostly embrace and lay claim to her heart, her body. He wanted to bring her home and defy anyone who stopped him. "D'ye also see how difficult ye make it to withstand each blow?"

Her smile on him warmed. "I am unsure of what I see. There are many facets to you, Patrick. You're cheeky with a rakish charm I'm sure gets you out of trouble. You know the right words to say and the right way to look when you say them."

"Ye dinna believe I speak in earnest?" he asked bending his head to her, whispering along her temple, her ear. "Ye dinna believe that ye make me doubt everything I thought I knew?"

"Damn your silver tongue, rogue," she breathed out as his mouth descended on her and his arms closed around her waist, drawing her close.

He wanted to run his lips over every inch of her. For now, he basked in the sweetness of her mouth. She tasted like daisies and for the maddest of all his moments yet, he feared his heart might just be completely lost. He may have succumbed to the wild, uncontrollable beast that was love. It stripped him of everything and everyone but her, here in his arms.

Molding his lips to hers, he kissed her until she fell weak against him. Holding her up in the crook of his arm, he withdrew just enough to look at her, heavy-lidded, lips parted and red from his kiss. He wanted more of her. All of her. He cupped her bare nape in his hand and tipped her head to receive him more fully.

He swept his tongue over the warm caverns of her mouth in slow, salacious strokes that made her tremble against him. He didn't want to let her go.

But he had to. He had to remember who stood between them. Kendrick Fergusson. But first, he ran his tongue, his lips, and his teeth down the long column of her neck. He drew in her scent with a long, deep inhalation, and then stepped away.

For the first time in his life, words eluded him. He watched her recover, touching her fingers to her smiling lips. He waited for his heart to slow down before he opened his mouth to speak.

"Charlotte."

They both turned to the sound of Hendry's voice as he entered the hen house a moment after they stepped apart. Patrick was glad he was still a wee bit muddleheaded from kissing Charlie. It stopped him from leaping for Hendry's throat.

He smiled stiffly instead.

"Campbell. What a surprise." The peacock strutted forward, his golden hair matching the color of the haystack Patrick wanted to toss him into. "Charlotte, Father wants you at the breakfast table."

"Tell him I had to feed the hens and now I'm going to return to El—"

"Tell him yourself. 'Tis enough that I had to fetch you. I'll not be your messenger."

Charlie fisted her hands at her sides and stomped off.

"Hendry," Patrick called out, stopping him from following his sister out. "Share a word with me."

Before Hendry could refuse, Patrick flung his arm around his shoulder. He could kill the bastard right now, or at least break a few of his ribs. "I know aboot Kendrick Fergusson," he said close to Hendry's ear. "Ye're goin' to meet me back here later and tell me what ye did with the lad's body."

"I don't know what you're talking about." Hendry tried to break free, but Patrick held fast.

"Ye killed him. In Dumfries. Of what else do ye need remindin'?"

Hendry's color drained so quickly Patrick thought the sniveling worm would faint. "Who told you this? Charlie? She's a lying witch who will—"

Patrick squeezed Hendry's throat between his bicep and forearm and pulled him closer. "Ye're goin' to tell me everything I want to know or I'm goin' to tell yer faither that ye insulted m' Campbell kin in such a way that m' only recourse is to summon m' uncle, the Duke of Argyll, to Pinwherry."

"What do you want to know?" Hendry relented after a moment of stunned silence, red-faced and short of breath from Patrick's hold.

"Later." Patrick released him with a smack on the back. "First," he said, setting his gaze on the door and the house beyond. "I will see to yer sister."

He started out, then turned back. There was something he forgot to tell the worm. "If ye ever cause harm to Robbie Wallace again or his kin I'll snap yer neck in two. Understand?"

Something . . . Perhaps in Patrick's deadly gaze, or in his hands rolling into fists at his sides, compelled Hendry to nod and keep quiet until Patrick was gone.

Chapter Twenty-Three

"*D*uff." Elsie tugged on his sleeve beside her. "Tell Patrick one of the stories you told me while I was abed. I know! Tell him about when the Lamont brothers tried to rob you!"

Sitting across from her at the supper table, Charlie smiled. Elsie was well. Her eyes sparkled like sapphires in the firelight and even the bounce in her golden curls had returned. Her recovery had been swift after two cups of butterbur tea, taken as Patrick prescribed, over a few hours. Patrick had remained at Elsie's bedside with her the whole afternoon, making Elsie smile, as he was so wont to do with folks.

But neither of them could get her to confess the name of the man she'd been meeting each time Charlie and Duff had left Pinwherry. Charlie still found it difficult to believe. Shy, meek Elsie doing something so bold! Was she in love with her mystery man? She must be if she was willing to defy their father. What of her and Charlie's plans to leave? Charlie would find out. For now, she was thankful that Elsie was well and there was hope for her future—whether she spent it with Charlie or not.

Charlie hadn't stopped her when she'd insisted on leaving her bed tonight and dressing for supper, and Patrick had agreed with her decision. If Elsie felt well enough to move about, she should do so.

Sitting with her now, Charlie wanted to celebrate. Patrick had done it. He'd brought Elsie the correct remedy. He saved her life.

She turned to look at him sitting next to her, his profile etched in the hearth fire behind him. He lifted his cup to his mouth, and from behind the rim he watched her father and brothers the way a wolf watches its prey. Thanks to Duff, Patrick knew what they'd done to Kendrick and his disdain was evident in his sharp gaze on her father and his forced smile when Duff began his tale.

Was he going to do something about it? Would he come back for her and take her and Elsie with him to Camlochlin? Did she truly want to live where he lived? Could she bear being near him, hearing his laughter, watching him open his arms to another woman?

His questions about her love for Kendrick had made her uncomfortable. Not because she was ashamed for loving a memory, but because she knew it was hurting Patrick to hear it—and because she was no longer certain she was still in love with Kendrick.

Sensing her gaze, Patrick turned his head and winked at her.

Her heart flipped. so hard she nearly hiccupped. She wanted to smile at him but his attention slipped back to her family. She drenched her gaze in the shape of his lips, remembering how she'd surrendered to them. She'd thought about his kiss all day. Twice she had to ask her sister to repeat her query. She'd thought about his mouth, and his intimate gaze shrouded in the shadows of his lashes. She'd basked in his playful grins and the melodic lilt in his voice while he melted her sister right out of her socks. Charlie wasn't wearing any or she would have melted right along with her. She hadn't thought about him leaving. She hadn't thought of Kendrick. She only thought of kissing Patrick, of being swept up in his burly arms and looking into his meaningful gaze before he kissed her.

He'd answered her prayer and brought laughter to her amidst all the worry. She knew a part of him lived the life of a careless scoundrel with no regard for any noble ideals other than to kick the dust from his boots. But there was a deeper part of him who rushed to the aid of a child and baled Robbie Wallace's hay. For her. She didn't want him to go. He hadn't kissed her in the henhouse like he wanted to leave.

Ye dinna believe m' heart can be won then?

Could it? Did she want to be the one who did it? She hadn't discarded her plans with Elsie, but was it wise to live with him on his homestead if something meaningful between them could never be? He made her want something meaningful, something filled with physical, soul-stirring passion and life-changing love.

He leaned in and without taking his gaze from Duff and his tale, spoke quietly in her ear. "Are ye also rememberin' our kiss then?"

She blinked and looked into his eyes when he turned to her. "Our...?"

"...kiss," he whispered and quirked one corner of his mouth. "In the henhouse. All of them, in fact. They haunt m' thoughts."

"Patrick." Elsie tore his gaze away and Charlie's breath along with it.

Their kiss haunted him too? Was it possible?

"Have you ever met any Lamonts?" Elsie asked him.

"No' to m' recollection."

"Campbell." Charlie's father snatched his attention next. "Don't you think we've avoided the topic long enough?"

"The Lamonts?" Patrick asked him. His tone was razor sharp rather than confused.

"Not the Lamonts," her father said setting down his cup. "You spent many hours unsupervised with my daughter a day or so past. Hendry told me that after he allowed Charlotte to accompany you both to the village, you refused to let her return home. You sent Hendry away with the promise that if she accuses you of taking liberties with her, you would take her as your wife." His dark eyes settled on Charlie and glimmered with both hope and a warning to her to see it fulfilled. "Do I have it all correct, Campbell?"

Charlie bit her lip hoping Patrick would agree and not tell her father about *her choice* to stay with him. Her father would know her choices soon enough when she left with Elsie. If he thought there was even the slightest chance that given the *choice*, she might run away without securing a prosperous marriage, he'd lock her in her room.

"Nae. No' all of it," Patrick said leaning back in his chair.

She slipped her hand under the table and pinched his thigh.

He flinched but that was the only sign of his distraction. "But 'tis a minor detail so I willna dispute it."

"Was his message to me correct?" her father pressed.

"Aye, 'twas," Patrick told him. "Has an accusation been made?"

Her father looked at her, waiting for her to accuse him

of taking liberties with her so they could be forced to marry and seal a Campbell union. She suspected she could fall deeply in love with Patrick. But she didn't want his promises if they came with a pistol to his head.

"I have no accusation against him, Father."

His expression went cold. Charlie matched it and glared right back at him. She wouldn't lie, and she wouldn't be forced to marry, not even to Patrick Campbell.

Her father was angry. Let him be, she thought, and then realized her hand was still on Patrick's thigh.

She moved it quickly and caught the hint of a smile on his lips.

"Cunningham," he said while her father was still glaring at her. "Let's finish this discussion after I spend the day with Charlie tomorrow."

Charlie held her breath then cursed herself for doing it. When had she become like every other wench in every village, fawning all over the charming Highlander? So what if he was staying another day? What did it mean to her? If he refused to take her and Elsie to Camlochlin, she'd never see him again. If that was what he wanted, what could she do to stop it? But what if that *wasn't* what he wanted?

What exactly did he want? Charlie thought feeling a bit flushed. Another kiss? Or perhaps he thought to whisk her off to the Highlands? But what about Elsie? She'd never leave without her sister.

Her eyes darted to Duff, who remained curiously silent. So, he'd protect her from drunken patrons but his promise to their mother didn't matter when a prosperous union was at stake.

When he smiled at her, she looked away.

"You ask much of me, Campbell," her father said, pulling Charlie's attention back to him.

"Ye ask fer much in return," Patrick countered. "Did I mention that m' kin have good relations with the queen?"

Charlie didn't have to wait to exhale a full breath when her father went from angry to beaming.

Sold to the man with good relations with the queen!

Charlie didn't know which of the three men at the table she should glare at first, the confident one, the quiet one, or the one who sired her? She didn't count Hendry, who'd remained quiet and skittish throughout supper.

Her father deserved the most contempt, so she chose him. It wasn't that she'd never consider becoming Patrick's wife. Just the thought of being in his bed, carrying his bairns, made her belly twist. It was because Patrick could have been anyone. She was nothing more than prized chattel to her father. It had stopped breaking her heart years ago, but it had never stopped being mortifying.

"That is," Patrick said turning to her, "if Charlie will grant me her company."

"Of course she will!" her father shouted, smiling and lifting his cup again.

"She's..."

Charlie didn't hear what her father was saying. The choice was hers. "Aye," she told Patrick softly, "I will grant it."

He smiled at her and brushed his fingers over her thigh under the table.

His touch was as hot as flame, igniting her skin, her cheeks. His smile deepened on her, as if he found her flushed face endearing. "If Elsie is up to it," he said moving his hand away, "she may come as well. We'll likely need her help with the lads."

"Lads?" she whispered back.

"Nonie and her brothers," he clarified, turning back to her father.

Charlie's heart could not have gone any softer. He was going to take them all on an outing tomorrow? She could hardly sit still. Oh, Elsie had to be up to it.

"So then, 'tis settled!" Her father gleamed with satisfaction.

Patrick shook his head, traces of the smile he'd given Charlie still apparent on his face. "There's still much settlin' to be done. Fer now though, I'll see to other things."

Her father laughed. "Like getting the queen to attend your wedding. Do you think she would?"

Charlie stared at him wishing she could throw her cup at him. She wasn't even promised yet and he was already planning the wedding. He didn't care if she was embarrassed or hurt, or angry. He only cared that he would be gaining power with a Campbell union. Power he'd lost to the Fergussons.

Patrick didn't seem the least bit fazed by her father's boldness. He set his jewel-cut gaze on Hendry, who responded by trying to appear even smaller.

"She might."

Patrick waited by the henhouse for Hendry to arrive. He didn't doubt the worm would come. The queen? Patrick smiled in the waning moonlight. He enjoyed waving *that* carrot at Cunningham.

Hendry would do what Patrick wanted because he knew his father would kill him if he did anything to jeopardize a union with the powerful Campbells—who knew the queen.

Confident, Patrick leaned against the wall of the henhouse and whistled. Soon, he'd have what he wanted and could return Kendrick to his father. What would he do after that? He stopped whistling and looked up at the stars.

Never had there been a time that the prospect of bringing home a lass hadn't scared the hell out of him. Or back into him, as Mailie liked to tell him.

Bringing Charlie home didn't make him feel any different. Warnings had been going off in his head since he'd left Tarrick Hall. They'd grown louder when he'd kissed her this morning, more consistent this afternoon while he'd examined the tilt of her raven brow, the quirk of her full, ripe lips when he was supposed to be listening to Elsie. And tonight, amidst opposing wars taking place in his head about what he was doing, and why he was doing it, he'd made plans to spend the day with her tomorrow.

Charlie was what he was afraid of. She was the one who could harness him, the one for whom he'd give up everything.

But he continued to ignore all the warnings, no matter how loud they'd become, because the thought of never seeing her again scared him even more.

Chapter Twenty-Four

Charlie stepped out of the house and pulled her cloak around her shoulders. She knew Patrick stood alone by the henhouse, for she had seen him in the moonlight from her window. What was he doing out here alone, staring up at the night sky? Was he thinking about her? About going home to Camlochlin?

Brushing away a lock of hair that had slipped free of her snood, she set her eyes on him and started off in his direction.

Coming closer, she realized that he wasn't facing her. She stopped moving when she heard her brother's voice on the other side of him, concealed by Patrick's broad shoulders.

"You expect me to remember where I left his body five years ago?"

"Aye," Patrick growled at him, "and ye're goin' to bring me to him."

Charlie's heart pounded so hard she was sure they heard it. They were speaking of Kendrick. Oh, why had Duff told Patrick? Why on earth did Patrick want his body? Was he truly talking about digging Kendrick up? Why? What could he possibly want with a dead boy's bones? Dear God, was she truly thinking about Kendrick's bones? She felt ill, and for a moment, slightly light-headed. Her eyes stung behind her lids. She'd somehow always kept herself from imagining her beloved's still body. She'd always preferred to remember his bright, wide smile and sapphire-blue eyes shining in the sunlight, his messy curls alive with all the colors of autumn.

"Be ready to leave in the morn." Patrick's crisp voice broke through her thoughts.

"We won't find him!" Hendry argued weakly.

"We better."

When Patrick turned to leave him, Charlie didn't run for cover but stepped into the moonlight. She wanted answers and she knew she wouldn't get them if she didn't catch them red-handed.

Patrick saw her first and went still.

She wanted to run to him, or never move again. Perched at the edge of a cliff, she looked out at an unfamiliar view. Did she want to risk it all and leap off into his open arms and carefree grins? She'd almost convinced herself, up until a few moments ago, that winning his heart might be possible, even worth the risk.

"Have ye been here long, lass?" he asked, looking at her in the soft moonlight as if she were the only one here with him.

"Long enough," she told him softly. Long enough to step back from the edge.

"Then you heard this outlandish notion of his!" Hendry propelled himself at her. "He wants me to find Kendrick!"

She hated to admit it but Hendry was right. It was mad. She nodded, her gaze on Patrick was hard. "Why?"

Patrick finally acknowledged Hendry with a murderous glare and then returned his attention to her. "May we speak alone?"

"Tell him to cease this quest before he gets us all killed," Hendry muttered as he passed her and headed back for the house.

Alone, she tilted her head to Patrick and waited. What could he possibly want with Kendrick's body? What kind of wretchedness did he possess? She wanted to ask him. She had to know. "Please explain what your intentions are with Kendrick's body."

She could barely breathe. She didn't want him to be like the rest, with secret, sometimes nefarious motives. She wanted the man she'd seen at Nonie's and Elsie's bedside. The one who might be even better than Kendrick.

"He was verra dear to me, Patrick," she continued, trying to keep the swell of emotions this night had caused from erupting. "What could you possibly want with what remains of him? Why would you disturb his rest?"

Was it a play of the moonlight on his eyes that made them shimmer—or something else?

"He isna at rest, lass."

"What?" Now her eyes filled with tears. "Why would you say that? I know what my brothers did to him, but surely the Lord—"

He nodded in agreement but held up his hand to stop her. "He needs to be returned to his father."

She closed her mouth. His father? That was why Patrick wanted him? To return him to his father? She wanted to find relief in his explanation, but did he not understand who Kendrick's father was?

"You intend to carry the body of Cameron Fergusson's youngest son to his door?"

"Aye, lass."

She wiped a tear from her cheek. God help her, who was he beneath his wicked smiles and gallantry that came so naturally he didn't realize he possessed it?

"You're correct," she admitted. "He should be returned to his father. He should never have been taken. I fear... I fear though that when his father lays eyes on him, his hatred toward us will be rekindled. This time, he may not leave without killing all of us."

"He willna return here."

When had he come closer? His hand reached for hers. His fingers played across her knuckles like a sigh.

"How do you know?" she asked, looking up into his eyes, her fingers involuntarily closing around his.

"Charlie," he said, his voice breaking on a silken breath. "I... I know that any man who had his son returned would be thankful, no' vengeful. I will tell him yer kin helped me in m' endeavor. Cameron Fergusson willna return."

He sounded so certain. Did she dare trust him? It wasn't just her life in jeopardy but Elsie's, as well. If the Fergussons returned would Patrick help her family fight them? Did it matter? Kendrick should be returned to his family. She certainly wouldn't stand in the way of that.

"M' hope is to put an end to this feud." His breath above her head was warm and close.

"Why?" she asked tilting her head. "Why do you concern yourself with it?"

His mouth slanted into a tender smile she wanted to kiss. "D'ye think so little of me then that ye dinna believe I would care about such things?"

No! No, she didn't think little of him at all. She hadn't understood why he wanted Kendrick, but now it made sense. He *was* that caring, concerned man she had seen with

Nonie and Elsie. He *was* different from the others. After all he had already done, now he wanted to return her Kendrick to his rightful resting place and end the feud! Surely God had sent Patrick Campbell to her. She was glad she hadn't killed him that day at the river. She didn't know if she could love him the way she loved Kendrick. She was afraid she could love him even more. But she wanted time to find out. He made her want a family, a husband, a different life than the one she'd been planning for years. She didn't want him to go, but she wouldn't beg him to stay. Perhaps, with him, there was a better way to get what she wanted.

"You're not so terrible, Mr. Campbell," she said pushing up on the tips of her toes. She wanted to kiss him. To be devoured by a hunger in him only she could satisfy, but how different would she be from the others before her if she gave in to him so easily? She pressed her lips to his cheek instead. "Goodnight." Smiling, she stepped away.

When he snatched her wrist and pulled her back, she nearly wilted in his arms. But she wasn't like other lasses, and if she wanted him she had to stop behaving like them.

She watched his mouth descending on her, felt his breath, warm and shallow on her lips. She didn't want to fight it. She wanted to kiss him like this for the next fifty years, not for only a few moments, like Bethany. If his heart could be won, she would win it.

She let his mouth cover hers, and let her body tremble against him for just a moment before she was completely swept away, and then she severed their contact and slapped the same cheek she'd kissed.

"If you're leaving," she told him while he rubbed his face, "or if you're planning on marrying another before you take me and Elsie to Camlochlin, there can be no more kissing between us."

"Are ye blackmailin' me then?" he asked, one corner of his mouth lifting in an admiring grin.

"Don't be ridiculous." She smiled and turned for home. "I'm just looking out for myself. You're not going to be around much longer."

He didn't agree or dispute her claim. He remained silent while he picked up his steps and walked with her—long enough to make her worry a little.

"Ye're clever," he finally said, angling his head to aim a grin at her that sapped the strength from her knees.

She realized at that moment that one of her favorite things to do was walking with him. From that first night he'd followed her to Robbie Wallace's, and all the strolls since then. He stirred her insides and he made her laugh. She liked him. That's how he was winning her, whether he was trying to or not.

"But I'm no' goin' anywhere just yet, lass. And dinna ferget ye agreed on an outin' tomorrow."

"But what of Kendrick?" she asked him. Oh, but it felt so odd to speak of him to Patrick—to anyone. She hadn't done so in five years. "You told Hendry to be ready in the morn."

"Aye." His humor faltered in his voice. "I did."

"I had hoped to spend the day with you." She looped her arm through his and snuggled just a bit closer. She liked the height of him, the breadth of him beside her. "But I will live through the day without you."

He chuckled above her but then grew serious again. "'Twill be more like three or four days dependin' on how hard we ride the horses. Kendrick is in Dumfries."

She nodded her head, remembering her brothers being away about that long when the boy had gone missing. Four days might be a bit more difficult.

"I'll leave fer Dumfries tomorrow night," he announced. "Nothin' will change in a day."

She stopped and turned to him. "You would change your plan on my account?"

"M' plan?" he asked, his tone, somewhere between startled and somber. "M' plan hasna changed. The children should have a day away from their chores and I will need yer help with them."

He could take them to the river any time. No, Charlie thought, working to conceal her smile, this quick turnaround had to do with her. He probably didn't like what was happening to him where she was concerned. And she hoped something was indeed happening. He kissed her with meaning and looked at her with desire that was deeper than the purely physical. He liked her and he wanted to spend the day with her, as well. If he didn't want to admit it—well, she'd just make him.

"If that's all that bothers you," she said, "I will ask Duff to take your place. I'm sure the children won't mind with all the excitement. He took tender care of Elsie. You've nothing to worry about. Go bring Kendrick home."

"As ideal as that sounds," he countered with feigned regret. "Duff needs to come to Dumfries—in case Hendry has forgotten which way to go."

Charlie abandoned trying to conceal her smile and aimed it at him. She'd expected him to fight—even to the death as she'd told him. If his reasons for wanting her with him tomorrow were of a more personal nature rather than needing her help with the children, he wasn't going to admit it easily. His mind and his tongue were quick like his fists. He'd won. Tonight.

"Verra well then, Patrick." She picked up her steps and leaned in close again. "A battle to the end it shall be."

Chapter Twenty-Five

Riding away from Cunningham House, Charlie looked up at the sun and smiled. It was so lovely to be going on an excursion with Patrick and Elsie, out in the sunshine, free to do what they liked, that Charlie didn't care where they ended up.

She looked toward Patrick riding just ahead and caught him watching her over his shoulder. He winked and she blushed.

"Do you like him then?" Elsie cut her an eager glance as she kept pace beside her on their way to pick up the Wallace children.

"Aye, I do," she confessed, turning her loving gaze on her sister.

"What if he was a Fergusson? Would you still like him?"

Charlie turned to look at her. What an odd question to ask. Why would Elsie bring up the Fergussons now?

"Well?" her sister asked with an impatient sigh. "Would you? Still like him?"

Images of Kendrick flashed across Charlie's thoughts. Aye, she could still like a Fergusson, but it wouldn't be safe for any Fergusson to lose his heart to a Cunningham. And what about her poor mother? Wouldn't liking a Fergusson betray Margaret Cunningham? Oh, what did any of it matter? Patrick wasn't a Fergusson. "What is all this talk of Fergussons about, El? Has Duff been talking to you again about Kendrick?"

Elsie shook her head. "Nay, but I think you should hear what he would say to you about it." Without waiting for Charlie's reply, she kicked her horse's flanks and caught up to Patrick.

She hadn't minded when Patrick had agreed to let Duff accompany them. Her brother would have likely followed them anyway.

Feeling her brother's gaze on her, Charlie turned to look at Duff riding close by. He smiled.

"Do you truly expect forgiveness from me?" she asked quietly.

"Nay, I don't." He shielded his pewter eyes beneath his lashes. "I know what I did was beyond redemption. I live with it every day. I seek nothing from you. I would only have you know that I'm sorry for not saving him. I would have you know that."

Charlie had forgotten how Duff had looked as a boy. His laughter was a memory that had also faded since the year Kendrick had disappeared. Before that, he was good-natured and a pain in her neck, always teasing her about Kendrick—or how she chewed. Always hovering around her whenever she was close by, protecting her long before he'd promised their mother that he would.

"I miss my brother," she spoke before she could stop.

"So do I, Charlie." He raised his gaze to hers, his

dark hair snapping across his face in the morning breeze. "I lost something of myself that I can never gain back again."

Something in his confession pulled at her heart. Duff was sorry. Was it enough? "If you're certain you can never gain this part of yourself back," she told him, "then cease mourning it and find a way to live without it. If there is a way to gain it back, then find it."

He nodded at her and smiled. She smiled back and then was gone.

Charlie suspected that the only reason little Jamie was squealing was because his three older siblings were. She didn't care. He was adorable. They all were, hopping and clapping with flaxen curls tumbling around their faces when Patrick invited them to spend the day at the river.

The river! She could have kissed Patrick when he'd announced it.

"And." Patrick leaned in closer to Mary. "'Twill give ye some time alone with Robbie." His smiled widened into a furtive grin. "I have wee cousins back home. I know how precious time alone can be fer their parents."

Charlie listened, wondering what kind of childhood he'd had. Was he afraid of marrying and becoming a father with no more time to fulfill his own desires?

"Aye, to sleep," Mary slapped his arm with her apron when he cast her a doubtful look. "I haven't had a good night's sleep since Robert came along six years ago."

His grin widened and amusement flickered across the surface of his eyes. Blazes, Charlie thought looking at him, he certainly was the most charming of rogues. She turned away to return her smile to the children.

"Sleep then," he told Mary, "and dinna worry aboot yer

babes. There are enough of us to make sure none of them venture into the water alone."

"Aye," Charlie validated with a playful cut of her gaze. "Patrick sacrificed much to acquire all the aid he needed."

"She embellishes." Patrick flashed his dimple at her first and then at Mary. "It required no sacrifice at all to spend the day with yer bairns." He bent a bit closer to Mary's ear. "And with her."

Charlie perked her ear. Did he just say it was no sacrifice to spend the day with *her*? Then she'd been correct last eve! He'd known what she'd been fishing for and he hadn't given it. What made him finally give it now? Did she really care why? Her breath grew short. Before she had time to ponder why it made her heart fly, she looked up at him and smiled.

He winked in reply. He. Winked. Was that amusement making his green eyes dance? What in blazes did it mean? Was this more of their cat and mouse game? Was he teasing her?

Very well, she was up to it, and now that she knew his weakness, this battle she would win. Her smile remained intact when she spoke. "Why, Patrick, are you expecting Mary and me to believe that I might be taming your wild heart?"

He chuckled and looked up toward heaven but he had no immediate reply. Was she suggesting the idea that he could actually love a woman was too preposterous to believe? Or was she boldly challenging him to admit he was losing the fight? He was unsure. Charlie could see it in his eyes.

Before he formed a reply, she winked at him then ushered the children to make ready for their outing.

There was much weighing on Patrick's mind as he rode his horse toward the river Stinchar with wee Jamie in his lap, but hell the sun was warm, the cool breeze fragranced with wild primrose and fern, and the sounds of children's squeals filled his ears when they saw a roe deer watching them from the trees. He wanted to enjoy the day, not spoil it by thinking about what was happening to him. Charlotte Cunningham had found a way under his skin. Of course, he wanted to spend the day with her. Of course it had nothing to do with needing her help with the children. He'd taken his wee cousins swimming in the bay of *Camas Fhion-nairigh* many times without incident. But he hadn't told her that. Hell, but she was a spirited lass, always challenging him. She seemed to know him better than he knew himself—a least as of late. He was losing his heart to her and she knew it and enjoyed torturing him with that knowledge. He wanted nothing more than to take her in his arms, but she withheld her kisses with blackmail.

He smiled while they traveled a path nestled into the twists and shade of the riverbank until they came to a small clearing surrounded by tall alder trees and downy birch. If she wanted him to stay so badly, he would, because well, he'd lost his damn mind.

Could he win her from Kendrick?

Tomorrow. He'd worry about it tomorrow.

The river flowed downstream like jewels glistening in the sun. It was here that she had stoned him in the head. Mayhap, she'd done more damage than he realized.

They stopped at the river's edge and after helping the children out of the four saddles, unpacked the large bag tied to Patrick's horse.

"Did you know this is one of my favorite places?"

He turned from ordering Jamie to stay close and offered Charlie a smile that was filled with more tenderness than he'd intended. Damn him, he'd become as soft as his cousins.

"I didna know that," he replied, taking note of the fullness of her coral lips and the sun in her dark eyes. "I'll make certain to bring ye here more often."

"Oh," she asked, her inky brow cocked. "You're staying then?"

"I might," he told her unfolding a large woolen blanket, which the children jumped on the instant it hit the grass. "If 'twill earn me a kiss, I'd consider it. What d'ye think, children? Should Charlie let me have a kiss?"

"Ew!" Andrew balked and made gagging noises.

"Why would you want to kiss her?" asked Robert.

"Oh, Robert," Elsie said helping Patrick unpack their lunch of black bread, fruit, various cheeses, and dried mutton. "In just a few short years you'll be thinking of nothing *but* kissing."

Patrick laughed at Charlie's suspicious glance at her sister and at the lad's vehement denial. He thought about how the affliction had only become worse for him since meeting Charlie. He had trouble taking his eyes off her when she bent to sit on the blanket and fit Nonie into her lap. Would she make a good mother to his bairns?

Damnation but he was willing to remain here for a kiss from her! For how long? What about Camlochlin? Would he take her and Elsie home? What about all his secrets? What about Kendrick's death?

"Can we go in the water, Patrick?" Andrew asked tugging on his hand and thankfully pulling him from his troublesome thoughts.

"We can do whatever ye like, lad." He tossed a pear to Robert. The lad caught it and sank his teeth into it.

"Are there frogs here?" Jamie lost all interest in eating and leaped up on his chubby legs, his wide blue gaze already searching the water's edge.

"Of course," Patrick answered feigning incredulity. "D'ye think I'd bring ye to a place where there are no frogs?"

The lad shook his head and aimed a smile at him that damned near melted Patrick's heart. He'd miss these babes when he left.

And what in blazes was he to do about Duff? His cousin lived with a great shame and bringing him home would likely bring shame to Will, as well. Still, Duff's life would have been very different if he'd been raised with his father in Camlochlin. Mayhap it was time for Will to face the consequences of his actions.

He sat on the blanket with the others and ate, refusing to darken the day with things he couldn't solve at present.

Later, they took the children to the water's edge and kicked at the small waves, splashing one another and laughing. They searched for frogs and helped Nonie pick daisies for her hair, and all the while Patrick's gaze followed Charlie, his heart delighting in the way she came alive in her freedom, away from Cunningham House. Unlike her sister's cumbersome wardrobe, Charlie's finely spun skirts lifted on the breeze and danced around her bare toes. She wore no flowery band above her brow to hold back her loose hair but kept the lush tresses tucked behind her ears with the aid of sprigs of elderberry. She was like something out of a fairy tale, both earthy and ethereal. Her eyes were lightly lined in kohl to accentuate their shape and the intensity of her gaze. Each time it met his, he felt as if he'd been struck in the belly.

The children finally grew sleepy by midafternoon and fell asleep sprawled on the blanket.

Looking at them, Patrick decided the day couldn't get any better—unless, of course, he could find a way to be alone with Charlie.

"Charlie," Duff said amidst the chattering birds over head, "did Patrick tell you that he knows my father?"

"Nay, he didn't." Charlie's smile faded when she looked at Patrick, misgivings replacing her pleasant mood. "What else haven't you told me?"

Chapter Twenty-Six

Charlie didn't know what to think of Patrick's claim that he knew Duff's true father, Will MacGregor. Will MacGregor of *Skye* to be precise—of those MacGregors who were kin to the Fergussons, making them kin to Duff. What did her brother think of this news that he'd killed his relative?

She looked at him sitting across from her on Patrick's blanket with Elsie's golden head resting on his arm. The haunting shadows darkening his gaze while he looked toward the river were proof enough of his shame. He'd lived with it for so long, it had become a part of who he was.

"Duff?"

He blinked and looked down at his knees and not at her.

"I don't know if it will help you or not but you have my forgiveness."

Elsie smiled and squeezed their brother tighter. "I told you she would."

Duff looked up from beneath his lashes and nodded at

Charlie, a trace of his loving smile tugging at his lips. "It helps."

She leaned in and flung her arms around his neck. Tentatively at first, his arm slipped around her, and then he drew her in and kissed her hair beneath his chin. Oh, she'd forgotten how much she'd missed him. She was overcome with how good it felt to throw off that burden of anger and began to weep.

She let go of him and rose to her feet. She didn't want to cry like some blathering fool and wake the children.

"I need to stretch my legs," she told them and walked off before she lost all control of her emotions.

Duff had a family somewhere else, a father, brothers, and cousins. Would any of them ever forgive him? She did and it made her feel weightless on her feet. She didn't know whether she would laugh or cry if she opened her mouth.

She almost reached the edge of the river when she felt someone come up behind her. She turned to see Patrick.

He crooked his mouth into a soft half-smile. "I needed to stretch m' legs too."

With the power to drag her deepest desires to the surface, he was the last person she wanted to see—and the only one she prayed would never leave.

She wasn't completely certain when it had begun, but he had somehow managed to penetrate every wall she'd ever built in defense of the men she knew and the ones who would never be. She'd thought he was like the rest, but he was so much more. He radiated light like the sun and refreshment like a cool breeze on a summer day. She enjoyed spending time with him, sharing in his carefree laughter and the rapture of their stolen kisses—kisses neither one could forget.

He tempted her to want more than the life she'd planned. He sparked an unfamiliar hope that more was possible.

She admired the strength it took him to deny his feelings and live a life bound to none. But that strength was beginning to get on her last nerve. He knew Duff's father and he hadn't told her. She wanted to trust him because she was falling in love with the stubborn Highlander, but his keeping such important information from her made her feel uneasy. What else did he keep from her?

"I didna tell ye," he said as if reading her thoughts like an open scroll on her face, "because I thought Duff should know before anyone else. 'Tis aboot him and his kin."

Charlie stared at him not knowing what to say and not knowing if it was his words or the way he looked at her while he spoke them that rendered her mute. She liked the compassion she saw in his eyes. His smile might be careless but his heart beat with the steady drum of an ideal he claimed too antiquated for the likes of him. It was what every other man had lacked. Compassion.

"I suspected he was Will's son even before Hendry told me," he continued and took her hand to walk with her along the bank. "After yer show of loyalty to yer brother's secret in the henhouse that day, I knew ye would understand m' reason fer not tellin' ye."

"I do," Charlie told him, looking down at their entwined fingers. She didn't pull away, too lost in the intimacy of his touch to separate them. She already loved walking with him. This subtlest of claims on her being thrilled her to her bones.

"What about the MacGregors?" she asked in an effort to keep her mind from abandoning her.

His hand grew warmer and a bit moist. He turned to offer her a casual smile. "What aboot them?"

"I understand why you didn't tell me about Duff's father,

but why didn't you tell me you knew the relatives of the Fergussons?"

He leaned in closer and dipped his face to hers, his vivid green eyes piercing and powerful, his smile slow and filled with natural charm. "Would ye have me tell ye everything I know?"

She stared at his full, red lips while he spoke, wishing he would press them to hers. She raised her gaze, taking her time to admire the fine sculpt of his nose. When she reached his potent gaze, she stared into his eyes and answered with a challenging smile. "Would you tell me?"

He didn't flinch but his thumb moved over hers. "Ye make me want to."

Was he sincere? Charlie wanted to believe so. It was a good start. Much more than she'd expected.

When he picked up his steps again and began telling her more, Charlie's emotions roiled within her— disappointment that he wasn't going to kiss her. (Why would he after she slapped him?) And elation that he was telling her more.

"I didna know aboot Kendrick," he told her while they walked beneath tall ash and beech, with the winding river running beside them. "I didna know the connection, so there was no reason to mention it."

She believed him. She had no reason not to. She couldn't fault him for any of his decisions. She likely would have done the same.

"Do you think Duff will want to go to Skye after what has happened?" she asked him as they rounded a bend and came upon a roe deer stopping for a drink. It fled even as Charlie smiled at it.

"I didna think he should at first," Patrick continued, "but the choice should be his."

Charlie looked at their hands again and then up at his handsome profile against the backdrop of trees and sky, his bronze hair ablaze in the sun. "Is it many days' ride to Camlochlin?"

He shook his head and set his gaze on the river. "'Tis no' too far."

She had the urge to smile at him—and perhaps kick him in the kneecaps. "Does it frighten you to think about me going there?"

"Why would it?" he asked with a suggestive quirk of his lips, and finally slipping her a side gaze.

"Because you think I will want to be with you."

He turned to face her fully. Sensuality deepened the green of his eyes and softened his mouth, making her feel less in control of her senses. "And ye willna want that?"

"Nay, I won't," she told him, managing a haughty tilt of her nose. "I don't want a husband. How many times must I remind you?"

"I'm known to be dense," he answered pulling her by the hand closer against him. "So ye're tellin' me that if I asked fer yer hand, ye'd refuse?"

"That's what I'm telling you."

His low, masculine laugh sent a tingle of fire down her spine. She pulled away, letting go of his hand at the same time.

"You're the kind of man who gets what he wants," she said, her eyes shining like polished onyx while his laughter waned into a smile. "Is it hard not having me?"

He stopped smiling altogether and reached her in two steps. "Aye, 'tis." He pulled her into his arms, staring into her eyes as if daring her to stop him. She didn't. She let his mouth cover hers with full, lush dominance. His arms closed around her and dragged her closer as his kiss deepened and she went weak in his embrace.

He kissed her with slow, titillating abandon, his mouth moving over hers with masterful leisure. He rubbed his palms over the swell of her buttocks, making her want to wedge her hips against his and feel his surging power. She opened again and again to his plundering tongue, running her palms down the sides of his face. She wanted him to never let her go, to kiss her just like this until their days ran out.

"Patrick," she breathed out on a lusty sigh, breaking their kiss. She wouldn't tell him what her heart was shouting. Proclaiming her love for him was the worst thing she could do.

"We should get back," she said against his lips, plump and red from so much kissing.

She leaned against his chest, drawing on her last reserves of energy to straighten up. "Duff will be looking for us."

He didn't try to stop her when she turned and started back toward the others. She wished he would have. She wished he didn't care if Duff found them locked in another embrace and accused them before her father so that they had to wed.

But apparently he did care.

She turned the bend and waved at Elsie in the distance. And what about her sister? Who was Elsie's mystery man? Charlie had to find out. Did this man know of Elsie's ailment? Did he plan on taking care of her?

"Yer brother wasna lookin'."

She glanced over her shoulder at Patrick coming up behind her and then returned her gaze to the blanket and to Duff sitting with the children gathered around him.

Duff had been following her to taverns. He likely knew about her thievery and visits to the Wallaces. "'Tis odd," she said softly as Patrick came up beside her. "He never let me out of his sight when one of my father's husband-hopefuls tried to court me. Yet he would trust *you* alone with me." She cast Patrick a curious glance. "Why do you suppose that is?"

He flashed her a guileless smile. "My endearing qualities?"

She rolled her eyes at him but had to laugh. He certainly lacked no confidence in himself.

"That," he continued as they walked, "and because I asked him if I could."

She slowed her pace and his as well when she pulled on his léine. "Could what?"

He looked at her and his smile warmed into something more meaningful. "Court ye, lass."

Chapter Twenty-Seven

They remained at the river for another pair of hours, picking berries, skipping rocks, and catching various bugs.

Patrick no longer questioned his sanity. He'd known he lost it days ago. He was surprised though at how quickly it had abandoned him. Enough to admit to her that he'd asked Duff for his permission to court her. Whatever it meant as far as his heart went, she knew it now too. He was losing fast.

Instead, he reveled in the children's laughter. They took turns riding on his shoulders or tackling him when he took a moment from their exuberant energy to rest. When they weren't climbing on him, they were begging Duff to spin them in circles or sparring with him with short branches. Jamie, small as he was, possessed an extra store of fearless bravado while he swung his thin "sword" at Duff's kneecaps. Charlie's brother appeared happier than Patrick had seen him so far. It seemed Charlie's forgiveness had given him some of the redemption he needed.

Patrick watched Charlie and Elsie traipsing through the

grass, hot on Nonie's heels while she chased a yellow butterfly, and he wondered what his life would be like with them in it. What would it be like to have bairns of his own? He'd never thought about being a father before he met Duff—and the facts of what Patrick could have left in his wake became clear. Or was it Charlie who stirred in him this deeply rooted desire to sire a child? If he decided to bring her to Camlochlin would his kin accept her? Could they forgive the Cunninghams for what they'd done to the son of Isobel Fergusson's favorite brother?

Soon it was time to bring the children back to their parents. He hated to see the day end, but he was ready to find Kendrick and bring him back to his father.

Any decisions and confessions to be made after that could wait.

He was stuffing leftovers into his saddlebag when he heard a woman shouting in the distance.

"Mary?" Charlie dropped the blanket she was folding and took off.

Hell. It *was* Mary. Patrick left what he was doing and pointed to Elsie. "Keep the babes here with ye. Let no' one oot of yer sight."

He ran, hearing Duff doing the same. What had happened to make Mary run all the way here? It had to be Robbie. Hell. Patrick hoped it wasn't Robbie.

"'Tis Robbie!" Mary confirmed by crying out as they grew closer. "My Robbie is dead!"

Elsie's breath had grown short soon after Mary's arrival. Duff returned her to Cunningham House with strict instructions on how to prepare her butterbur tea.

For a few moments on the trip back Patrick thought about leaving. He'd spent the day with these babes, watching them laugh and play. Now, he was going to have to watch them weep for their father.

But that thought didn't last long before he felt thankful that he was here with them. That Charlie was here and Mary wasn't alone. They'd help this family through it.

He still didn't know what had happened. He learned from Mary between her sobs, that her husband had simply collapsed. He'd cried out and clutched his chest and then fell to the floor dead.

According to her, he was still there. In the kitchen, at the foot of his chair.

When they reached the house, Patrick helped Mary and the children dismount and then informed Charlie that he was going inside. "Keep them oot here with ye fer a bit, aye, lass?"

She nodded and gathered Mary and the children around her when she sat on the grass.

Patrick entered the house and hurried to the kitchen. He pushed the table away and bent to Robbie's body. There was a chance he was still alive. Patrick pressed his ear to Robbie's chest, listened, and then cursed the booming silence. He didn't want the children to see their father this way, so he fit his arms under Robbie's shoulders and knees and lifted him up. He carried him into the backyard and set him down gently on the grass. Damnation, he thought, while he straightened and headed for a line of fresh linens blowing in the breeze. How was this family going to survive without a husband and father to see to them?

He yanked on a bedsheet, pulling it from the line, and covered Robbie's body with it. He would enlist Duff's help to bury him tomorrow.

When he returned to the kitchen, he pressed his hands to the table and let his head sink between his shoulders. He remained that way while a sickening wave of heat coursed through him and stole his breath.

He thought of the babes outside the next door. Of Nonie and her nightmares, spurred by Hendry's punishment of her father. He closed his eyes in defense of the burning sensation behind them.

"Patrick?"

He opened his eyes and saw Charlie standing across the table, her large eyes glistened with unshed tears in the candlelight.

"Mary asks that you tell them. She cannot."

He shook his head, afraid to speak and hear the quaver in his voice.

"I will help you, Patrick," she said, stepping around the table and reaching for his arm. "Come, Mary needs us."

He ground his jaw and bit out an oath under his breath. He wasn't a champion…a hero. He'd never wanted this kind of weight on his shoulders.

"Patrick."

He nodded and pushed off the table. He'd let his heart open to this family. Nonie and her brothers had snatched it when he wasn't paying attention.

When he stepped outside, they ran to him. He sat on the small stair at the entrance and closed his arms around Nonie and Jamie when they crawled atop his knees.

"I have sad news fer ye, children. Now I know ye're just babes, but yer mother is goin' to need ye to be strong fer her, aye?"

When they all nodded, he looked up at Charlie and grinded his jaw. She offered him the scantest of smiles. It gave him the strength he needed to continue.

The children didn't cry as much as he'd feared and he suspected they didn't fully understand. He carried Nonie and Jamie to the kitchen where Charlie began preparing their supper.

Dusk had settled and no one ventured into the yard. The children could say their farewells at the gravesite in the morn. There was no need for them to see him under a bedsheet.

"We'll stay here with ye tonight, Mary," Patrick told her after the children were asleep and the house was quiet. "Yer husband will have a proper burial tomorrow. We'll see to it."

Mary nodded and wiped her nose. "I want to say farewell to him now. Take me to him, please."

Patrick rose from his chair and after a glance toward Charlie, lit a lantern, and escorted Mary outside.

When Robbie's covered body came into view, Mary wept and held onto Patrick's arm. He helped her go to her husband and then backed away from her when she fell to her knees.

Illuminated by his lantern set beside her, Patrick watched her. This was what love did. It broke a person to pieces. He'd seen it before. His father had nearly lost his mind when his beloved Isobel suffered a particularly bad breathing attack and she turned blue-gray in his arms. And again when his aunt Davina had become ill and his uncle Rob carried her frail body around the halls expressing his love in quiet whispers breathed into her hair. No one in Camlochlin had believed he'd recover without her.

But watching Mary speak her soft farewells to her husband pierced him in the heart like nothing before it.

He heard Charlie's approach and turned to kiss her brow when she rested her head on his arm. Sharing this moment with her felt deeper and more intimate than anything he'd ever felt before. It made his hands shake and his guts ache.

They remained silent while Mary wept and finally bid her last farewell.

He stepped back when Charlie gathered her friend up and helped her back to the house.

Patrick watched them go, the world, as he knew it, shifting from its place. How could he leave now? Mary's rent didn't get paid even *with* a husband. How would she manage all their lives on her own? How would Charlie ever leave if she gave every coin she had to help?

What the hell had he gotten himself into? It was his fault for staying so long and getting attached to these people.

He'd always run from the duty of being responsible for others. He had no idea how to react to the change. He could flee now—just run to his horse and go, leaving this all behind. Or he could return to the house and face the challenge head-on. His decision wouldn't only affect the six people inside, but Cameron's son would never be returned to him if Patrick left. Duff would never know his father, or Will, his son. But nothing made his decision easier than the thought of what Hendry would do to these women. To the babes.

He straightened his shoulders and moved to stand over Robbie Wallace. "I'll take care of things, Robbie. Ye rest now."

His hands were still shaking as he headed back.

Chapter Twenty-Eight

Charlie left the house and drew in a fresh breath of air. She had to get away, just for a few moments. She'd sat with Mary in her small bedroom off the kitchen and soothed her for hours. Her heart broke for her friend and she suffered through the same fears about Hendry that Patrick had. She'd thought about it all night. She needed to be outside, to smell the night blossoms and gaze at the stars, remembering that there was a Master Plan for everything.

She looked toward the fields in the distance, dipped softly in moonlight, and started toward them.

She hadn't seen Patrick for hours and guessed he slept in the chair by the children's bed. Just as well. She didn't want to saddle him with her troubling thoughts. Why hadn't he left? Any other man would have taken off by now.

She was halfway across the field, thinking about how thankful she was that he was still here when the sound of a horse's hooves pounding the earth was suddenly upon her.

"Hell, lass!" Patrick tugged on his reins, stopping his mount just inches away, and swung his leg over the saddle. "I nearly rode straight into ye!"

She opened her mouth in defense and then shut it again when he dropped to his boots before her, close enough to overpower her senses. The scent of the earth wafted off him and saturated her, the touch of his breath across her cheek wielding a flame across her spine.

"Where are ye off to this time?" he demanded, his smoldering gaze burning holes in all her defenses.

She held herself rigid, steady. When had she given him this much power over her?

"I don't like your tone." She stepped around him and continued on her way.

He caught up, leaving his horse where he'd stopped it, and blocked her path. "Ye dinna like the tone of concern?"

"I've been coming out here alone at night for years, Patrick." She tried to step around him but he moved with her and she walked into his chest. "I won't stop because of your disapproval," she said breaking free.

"I dinna disapprove of yer courage and steadfastness to see to yer sister's needs and risk yer life fer a year and a half," he told her. "I just dinna think ye use enough caution in yer much sought after freedom, and it concerns me. It might no' seem as dangerous here as 'tis in other places, but have ye fergotten aboot the Dunbars' attack?"

What other places? Charlie wondered. Did he mean wherever he thought she was going when she left Pinwherry behind? Was he telling her that it wasn't Camlochlin? The way he'd spoken of it that day in Robbie and Mary's kitchen made her imagine an impenetrable fortress far into the clouds, hidden from the world. No doubt there, where values and integrity were nourished, a lass was in no danger walking alone at night. His *other places* didn't include his home.

She tried not to let her disappointment escape her lips when she replied. "I wouldn't wander off in places I don't know. And of course, I remember the Dunbars' attack. I'm not an imbecile." She gave him a pointed stare and rested her palms on her hips. "Do *you* remember the man I took down in Blind Jack's?"

"Och, hell, ye're stubborn."

She moved around him again and felt a smile creep along her lips in the dim light. She concerned him. All hope of going to Camlochlin wasn't gone.

"Where are you coming from?" she asked him when he appeared at her side. "Are you going to Dumfries to get him?"

"Nae. Kendrick..." he said and paused to give her a pointed gaze, "...will have to wait. Accordin' to Duff, Hendry has disappeared."

"Disappeared?"

Patrick held his arms out. "'Tis what I was told. He left sometime this morn and hasna returned."

"He doesn't want to bring him back," she muttered in a low voice. Hendry was so much like their father. "Why would he want to help you? He —" He'd been to the house? "How is—"

"Elsie is well," he told her. "I checked on her first."

She could just make out his irresistible grin under the stars.

"In fact, she is the reason I went back. 'Twas late and I saw no reason to wake ye. Even if Hendry hadn't run off, I would no' have gone to Dumfries tonight but would have returned to ye."

He'd gone to check on Elsie? He would have returned to

her? Blazes, how was she supposed to resist falling in love with him? But did he love her? Why would he? What made her different from the others? Mayhap she was no different at all.

"I wasn't asleep," she said softly, too weary to think on it all now. "Mary fell asleep a short time ago. I just needed some air."

Patrick turned and whistled for his horse. The beast came without hesitation. Charlie wished her horse would do the same, but she guessed Patrick needed his ride always ready to make quick escapes. She didn't.

She watched him pull something from his saddlebag and then turn back to her holding up the folded blanket. "Just us this time."

Her heart went warm and when he moved closer and closed his arm around her shoulder, she sank into his strong arm and rested her head on his chest.

"Are ye cold, lass?"

She closed her eyes, loving the sound of his voice, the feel of his arm around her, his body warming her. "Nay, I'm not cold."

They walked that way together across the field to the heather-lined muirs beyond. She likely wouldn't have come this far alone in the dark. Traveling to pubs in other villages was a necessity. She'd had no choice. Venturing so far off for pleasure was different. But Patrick was here and she felt safe.

In fact, she felt every concern melt away when a cool breeze filled her lungs with the fragrance of heather. Shafts of waning moonlight speared the gossamer mist drifting across the muirs and fell on pools of silvery-purple blossoms and glistening dewdrops.

She'd seen the heather muirs in daylight, but never at

night. It was a place taken from her dreams and spread out before her. Oh, but she was glad that places like this truly existed in the world she knew.

She drew in a deep breath, letting it fill her, cleanse her, and then looked up to smile at Patrick. "I feel alive again."

He looked into her eyes for a moment, without speaking a word, and if Charlie didn't know any better, which she didn't, she'd have thought he was gazing at her as if he loved her. She hoped he'd tell her something that would convince her that a future with him was possible. But he stepped away and unfolded the blanket.

With a snap, he set it atop the heather and offered her a seat on the billowy wool. He sat beside her and spoke softly against her ear. "It has been a difficult evenin'. Take yer rest here in m' arms."

Charlie was tempted to weep—and for so many reasons. For Mary and her bairns. For herself if she couldn't do enough to claim this man's heart. Oh, how could she have let herself fall in love with a beautiful scoundrel among women? But that wasn't the Patrick she had come to know. Of course, he knew all the right things to say and if they didn't work, his easy, inviting smile usually did. But that was only one layer of him. He had many. And Charlie wanted to peel them all away until she reached his heart.

She sank into his embrace and let him hold her with nothing between them but the fragranced air.

"The world," he finally said against her forehead, "is no' yer responsibility. Sometimes, ye canna help everyone. The weight of it will become too heavy."

She tilted her face to his. "I know I cannot help everyone, but I will help everyone I can. How is doing that too much weight to carry?"

"I dinna know, but I—"

"Is that what you truly believe, Patrick?"

He exhaled a heavy breath above her and seemed to be pondering his words before he spoke them. "We are verra different, Charlie." She was everything he wasn't, and everything he wanted to be. "Ye care fer all, while I care fer few."

She blinked. Was he telling her...?

"Ye bein' among the few, of course."

She let out a soft breath she didn't realize she was holding. He cared for her. He wanted to court her. What did it mean? What did it mean for a rogue? Had she won his heart?

She smiled up at him, hoping he could see her and how happy he made her in the moonlight and mist.

"I know many but I don't like them all," she assured him.

"And me?" he fished with humor lacing his voice.

Goodness, but he always made her smile.

"I like you. Of course. I *wouldn't* like you," she added lifting her hand to his bristled cheek, "if you were an uncaring lout. You have proven to me with Nonie, and Elsie, and even Duff that you're not." She ran her thumb across his bottom lip. "You're more like your Sir Gawain than you realize, Patrick. Does that trouble you so?"

"Ye trouble me, lass," he said softy, his breath falling on her chin. "Ye, and what ye're doin' to me."

"What am I doing?" she whispered, angling her head to meet his hovering mouth.

"Ye're changin' m' world."

She had no time to react to his declaration. His mouth descended on hers with the same breathless urgency she felt. She had no time to think, only feel, thrill, exalt in his touch, his tongue.

He cupped her face in his hands, deepening their kiss and sending wicked fires down her spine. When he drew her down, she didn't object. The soft heather felt like clouds beneath her back. Patrick's body was much harder above. She knew it was a dangerous position to be in with him, but she didn't care. She didn't care about teasing him with what he couldn't have. She wanted to give him all.

His bristled jaw scratched at her face while he moved his lips over hers, his tongue taking the deepest corners of her mouth. She squirmed, wanting more and not knowing what to do about it. He groaned at her movement beneath him and slid his hands down her neck and over the mound of her breast. He made her forget Kendrick's kiss, his quiet, unsure hands, as fire shot through her and she had the urge to sit up and tear Patrick's clothes away...or run.

She did neither but let the sensation of his rough hand thrill her. His touch tightened her nipple. It pushed upward through her gown, aching, aching for more. His fingers found it and for a moment so agonizing, Charlie nearly cried out, he dipped his face and closed his lips around the taut bud.

Lights, in hues painted silver and purple, burst before her eyes, while deep crimson ignited her nerve-endings.

He made her feel wicked, like some wild thing he'd caught and was about to conquer. And she couldn't wait. She tugged at his shirt and he at her skirts. Her body pained her somewhere below her navel, for something she wasn't quite sure of.

She'd spoken to Mary, briefly, about the art of love-making, but they ended up giggling through most of it. Once, during one of her visits to a tavern not far from here, she'd seen a serving girl pull up her skirts and straddle a customer in his seat.

She thought about straddling Patrick. Was she so bold? Nay! She shook her head then drew her lower lip between her teeth. Oh, to hell with logic, she thought while flames scorched her blood. Instinctually, she jutted her hips upward then pulled on his shirt again. She arched her back when he moved his face to the valley between her breasts and pulled at the laces of her hand-sewn corset with his teeth. They came undone with one last tug and her corset sprang away from her bosom.

She lay there, exposed to his hungry gaze and ready to surrender all.

Chapter Twenty-Nine

$\mathcal{P}$atrick's heart battered against his ribs while he gazed down at her, the bonnie curve of her jaw caught in slivers of moonlight, her black hair spread out like a nimbus around her face—the face any goddess would envy, and the heavy rise and fall of her bare breasts, their erect nipples reaching for his mouth. His blood rushed through his veins, the way it did before a fight. She intoxicated him, filled him with desire to take her, to fill his days and nights with her, and only her, to make her feel alive every day.

A wave of nerves washed over him, and for an instant he felt like a fresh young lad. He settled himself quickly enough and yanked his shirt over his head.

He wanted to devour her. But one didn't devour perfection, one lavished in it.

"Ye honor me, lass," he whispered, lowering his body over hers.

"Oh, Sir Gawain," she replied softly, closing her arms

around his neck and dipping back her head. "You and your dusty old ideals."

Hell, she made him laugh, even now, when he was thinking about ravishing the throat she offered. "That would make ye m' crone."

She laughed with him but pinched him on the side. He caught her wrist and held it over her head while he captured her laughter with a kiss.

He loved kissing her. Her plump lips yielded to him with just enough resistance to make him snap. She matched him in fervor, not backing down when he spread his tongue over hers or paused to nibble her lips before returning like a starving waif.

And to think, she would have kept this from him if he'd decided to leave. She was clever. For he did not think he could live without ever kissing her again.

She groaned into his mouth and he went hard against her thigh.

When she tried to push him off, he feared he'd gone too fast. He rolled off her and to his surprise and delight she rolled on top of him and sat up, straddling him.

Patrick had known from early on that if he'd had his way with her she wouldn't be afraid. She was like a wild mare, her mane falling around her shoulders, her gaze languid, and her breasts dangling in front of him. He leaned up and took one into his mouth, sucking her and laving over her sensitive bud with his tongue.

When she remained stiff atop him, he realized, smiling on his way to her throat, she didn't know what to do.

It shook him to his core that this glorious maiden would offer herself to him. What had he done to win a heart such as hers?

"We're goin' to have to marry," he teased lightly while

he ran his palms down her back. He cupped her firm, round buttocks and dragged her over the length of his upright cock, awaiting freedom from his breeches.

After a moment of surprise, she smiled and closed her eyes and then moved over him like a burning flame. "We don't *have* to marry."

She leaned down close to his mouth, still moving, rubbing her hot crux up and down him until he thought he would burst. "'Tis not too late to stop."

She ceased her movements and was ready to swing her leg over him when he sat up, took her in his arms, and switched places with her. "'Tis fer me, lass," he said, leaning down to kiss her.

When she made no protest, he shifted and tugged at his belt and breeches. She pulled at the laces in the back of her skirt and wriggled free beneath him.

"Will it hurt?" she asked, sounding like wings on the wind.

"Aye, would ye have me stop?"

"Nay, don't stop. Am I a fool, Patrick?" she bid him, going breathless when he dipped his mouth to her neck.

"I hope so, love," he murmured and then ran his tongue down the puckered flesh of her breast. "This madness is no' something I want to suffer alone."

"Poor rogue," she cooed, running her soft palms over his back. "How difficult this must be for you."

He chuckled and kissed her taut nipple then leaned up and looked into her eyes. "'Twill likely be more difficult fer *ye*." He pushed her legs apart with his knees. She gasped at the unyielding lance poised above her entrance. "But dinna fear," he continued in a husky whisper. "I know what I'm doin'."

But he didn't. He knew nothing about making love to a

lass who meant more to him than a bed, his next meal, or any subsequent empty adventure.

Her naked body swathed in moonlight made him feel untried, unsure, and clumsy for the first time in years.

He would learn her, he thought, resting his rigid body atop her. He would not plunder her but proceed with care and caution to cause her as little pain as possible. He reached his fingers to her lips and glided them to her chin, down her neck, kissing where he touched. He would learn what pleased her. He inhaled her scent and let it stir the scalding cauldron deep in the pit of his belly. His body burned, and his heart with it as he fired a path with his tongue, his teeth, between her breasts—over them, drawn by her firm, erect nipples.

His touch was the perfect combination of skill and raw sensuality. Charlie could do nothing more but be ravished by him, forgetting, for the moment, the thought of his daunting erection so close.

She'd never done anything like this before. She never thought she would. Not only was she lying in the heather muirs with nothing covering her but the moonlight, she was lying beneath Patrick, clutching him to her, eager for every inch of him.

She wasn't afraid. Not of him. She refused to be afraid of anything tonight.

When he withdrew from her breasts to lick a titillating line down her belly, she fought to control the urge to stop him from going farther. Judging from his path, she suspected where he was going. Mary had never told her anything about this and she'd never spoken to any of the girls from the taverns about what they may or may not have done in their lovers' beds.

"Patrick," she asked with measured apprehension, "are you going to…kiss me…there?"

"Aye, lass." He looked up briefly from kissing her and ran his palms over her thighs. His fingers stopped at the thin leather strips that secured her blade and her sling. He tugged on them and pressed his mouth to her thigh. "I'm goin' to kiss ye and more."

She had no intention of stopping him so she waited, trusting his promise that he knew what he was doing.

Continuing downward, he slipped the heavy weight of his ready lance away from her and pressed his lips to the sensitive flesh below her navel, and then spread her wider. Moving lower still, he darted his masterful tongue over her entrance and drew her crux into his mouth. He pulled on her with tender insistence, kissing and licking her intimate folds before returning to the tiny flame that threatened to consume her.

She closed her eyes and bit her lower lip as passion seized her. Her body went taut. Her back arched involuntarily and her hands clenched fistfuls of his hair while he drank from her. She cried out, unable to stop herself from doing so. This was truly happening. She was about to give up her virtue to a rake. Aye, he might be the most honorable man she'd ever met, but when it came to women, his armor needed polishing.

She wanted to be the woman to do it.

She had to. She was in love with him despite every nerve in her body screaming to use caution. She didn't want to lose him too.

His teeth scraping against her sent fires down her spine. She couldn't imagine how scandalous this was. It made her smile and spread her thighs wider.

His tongue swept over her and flicked across her swollen bud. She grew hotter, wetter, wild for more.

When she thought she might weep with need, he rose up on splayed palms and tilted his hips. She could see the intensity in his glittering eyes when the tip of his shaft pressed against her moist entrance. He pushed, entering her with slow deliberation.

A sharp pain stabbed her and she gritted her teeth. He saw her discomfort and gathered her into his arms. "Ye drive me mad," he whispered across her ear. The power of his gaze when he stared into her eyes made her weak and willing, but when he began to move inside her again she moved with him.

Soon only the painful throb of desire remained.

Instinctively, she raised her knees and coiled her legs around his waist.

He groaned and thrust deeper, watching her as he claimed her. He retreated and returned with long, languid strokes that pulled cries from her parted lips.

He lifted her to the clouds, floating with her on wings made of passion and intimacy. She closed her eyes and held him as waves of ecstasy washed over her, freeing her from every other thought but one. Him. She ran her palms down his powerful arms, the flare of his corded back, and lower to his taut buttocks straining at his powerful thrusts. Eyes closed, she moaned, delighting in the way he filled her.

She took his deepest plunges and writhed beneath him as blinding, uncontrollable spasms of pleasure coursed through her. She tossed back her head, unfamiliar with the view from *this* precipice. It was a land of dark, tantalizing temptation. She didn't know where it would lead and she didn't care. His body felt too good. With one final cry, she let herself fall over the edge.

He caught her in a burst of radiant color. She dug her

nails into his flesh and held on as her body convulsed, tightening and relaxing around his thick cock.

She heard a tight sound from him and looked up in time to see him lost in rapturous ecstasy as he drove himself into her quicker, deeper. Finally, he sank into her one last time, filling her to the last drop.

She became aware of his weight almost instantly. His muscles trembled against her flesh. She basked in the feel of so much man in her arms. She held him while they breathed into the other's neck.

Oh, how could anything feel so exhilarating? How could she feel so happy she feared she might drift away on the next breeze? Especially after her night with poor Mary? It had to be the rush of emotions Patrick had just pulled from her that made her want to cry now.

He must have sensed the well of emotions roiling within her. Lifting his face, he gazed down at her. "What is it, lass? Did I hurt ye?"

She shook her head and rested in his embrace when he rolled onto his side and gathered her in his arms. Was she truly changing his world? What did it mean? Had he been jesting when he mentioned marriage? Oh, what was she to think?

She wouldn't ask him. She didn't want to ruin what they had just shared by seeming needy. She had no idea how she should behave. She'd jumped over the cliff and now she didn't know where she was. Would he seek her out again? Would she surrender to him again?

"What troubles ye, Charlie?" He ran his fingers across her jaw, angling her face to his. "Tell me."

"I was just remembering Mary." It wasn't completely false.

"Aye, the days to come will be difficult for her."

"I must help."

"Aye, Angel." He kissed her forehead. "I know."

She didn't want to do it alone. For the first time in her life she wasn't sure if she could bear the responsibility by herself. "Patrick?"

"Aye?" he whispered.

"Can we stay here for a little while longer?" She didn't want her time with him to end.

"We can stay fer as long as ye want."

Charlie wanted to stay wrapped in Patrick's arms forever but they had to get back to the house by morning. She wanted to be there when Mary and the children woke up.

When Patrick stood up to dress a little while later, she basked in the sight of him, fully naked, clothed only in moonlight. Pale luminescent light danced over his muscular arms and the sculpted hills and valleys of his tight abdomen. A light dusting of hair spread across his chest. His legs were long, with well-muscled thighs and shapely calves still encased in his hide boots.

She did her best to keep from staring at that part of him that had been inside her, but hell. Blinking at it now, she marveled that he'd managed to impale her to the hilt.

The dull ache between her legs testified that he'd managed it all right. And well.

He caught her staring while he tied his breeches and smiled. She blushed then realized that he was staring too.

Blazes, she was bare. Instinctively, she drew her arms up and covered her breasts.

"Dinna hide yer beauty from me, lass," he said, his voice a mellifluous sigh as he bent to take her hand and pulled her to her feet. He drew her close and kissed her, setting her nerve-endings on fire all over again. "If it were up to me, I'd never have ye dressed again."

She smiled against his lips. She felt the same way about him. But they had to get back. Dawn was about to break and begin the day. Duff would be arriving soon to help Patrick bury Robbie. At the thought of it, her eyes grew moist again. She withdrew from his embrace and reached for her skirts.

Patrick watched her for a moment and then moved to tie the laces of her corset. His breath fell softly on her bosom while she gazed at him, taking in the length of his thick downward lashes, the straight, noble lines of his nose.

He didn't speak. He didn't tell her not to cry. He didn't try to convince her that all would be well. He simply let her mourn, her tears falling on his deft fingers. When he finished with her laces he pulled her in again and kissed the folds of her hair, then, "Are ye ready to go back?"

She never wanted to go back. They had to bury Robbie. Where was Hendry? Who had captured Elsie's heart? Patrick would soon be leaving to find Kendrick's body. She didn't want to face any of it. But she nodded and swiped her tears away. "Aye, I'm ready."

Chapter Thirty

Pewter clouds rolled across the pale sky, spilling rain on the misty earth below, and on the folks who came to bid Robbie Wallace farewell. Many of the villagers followed Charlie while she led Mary and the children toward the hillside overlooking the Wallaces' small holding.

Having arrived hours earlier to make a place for Robbie in the ground, Patrick and Duff were already there waiting.

Patrick swiped the rain from his eyes and watched the procession. He hadn't met the people of Pinwherry yet, but one look at their tattered clothing and gaunt features proved their lives were difficult under Allan Cunningham, who was not present.

His gaze swept over their lady, filling his vision with her, making his other four senses come alive.

Of all the lasses he'd ever known, none were like Charlie. She defied danger and her kin for the safety of others. She wondered how many of them she had helped in the past. She couldn't do it all on her own—but he'd hesitate to ever tell her so again. The last time he tried, her response was swift and laden with disappointment in him. Her simple question asking him how helping everyone she could was too much weight to carry, stung because he'd always shrugged òff any weight at all. It also brought to full light the differences between them.

He'd lived his life like an indolent rogue, defying the wind and its words.

But the winds were shifting and she was the navigator, seeking the best in him. Duff was there too, reminding him of the possible consequences of his lifestyle.

It seemed, Charlie knew just where to look. His gaze fell to Nonie. He winked at her and gained a smile in response.

Hell, he loved her. He loved her brothers. His gaze rose back to Charlie. He loved her.

He was silent while the priest recited from the Holy Book, his thoughts in a state of being he knew nothing about. He loved her. He'd let it happen. It had to be love, or something even stronger, more wild and uncontainable than anything he'd ever experienced before. She consumed him, both awake and asleep. Whenever she came into his vision, his heart pounded with a force that sometimes made him a wee bit light-headed. He felt inept and unskilled in her arms, intoxicated by desire to know her in his bed and out of it.

Did he want to be bound to her for the remainder of his days?

He suspected he did since the thought of living his life without her made him want to groan and punch someone in the face.

How would he tell her? When he'd quipped about it last eve, she hadn't seemed overly excited. He had to tell her who he truly was first. A Fergusson. Kendrick's cousin. An outlawed MacGregor. Duff's cousin. Would she forgive him for keeping it from her? What about Kendrick? Would she continue to cling to him?

"Patrick?" Wee Jamie tapped him on the leg, thankfully pulling Patrick's attention away from things that vexed him. "Can I dig next?"

"Another day, lad." Patrick bent to scoop him up his arms.

Was he staying? Could he leave the babes? Would Charlie be able to go?

He stepped out of the way when Mary urged Robert and Andrew past him to toss handfuls of dirt into their father's grave. He watched Charlie move closer, her long black hair clinging to her body like a mantle. She lifted her face and their gazes met. He wanted to tell her. All of it, and he wanted to trust that he could win her back after that. He believed he was ready to start a new life and he wanted to live it with her. He reached his hand toward hers, wanting to tell her that he wasn't leaving, not until she left with him.

A much smaller hand fit itself into his first. He smiled down at Nonie, feeling privileged that she chose his hand to hold when her turn came to bid her father farewell.

The rest of the morning passed with more prayer, more tears from Robbie's widow and children, who cried mainly because their mother did. Patrick was glad to be there to comfort them.

Finally, when the clouds parted, they all made their way back to the Wallace holding to eat, drink, and help Mary through her difficult day.

Patrick strolled back with Jamie on his shoulders and Charlie at his side.

"How is Elsie this morn?" he asked her.

"Duff says she is better, but he didn't think she should be out in the rain so he didn't let her come."

"'Twas a good decision."

"Aye," she agreed, smiling up at him and then at Jamie.

Now seemed as good a time as any. He didn't know why he hadn't told her last night while he made love to her. Hell, he couldn't think of that now. He'd struggled at the gravesite not to think of it. Reminiscing about the carnal pleasure they'd shared during such a time as this didn't seem right.

"Tell me, lass," he said, determined to press on. He bent slightly to her. "Would ye protest me stayin' here?"

Hell, he loved looking into her eyes and seeing every emotion that possessed her.

"Staying here? In Pinwherry?"

"Aye." He nodded, making Jamie laugh above him. "With ye."

Her glorious eyes opened wider. Her lips parted, drawing his eyes to them. "Me?" she breathed.

He was about to reply when a woman somewhere just ahead screamed. Patrick lifted Jamie off his shoulders, handed him to Charlie, and ran ahead.

Almost immediately he saw the reason for the outburst. A man, at least Patrick thought he was, stumbled toward the crowd. He didn't make it far when his wobbly legs failed him and he crumpled to the ground.

Patrick reached him, and with the people gathering around, bent to the stranger. His eyes were closed, his breathing shallow. He was covered in dirt and grime from the top of his head to the soles of his bare, bleeding feet. He appeared to have walked through hell.

"Who is he?" someone asked.

"Is he dead?" asked another.

Patrick dipped his ear to the stranger's chest. His cheek hit bone. The wretched soul was breathing. "He needs care."

"Come," Mary stepped forward, "bring him to the house. 'Tis closest."

Patrick shoved his arms under the man and lifted him with little effort. There wasn't much left of him beneath his torn, dirt-encrusted clothes. "We have to clean his feet," he told Charlie who kept pace at his side, Jamie traded off to someone else.

"What do we do?" she asked him, her eyes looking over the poor stranger.

"Put fresh linen on the babes' bed. We need scaldin' water and rags." He didn't remember seeing any herbs growing in Mary's yard, but there was another way to destroy infections. "I need honey and yarrow."

When they reached the house, she gathered up Mary and raced with her and some of the other lasses inside.

He carried the man to the children's bed and removed the stranger's mud-soaked shirt while fresh linens were prepared and laid. "Duff," he said, without turning to him when he set the unresponsive stranger on the bed. "He'll suffer fever. I'm goin' to give ye a list of things I need from Alice's kitchen that will help."

"I cannot read," Duff told him. "But tell me what you require and I'll get it."

Patrick did so while Mary set to boiling water and Charlie waited for more instructions.

"We need a basin," Patrick told her, rolling up his sleeves. "His feet must be cleaned and tended to else he'll lose them."

"He will not lose them."

Patrick turned his head to look at her. She smiled at him. He smiled back, appreciating her confidence. He was no healer. In fact, he'd left men bleeding and broken after a fight. He'd never tried to heal any of them. He knew the remedies for many ailments but he'd never put any of them to work before Elsie's butterbur.

When he had everything he needed, he set about cutting the stranger's tattered pants away and then proceeded to tend to him. The man did not react or respond during his care, which worried Patrick. Still, he worked while Mary returned to her children and her guests. Charlie hadn't left his side, watching everything he did and gracing him with more encouraging smiles. When he was satisfied that the poor man's feet were as clean as he could get them, he applied the honey to fight infection then wrapped each foot in clean rags.

"It looks as if he's been walkin' fer quite a while," he said, stepping back from his work and washing his hands.

"Do you think he's a thief?" Charlie asked, gently lifting the man's grimy head to the pillows. They could clean the rest of him later.

"I think anyone who is as thin as he is likely had to rob fer food. He wasna good at it by the look of his bones.

"Ye dinna recognize him from yer travels?"

She shook her head, coming around to his side of the bed. "Should I cover him?"

"Aye, but leave his feet uncovered. Nothin' is to touch them."

He fell into the chair by the children's bed and exhaled a long breath. He wasn't tired from not sleeping all night and digging all morning. Oddly, his body felt refreshed, revived. He looked over at the bed. "I dinna know if anything will help him."

She came to him and fit herself into his lap. "Whether it does, or not, you've done everything you can."

He looked at her and nodded. Hell, he loved her face, the sensuous curves of her mouth. He wanted her to know how he felt. But he had to tell her the truth first. "Take a walk with me, lass. There are things I would have ye know. There's nothin' more we can do fer this man presently."

She followed him out of the room, and after letting the people of Pinwherry know the condition of the stranger, slipped out of the house with him.

"You're behaving strangely," she told him while they walked together through the field.

"Am I?"

She nodded and took his hand. "You're solemn. What troubles you?"

"Solemn things," he told her quietly. "Things I wouldna tell ye on a day when even the sun hides its face. Things I must tell ye now while I have the courage."

"It sounds like whatever 'tis, I won't like it."

"Ye willna," he said hoarsely.

"Well go ahead then." She held his hand a little tighter. Somehow, it hooked Patrick worse than the priest's words over Robbie Wallace.

Hell, where should he begin?

"I wasna truthful aboot how I know Duff's faither."

"Oh?" she asked nervously. "How do you know him then?"

"Will MacGregor is...he is m' cousin. He lives in Camlochlin with the rest of m' kin." There. He said it. She didn't let go of his hand. There was more. He couldn't stop now.

"You said Will MacGregor was from Skye," she interrupted as the full weight of the truth began to dawn on her. "Are you telling me you're kin to the MacGregors of Skye?"

"Nae, lass. I *am* a MacGregor from Skye. Camlochlin is in Skye. 'Tis where we all live."

She shook her head as if still confused and let go of his hand. "I don't understand. You said you are a Campbell."

"Campbell blood runs through me but m' faither is a MacGregor."

She backed away from him slowly. His heart sank when he reached for her and she held up her palms to ward him off. "I don't understand this, Patrick." She looked around her as if she were lost, her eyes misted with tears. She closed them to stop any from falling. "I don't want to," she said, opening her eyes and setting them on him. "You're a MacGregor from Skye, so you also deceived me about your ties to the Fergussons."

It was what he'd wanted to tell her, but hearing the words spoken aloud made him want to turn away. He'd deceived her, not about trivial things, but about truths that might have caused her to make different decisions about him. He saw the accusation in her eyes. The shame of what she'd let him do to her last night. He was a cad and nothing more. A dark, somber wave washed over him like nothing he'd ever felt before. He feared that if he didn't correct this now, he might not get the chance again.

"Patrick?" her voice snapped like a whip. "Do I have that right? Do you have ties to the Fergussons?"

"Charlie, let me first say this—"

"Do you?"

"Aye, I do, but the reason I kept it from ye isna—"

"What kind of ties, Patrick?" she demanded. "Blood ties?"

Hell, he should not have told her. Nae, he had to tell her the truth. Whatever the consequences he had to do the right damned thing. Damn it. And he might as well go headlong into it, the way he did with his fists. The quicker it was over with, the less damage was done.

"Aye, they are blood ties," he admitted. "M' mother is Cameron Fergusson's sister." He moved toward her again when she moved farther away. "I truly didna know how to tell ye, lass. M' reasons fer keepin' it from ye changed, but m' reason fer tellin' ye now never will. I love ye, Charlie. I dinna want to keep anything from ye."

"Well then, that makes it all right," she said crisply. "A man, who has no idea what love even means"—her voice rose in pitch—"loves me! What should I care that he lied to me about being kin to men who left only six people alive when they last came here?"

He held up his palm. "I would speak with ye aboot that, lass."

She took a step forward and slapped his hand away. "Do you think I'd believe anything you say? Did Cameron Fergusson send you here to kill Duff and Hendry? I know you wouldn't be opposed to hurting the latter."

"M' wantin' to harm Hendry has nothin' to do with the Fergussons," Patrick defended. "And as fer them sendin' me here, I was on m' way to visit them fer the first time in ten years the mornin' yer stone struck me."

Her dark glare faltered as another terrible truth dawned on her—one he could not defend or deny. "You're Kendrick's cousin."

Finally, he lowered his gaze at the disgust in her expression.

"Does it satisfy you to know that you succeeded where my father failed?"

"Charlie, nae. I—"

She yanked her hand back when he reached for it. "I was a fool. The victory is yours. I'm certain you'll display it proudly on your belt."

She didn't wait for his reply but left him there to look after her as she ran away.

Chapter Thirty-One

Charlie didn't race back to Mary's, but to her sister. She needed someone to spill her heart out to, and poor Mary had her own sorrows. Elsie would listen and kiss her head. Elsie would tell her she was right to hate Patrick.

She quickened her pace as tears welled up in her eyes.

Patrick was a Fergusson. The men at Tarrick Hall were his uncles, and he expected her to believe his coming to Pinwherry was coincidence? She wasn't that big of a fool. But she was! She'd fallen for his handsome face and well-practiced gallantry. He was a seducer and she'd let him seduce her. Worst of all, she'd let him take up residence in her heart where his cousin belonged. He'd known Kendrick was his cousin. He'd known Charlie loved him. All the time he'd let her go on about him, he knew and he still tried to win her. Why?

Would her blood ever feel warm in her veins again? Would her heart stop breaking? He was Kendrick's cousin. She'd betrayed—nay, they had both betrayed Kendrick's memory. What would Kendrick's father think of that? Dear God, Patrick was Cameron Fergusson's nephew.

She had to hold her hand over her mouth to stop from crying out. She'd been correct all along and *still* she'd let herself fall in love. She was a fool just like the other women who believed the lies of a snake!

Every man's purpose was driven by lust, greed, power, or pride. Patrick had taken her, and for that—well, to be truthful, she would remember it for the rest of her life. But he hadn't pushed. Lust didn't drive him. No one in the village had coin, so greed wasn't a possibility. He had no power to gain from her father.

Pride.

Kendrick, his cousin, had been killed. What would he do after he retrieved Kendrick's remains? Would his uncle finally have the proof he needed that the Cunninghams had murdered his son? Would he come back to finish what he'd started five years ago? Was Patrick here to avenge his kin?

What could she do about it but warn Duff and escape with Elsie?

She swiped a cursed tear from her cheek, but more came when she remembered that Camlochlin was in Skye. He'd never had any intention of bringing her there.

She stopped for a moment to cover her face with her hands and weep at her foolish heart. Had anything about him been real?

She heard a horse barreling toward her and looked up to see her brother returning from their home and leaping from his saddle before the beast came to a halt.

"What are you doing out here?" he asked her with something wild in his eyes. "Why do you weep? Have you heard something?"

She wiped her eyes. Something was wrong. "Something about what?"

He seemed to shatter into pieces before her eyes. She hadn't seen him in such despair since the night he and Hendry returned from their trip to Dumfries five years ago.

"Is it Elsie?" she shouted as nausea overwhelmed her.

"She…"

Charlie blinked. Her breath faltered. She what?

"…was not in her room when I checked on her before I left. I have searched everywhere, but I cannot find her."

Charlie's blood boiled. How could her sister run off to her admirer when they were burying Robbie?

"I am not the only one who has been sneaking off, Duff," she tried to reassure him.

He shook his head. "I fear the Fergussons have taken her."

Oh, blast this damned feud for somehow always being included in everything. "Why would the Fergussons have taken her?"

"Hendry has returned, Charlie," he told her, visibly trying to keep himself calm. "He killed a man. A tenant of the Fergussons."

She refused to faint. She would not do it. Nor would she fall apart. If, heaven forbid, the Fergussons had taken Elsie, Charlie knew who could get her back. Patrick had said he loved her. Now, he could prove it. If he refused, she'd find a big enough rock to kill him.

"I'm going to get her, Charlie," her brother promised. "I was coming to tell you so that—"

"Nay! You cannot go!" She snatched his sleeve. "You'll have no chance against all of them. Don't be a fool, brother! You will not be a hero. You'll be dead, and so will Elsie. Patrick must go."

"Charlie, I'm going," he said firmly and unclenched her fingers from his wrist. "Stay here, where I know you're safe with Patrick."

"Patrick is a Fergusson!" she called out when he moved to return to his horse.

He stopped and turned to her. "What? How do you know that?"

"He just told me," she said going to him. "He's Cameron's nephew. Now you understand why Patrick must go?"

She searched his gaze and backed away, hoping he listened. "There isn't time to tell you more. Patrick is the only one who can help us."

Before he answered, she turned and took off running for the house.

A moment later, she was scooped off her feet and deposited onto Duff's lap while he thundered toward the Wallace holding.

Patrick had to help them, Charlie thought, slipping from her brother's saddle when they reached the house a few moments later. How would they get Elsie back if he didn't? Duff, Hendry, *and* her father couldn't fight off the Fergussons. They would all be killed.

She burst into the house and ignoring the villagers gathered about, she rushed into the children's room. She found Patrick asleep in the chair, the stranger still unresponsive in bed.

Wasting no time, Charlie hurried to Patrick and fell at his feet. "Wake up! Wake up, Patrick!"

He came awake immediately and sat up. "Charlie, what—"

"Elsie is gone. We fear the Fergussons have taken her."

"They wouldna do it." He rose from the chair and pulled her to her feet. She searched his gaze for the truth. He turned it on Duff. "They wouldna."

"I think they did," Duff growled at him.

Charlie wouldn't have them fighting now. She hurried to stand between them and faced Patrick.

"They might because Hendry killed one of your uncle's tenants."

"Hell."

Charlie nodded. He finally understood. "If she's at Tarrick Hall, I'll bring her back."

She hadn't even asked him yet. She hadn't needed to promise him anything. He was going to help!

"Charlie?" he said, urging her to look at him. "I will find her. Dinna fear, aye?"

He smiled when she nodded and then stepped around her.

"I'm coming with you," Duff insisted, blocking his path.

"Nae," Patrick told him. "I'll no' have any killin'. I'll be back before nightfall with her."

"And what if you had something to do with this," Duff accused, not moving, "this would be the perfect opportunity for you to slip away and never return. We'd never see you or Elsie again."

"But ye will see her again. Tonight, if the Fergussons have her. Ye have m' word."

"The word of a snake?"

Patrick shook his head, unfazed by Duff's insult, or knowing it was true and not bothering to deny it. "The word of yer cousin."

Damnation, she'd forgotten to tell Duff that part.

"I too am a MacGregor, and when this is all over I'm goin' to take ye home to meet yer kin. Now please, move aside and stay alive so I can keep m' word to ye. I'm tryin' to be a better man so I can win back yer sister."

He turned and flashed her a confident smile then left the room when Duff moved to let him pass.

"He's my cousin?" Duff asked her when they were the only two left standing.

"Aye, he is. We'll speak of it more when he returns." She patted his arm with her gaze fastened on Patrick's departure. "Have a seat and give yourself a moment to absorb it, brother. I know 'tis all a shock." She took a moment to smile at him. "It was for me as well. I will return in a moment." She broke away. "I wish to remind Patrick to leave us with instructions for this poor stranger."

"Whoever Patrick is," Duff said, stopping her. "Elsie is my sister. It should be me who brings her home."

"Why?" she asked succinctly. "Why does it have to be you?" She sighed looking at him and shook her head. "You're as prideful as he is." And as noble. Aye, as worried as she was about Duff going to Tarrick Hall, it warmed her heart toward him that he was willing to risk his life for their sister.

"Duff," she led him tenderly toward the chair. "Stay here for me. We've lost many years. I'd like them back."

She leaned up and kissed him on the cheek, and then hurried out of the room.

She spotted Patrick leaving Mary's side after a word with her. Hopefully to tell her how to continue treating the man in her children's bed.

She watched him leave the house and without making herself known, crept out after him. The thought of following him hadn't crossed her mind until Duff had brought it up. What if he was correct? What if Patrick had achieved his purpose and was now escaping without injury?

She had to go for Elsie's sake. She prayed that once her brother discovered she'd gone, he wouldn't follow her. But if he did, and he was correct about Patrick, they'd surely never see Elsie again. If they both died fighting to rescue her, then so be it.

If Duff was wrong, hopefully they wouldn't be so far ahead when he realized she was gone that he couldn't catch up. Once he did, she could ask Patrick to tie him to a tree.

She had to go because she needed to know who Patrick MacGregor was. Not by name or by blood, but what kind of man he truly was. It was why she was taking such a chance following him straight to her father's enemy's door. She had to know, once and for all, if there was anything redeemable about him.

No one saw her leap into her saddle and take off in Patrick's direction, keeping a safe distance behind as his horse's hooves tore up the ground.

Duff hadn't shown up after an hour, and Charlie couldn't believe how much her arse hurt. She'd never been in the saddle this long. She'd managed to stay behind at an even pace without being discovered, but there were more trees up ahead and she didn't want to get lost by staying too far behind.

She had no choice but to speed up her mount. At the same time she did, she picked up a sound behind her. A horse. She turned, expecting to see Duff, and finding not one, but five horses bearing down on her.

One in particular was almost at her horse's flank. She had no time to reach for her sling, no time to do anything but kick her horse and fly.

Chapter Thirty-Two

Patrick heard his name faint on the wind. He turned and saw Charlie thundering toward him with five riders at her back.

Cursing, he swung his mount around and yanked on his reins, drawing the horse up on its hind legs, clawing the air with its front. The instant all fours hooves were back on the ground, the beast took off at a full gallop.

Patrick saw Charlie pass him and come back around to stand with him. In one beautifully fluid movement her spine straightened like some Pictish queen readying for battle, her well-worn and well-loved leather sling swinging over her head. There was no time to think about how glorious she was to him. The lead rider was closing the gap.

"Aim fer heads," he told her then rushed into the mêlée. "No' mine!"

He preferred to fight on his feet, but horseback would have to do. He was going to need a sword. His quick eyes found only two men carrying them. The closest rider wasn't one of them. Patrick was going to have to waste no time going through him first.

As he thundered closer with no sign of slowing down, his opponent hesitated. Patrick prepared to hoist the thief out of his saddle and bust his jaw.

A stone whipped by his ear and struck the thief between the eyes, felling him from his horse. This one was no longer a concern.

Patrick smiled as he charged on toward the sword-carrier. When it looked as if they were about to collide, Patrick veered left to pass him. He let go of the reins first and reached out to grab the thief by his neck. Without slowing his pace, he soon held the man suspended a few feet above the ground. He wasn't so strong that he could keep up this feat for longer than a few moments, even less with one hand. But that was all the time he needed to swipe the thief's sword and drop him.

Though he hadn't felt the weight of such a blade in a while, the hilt felt familiar and his muscles took over. He reached the next rider and swung a mighty arc across the thief's chest. The man went down spurting blood. Patrick turned to the next, and kicked his horse's flanks, charging forward. The second rider with a sword held it aloft, ready to bring the rusty blade down on Patrick's head.

Patrick blocked with his blade, which was in no better condition. No stone came from Charlie. That wasn't a good sign.

Eager to see to her, he flipped his hilt into his right hand and brought his sword down against the other with a powerful blow that broke both blades. His opponent took a moment to look at the stump at his hilt. Patrick didn't. He dropped his and moved in a blur of speed, grasping the man's closed fist and using the hilt to knock him out, along with what few teeth he had left.

Free, Patrick whirled his mount around and found Charlie not far from where he'd left her. Two men, including the lead rider and the original owner of his sword lay unconscious or dead from one of Charlie's stones.

The last rider had her out of her saddle and in his grips, a rusty blade held to her throat. Patrick's bones shook at the thought of her dying at the hands of a thug. But this braw lass was having none of it. She tucked her hand beneath her skirts. When it reappeared, her fingers were closed around the hilt of her small black blade. Without hesitation, she sank the blade into her captor's belly. He pulled away, writhing when Charlie turned, snatched back her blade from his flesh with her left hand and punched him in the face with her right.

Patrick raced forward, unable to stand by, no matter how good she was. But he was too late. Charlie's hard, swift kick to her captor's groin took him down before Patrick could.

Dismounting, he went to her and gave her a slow looking over. "Are you hurt anywhere?"

"Nay," she told him, out of breath. "Are you?"

He gave her a smirk like she was mad. Then he grew serious again. "What are ye doin' here?"

"I want to see to my sister, not sit around waiting."

His gaze met hers. He could easily believe that she didn't want to sit around waiting to hear news of her sister, but there was more to it. He saw it when she looked away first. "Ye dinna trust me."

"You are calling me a liar," she countered. "You of all people."

Hell, she had a point. Still... "If ye were set on comin' why did ye follow me in secret?"

She appeared to be thinking of her answer then stopped and scowled at him. "All right then, if you must know the full truth of it. Nay, I don't trust anyone with my sister's life. I—"

He stilled her words when he dipped his mouth to her ear. "Ye're safe with me, lass. As are yer kin. Ye have m' word."

She looked up at him. There was nothing warm in her gaze. "Your word means verra little to me, Patrick MacGregor. I trusted you."

"Ye still can," he promised. Hell, how would he convince her? He was sorry he hadn't told her the truth. He understood her anger, her resistance. He ached to kiss her, but he didn't. Instead his gaze moved over her face, her hair, and back to her. "Fergive me, Charlie."

But she shook her head and stepped away from him. "You expect me to believe you now that you care for me? A Cunningham?"

"I dinna give a damn what ye're called. Ye're a lass who has no trouble tellin' me what she thinks, and withoot any sugary pretense." His impish grin returned. "I like it. It keeps me on m' toes."

"If you find this amusing, then I've nothing more to say."

"Ye please me. Is that so terrible?"

"You are insufferable," she said moving toward her horse. "Do you get out of everything with charm?"

"I used to."

She shoved her foot into the stirrup and lifted herself up. "Give me one reason I should trust you now when you've been nothing but deceitful."

He bounded up into his saddle and nodded, giving her the point. "No' everything was untrue," he told her having no defense in her charge but one.

"The rest doesn't matter," she replied and rode away.

Patrick followed her. He wanted to tell her everything in his heart, but he'd never told anyone before. He didn't know where to begin or if it would matter to her anymore. He certainly couldn't tell her from his saddle while they thundered through Colmonell. Colmonell. What would his uncles think of her? What would his kin at home think of her? Would they believe he'd betrayed them by falling in love with her? He wanted to take her back to the heather muirs and forget the rest of the world. He wanted to promise her that he would never deceive her again.

"Patrick," she called, slowing her horse and turning to him, her face pale. "We didn't bring any butterbur! What if Elsie is ill? If she was kidnapped, she may need it!"

"There's plenty of butterbur around Tarrick Hall," he soothed, riding back to her and stopping at her side. "We'll be welcome to it if we need it. If Elsie is even there."

She stared at him as one moment passed to two as if waiting for him to realize what he'd just said. When he didn't, she reminded him. "You said there was no butterbur in Colmonell."

Hell.

"You cannot remember all your lies, can you?" She shook her head at him and rode away before he had time to reply.

"Charlie." He caught up to her and moved his horse close. "How was I to tell ye where I'd been withoot revealin' everything else?"

"Why didn't—" she began and then stopped, her eyes growing wider on something behind him.

Patrick found out what... or who it was a moment later.

"What are ye doin' on my land? Start explainin' or I'll kill ye where ye stand."

Patrick took a moment to wink at Charlie before turning around to face their attacker.

He smiled at the man standing at the tree line, a sling and a stone ready to fly. "D'ye stand aroond every day waitin' fer someone to throw yer rocks at, Uncle Tamas?"

* * *

Tamas Fergusson. Charlie hadn't seen him since she was a child. He hadn't changed. He still had the same dangerous, almost feral look about him, and the same fiery hair as Kendrick's.

And all at once she was there, plunged into her past by the sight of Tamas and his sling—a young lass skipping in the field with Kendrick hot on her heels. Tamas's voice calling to his nephew. He'd made something for him. Kendrick's own sling. The sling Kendrick had later given to her.

"Patrick?" His uncle put away his weapon and smiled at him. "What brings ye back so soon? And who is this?"

He didn't recognize her. Then, Patrick hadn't told his uncles about her, or where he had been staying.

She was still reeling from the discovery that Patrick had visited his uncles the day while Elsie had grown more ill, when he had supposedly gone to Craigneil. What had they spoken about? Kendrick, no doubt. That was why Patrick had seemed so angry at Duff after he'd returned. It was the first time Patrick had heard about what her brothers had done.

It proved, at least, that his arrival in Pinwherry that morning by the river was purely coincidental. He hadn't stayed for any hidden purpose. Had he stayed for her?

"Uncle," Patrick said gently from his mount. "I've come fer the gel."

Tamas looked at her again, this time his creased eyes lingered on her as if her face were familiar and he was trying to place it. He shook his head. "What d'ye mean ye've come fer her?"

"He means my sister," Charlie told him, her gaze on him, clear and somber. "Elsie. Elsie Cunningham."

Chapter Thirty-Three

Tamas Fergusson didn't have much of a reaction to Charlie's introduction. He looked angry, but then, that's how Charlie remembered him always looking.

"Charlotte Cunningham," he said, remembering her. "What makes ye think yer sister is at Tarrick Hall?"

"Is she?" Charlie asked him, lifting her brow. She wasn't about to tell him what her idiot of a brother had done. If the Fergussons didn't know Hendry had killed one of their tenants, she didn't want to tell them and have them come riding into Pinwherry to exact revenge—if they didn't already have Elsie. Besides, they were wasting time. "My sister suffers the ailment of asthma. She may need butterbur. If you have her—"

He scowled as if a bug had just flown down his throat. "The Fergussons dinna kidnap lasses." He turned his frosty gaze to his nephew. "Ye came fer butterbur last time ye were here. Have ye been livin' with the Cunninghams, then?"

Patrick's heart reverberated through him, making him

feel ill. There was nowhere to run from the betrayal tainting his uncle's angry gaze. Just as there was nowhere to run from Charlie's. Was this what trying to do the right thing cost a man? Honor was as bad as love.

Still, he was done running. "Aye, Uncle, I have. I should have told ye, but—"

"He keeps many secrets," Charlie interrupted, casting him a scathing look.

He offered a repentant nod. "I'll explain it all later, Uncle Tamas. Is Elsie at Tarrick Hall?"

Tamas shrugged his plaid-draped shoulders. "I dinna know. I havena been to the house all day." He turned on his heel and started for the house. "Come, we shall find oot, and then ye can tell us what the hell ye're doin' with *them*."

Charlie's belly sank. Their hatred for her family was still strong, and why shouldn't it be? Hendry had killed their youngest. Was she walking into a trap? Would Patrick's uncles try to kidnap her too? Would Patrick let them?

No. She wasn't a coward. If Elsie was at Tarrick Hall, Charlie would get her back or die trying.

Keeping her misgivings to herself, she followed Tamas to the house.

They were met at the door by Annie Fergusson, Kendrick's mother. Charlie bit her tongue to keep from weeping at the sight of her, the memories of her laughing with Charlie's mother and her teasing Charlie about marrying her son. She'd changed more in five years than Charlie would have expected. Her hair was still a beautiful shade of vermillion, but her wide, bright eyes had lost their luster.

Suddenly, Charlie felt ill. She didn't want to be here. She didn't want to see the terrible hatred in their eyes when they laid them on her. She'd loved these people once, thought of them as family.

She wanted to look away from Annie's gaze as she studied Charlie upon her horse. Her smile faltered only for a moment, but then returned, warmer than before.

"Charlie, how nice to see you again."

Tamas mumbled something unintelligible and then stepped into the house.

"Mrs. Fergusson," Charlie said softly after she dismounted. What should she say? Should she fall to her knees and beg forgiveness for what happened? "You're verra kind."

"What brings you here, my dear? And with Patrick?" Annie slanted her gaze at her nephew, then back to her.

"We're—" Charlie stopped speaking when Cameron Fergusson appeared at the doorway and took his place beside his wife. She choked back a sob when she saw him and prayed her tears wouldn't fall. This was the man who had killed her mother, not the father she remembered with clear green, soulful eyes and a gentle smile. He'd aged but he still wore the same handsome face as Kendrick. He didn't smile but he didn't scowl at her as his brother had. No, his expression was more like Charlie's, filled with guilt and sorrow.

"Miss Cunningham," he greeted her quietly, "please come inside."

He stepped aside to let her and his wife enter then waited for Patrick and greeted him on the way in.

Memories of being here before flooded Charlie's thoughts. Tarrick Hall was nothing like Cunningham House. Spacious and brightly lit with wood and candle chandeliers, colorful tapestries hanging on the walls, and enormous, ornately carved hearths, Tarrick Hall was a warm, inviting home, sprinkled with the delicate laughter of ladies and the raucous banter of mighty men.

She was led to the great hall and a long, polished wood table, joined a moment later by the Fergusson family.

It was intimidating being in the presence of the men who'd killed so many to avenge their youngest. Charlie had watched them from the stairs that day, lifting their bloody swords and raining down terror on anyone in their path. She'd seen what men were capable of, and though she understood their rage, she never wanted to be around it again. But with the exception of Tamas, the men welcomed her with courtly bows and warm smiles. Whisky was served in small wooden cups, which the men downed in a single gulp.

As much as Charlie knew that this could be what was needed to end the hostility between the clans, she'd come here for her sister. She was about to speak up, when Patrick did it for her.

"Uncle Cameron, Miss Cunningham's sister has disappeared."

"Aye, Tamas mentioned it," his uncle said, settling his regretful gaze on her. "I'm verra sorry, but what does that have to do with us?"

"We were hoping you might know where she is," Charlie told him.

His gaze rolled off her and onto his brother Tamas. "Does this have something to do with Hendry Cunningham killing Ennis Ogilvy last night?"

Tamas shrugged. "If it does, I know nothin' of it."

Charlie's stomach knotted. Then they knew about their dead tenant.

"My brother is a fool!" she blurted, her fears springing back to life. "He will get us all killed!"

"Nay," Tamas answered. "No' all of ye."

"Certainly not your sister," Cameron assured her. "No one here would bring her harm, I assure you. They would answer to me, and they don't want to have to do that. Your sister is not here."

Charlie wanted to believe him, but then where was Elsie? Was she hurt? Losing breath? She couldn't stay but as she was about to rise from her chair to leave and continue searching, another, younger man stepped into the hall after just having entered the house.

He was handsome, tall and broad shouldered, with dark copper hair and summer-green eyes. The smile he wore faded when he saw Charlie.

"Shaw," Cameron called out to his oldest son. "Come greet Miss Cunningham. You remember her, aye?"

Kendrick's eldest brother, Charlie recalled. He'd always been kind to her and Elsie. In fact, Elsie had fancied him and...A thought occurred to her. Could he be the man whom Elsie had been sneaking out to see?

"'Tis good to see ye again, Shaw." Patrick stood from his seat and offered Shaw a cup and a friendly grin. "We just arrived. We didna see ye on the road. From which direction did ye come?"

Charlie understood Patrick's query and noted with pride in him how astute he truly was.

"From...ehm..." His gaze flicked to his father then back to Patrick. "I was visiting a friend."

Fortunately for Charlie, Shaw wasn't nearly half as skillful at deceit as his cousin. She wasn't the only one who took note that there was something he didn't want them to know.

"Oh?" his father asked, raising a brow. "Who were you visiting?"

After a moment of silence, his uncle John spoke. "You haven't, by chance, seen Elsie Cunningham in your travels, have you? She's gone missing."

"And the Cunninghams here," Tamas Fergusson cut her a glance, "believe we had something to do with it."

They ruthlessly broke him down in three single steps. Charlie was thankful.

"We did. *I* did," Shaw confessed. "I was with her."

The hall went silent. Charlie could hear her heart thumping. If Elsie had been with him, then she was likely safe.

"Where is she now?" Charlie asked him.

"Home." He looked into her eyes and she could see his heart there. He cared for Elsie. "I brought her home. Fergive me fer causing ye to worry."

She nodded. How long had they been meeting? Charlie smiled thinking she was so clever sneaking off in the night to visit the village and neighboring pubs—when Elsie had been doing the same thing to meet a young man, and no one suspected it, not even Duff.

"That's why ye always fought us on whether or not to go to Pinwherry and finish what we started," Tamas accused.

Charlie's smile softened on Shaw, silently thanking him for that.

"Shaw." His father stood from his chair. His mother cast her a worried look. "How serious is this. What have you done?"

Shaw paled but straightened his shoulders and met his father's gaze. "'Tis serious, Father. I love her."

Charlie closed her eyes, half elated for her sister. The other half mourning the life they'd planned, the life Patrick MacGregor had made her doubt she wanted.

Tamas shouted an expletive. John quieted him.

"Are you telling me," Cameron continued, "that you've been secretly courting a Cunningham and kept it from me?"

"I didn't want you to think I had betrayed you. I know what they took from you."

"And from you," his father reminded him, keeping his temper in check. "From all of us. I will not lose another son to Allan Cunningham's treachery." He turned to Charlie and his gaze softened for a moment before hardening again. "Your father is a treacherous man. Tell your sister it is over."

"I will not," she said staring up at him, not caring who he was. "Let your son break her heart. I will not do it."

He looked about to speak when Annie stepped in front of her husband. "Has Allan Cunningham also taken your good manners, Cam? And in front of Tristan's son?"

He looked over Charlie's shoulder at Patrick and then lowered his gaze.

"All of you," Annie turned on the rest of them. "Charlotte Cunningham is here as our *guest*. She had nothing to do with Kendrick's death, and I won't have her insulted in my home."

Like chastised puppies they looked away or lowered their heads.

Kendrick had adored his mother, and so had Charlie. She still did.

But she refused when Annie invited her to stay for supper. They still had at least four hours of daylight left and after her encounter with thieves earlier, she'd prefer not to travel so far in the dark. Besides the Fergussons had family matters to discuss and Charlie wasn't part of their family.

After a sincere apology from Cameron Fergusson at the door and an embrace with Annie, Charlie left Tarrick Hall with Patrick.

"D'ye think Elsie loves him?" Patrick asked her as they rode.

"Aye. I worry to think how she'll take it." She blinked the mist from her eyes. "But I will help her get through it."

"I know."

She made the mistake of looking up into his verdant

gaze. Oh, she could see every color of autumn glinting in his whiskers. His decadent lips curling into a smile while she admired him.

She had to keep a clear head. He'd lied to her. He was kin to her family's greatest enemy. The hatred still festered on both sides. His uncle had proven it. His family at Camlochlin would hate her too.

"You think you know all about me, don't you."

He grinned, making her heart flip. "I know what's important. That ye're a kindhearted, compassionate lass who can fell a man with her smile or her stone. I know ye make me want to be a better man."

She had no argument for that so she kicked her flanks and took off. Better not to consider forgiving him when there were so many reasons they could never be together.

They rode toward Pinwherry in silence. When Patrick veered from the road and entered the woods, Charlie followed, calling to him. "Why are we going this way?"

"'Tis a shortcut."

He led them through the filtered sunlight of a forest alive with the chatter of birds, buzzing insects, and critters dashing into the summer bramble.

Charlie had never been in the forest. If she had to travel to a pub, she avoided the trees. This place was magical. She wanted to leap from her saddle and traipse on her bare feet like a woodland nymph, basking in her freedom—freedom Patrick always provided.

Soon, the trees began to thin out, finally leading them to a place Charlie often dreamed of.

Rarely cultivated, the muirs were overgrown and wild, tangled bushes of blackberry and currant lined most of the perimeter. Rabbits rested within the thick stalks, hidden from predators in the lush heather. Charlie took a moment to marvel at the lavender carpet spread out before her, aglow in splashes of sunlight and dragonflies.

When Patrick slowed his horse and dismounted, she wanted to run free. What were they doing here? What would she do if...

"Let's walk a wee bit, aye?" He held his hand up to help her dismount.

She accepted and landed on her feet. "And discuss your secrets?"

His brow rose, along with one corner of his mouth. "If ye like."

She nodded and walked beside him.

"Where would ye like to begin?" he asked.

"I don't know. I don't know what difference any answer would make. You tell me that you care for me, but how do I know you're not deceiving me again?"

He thought about his reply for a moment and then turned to her. "Before m' uncle came upon us, ye said the rest of what I'd told ye didna matter. But 'tis the only thing that *does* matter. I know it must come as a shock fer ye to hear me speak such words. Imagine what is goin' on in *m'* head. All I want is to be with ye." He smiled and shook his head as if what he'd just said was the most preposterous thing ever to come out of his mouth. "Ye're all I think aboot," he said, seeming to forget why he was smiling. His gaze intensified, colors changing in the golden light, breaking through her every defense. "Ye drive m' every ambition, Charlie. I dinna know how it happened. There was me, and now there is only ye."

Her knees threatened to give out beneath her. She believed him and it hit her like a wave, pulling her under. Patrick was telling her the truth. He was losing his heart to her.

"I'm no' here to betray ye, or yer kin," he told her. "I want to help end this feud. Dinna doubt me in that."

If he could end it, they could be together. Elsie and Shaw could have the life they wanted. "I won't," she answered on a billowy sigh.

He made her insides burn. No other man would. She did her best to conceal the dreamy grin she wanted to offer him. Patrick was going to change her future, one way or another, whether he stayed or left without her.

What did winning his heart mean for Charlie? Would he take her to Camlochlin? Take her as his wife? But she couldn't leave the villagers yet. Too many still needed her. Duff would be leaving too. There would be no one here to protect them from her father and Hendry.

She didn't want to live her life pining over him if he left. But there were still things she needed to know.

"Why didn't you tell me the truth?" she asked, looking out over the muirs while they walked. "I understand that my own warning stopped you from revealing you were a Fergusson." She turned to him. "But you knew what your being a Fergusson meant—about the feud, about Kendrick, about everything. You should have told me. You should have told Duff you were his cousin. Neither one of us would have turned you over to my father. And so what if we did? What could he do to you?"

"Yer faither didna matter to me," he answered. "Ye did. I didna want to be yer enemy, or to be driven from yer home. I was mad. I still am. The longer I waited to tell ye the truth, the more difficult it became, and then when I found oot aboot Kendrick, I knew I'd lose ye if ye discovered m' secrets."

"I see," she said while her stomach knotted and her blood felt hot in her veins. Why did his explanations pull at her heart and make her forget everything else?

"Ye have a reason no' to believe me, but m' words to ye now are true. I will prove them to ye. Will ye let me?"

He reached for her hand and she took it, loving the intimacy of it. "Aye, I'll let you."

They walked to a tall stand of heather, where Charlie dropped his hand and fell into the lush flora. She smiled up at Patrick with heather tickling her cheeks. She loved being here. She loved Patrick for bringing her.

"Is there heather at Camlochlin?" she asked him.

He nodded and sank down next her. "'Tis everywhere, outside the castle and inside. Every wife has bundles of it arranged on her night table, save one, who prefers orchids."

"Every wife?" Charlie turned toward him and leaned up on her elbow. "Tell me why? Who picks the heather?"

"Their husbands," he told her, lying beside her in the same position. "M' grandfather started pickin' it fer m' grandmother when he brought her to Camlochlin as a symbol of his love fer her. Other husbands began doin' it, and soon every lad was taught the art."

"Art?"

"Aye, heather is verra difficult to gather. The flowers are delicate and the shoots are strong. Pull with a rough hand and ye lose the flowers, with too much hesitancy and the roots will not budge. M' grandsire is said no' to have ever lost a petal."

"'Tis all verra romantic."

"They think so."

"You don't?"

"What's so romantic aboot flowers?"

"Nothing. The romance is in the picking. Didn't you learn anything living among such men?"

He reached for her cheek and ran his knuckles over it. "I

learned that 'tis possible fer a man's heart to belong to one woman."

She tossed him a playful smirk. "And you quickly rejected that notion."

"I did," he laughed, then slipped his hand around her nape and drew her mouth closer. "Until I met ye."

Was it all true? Charlie hoped it was as Patrick pressed his lips to hers. Did she drive his ambitions? Oh, but if it were true...if it were true she would forgive him anything—promise him anything.

She'd already jumped over the precipice to be with him. It was time she started trusting him.

Abandoning her doubts, she pushed off her elbow and coiled her arms around his neck. He withdrew only to kiss her lips again before he devoured her. Oh, but he knew how to kiss. His mouth caressed hers, molded to her, angling to take her more deeply. He traced her with his tongue and nibbled her with his teeth.

She made no objection when they sank into the heather locked in passion's embrace. She wanted him in her arms. She wanted his heart and everything that came with it.

She withdrew and looked up into his eyes. "Are you going to take me to Camlochlin?"

"Aye, lass." He smiled at her and dragged the pad of his thumb across her lower lip. "If ye still want to go."

"I do," she told him on a whispered breath. She didn't care where he took her as long as he stayed with her.

He undressed her slowly, baring her skin to the late afternoon sun and heather-scented breeze...and his kisses. Modest in the light of day, she tried to cover herself with her arms, but he gently pulled them away, taking in the vision of her with something akin to worship in his gaze.

It emboldened her to lean up and pull him out of his shirt.

When he helped her rid him of his breeches and boots, she kissed him running her palms over the hard planes of his back, thrilled and apprehensive that they were naked under the sun. She didn't worry that they would be seen. No one from the village came to the muirs.

They were alone, the only two people in the world, and the world was theirs.

Chapter Thirty-Four

$\mathcal{D}$uff sat in the chair by the bed, wondering if he'd made the biggest mistake of his life by letting Patrick go, and not going after Charlie when he realized that she'd gone after him. If the Fergussons were holding Elsie for ransom, he could have used Patrick as a bargaining piece.

But Charlie was correct. More than likely she would lose them both if he went. He had no choice but to put his trust in a man who had cleverly deceived them.

He was thinking of ways to hurt Patrick if he didn't return with both his sisters safe and sound. Duff would go to Skye to find him if he had to.

Skye.

He was still thinking of it and Patrick's promise to bring him there when the man in the bed uttered a word on a soft, crackling voice.

"Wah...gah."

Duff bolted to his feet. Water! "Aye, aye, 'tis coming." He hurried to a jug of water and poured a cup. "Her you go, friend." He held the cup to the man's lips and slipped his hand behind his head to support him while he drank.

"Not too much now," Duff told him gently and smiled when the man looked up at him. His eyes were a striking shade of blue against the dingy color of his skin.

Duff looked into them and felt his belly flip enough to make him ill. Where had he seen—?

"Nay," the man cried out and tried to move his scant body away. His eyes grew even bluer when tears filled them to the brim. "It cannot be you, Duff Cunningham. It cannot be you."

Duff swallowed and wished he'd gone to church more often. There, he could have learned more about a man coming back to life.

"Kendrick?" Duff's heart welled over even as his mind refused to believe who he was speaking to. How was it possible? "Kendrick, you're alive." He wasn't dead!

He wasn't dead!

Patrick's body was hard and ready to take her, but he wanted to take his time with her. She was an untried virgin just a day ago. He didn't want to hurt her or make her dislike lovemaking. He intended on making love to her often.

Presently, he basked in the supple fullness of her breasts, shaping them in his hands, kissing each in turn and tugging gently on her tight nipples until she writhed beneath him.

She took her fill of him as well, kissing his chest and biting his shoulder, tempting his restraint to falter.

When she opened her luminous eyes and gazed at him, he felt his heart falter as well. He wanted a life filled with her. Only her.

"Do I truly drive your every ambition?" she asked on a gasp.

"Aye, lass, ye do."

"Show me." She smiled and spread her legs high around his waist.

His control snapped. He rose up like some fabled, fiery beast and did as she asked.

He wasn't sure he could hold himself back with her. A power he had no control over swept across his heart like wind across the muirs. It made him drunk with desire for her, willing to give up all. For her.

He sank into her and stretching over her body, kissed her hungry mouth. He retreated and returned, then had to stop himself.

This was more than he'd ever done before. It meant more to him. Everything to him. He wanted to breathe with her, bind himself to her, brand her as his.

He plunged deeper. She grew warmer and wet around him. He swelled inside her, on the verge of bursting. He dared a look at her and found her glorious head thrown back in ecstasy, her tight, erect nipples pressed to his chest. Hell. He had to stop again.

Lying sill atop her, he smiled when she lifted her head. He moved over her, settling deeper. He couldn't get deep enough. He kissed her parted lips once, twice. "Ye bring me pleasure, lass, and I'm findin' it more and more difficult to contain."

Her haunting lips curled into a smile, captivating him. "What is this power I have over you, MacGregor, that one movement..." She undulated her hips beneath him. "Can tempt you to snap?"

He looked at her, wondering how he'd survived all these years without her. "It must be love," he whispered, dragging his mouth across hers, and answering her thrust with a long, salacious one of his own.

"Aye." She closed her eyes and breathed across his lips before he kissed her. "It must be."

How had it happened? he pondered, drawing his head back to look at her. Love, the thing he feared, had found him. Oddly, he wasn't afraid anymore. "Ye exhilarate me, Charlie. Ye're all I need. All I want."

He made love to her two more times that afternoon. No thing and no one existed, save her, her lithe body pressed to his while he took her from behind on their knees with his mouth at her throat and her breasts in his hands.

He proved to her that she drove his every ambition while she moved, impaled to the hilt, atop him. Och, but that time had been especially exhilarating to watch her thrill at being in control of their pleasure. She moved him, changed him and he never wanted to go back. They found their release together and laughed when it was over.

He held her close in his arms, fully aware of the power of what his heart felt for her.

Gone were the nagging doubts that haunted him before he met her. His convictions had changed and he was glad. In fact, he never felt happier—or more tired. Neither of them had gotten much sleep last night.

They would leave soon, see to the stranger, and then they could both get some sleep.

But not yet. He didn't want to let her go yet.

How was it possible to bind oneself to another and feel so weightless? Had he ever felt as alive as he did now? Hell, if he'd known love felt like this, he would have considered it sooner. But no. He was glad he discovered it with her.

"Charlie, ye've become m' only love."

A moment later he realized she was asleep. He held her for a little while longer, but he didn't want to fall asleep as well. If they slept through the night, Duff would come looking for them, and Patrick didn't want them found like this.

Smiling, he kissed her head then disengaged himself from her and sat up. He looked around at all the purple and saw it a little differently. He shook his head at himself and chuckled. What the hell kind of pansy had he become to let the sight of heather choke him up? It reminded him of home, and of her. The sight of it anywhere would always bring him back to this place.

He understood now why his grandsire always picked the fragrant shrub for his wife.

Rising to his feet he bent again to pluck a shoot from the ground without losing a single blossom. As a lad, he'd hated his lessons in the heather-carpeted glens outside the castle, but he'd learned the proper way to break the shoot and mastered it until he had nothing left to learn and was set free to cause trouble with his cousins.

He walked around now, picking only the fullest shoots, from pale lilac to deep purple until he had a large bundle clasped in his hand.

He was a MacGregor, after all.

Feverish and foolish, mayhap, but still, a MacGregor.

Charlie dipped her face into the spray of heather clutched in her arms and inhaled. She'd done the like at least seven times on the way back to Mary's house. It was a tradition for the men in Camlochlin to gather heather as a symbol of love to their wives.

It was a lovely tradition and if she ever heard another unkind word about Patrick's kin, she would remember only the tales Patrick had told her.

Patrick loved her, she thought, smiling into her heather, loving the feel of his arm around her waist, holding her steady against the swift pace of his horse. He loved her and he found no difficulty telling her how it stunned him.

Poor rogue. He was as innocent about love as she was.

Whatever was going to happen now? She thought she should know for certain, and avoid anything unexpected later.

"I cannot go with you to Camlochlin yet," she told him, lifting her face from the petals. "I cannot leave everyone... Mary and the children, to Hendry."

He nodded, his eyes set on the Wallace holding. "I know. We'll wait until we find a way to keep them all safe."

"We will?" She gazed up at him. "You'll stay?"

"Of course I will." He met her gaze and smiled. "Do ye think I'm goin' to give up kissin' ye?"

"What about your family? They will not approve."

"They will in time."

"And my father?" she asked him, stopping him with a palm on his chest when he dipped his mouth to hers.

"M' aunt's sister is the queen," he replied with a flash of his dimple. "Yer father willna object to our weddin'."

His aunt's sister was who? Their what?

Every other thought fled at his kiss.

Chapter Thirty-Five

*P*atrick didn't take Charlie directly to Mary's, but to Cunningham House first to check on Elsie. Charlie hadn't seen her sister since yesterday. They'd never gone so long without being together. And there was much Charlie wanted to discuss with her.

But her sister wasn't in her room, or anywhere else in the house. Panic settled over Charlie quickly. Had Shaw deceived her? While she ran to his parlor to find her father, she wondered how the happiest day of her life could become the worst.

Alice the cook stopped her in the hall. "There you are, Miss," she said, wiping her hands on her apron. "Your sister said to tell you that she's with Duff at the Wallace holding, and for you to make haste in getting there."

"Why? What's happened?" Charlie's heart slowed a little, but the very thought of harm coming to her sister made her ill.

Alice shrugged her meaty shoulders and turned to head back to the kitchen.

"Mayhap, 'tis the stranger," Patrick said behind her. "He may have worsened. We should go."

Aye. The stranger. Charlie nodded, thankful and guilty for the relief Patrick's sensible explanation provided. She hoped the man's condition hadn't worsened, but she was glad that Elsie was with Duff.

They hurried back to the stable and retrieved Patrick's stallion. Her own horse would take too long to saddle.

She didn't realize she was still clutching over a dozen stalks of heather in her arm. She wasn't about to leave them in the stable for the horses to eat. Besides, carrying them helped her remember the best part of her day.

Was she truly going to take a husband? She never would have believed it. She hadn't loved anyone since Kendrick. She never thought she would. How could she when she'd kept him alive in her heart, in her thoughts and convictions?

She hadn't been looking for a hero, a champion. She didn't believe any more existed. She'd never expected to find him in a rogue with laughing eyes and a silver tongue.

In a MacGregor with Fergusson blood.

But, oh, that silver tongue spoke the most heartfelt words her poor ears had ever heard. Who could compare to Patrick MacGregor?

They reached the house and found it empty. The guests had all gone home. Silence greeted them as they entered. Where were the children? Mary?

"Elsie?" Charlie called out and hurried toward the bedroom.

Her sister met her at the doorway. Her breath didn't appear labored but she looked at Charlie with wide, anxious eyes.

"Where have you been?" she asked Charlie, wringing her hands through her thick, woolen skirts.

"Is everything all right?" Charlie put to her instead. "Where are Duff, and Mary and the children? Are you ill?"

"I'm well," her sister answered, then chewed her lip. "Duff took an elderly woman home and Mary and the children went with him."

"They left you here with a man we don't know?" Charlie demanded and stepped around her sister to check if the stranger was awake or not. Was that her cousin Caitriona standing by the bed?

"We do know him," Elsie told her softly.

"We do?" Charlie asked her, moving toward the bed. She saw a movement. His hand. It moved and it was clean.

As was the rest of him.

"Who is he?" she heard Patrick ask her sister, following her into the room.

The stranger's skin was pale, his lips cracked and dry. His nose looked to have been broken more than once. He was awake and when she stepped up to him, he turned his eyes on her. They misted with tears almost instantly.

Who was he and why would he weep at seeing her? Why did her heart begin banging against her chest again? She was barely aware of Patrick coming to stand beside her or Cait stepping away.

"Charlie?" the man said in a weak, shaky voice. "Am I dreaming?"

Was *she* dreaming? Why did she feel like she'd heard him speak her name a hundred times before?

"I've dreamed of you," he went on. "Every day, Charlie. Your smile kept me alive."

Charlie stared at him, then at Elsie. Her sister smiled faintly and wiped a tear from her cheek. No, Charlie told herself looking at him again. No, it couldn't be. He was dead.

"I know how I must appear to you," he continued torturously, "but 'tis I, Kendrick."

Charlie dropped her bundle of heather to the floor and lifted her hands to her mouth. It was Kendrick!

The room was spinning. A cry fought for release from her throat. Kendrick! Here. Alive. Speaking to her. She'd never hoped to hear his voice again. Her Kendrick wasn't dead!

"Kendrick?" Was this her voice speaking to him? Waiting for him to answer?

"Aye, Charlie." He smiled at her and memories of his face flooded her thoughts. "'Tis I."

It was him. Her Kendrick, back from the dead. God help her, she almost fell to the bed, keeping herself upright by sheer force of will.

"All these years I've thought of you, believing you were gone…and now…here you are. How…how is it possible?" she heard herself asking him, looking at him, soaking in the sight of him. It was Kendrick! She simply couldn't take it in fully. "My brothers. Hendry—"

"Aye, he stabbed me and left me for dead. But I lived."

"How?"

Charlie looked up at Patrick when he spoke. He looked as shocked and confused as she.

"Who are you?" Kendrick asked him.

"This is your cousin," Charlie told him, still stunned to be speaking to him again. "Patrick MacGregor."

"I remember hearing of them around the table." Kendrick's smile was almost as warm and welcoming as Patrick's usually was. "My aunt Isobel wed a MacGregor."

"Aye, Isobel is m' mother," Patrick told him, sounding hesitant, heavy, as if the world had just crumbled around his feet and left him standing in the rubble.

Charlie's smile faded. The love of her life had just returned to her, and Patrick was watching. Had she told him she loved him while they…Her gaze flicked guiltily to Kendrick. Kendrick! She still couldn't take it in. All the years she'd cried for him, pined over him, believed she could never love anyone but him…But she did love someone else. She loved Patrick.

"Do you know my father then?" Kendrick asked him, his voice hopeful and dreadful at the same time. "Is he well?"

"He will be better when he sees ye," Patrick assured him in a gentler tone Charlie didn't know how he pulled off. His calm expression looked as if it were about to dissolve into something more excruciating. "Are ye up to tellin' us what happened?"

Kendrick nodded and coughed into his hand. Caitriona hurried forward with a cup of water, or mayhap tea, for it soothed him and he smiled at her.

Charlie watched Cait with a measured smile. She'd barely seen him in the last five years and now, when Kendrick had returned, so had Cait. She cared for Kendrick. Charlie had always suspected it, but Kendrick's heart had been loyal only to Charlie.

"Hendry left me in Dumfries, bleeding out in a ditch," Kendrick continued. "I don't know how long I was there before an old man happened by and took me home."

Charlie felt as if she couldn't breathe. How could her brother have done something so vile? She wasn't sure she wanted to hear the rest, to hear how he ended up like this, with barely any meat on his bones, filthy, sickly…She wiped her eyes and reached for his hand, aching to comfort him.

"When I was well enough," he told them, "I left and began my journey home. With no coin, I had to steal to eat. I was caught and sent to the colonies as an indentured servant. I was put to work and beaten by almost every owner I had."

Beaten by his *owners*? Charlie couldn't bear it. She hung her head in shame at what her family had done and let her tears fall freely. Five years of fear and torture inflicted on him just to keep her from marrying a Fergusson. She wiped her eyes and looked at Patrick. Surely, Allan Cunningham could not do the same thing to him. Patrick was a man, not a boy, as Kendrick had been.

"Thoughts of you and the laughter we shared helped me go on," Kendrick confessed, pulling Charlie's woeful gaze back to him. "I vowed to myself that I would return home and see you again...see my father and mother again. Three months ago, I managed to escape the bonds of my servitude and stowed away on a ship bound for Scotland. It took much to return, but I finally made it."

He smiled and it was as if nothing had changed between them. But so much had. He'd gone through it all because of her and had gone through more to return to her. A sennight ago she would have rejoiced, climbed into bed with him, and promised her life to him—as she had when they were younger. But then Patrick had stumbled into her life, swept out the cobwebs, and spread laughter and life into the ghostly chambers of her heart.

"Ye're here now," Patrick told him with another forced smile. "Ye're safe. As soon as ye're well enough to travel, I'll bring ye home to Tarrick Hall."

"You have my thanks, cousin." Kendrick looked at Charlie again and gave her one last smile before he fell asleep.

"Charlie." It was Elsie. She'd come to stand by her sister and rested her hand on Charlie's shoulder. "Why don't you go rest? Cait and I will see to Kendrick."

"Nay." Charlie shook her head. "I wish to remain with

him." Kendrick deserved that, didn't he? He'd meant more to her than anyone in her life besides Elsie. He'd been ripped from his family's arms and shipped across the world, where he was forced to be a servant by abusive men because of her! She would see him back to good health. She would have done it for anyone, and Kendrick was so much more than that.

"There's nothin' ye can do fer him presently, love," Patrick said in a gentle tone. "Come, share a meal with me while he sleeps."

She couldn't. What if he brought up Camlochlin or their life together? What was she to tell him? How could she leave Kendrick after all he'd suffered? "I'm not hungry," she told him without looking at him. "You go eat. Elsie will fix you something. Won't you, Elsie?"

"Of course."

Charlie watched her sister turn to leave. Patrick nodded but then paused and bent to pick up the heather strewn on the floor. Her belly sank and she felt queasy for a moment at the solemn expression he wore.

She turned to speak a word to him. She understood what the heather represented. She hadn't meant to drop it and send it scattering as if it meant nothing to her. She was sure he knew that.

Her gaze returned to the man in the bed.

Kendrick. He'd returned from the dead. Oh, how she'd missed him. When she thought about the life he'd suffered, she sniffed and wiped her eyes again.

She heard Duff return to the house with Mary and the children. She would greet them later. She expected Duff to come to her, but Elsie appeared beside her instead.

"Forgive me, Charlie. Patrick told me how terrified you were for me and how brave you were facing thieves and then his uncles." Tears filled Elsie's large eyes. "Forgive me for putting you through that."

Charlie smiled and took her hand. "First, does Duff know about Kendrick?"

Her sister nodded, casting Kendrick a pitying glance.

Charlie wondered how it had felt for her brother to know Kendrick was alive. Was he delivered from his terrible guilt, or more reminded of it?

She looked toward the door, hoping to see him, but he'd likely stopped to speak with Patrick.

"He also knows about Shaw," Elsie continued. "I had to tell him when he found me at the house."

"How is he?"

"I don't know. He wasn't here long enough to speak to."

They would find out soon enough. Her smile restored, Charlie smiled at the person she loved most in the world, besides Patrick. "Tell me about Shaw."

"Oh, Charlie, he's wonderful! I wanted to tell you so many times—"

"'Tis dangerous and reckless to go out alone."

"He always meets me just beyond the fields."

Charlie listened while her sister told her about Kendrick's brother. Shaw sounded like quite a nice fellow. Elsie sounded very much in love. Charlie's heart broke thinking about what Cameron had said. Should she tell her? Would it be any easier hearing it from her? No. And Kendrick was alive. Surely this changed things with the Fergussons, perhaps even with the MacGregors.

She stayed with Kendrick long after her sister left. Poor Kendrick. She wanted to be the first thing he saw when he woke. It was the very least she could do.

Chapter Thirty-Six

$\mathcal{P}$atrick hadn't been speaking with Duff as Charlie had assumed.

He'd needed air and had stepped out into the backyard after speaking with Elsie. Kendrick was alive. He was thankful, happy for the lad, and for Cameron. It would be a good reunion. It was another reunion that vexed him now.

The only man Charlie had ever loved had returned from the dead and she refused to leave his side. Thankfully, he had no more time to think about it when someone called his name from inside the house.

Patrick smiled. The children had returned and rushed toward him when he went back inside.

He'd seen Duff over Nonie's head after he'd scooped up her and her brothers. He realized in an instant that Duff knew the man in the other room. They would speak of it later, that, and other things. Patrick owed him explanations.

But the children insisted he put them to bed and tell them a story, so he followed Mary to her room, carrying all her children to her bed.

"Patrick?" young Andrew asked, dangling from Patrick's shoulder. "Everyone was crying because of Papa. Is he not coming back?"

"Nae," he said softly to them. "He isna comin' back. But ye'll see him again someday." He caught Mary's eye and smiled when she turned to look at him over her shoulder. "And until then, ye must listen to yer mother and dinna vex her. Aye?"

They all nodded and he somehow kept his heart together.

"What story will you tell us?" Jamie asked while his mother undressed them.

Patrick thought about it. They deserved a good tale. He remembered just the one. "I will tell you of the greatest knight who ever lived."

"Sir Gawain!"

"Nae, Robert, no' Sir Gawain," Patrick told him. "Sir Galahad."

"What's so great about him?"

Patrick smiled, drawing in their attention. "He pulled a sword from a stone."

Later, when they were asleep, he kissed each head, happy that they'd enjoyed his story of young Galahad and the sword that had been waiting for him. He'd always enjoyed that story as a child. He'd forgotten it. He'd forgotten much. It was time to go home. And home was wherever Charlie was.

But Kendrick had returned and Charlie had all but forgotten Patrick was even there.

All these years I've thought of you, believing you were gone... and now... here you are.

Here he was, back from her memories and in the flesh. Would Charlie want to be with him again? What the hell would Patrick do if she did?

He left the children and ran straight into Duff. He looked over his cousin's shoulder for any sign of Charlie. His teeth ground together. Was she still at Kendrick's bedside?

How was Duff taking it? "How are ye, cousin?"

Duff stared at him for a moment and then smiled. "I'm happy he lives."

"As am I," Patrick agreed.

"Share a cup of whisky with me, Patrick," Duff offered. "There's much to discuss between us. Don't worry about Kendrick. I've seen to his feet with Elsie and Caitriona's help."

Patrick didn't refuse and followed him to the kitchen. They discussed secrets, Patrick's and Elsie's, and truths, the MacGregors, and even weddings.

When they were done, Mary offered to make them a plate of food from her neighbors. They hadn't had much to give her but gave her what they had. Patrick refused. He was exhausted and wanted to check on Kendrick.

He stepped into the room alone and noticed Charlie asleep in the chair. Kendrick hadn't awakened yet.

Patrick checked his patient's feet and was impressed at how well Duff and the lasses had cleaned and wrapped them.

His gaze slipped to Charlie. Was she happy Kendrick was back? Of course she was. They all were. What did it matter that she'd loved him once, a long time ago?

But she hadn't left his side. Would she show Kendrick his sling so carefully kept upon her thigh?

His eyes lingered on the curve of her cheekbone, the grace in her jaw. He thought about the heather muirs and her beautiful smiles. Their future. He wanted one with her. Kendrick's return wouldn't change that.

He wouldn't let it.

He felt Kendrick's forehead. No fever. That was a good sign. The faster Patrick could get him home to his father, the quicker the true healing could begin.

"Patrick?"

Her soft dreamy voice nearly buckled his knees. "Aye, love?" He went to her.

"Has he awakened?"

"Nae, sleep is best fer him, as 'tis fer ye. Come, let me take ye home to yer bed."

She shook her head. "I don't want to go so far."

From him. Patrick looked at his cousin. Hell, what would he do if she chose Kendrick?

"But I admit," she continued, drawing his gaze back to her, "I am weary and in need of rest. There is no room in Mary's bed. Will you take me outside and sleep with me, Patrick?"

Relief flooded through him and he scooped her up before she could change her mind. He carried her, cradled in his arms through the house, to the kitchen's back door.

"Patrick?"

"Aye, lass?" he whispered into her hair as he took her outside.

"He cannot return to Colmonell like this, barely able to keep awake. He is going to have to stay here for now."

He knew she was right. Kendrick's body was in no condition for the journey. He could die before they reached Tarrick Hall.

"I cannot leave his convalescence to Mary when she just lost her husband."

Again, she was right. He bent and lowered her to the grass. This behavior of hers was nothing peculiar, he thought as he snatched a bedsheet from the line and returned to cover her. It was who she was, the lass he loved. An innate leader with a compassionate heart, who was responsible for everyone else. She took care of her sister, the villagers, and the chickens. It was only natural for her to want to take care of Kendrick.

He slipped beneath the bedsheet and gathered her in his arms. "We will tend to him."

She snuggled deeper into him and sighed against his chest, making his heart swell with emotions given to her alone. "Did you speak with Duff?"

"Aye, he is glad the lad is alive. We shared drinks and I put things right between us."

"That's good. And the children?" Her voice grew softer, slower. "How are they after today?"

Patrick kissed her brow. Even half asleep she considered others. "All dreaming, I hope, of swords in stones and... Charlie?"

A tiny sound escaped her. She was asleep, and soon Patrick joined her, sure in the knowledge that Charlie loved him.

That certainty began to chip away over the next three days. Three days of listening to Charlie laugh with Kendrick at his bedside. She doted on his every wish and even told him how handsome he still was, after Patrick and Duff bathed him and cleaned his hair. She was first to his bedside in the morning and last to leave it at night. With nothing left to do for him, even Caitriona went home.

Patrick couldn't have been happier when he awoke on the third morning to find Kendrick taking small steps on his feet. He just wished Charlie wasn't under his cousin's arm while he did it.

Patrick tried. He fought battles with himself that made the ones he'd had for coin laughable. Even knowing Charlie was kind and attentive to any who needed her, her attention to Kendrick was becoming harder to endure. He thought about telling her, asking her if she still harbored feelings toward Kendrick. But he didn't want the answer. And he especially didn't want her to think he was some jealous fool. He just wanted Kendrick to go home, and he felt like hell over it. He didn't like these feelings of jealousy. He'd never suffered anything like it before—the pain in the pit of his gut, staying awake all night with images of Charlie waving farewell to him as she left to begin her life with his cousin, his heart breaking.

"Ye're doin' well," he said entering the room and coming to stand face to face with his upright cousin. He slipped his gaze to Charlie and winked at her, feeling sick with the desire to remove Kendrick's arm from around her shoulder.

"I'm feeling well, thanks to you and Charlie and the others. You've all been very kind."

Hell, why had Patrick cleaned him up so well? He should have at least cut off Kendrick's bronze curls so they wouldn't fall over his eyes when he turned them on Charlie. He was gaunt, his complexion sallow, but Charlie beamed at him as if he were more striking than the vales of Camlochlin.

"I'm goin' to Colmonell today," Patrick announced, keeping his practiced, weary smile in place. He should have gone straight to Colmonell to tell his uncle the good news the moment he discovered who Kendrick was. He hadn't wanted to leave Charlie alone. Pitiful fool that he was. "I dinna think ye're well enough to leave yet, but yer faither should know ye're alive."

"I would be in your debt, cousin," Kendrick told him, his arm still around Charlie.

Patrick nodded, reminding himself for the hundredth

time that this was his cousin. "I'll be leavin' shortly," he said, offered them both his best smile, and left the room.

He'd found it easier over the last pair of days not to stay in the room with them for too long. He could control his thoughts better without the two of them smiling and laughing together. He was glad to be going to Colmonell today. The time away was just what he needed. If Charlie still loved Kendrick, Patrick's being here wasn't going to change it. His uncle needed to be told.

Chapter Thirty-Seven

"We weren't expecting you back so soon," Patrick's uncle John said, ushering him into Tarrick Hall. "Is all well?"

Nay, everything is not well, Patrick lamented silently. *I'm losing the only lass I've ever loved.*

"Verra well, Uncle," he said out loud. "Fetch yer brothers please. I have news."

Watching John take to the task, Patrick's heart drummed in his chest. How should he tell Cameron? Would the shock be too much for him?

He waited until everyone had gathered into the great hall and asked for whisky to be served. There would be much celebration.

"What is it?" John asked him. "You look about to burst. Is it good news from home? Your mother?"

"She's likely with child again," Tamas guessed, reclining in a chair beside John's.

"Have you found Miss Cunningham?" Annie asked.

"Why don't we let the lad speak," Cameron said, taking a seat after his wife. "Go on, lad."

"Uncle Cameron," Patrick's voice shook when he turned to him. "Take yer wife's hand. She will likely need it."

"Is it about Shaw and Miss Cunningham?" Annie begged.

"Nae," Patrick told her, bracing himself. "'Tis Kendrick. He lives."

As he suspected, the ground fell away. Everyone came to his and her feet, save Cameron. He sat in his chair staring at Patrick, his hand rising with his wife as she stood. Patrick hadn't moved his gaze off his uncle in the commotion.

"I hope you have proof," Cameron told him, "or what you did here today is unforgivable."

"I have seen him, spoken to him."

"Where?" Now Cameron rose to his full height. "Take me to him."

"Aye, take us!" his uncles and cousins demanded.

Patrick leaped from his chair to ward them off. "Nae. His father only, fer now."

"Patrick." Cameron was upon him in a single stride. "Where is he? How do you know 'tis him?"

Thankfully, Patrick had prepared himself for the whirlwind. But who could prepare for the emotion of finding out your child wasn't dead?

Patrick did his best to remain calm and steady while he spoke. "He's in Pinwherry."

"They had him all this time!" Cameron's son Tam accused.

"Nae!" Patrick held up his hand. "He's been…Hell, I'll let him tell ye his tale. I found him stumblin' into Pinwherry in poor condition. His feet were bare and raw and caked with weeks of dirt. He is being nursed back to health in the house of Mary Wallace, by Charlie, Duff, Elsie, and Caitriona Cunningham."

His uncle Cameron took him by the collar of his shirt. "You left him with them?"

"Aye," Patrick told him evenly. "I did. Charlie lost him too."

"And Duff? The one who—"

"Kendrick will tell you himself that Duff didna put a finger to him. 'Twas Hendry, and he has disappeared again. And Duff is a MacGregor. Will's son," Patrick supplied when his uncle opened his mouth to speak and nothing came out. "They are helpin' yer son recover. Never leavin' his side."

"Let's go and get him back," Tamas said. "Enough wastin' time."

"He isna well enough to travel, or I would have brought him with me."

"Ye're no physician," Tamas pointed out.

"Everything yer sister knows aboot medicine, she taught to me."

When Tamas made no other reply, Patrick returned his attention to Cameron. "Allan Cunningham doesna know aboot Kendrick. If ye all show up on his land, he's likely to start shootin' his pistol. I know ye can overtake him, but ye have yer son back. This war needs to end before anyone else dies."

Cameron let him go and looked at his wife. "Our Kendrick may be alive, Annie."

"Go find out, my love. Hurry back to tell me."

They were leaving now. Turning to go, Patrick paused and looked at the rest of his kin. "Trust me," he told them. "And celebrate Kendrick's return."

His aunt smiled, as did Shaw and John. Tamas stared at him with narrowed eyes. "We'll see."

* * *

"Five years, Patrick," His uncle exhaled heavily as he dismounted in front of the Wallace holding. "Five years I believed him gone from me. Can this be?"

"Aye, Uncle," Patrick promised him. "It can.

"Remember," Patrick reminded him as they approached the door. "Duff Cunningham is no' a threat."

Cam nodded and cast him an anxious glance. "Think you Kendrick will recognize me? Will I recognize him?"

Patrick smiled and ushered him inside. "Ye've had a hard life, Uncle," he said tossing his arm around Cameron's shoulder. He pointed to the doorway down the hall. "Go inside and see yer son."

Cameron stepped forward slowly and then hurried forward. He stopped at the entrance, his eyes fixed on the man sitting up in the bed.

"Kendrick?"

His son looked away from Charlie's smiling face and his eyes glistened with tears. "Father."

Cameron ran to him and cupped Kendrick's face in his large hands. He studied him, his eyes, eyes he knew. Tears fell down his face onto the bed, into his son's shoulder when he pulled him into his arms.

Patrick wiped his eye and caught Charlie smiling at him. He winked at her, forgetting that an instant ago he was angry that she was here yet again.

She left her chair and went to him. "There's something I would speak with you about."

"Of course," he said and led her out. They met Mary in the hall and Patrick forgot about the man in their bed and what he still meant to Charlie thanks to the children running around his legs. He wanted this. He looked at Charlie. And he wanted it with her.

They followed the brood into the kitchen, where they met Duff and Elsie.

"Cameron is here," Patrick told his cousin then bent to the children. "Go play in the yard. I'll join ye shortly." He wanted to speak with Duff about fighting and he didn't want them here to hear it.

"Do I have yer word that ye'll no' try to harm him?" he asked him when the children ran outside.

"Aye, ye have it," his cousin told him, "but 'tis difficult knowing he killed my mother."

"Kendrick thirsts." Cameron's voice drew every eye to where he stood in the doorway. When Charlie hurried to fetch Kendrick some water, Cameron held up his hand and smiled at her. "Thank you, Miss Cunningham, but let me see to him now that I am here. You have my deepest gratitude for all you've done already."

She nodded and he waited while she filled a cup.

"Your mother was my friend," he told her in a quiet, quavering voice. His gaze fell on Duff and on Elsie. "I know it won't bring her back and I take full responsibility for it. The fault of it lies with me. But I would have you know that it was a terrible accident." He took a deep breath then continued as if he'd been waiting for years to tell them. Patrick knew he had. "We had come here to exact vengeance from your father. Because of my past friendship with your mother, I decided to spare her sons, and her of course. But she hadn't known. When we attacked, cutting a path to Allan Cunningham, your mother had leaped in front of us, cutting off our path to plead for her family's lives.

"Even covered in blood, I wasn't satisfied. I'd come to kill the man responsible for taking my son. Nothing was going to stop me.

"Ignoring your mother's pleas, I...I shoved her away. She fell and landed on a guardsman already splayed out on the floor. His blade, exposed and tilted across his chest..." He stopped for a moment to try to gather himself. Patrick knew how difficult this was for his uncle. But it was time to heal.

"When I saw what I had done, I went to her and lifted her from the blade. I carried her to a cushioned chair and fell at her feet to plead her forgiveness. I don't know if she would have given it. I left Cunningham House ashamed of my blood-lust." He lifted his gaze from the ground and set it on Duff, then at Charlie. "We have done things we regret. I hope you can all someday forgive me."

For a moment, no one spoke. Patrick hoped it was enough.

Duff moved forward and Patrick readied himself to break up a fight.

"We were commanded to take your boy to Dumfries and kill him. I like to think 'twas my age that made me so fool-ish." Duff reached him and sat on the edge of the table. "I wanted to please the man who raised me, to finally be ac-cepted as his son, so I agreed to do it. I took him from you and cast him into a life worse than death. If anyone pleads forgiveness, 'tis I."

Patrick smiled watching him. Duff was a good man, a MacGregor, for certain. Will would be honored to call him son.

"You have it," Cameron replied.

Charlie stepped forward and handed Cameron the cup of water she'd been clutching to her chest. "You'll stay for supper then?"

Cameron accepted the cup and smiled.

"And later," Patrick's uncle added. "We can discuss the marriage ceremony."

Elsie hurried forward, her blue eyes sparkling. Patrick was glad she looked healthier than when he'd first arrived. And now she was going to wed Shaw. She'd be a Fergusson. He was happy for her.

"I'll be a good wife to your son, Mr. Fergusson," she beamed.

Cameron looked a wee bit lost for an instant and then his grin widened. "Aye, ye and Shaw. We'll make it a double ceremony." He smiled at them all and then turned and continued down the hall.

What? Patrick's smile faded. A double ceremony? No damn way in hell..."Uncle!" he called out, catching up to him. "What's goin' on?"

Cameron opened his mouth to speak and then rethought his words. Finally he said with a sigh, "I understand that Charlotte Cunningham may have caught your eye, but Kendrick loves her."

"He told this to you?" Patrick's heart drummed in his ears, the sound of war. "Ye were barely in there long enough to—"

"When I asked him how he lived, his reply was *her*."

Patrick turned to look at her. She looked away, unable to meet his gaze. Nae! His heart battered against his ribs as if it sought to break free and fly to her. Nae, his jaw tightened. He wouldn't lose Charlie to Kendrick.

"You must know," his uncle continued, dragging his gaze back to him, "that if his love for her has remained true after all this time, he should have her."

Nae. Patrick shook his head and ran both hands over his face. Nae. He didn't know that. All he knew was that he was ready to put away his careless ways and be responsible for someone else. Her. He'd given his heart to her, his soul. For what? To have Kendrick return from the damn dead and reclaim her? Nae! He turned to her again with his heart in his eyes. "What d'ye want, Charlie?"

Her eyes were large and liquid in the soft candlelight. She couldn't say. She didn't have to. Patrick was certain his heart was about to stop for good and he'd drop to the floor dead at her feet.

Cameron placed his hand on Patrick's shoulder. His eyes, pouring over his sister's son, were filled with love and hope Patrick hadn't seen in him.

"She was about to agree to Kendrick's proposal when we entered."

Patrick must have looked like he was about to be ill or about to start breaking jaws because his uncle moved in closer and cupped his face in both hands. "Lad, she cannot mean that much to you. You haven't known her long, have you?" He didn't wait for an answer. "I would see him happy, nephew. Make this small sacrifice for him, and I'll be sure to write your father about it. Think on it please. Now, I must go. Kendrick's waited long enough."

Patrick watched him enter the room and wondered what kind of monster he'd become to hate Kendrick.

He needed to be away from here. He needed to plot his course of action with a clear head.

He strode past Charlie, not answering her when she called out and headed for the door. He didn't want to speak to her or look at her. He couldn't have been this big of a fool. He didn't care what Cameron wrote to his father, but this was kin. He could only go so far. How far would that be? He didn't want to talk. He wanted to fight. He left the house before he could consider it further and strode toward the fields. He wouldn't go too far in case his uncle tried to have them wed by the village priest.

The thought of Charlie spending her life with anyone but

him made him want to do more than just bust some bones. He tried to plan the best way to convince Cameron that he wasn't giving her up, but he couldn't think straight. His head felt as if it were about to burst, his heart felt the same.

Was it wrong of him to keep her from a man she's loved her whole life? Was he still nothing but a selfish bastard? He wished he could speak with his father and mayhap gain some insight on what the hell was happening to him. He'd never felt this kind of pain before. What would his father have to say to him? Hadn't the men of Camlochlin risked all for love? Had any one of them given up his woman? His father would tell him to fight for her. But how far?

And what was there to fight? Charlie wanted Kendrick. She couldn't even look at him. Patrick had known she loved his cousin. His sling at her thigh attested. He should have left her to her ghost.

He sank to his knees at the twisting ache in his guts, his chest.

Chapter Thirty-Eight

Charlie watched Patrick leave and looked at the doorway to the sleeping quarters. Her indecision as to where she should go kept her rooted in her spot. She wanted to go to the room and tell Cameron Fergusson that there was no future for her and Kendrick. But how could she turn her back on the boy she loved so deeply? He'd grown to manhood in a world of beatings and chains and fought his way to the brink of death, for her. How the hell was she supposed to tell him the truth? She'd actually considered agreeing to his proposal. But guilt and regret were prisons she no longer wanted any part of. And Kendrick deserved more.

She looked toward the front door and thought of the man who'd set her free. Was Patrick leaving? Dare she chase him?

She took off running. He'd told her he loved her, and she believed him. Then why was he giving up so easily? Had he given up already? He rarely requested her company of late. When he checked on Kendrick, he spoke briefly to her then left. She'd wanted to speak with him about Kendrick's proposal. Did he still love her? Was she giving up her child-hood love for a man whose fickle heart had changed once again? But she knew he loved her when he'd looked at her, his heart laid bare before her. Why hadn't she told him then?

When she stepped outside, she was surprised and utterly relieved to see his horse still tethered to the small post. She looked around. He couldn't be too far. He'd either gone right toward the village, or left to the fields.

She lifted the hem of her delicate skirts and ran left.

When she saw him kneeling in the grass, she stopped and clutched her hands to her breast. He looked anguished and in terrible pain.

"Patrick?" she said, reaching him. She fell to her knees before him and cupped his face in her hands. The long spray of his lashes were dark with moisture around his somber gaze. "Are you unwell?"

He nodded. "A plague."

"What do you mean, please be serious. I'm concerned."

One corner of his mouth quirked, but it was void of any humor. "'Tis love. It has befallen me."

She blinked and removed her hands from his face to fold her arms across her chest. "*Befallen* you. Like a curse. A plague."

"Aye, I—"

She gave him a shove backward and bounded to her feet. "And here I was concerned over you."

He rose and caught her arm when she moved away. "What would ye call it when ye're willin' to fersake all oth-ers fer the sake of one? Or the gnarled talons clawin' away m' insides and threatenin' to leave me in ruins? How would ye describe the feelin' of drownin' with no one around to help, every damn wakin' moment? I want to say, the choice is yers." He shook his head, his eyes glistening under the sun. "But I canna speak the words. I want to fight fer ye. I want to fight him and it shames me."

She returned to him, her eyes, wide, warm, and worshipful. "I choose you, Patrick MacGregor. What do you think I meant when I told you that you'd succeeded where my father failed?" When he shook his head, she smiled and reached up to run her fingers over his strong jaw. "He tried to kill Kendrick to make me stop loving him. There will always be love in my heart for Kendrick but you are the man I want in my bed every night." She stepped into his arms. His smile made the backs of her knees burn. "You are the man I want to father my children, and grow old with. 'Tis you I want. I love you, and only you. God and all his angels help me."

She lost herself in his laughter and his passionate kiss.

They stood at the entryway on the brink of possibly starting another feud—or ending one. Patrick prayed he could convince his uncle what Charlie meant to him, and that Charlie could help Kendrick understand. They were going to claim their futures, defy anything that came against them, together. She'd been at his side during every battle he'd faced since coming here, sometimes dragging him into the glaring light of self-examination. When the thieves had attacked them outside Colmonell, her stones had flown with pinpoint precision, saving his arse. Looking at her, Patrick doubted it would be the last time they would stand united against whatever cause Charlie took on next.

His gaze drew hers. He smiled like a fool, drinking in the sight of her delicate jaw, the shape of her lips angling upward. "I love ye, lass."

He saw her reply in her eyes before she spoke. He'd won her. "I love you, as well, Patrick."

She moved against him with haste and reached up to press her lips to his. She turned away and stepped inside. Patrick hung back, his ear alerted to a sound.

He turned toward the kitchen. Were the children still outside? Another sound turned his blood cold.

A child's muffled scream.

He reached the kitchen before the cry ended and passed Duff and Mary on their way out.

"Children!" Patrick shouted, spinning in a circle as his gaze scanned every direction.

"Jamie!" Mary screamed.

Patrick turned to see the lad running from the barn. Was that... blood on him? Patrick ran to him. "Nonie!" he roared toward the barn. "Robert!"

Robert and Andrew ran crying from the barn next, stilling Patrick's breath as he caught them in his arms. "Where's Nonie?" he asked while he quickly examined Jamie for any wound.

"'Tis not his blood," Robert sniffed and wiped his eyes.

"Nonie bit the monster," Andrew cried. "He was holding her and Jamie and she bit him."

"Hendry!" Duff's voice resonated off the distant trees, and through Patrick's soul. "What the hell are you doing? I'll kill you, you bastard! Let her go!"

Patrick rose up from the children. Nonie. Hendry stood at the barn doors holding Nonie by the hair. At Duff's threat, Hendry produced a knife and held it to her throat.

Patrick caught Nonie's eye and he winked, though he felt like he had no air left to breathe.

"What d'ye want, Hendry?" he asked with deadly calm.

"I must pay a debt. You know how I enjoy the card tables." He grinned at Duff and Patrick fought not to rush at him and break every bone in his face. "I want my sister.

She must marry Alistair Dunbar or my life is forfeit. So you see?" He tugged Nonie's head back by her hair, exposing more of her thin throat. "I'll do whatever I must to have her. Bring her to me now."

"You offered up our sister at a game of cards?"

Patrick turned to glare at Duff. He was going to get Nonie killed if he tried anything. This wasn't the time to lose his temper over how Charlie had been treated. Hendry would never have her, nor would the Dunbars. It was not something to worry over.

"Let go of the lass," he called out to Hendry and returned his gaze to him, "and I'll bring Charlie to ye m'self."

"Why? Did you tire of her already?" Hendry laughed. Did all her pining over poor dead Kendrick finally get to you?"

Patrick was supposed to be proclaiming his love for her, instead he stood here, preparing himself to denounce her.

"Aye, I—"

"You're a liar, Monster!" Nonie shouted. "Kendrick isn't dead!" She sank her teeth into his arm for the second time and bit him.

Hendry threw back his head at the pain in his arm at the same instant Charlie's stone flew at his head. The stone struck him in the cheek, tearing skin away from bone.

Patrick took advantage of Hendry's moment of shock and pain and leaped at him.

"Run to yer mother!" he shouted at Nonie as Hendry's grip on her loosened and he fought to remain upright.

The lass broke free and ran as Patrick reached Hendry and took hold of him.

Patrick had never wanted to kill a man, until now. Clutching Hendry's léine, he balled his free hand into a fist and hit him. And again. Three direct blows to the face was enough for the worm, and his legs collapsed beneath him.

Patrick wanted to kill him. But he stepped away and turned to Charlie. Hendry was still her brother.

He moved toward her and saw his uncle appear at the doorway, his pistol raised and pointed at Patrick.

What in blazes—

Patrick heard a sound behind him and ducked. Cameron's pistol ball shot above his head and hit the bloodied man rising to his feet.

Hendry fell to the ground.

Thankfully, Mary had brought the children inside while Patrick was punching Hendry. Charlie looked away from Hendry's body and disappeared into the house. Duff passed him, moving toward his brother.

"Uncle?" Patrick went to him. Cameron's eyes were wide, his brow still furrowed. His pistol still held aloft, shaking in his hand. "Are ye well?"

Cameron blinked and looked at him. He nodded, shoving his weapon beneath his belt. "I am now."

Patrick held Charlie in his arms within the starlit muirs. The day had been long and difficult and they wanted to be alone. He'd spoken to her briefly about the death of her brother. But her solemn reply was correct. Hendry had brought it on himself.

"Do ye think Kendrick took yer confession well?" Patrick asked against her brow.

"I think he is going to need a long time to heal from his past," she replied softly. "Caitriona has asked to go to Tarrick Hall to see to his mending. She's loved him all along. I think I always knew."

Patrick was glad. They would be here too if Kendrick needed them. Patrick would remain with Charlie in Pinwherry until her father was properly taken to prison for conspiring to kill a boy. Patrick would ask Daniel Marlow, a general in the queen's army and his cousin by marriage, to see it done.

After he knew the people of Pinwherry were safe, he would take Charlie and Duff to Camlochlin to meet their new kin, and then return here.

"Do you think your uncle will ask me?"

It was Patrick's idea to tell him he'd handfasted with Charlie in the presence of a priest just a few days ago. He didn't mind telling an untruth every once in a while. It was Charlie he was worried about. According to her, she did her best never to lie. He hoped, if asked if they were already wed, she wouldn't try so hard.

He wouldn't keep her dishonest for long. If the priest were here, he'd make her his wife right now. If Duff wanted to remain in Camlochlin, Patrick would stay here as liege.

It meant responsibility. Duty to every one of his tenants, the weight of a village on his shoulders. But hell, he was strong. Built for fighting. And he wasn't alone. He had her. This was what he wanted—the challenge of a new life with the only woman he ever loved.

Epilogue

$\mathcal{P}$atrick stopped his horse at the crest of a deep sunlit vale, cradled beneath the vast slopes of Sgurr Na Sti. His gaze scanned the jagged horizon of the Cullians beyond and Bla Bheinn to the north. Many kisses had been shared by many generations on the braes of Bla Bheinn.

He turned when he heard a sound from Duff on his left. His cousin was staring into the vale where sheep and cattle grazed, and children played around stone-roofed cottages.

"Ease yer concerns, cousin. All will be well there."

"'Tisn't that," Duff said and spread his gaze to the west of the glen and the frothy caps spilling onto a pebbled beach, where a lass had paused to dip her feet. "This could have been my home," he said, his voice laden with regret.

Patrick didn't worry too much over it. His cousin would be well here. Camlochlin had been built to heal. "'Tis yer home *now*."

It was Patrick's home and his heart swelled with love for it. More than the stone fortress with turrets rising from the mountain behind it, or the houses scattered around it, built by the masterful hands of the Grants, the land beckoned him home.

He turned to the braw lass saddled to his right. She'd crossed the cliffs of Elgol on her horse without so much as a peep, though she purged her lunch as soon as they were back on solid ground.

"Feelin' better, m' love?"

She turned to him and he was surprised to see her eyes moist with tears. "Camlochlin?"

He nodded and she turned back to the view before her and smiled. "You described it well. I don't want to ride there," she decided and dismounted. "I want to run."

Dropping her reins, she lifted her earasaid and her billowy skirts beneath it, and set off over the crest and onto the wind-blown heather-carpeted hill. She spun around to aim her most radiant smile at him and then continued on her way.

She fired his blood and made his heart race. "Bring the horses doun, will ye?" he asked Duff while he dismounted and handed his cousin the reins. "I'll wait fer ye at the bottom."

Casting him a grin, Patrick took off after her.

Hearing him behind her, she turned and laughed, picking up speed. He let her run until she tired and then scooped her up and set her down over his shoulder.

Her laughter filled the braes and drew the attention of some of Camlochlin's inhabitants.

"Patrick, put me down!" she shrieked and pounded her fists on his back. "I'll not meet your family tossed over you like a sack of grain! Now, put me down!"

She'd learned a little trick from Nonie and promptly bit him on the shoulder.

He howled and tripped and they both landed with a heavy

thud. After they retrieved the breath that had been knocked out of them, they sat up and laughed.

They became aware of the man standing over them. Charlie looked first, from his kid-skin boots, up his long, deadly Claymore, dangling from his hip, to the drape of his plaid over the expanse of his shoulders. She gulped and blinked up into a gaze as powerful as the seas.

Patrick smiled and stood to his feet, bringing à mute Charlie with him. Callum MacGregor still had the same effect on people.

"'Tis good to see ye, grandsire."

"Patrick?" His aunt Davina rushed toward him on bare feet, leaving the whitecaps behind. "Is that you?"

The current laird's wife reached them the same time Duff did. Seeing him, Patrick's grandfather slipped his arm around her.

Ever the unflustered Lady of Camlochlin, Davina turned her wide gaze on Charlie. "Do we have this lovely maiden to thank for bringing you home to us?"

"Aye," Patrick told her and presented Charlie to them. "M' wife, Charlotte—and her brother, Duff."

Callum watched Duff dismount with a scrutinizing eye. Patrick wondered, while Davina took Charlie by the hand and under her wing, if his grandfather saw the stark resemblance.

"Her brother?" he asked.

Patrick smiled. "I found him in Pinwherry, fostered by Charlie's father, Allan Cunningham."

Callum's gaze slipped to him. Patrick's grin faded. "'Tis a long story, grandsire. One which I will explain to everyone at supper tonight."

Mollified, the Devil MacGregor returned his attention to Duff. "Yer faither will be happy to meet ye."

Duff smiled for the first time in days. "Do I resemble him so much that you already know who he is?"

Callum nodded. "Ye're Will's." He held out the crook of his elbow to Charlie. She accepted, looking suitably overwhelmed. "Though I dinna know how I feel aboot ye if ye let yer sister wed this wanderin' rogue."

"Wanderin' no longer," Patrick corrected, catching up, Duff just a step behind. "I've been hit with the fever and awaken from m' bed each morning freshly delirious."

Both his grandfather and his wife smiled at him.

Patrick entered Camlochlin the same way every one of her children who'd been away for any length of time did when they returned—with awe at its warmth and familiarity.

But being reunited with his father was by far the best part of being home. Patrick had much to tell him. Things he suspected his father would be glad to hear.

His mother, as beautiful as the day he'd left her, doted over Charlie, as did the rest of the women. His uncles and cousins greeted them and marveled at Duff, eager for Will to arrive when one of Patrick's younger cousins was sent to fetch him from his home.

Duff was sharing a cup of brew with Callum when his father finally arrived.

After greeting Patrick with a great bear hug, and Charlie with a more delicate embrace, Will turned to Duff and smiled.

There was nothing unusual about Will's lack of interest in the people milling about around him, staring and waiting like they hadn't been fed in a sennight and food was on the way.

"Will Mac—" He stopped his introduction and gave Duff a more careful looking over. "MacGregor," he finished. "Have we met?"

"Aye," Callum said, and spotting his wife on the other side of the great hall, pushed off the wall. "He's yer son."

Charlie sat at a long polished table in the great hall. All around her sat MacGregors and Grants, young and old, laughing, bickering, toasting their cups to this thing or that.

She listened with one ear while Patrick told them her and Duff's tale and everything that had happened with Kendrick. They asked questions, but soon their merriment returned. It was as if nothing beyond the water concerned them overmuch.

She watched her brother smiling while he spoke with his father, Will MacGregor taking in every word and smiling with him. She knew she'd lost her brother to their family before he told he didn't want to go back.

She didn't blame him. Why would any good man want to live in a cruel world? Patrick would. He'd return to Pinwherry with her and help her follow her heart and change the lives of the people who lived there.

And then they would return to Camlochlin, perhaps with Elsie and Shaw, and raise their bairns with a family the size of an army. She smiled thinking of it and felt her husband's mouth caress her neck.

"Are ye thinkin' aboot kissin' me in the heather?"

She giggled and slapped his arm but turned to him, her lashes low, her smile, promising. He made her insides burn. No other man would. "When can we leave?"

Lachlan MacKenzie, Dragon Laird of the Black Isle, will do anything to be reunited with his little girl...even kidnap Mailie MacGregor from her family at Lord Sinclair's request. Grab the lass, deliver her to the man who desires her hand in marriage, and finally be reunited with his daughter— that's Lachlan's plan. But he never expected to want the beautiful, spirited Mailie for himself...

A preview of
Laird of the Black Isle follows.

Chapter One

A thin layer of mist from the Moray Firth drifted through the cold, still forest. A fine dew settled on the still, russet leaves of downy birch and ancient rowan and clung to the underbrush.

A lark soared above the canopy, but made no sound to disturb the serenity of silence around the man peering down the length of his arrow.

As still as the roebuck a few feet away, the only sign of the hunter's presence was his breath against the morning air. His hooded plaid of dark and light green and brown blended in well with the forest. His bowstring made no sound as he pulled it back, the muscles in his arm bulging. His gaze was steady, his breath unchanged. It wasn't until he thought about all the food the beast would provide did the buck lift its head.

It was too late. The arrow found its mark. The deer fell and the man finally moved.

The buck was large and would be heavy but the hunter's shoulder was the only way to get it back.

He looked down at the fruit of his labor and was grateful for the deer's sacrifice. During his station in the Colonies, an old Iroquois chief had taught him that every life had a purpose.

The buck's purpose was to provide food—at least it was today. He often wondered what was his?

He bent his knees and with a solid grunt from his belly, he hefted the animal over his shoulder. He stood, steady on his hide-encased legs, and then took off running.

His boots crushed the leaf-carpeted ground as the sounds around him grew. Birds burst from the treetops at his disturbance, smaller animals scurrying out of his path.

He was in no hurry to get back to his life in Avoch, but the way he chose to live it required that he keep fit.

By the time he broke through the forest, his thighs burned and his breath came hard.

He ran past the harbor, giving no greeting to the men loading their fishing nets and no notice to the screaming gulls above. He didn't slow, hoping to be gone before the rest of their families awoke.

His body nearly spent, he finally slowed his pace when he reached the sleepy village of Avoch. A cock crowed at the breaking dawn. He quickened his gait and pulled his hood farther over his head, hiding his face, lest he be recognized by anyone leaving his cottage to take his morning piss.

Just a little farther. He looked up at Avoch Castle perched at the top of the hill, its dark, jagged turrets piercing the gossamer mist that surrounded it. Built in stone nearly two centuries ago, the castle had many ghosts, but it was the last two to arrive who haunted him. Though it was in no state of disrepair, for he had made certain to fill every hole in every wall and maintain his privacy, the castle looked uncared for and deserted set against the bleak backdrop of a gray March sky. A shell, as lifeless as the man who lived in it.

Determined to his task, he kept moving and collided with a lad appearing out of the settling mist. The hunter's solid form knocked the boy on his arse.

Watching the figure go down, he wondered if he should drop the buck and help. He maintained his position as the bucket the lad had been carrying in one hand hit the ground and rolled away. A younger lass, whose hand he held with the other, did the same.

The hunter's dark eyes fell to her. She looked to be about six summers—the same age Annabelle would have been. Belle's nose might have been as small as this one. He blinked and looked away.

"Look where ye're goin!" the lad shouted at him. "Have ye no—"

His tirade came to an abrupt halt when a ray of light from the rising sun broke through the thick clouds and settled on the hunter's face beneath his hood.

The lass gasped while the lad scrambled to his feet on shaky legs.

"Laird MacKenzie! Fergive me! I didna see ye, though I'll admit ye're difficult to miss." The lad looked to be roughly nine, mayhap ten, and seemed to be bent on getting his master to smile at him. "I'm William. I was just fetchin' water fer—"

Lachlan MacKenzie, Dragon Laird of the Black Isle, thought about removing his hood. The full sight of his scarred face usually silenced flapping tongues, but he'd already frightened the girl.

With a will of their own, his eyes fell to her again. She was staring up at him, her round face tilted—

"That's Lily." The lad moved toward her and bumped his elbow into her arm. "Lily, quit starin'."

Lachlan stepped around them and continued on his way.

"D'ye need help with that buck? What are ye goin' to do with all that meat?"

Lachlan wasn't about to tell him, though William would discover the answer this eve. He scowled at the ground as he walked. He didn't want the villagers to know any of the food he sometimes provided had come from him. He had no need for friends, or family. He'd already lost everything he had ever wanted.

For the most part the people of the Black Isle were self-sufficient. As earl there was little to do but attend stately gatherings from time to time. As laird, he was bound to his tenants and he did what was required of him.

He stepped through the short outer wall and turned to make certain William wasn't following him. The wall should be higher. He'd work on it, he thought and stepped up to the thick, carved doors.

He didn't think about his life beyond this point. He simply lived it, alone in a castle with twenty-two rooms.

He pushed open one of the doors and stepped inside, ignoring the ghostly cry of the wrought iron hinges and creaking wood. He pushed the door shut with his heel. The resonating boom stirred the empty halls and then died.

He carried the buck to the enormous kitchen, one of only three rooms in the castle in which he kept the hearth burning, and dropped the carcass on the carving table. He bent backward to crack his back and then unclasped his bodkin and removed his plaid. He picked up a large knife.

Butchering had stopped making him ill years ago. He'd learned how to hunt and prepare his kill during his time in the Royal North British Dragoons. It was how he'd found the men who'd killed Hannah, his wife, and their daughter, Annabelle, two years ago and put an end to them.

He scowled when a knock came at the front door. William. The lad needed to know that his laird wouldn't stand for being bothered by anyone.

With his knife in his hand and his hands and shirt covered in blood, he went to the door and swung it open.

It wasn't William.

"What can I do for ye?" he asked the man standing across the threshold. His unexpected visitor was several years older than Lachlan, and shorter by at least two heads. He wore a clean, un-tattered plaid and bonnet. One of the neighboring barons? Lachlan had never seen him before.

The stranger trembled once, and deeply in his polished boots as his pale eyes took in the sight before him.

Lachlan hadn't become so unrefined that he couldn't comprehend how he must appear. He thought about wiping his hands but there was little of him clean.

"Lachlan MacKenzie, Earl of Cromartie?" the man asked, backing away from him, his eyes fastened on the lacy scar marring the left side of Lachlan's face. "I am... ehm... I am Robert Graham, emissary to Ranald Sinclair, Earl of Caithness."

Caithness? What the hell did they want with him?

"Might I come in?" he asked, looking like he'd rather be anywhere else. "There is a matter of great urgency I need to discuss with you."

"I dinna concern myself with things so far off," Lachlan told him. "Whatever Sinclair wants with me, my answer is no." He stepped back to close the door.

The emissary held his hand up to stay him. "You'll not want to say no to this."

Curious by the man's certainty, Lachlan stepped aside allowing him entry and tucking the knife into his belt. "This way." He led his guest to his study. There was blood everywhere else.

Lachlan watched Graham look around, surprised by the books lining dozens of hand-carved cases, all softly lit against the light of a dozen candles and the deep hearth.

"Have a seat." He offered the only chair in the room, placed close to the fire.

"You live here alone?" Graham asked while he sat.

Lachlan took hold of a poker and stirred the embers in the hearth. "Why does Sinclair disturb me?"

"He sends you an offer, MacKenzie."

Lachlan thought about picking him up, carrying him to the door, and throwing him out. What *offer* was urgent? What kind of *offer* did this little worm think Lachlan could not refuse?

"What is it?" he asked, returning the poker to its place and coming to stand over the chair. He took no mercy on the emissary when Graham shrank back.

"Lord Sinclair...needs you to bring someone to him," Graham sputtered. "For your trouble he will pay you something priceless."

Impossible. Whatever was priceless in Lachlan's life was gone. But his curiosity had been piqued.

"Why doesna he go fetch this person himself?" he asked, folding his arms across his chest. "Why is he making this offer to me?"

"You've been a Scot's Grey for almost a decade, a colonel with—"

"That ended two years ago."

"Aye, but you gained renown for your great brute

strength and deadly proficiency with any weapon. Getting hands on this person requires a man of your expertise."

"Why?" Lachlan asked. "Who is it?"

"She is my lord's beloved, Miss Mailie MacGregor, of the MacGregors of Skye. Her father has refused Lord Sinclair's offer of marriage, though she cares deeply for my lord."

Lachlan smiled but his gaze was hard as the rest of him. "Sinclair wants me to kidnap a lass? A *MacGregor* lass? He thinks me a fool."

"He thinks you are a man with nothing to lose," Graham corrected him, looking a bit more confident since Lachlan hadn't killed him yet. "And if rumor is correct, and that is the blood of game covering you, you are an excellent hunter. You can grab Miss MacGregor and be away before you are discovered. She is on her way to Inverness with a small party as we speak. She should arrive sometime tomorrow. After that, she returns to Camlochlin and any chance we had will be gone."

"Will Caithness not be the first place the MacGregors look fer her since Sinclair was refused her hand?"

"They might, but she won't be there."

Lachlan unfolded his arms and clenched his fists. "Would ye like to walk oot, or be tossed?"

"MacKenzie." Graham leaped to his feet, choosing to walk, though he was daft enough to open his mouth again. He spoke quickly. "As payment Sinclair will give you the name of the man who has your daughter, Annabelle."

Lachlan took a moment to replay over in his head what he'd just heard. When he was sure his ears hadn't deceived him, he grasped the smaller man by the collar and yanked him close. "Ye enter my castle and dare speak of my daughter? Ye dare speak her name?"

The older man gasped and looked about to faint. "My lord, hear me please!"

Lachlan wanted to snap him in two, but flung him back into the chair with a warning. "Take care what ye say next, emissary. If it is to deceive me, ye and Sinclair will discover why I'm called the Dragon Laird."

"There is no deceit here," the emissary vowed, clutching the arms of the chair. "Lord Sinclair has recently discovered the whereabouts of your daughter. Anna— She is not dead."

When Lachlan moved for the chair again, Graham squeezed his eyes shut and cringed. "Sinclair will give you the location and the names of the people who have her!"

Lachlan hated him for making him say it. "My daughter is dead. I saw her body, killed with her mother and burned by a band of rogue Jacobites who were angry that I didna fight fer James Stuart."

"That's what they wanted you to believe, my lord."

"Who is they?" Lachlan grounded out. "—and it had better be good. I am close to killing ye."

"The people who have your daughter. The ones who paid those Jacobites to take her and kill your wife."

Lachlan's head was spinning. Why was he listening to this? Was he so desperate for any spark of hope that might bring his life back? Why would his enemies want his daughter? Why would they go to such lengths as to kill another child to trick him into believing Annabelle was dead? He wanted to laugh, but the memory of his discovery was too devastating. "My daughter was there with her mother. I saw her body."

"No." Graham shook his head. "It wasn't her."

The idea that any man, or group of them, could do such a thing to not one, but two children made him glad he'd slaughtered them all. They were in hell, where they belonged.

"Your daughter is alive."

Could it be true? Could Annabelle be alive? It was too much to hope for. He wouldn't let himself. He ran his hand through his dark mane and fought to control the beast welling up inside of him. If this was some kind of trick, he'd kill everyone involved. He'd seen her body. He closed his eyes as if that would somehow vanquish the memory of carrying her from the flames.

"Who has this child and why does Sinclair believe she's my daughter?"

"Sinclair had heard rumors at the time of the tragedy that these people had arranged it," Graham told him. "He recently paid them a visit and met her. He said she looks to be the age of six or seven, with long dark hair, which she uses to cover the scars on her arms."

"Scars?" Lachlan hated himself for falling for this tale.

"Burns from the fire—like yours. It appears she tried to hold onto her mother when they took her."

Lachlan leaned on the chair for support. His belly burned with flames he knew could never be quenched. He didn't want to go back to that day and Sinclair's emissary was forcing him to. "I'm going to kill ye if what ye're telling me is untrue."

"It is all true," Graham assured him. "When my lord asked for her name, she gave it. Annabelle, a fostered child of her captors."

Annabelle. His heart thumped hard in his chest "That doesn't make her my daughter."

"Are you not curious?"

Aye. Aye, he was. "Who are they?" Lachlan bent over the chair. "I'll go to them and see fer myself."

Graham offered him a quavering smile and held up his finger. "I don't know who has her. Do you think Sinclair would send someone from whom you could torture the information? Only Lord Sinclair knows and he will be glad to tell you."

Lachlan stared at him. "Sinclair will tell me where the child is, who he thinks is my daughter, on the condition that I kidnap the daughter of a Jacobite warrior."

"'Tis not a condition, MacKenzie, but a favor, a gesture of thanks for reuniting you with your daughter."

Lachlan's smile was deadly. "Tell Sinclair I'm coming to Caithness for him. I'll get the name withoot kidnapping a woman."

"He is not in Caithness," Graham let him know. "He thought you might feel this way. He is no fool. The MacGregors will suspect him so he cannot be in Caithness when she is taken. You will keep her hidden until things settle a bit. I will return to Caithness with news of your agreement and have word sent to him. He will then agree to meet with you."

Lachlan plucked his knife from his belt and stepped closer to the chair. "I should kill ye and send Sinclair your head. Do ye think my answer to his offer will be clear enough?"

The emissary bolted out of the chair and ran for the door without giving him an answer.

Alone, Lachlan fell into his chair. He wondered if Sinclair was in Caithness or not. He'd like to go there and kill the bastard for giving him false hope.

His daughter was alive. As if it were possible. But what if it was? His heart raced. Shouldn't he do whatever was necessary to find out? He hadn't given up finding the men he believed had killed her. If there was any chance that Sinclair was being truthful and there was a girl who could be his daughter, he had to find out.

But kidnapping a lass from her family...her *MacGregor* family was not something he looked upon lightly. Besides that, they'd kill him if he were caught.

Memories of Annabelle's face, her soft voice, her scent rushed through him.

He wouldn't let himself get caught.

New York Times bestselling author Paula Quinn lives in New York with her three beautiful children, six overprotective Chihuahuas, and three small parrots. She loves to read romance and science fiction and has been writing since she was eleven. She loves all things medieval, but it is her love for Scotland that pulls at her heartstrings.

You can learn more at:
  http://pa0854.wixsite.com/paulaquinn
  Twitter: @Paula_Quinn
  Facebook: facebook.com/pages/Fans-of-Paula-Quinn/

Fall in Love with Forever Romance

SUGARPLUM WAY
By Debbie Mason

The *USA Today* bestselling Harmony Harbor series continues! As a romance author, Julia Landon's job is to create happy-ever-afters. But she can't seem to create one for herself—even after a steamy kiss under the mistletoe with Aiden Gallagher. After a bitter divorce, Aiden has no interest in making another commitment; he just wants to spend quality time with his daughter. But with Christmas right around the corner, both Aiden and Julia may find that Santa is about to grant a little girl's special wish.

Fall in Love with Forever Romance

TOTALLY HIS
By Erin Nicholas

In the newest of *New York Times* bestselling author Erin Nicholas's Opposites Attract series, actress Sophie Birch is used to looking out for herself. When her theater catches fire and a cop scoops her up to save her, she fights him every step of the way...even though his arms feel oh-so-good. Finn Kelly can't help but appreciate how sexy the woman in his arms looks...even if she's currently resisting arrest. But when Sophie finds herself in trouble again, can Finn convince her to lean on him?

Fall in Love with Forever Romance

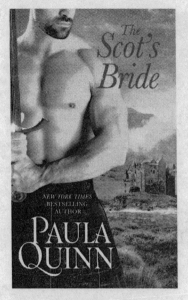

THE SCOT'S BRIDE
By Paula Quinn

For readers of Karen Hawkins, Monica McCarty, and Hannah Howell. Charlotte Cunningham refuses to abide by Patrick MacGregor, the barbaric highlander assigned to keep her out of trouble. But what's Charlie to do when her biggest temptation is the man charged with keeping her a proper young lass?

Fall in Love with Forever Romance

BACK IN THE GAME
By Erin Kern

Fans of *Friday Night Lights* will love the heartwarming Champion Valley series by bestselling author Erin Kern. Stella Davenport swore she'd never let anything get in the way of her dream—until sexy, broad-shouldered Brandon West walks back into her life. Brandon knows that love only leads to heartbreak, but Stella is a breath of fresh air he didn't even know he'd been missing. When she's offered her dream job in Chicago, will he be willing to put his heart on the line?

LETHAL LIES
By Rebecca Zanetti

Long-buried secrets and deadly forces threaten Anya Best and Heath Jones as they hunt down the infamous Copper Killer. Will they find love only to lose their lives? Fans of Maya Banks and Shannon McKenna will love Rebecca Zanetti's latest sexy suspense!

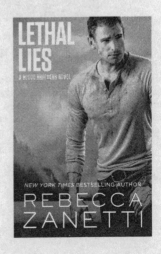